DELIGHTFUL SINS

NORTH SHORE STORIES BOOK THREE

LOLA KING

Cover art by Wild Love Designs
Editing by Mackenzie at Nice Girl Naughty Edits
Alpha reading by Lauren Pixley
Beta Reading by Ratula Roy

I tried to be perfect, but nothing was worth it. I don't believe it makes me real.

Sum 41

This book is for all the women who are angry.

PLAYLIST

Ghost of You - 5 Seconds of Summer
Pac Ave - Diggy Graves
Erase You - Point North
Trouble - Adam Jensin
toxic energy - blackbear, The Used
Welcome To Hell - Sum 41
Bad Bitch Energy - Damien Styles
LIGHTS OUT - Kxllswxtch
dying on the inside - Nessa Barrett
All the Things I Hate About You - Huddy
EAT SPIT! - Slush Puppy, Royal & The Serpent
MakeDamnSure - Taking Back Sunday
roses red - Jeris Johnson
Fool & The Thief - THE HARA
CODE MISTAKE - CORPSE, Bring Me The Horizon
deathwish - Stand Atlantic, nothing.nowhere.

HELL REPLIED - Grey
Red Flags - Gomey
ALL ABOUT ME - Lilyisthatyou
Na Na Na - My Chemical Romance
Prescription Kid - KID BRUNSWICK
RUN UP! - iamjakehill, Josh A
Young God - Halsey
KULT - Steve Aoki, grandson, Jasiah
Loser - Sueco
pretty poison - Nessa Barrett
Honest - Bazzi
Ghost - Halsey
Gasoline - Halsey
Pieces - Sum 41
With Me - Sum 41
Scumbag - Goody Grace, blink-182
you broke me first - Tate McRae
Strange Love - Halsey
FIGHT MODE - Beauty School Dropout
Pretty Little Addict - Haiden
hell is a teenage girl - Nessa Barrett
A$$A$$IN - Beauty Shool Dropout
Trick or Cheat - Diggy Graves
MAKEUP - Chris Grey
Use Me - Emerald Royce
Love Is Madness - Thirty Seconds to Mars, Halsey
Circus Psyho - Diggy Graves
Angels Don't Cry - Ellise
I Need You - Chri$tian Gate$
Devil In Me - Halsey
I'm Not Okay (I Promise) - My Chemical Romance
Roses - Awaken I am
Cute Girl - Diggy Graves

WE MADE PLANS & GOD LAUGHED - Beauty School
Dropout
Supposed to Be - Presence
Sorry - Halsey
All I Want - Kodaline
HONEY (ARE U COMING?) - Måneskin

1

ELLIOT

Three months earlier...

Pac Ave - Diggy Graves

Alexandra Delacroix notices the second our car parks in front of Xi's house. She gasps, her eyes rounding with fear. She's wearing a large t-shirt that must belong to her boyfriend.

I wonder if Xi realizes how much of a lucky motherfucker he is. The Kings and the North Shore Crew have been at war since before Ethan and I even joined. Xi used to be part of NSC, our enemy since my brother and I are part of the Kings. Yet the fucker managed to strike a deal and leave his crew so he could peacefully be with his rich princess. His house is neutral territory now...or so he wishes.

The city of Silver Falls is split in two by the Silver Snake River. The south of the river, or what we call South Bank, is where the average middle-class American lives. Spacious, full of lovely families, a beautiful newly built mall, restaurants, and even a trail that leads to the Silver Falls, where middle-class families can go picnic on the weekends.

We don't live there. We live north of the river, also known as the North Shore. A place destroyed by the war between our two gangs, and where flowers are crushed under our boots before they have a chance to grow. A place we've had control of for over three years, forcing NSC to live on our scraps. Our boss struck a deal with the American Bratva, and thanks to the support of the Wolves, we are practically indestructible. NSC is trying to do the same with the Cosa Nostra, and they'll fucking die trying.

But that's not why we're here today. Xi Benhaim might want to leave the war behind, but he's got something we want. Something we *need*.

I grab the gun from the glove compartment and load it.

"Patience, brother," Ethan says calmly.

My stepbrother and I don't always have the same way of doing things. He's quiet, composed, *patient*. Or so everyone thinks.

I'm a ticking time bomb. Especially since we started looking for our mutual ex-girlfriend.

Two years ago.

If that's not being patient, I don't fucking know what is.

He pushes the gun down with a hand on the barrel. "He's coming."

Xi bursts out of his house, topless, and his own gun tucked into his jeans. I can see the three ugly scars he still has from the time our best friend Caden stabbed him.

Things have changed since then. Caden and Billie Scott fell in love, despite being from different crews. Xi, who used to be in love with Billie, got over his stepsister and found himself a girl from a nearby town called Stoneview, where

CONTENT WARNING

This book is a dark romance for 18+ readers only. It contains scenes that may be triggering to some readers, including: Dubcon, kidnapping, murder, torture, blackmail, manipulation and control, extreme and toxic jealousy, police violence, SA, mention of SA + remembering SA on a minor, mention of childhood abuse, mention of past bullying, body dysmorphia, eating disorder, mention of death of parents, and mention of suicide

Like in all my books, the characters who are involved romantically are toxic, my MMCs close to non-redeemable and manipulative. I do not approve of this in real life, and in fact, actively tell you to keep this to fiction.

This book includes kinks such as: bondage, pet play, degradation/humiliation, impact play, collaring. My books are *not* guides to BDSM. There is *no* real BDSM in this book.

This book is for people who want to dive into their fantasies safely, on the page. Please, be aware that the fantasy starts on the next page, and you are entering at your own risk—there will be no further warning and no safe word.
The only safe word/gesture at your disposal is to close the book.

Always play safely and consensually.

Lots of Love,
Lola

PROLOGUE

JADE

Ghost of You - 5 Seconds of Summer

"If we don't get her to a hospital within the next ten minutes, she's dead."

"Jade..."

Such a beautiful voice. It sounds like an echo lost in a mountain. It beats in my ears with a need for me.

"Jade...baby, please open your eyes."

A deep breath swallows the last note of his plea. The scattered kind, broken down by meaningful sobs.

"If you open your eyes...I swear...I swear I will make it right."

There's a void inside me. Something that grabbed me a few minutes ago when that gun was aimed at me.

I cough when I try to breathe. It tastes like blood in my mouth. It tastes like death in my heart.

My chest constricts when the car hits a bump.

"Small breaths..." That's a new voice. "Hold on for us, Mi Cielo. Please, hold on. Kay, take the next right."

"My love..." Elliot's voice barely makes it past the ringing in my ears this time.

Those breaths are becoming really fucking hard to take. I cough and feel the burst of blood spurting out of my mouth.

That must be all over Elliot now.

The light is too bright when I try to open my eyes. Like a flash right in front of my face.

Click. Here's your last shot as a woman alive.

I can feel a slap on my cheek, barely. Like being hit by soft cotton. My body shakes from the cold coming from within me.

"Ethan." Elliot's panic has gone up a notch. It's desperate now. "She's not..."

Isn't it insane? That I still feel conscious, perfectly knowing my breathing has stopped and so aware that there's nothing to do about it.

This is the end.

billionaires like her live. If the South Bank feels out of reach, then Stoneview isn't even in our stratosphere.

Through the changes over the past years, something stayed exactly the same: Jade is impossible to find.

Ethan and I get out of the car in tandem. I round the front to face the man who has what we want.

And then our passenger gets out as well.

"I'll be doing the talking," Caden says just before Xi gets into earshot. And I'll let him. I'm not patient, but I'm a man who always has a plan. Today, my plan was to bring someone Xi will want out of his sight even more than Ethan and me. And that someone is Caden King.

The NSC man doesn't bother with formalities. He stops just short of barging into us and eyes us one after the other, his nostrils flared and jaw clenched.

"Emma and Kayla had a talk," he growls low. Emma Scott is the head of NSC, and Kayla King is our boss and Caden's sister. "This very house is on neutral territory. Keep me out of your shit because I've left it all behind. Did you fuckers not get the memo?"

The two women at the head of our opposite gangs rarely discuss anything, but Kay made us aware of the new rule. Xi Benhaim is out, and his house has turned into neutral territory. It's crazy what love can do. I wonder what Emma offered for Kay to agree. Both are ruthless businesswomen.

What they didn't anticipate is that Ethan and I don't give a shit about their little truce. We want to find the woman who betrayed us, and Xi has the information we want.

"Same," Cade chuckles. "Isn't life on the right side of the law just so boring? I'd give anything to stab a fucker three times in the stomach again."

Xi narrows his eyes at his lifelong enemy.

"But Billie won't let me." My best friend sighs

dramatically. "And you know what they say. Happy wife... happy Caden King when he makes her scream his name. Or something like that."

Cade's attempt at taunting Xi doesn't even make him blink. The man is so taken by Alex Delacroix, I don't think he remembers Billie's last name.

I'm ready to start threatening him, maybe mention his girlfriend standing by the window and watching us with the clear order to stay inside the house.

Before I can say anything, he addresses Ethan and me.

"I want you to know that if sparing your life wasn't in the deal Emma made with Kay, you would both be six feet under for what you did to Zara."

Ah, yes. I forgot to mention we killed his childhood best friend in our search for Jade. Xi is the only one with the information, and we needed to convince him. Not our proudest moment, but not the worst thing we've ever done either.

"Fucking do it," I sneer. "Just try."

"No," he says sternly. "It's part of the deal, and I'm a man of my word. It's keeping me out of this war, and that's all I want. My life is about protecting the woman I love, not avenging the dead."

He lifts his hand, showing us the ripped piece of paper he's holding.

"That's where Jade is hiding. I'm going to give it to you and never see your fucking faces again, that clear? Come near me, my woman, or my family, and you'll wish you were never born. Deal or no deal." He shoves the paper into Ethan's chest, my brother barely catching it in his hand, and walks back to his house.

Completely unafraid, like an invincible man, he turns his back to his enemies.

"Love truly fucks a man up," I say, shaking my head.

"In the best way, my friend." Caden smiles. That fucking creepy smile he does so well.

I look at the window again, watching Xi wrap a hand at the back of Alexandra's neck. He watches us until we go back into the car and disappear.

Ethan gives me the crumbled paper, and I unfold it as he rounds the corner and drives us back to Kings' territory.

420 Old Montauk Highway, Montauk, NY

"What the fuck?" I mutter to myself. Ethan stays silent, waiting for me to continue. "She's on Long Island."

"Long Island?" he repeats.

"Fuck," I chuckle to myself. It turns into a laugh until I feel tears at the corners of my eyes.

When I can finally breathe again, I become so serious one could think my dog just got ran over. "The fucking bitch found a sugar daddy to escape us." She always knew how to slither her way into men's beds for her own benefit.

I watch Ethan's jaw work from side to side. "Huh. Looks like we're going on a road trip."

2

ELLIOT

Erase You - Point North

"You what?" Kay's angry eyes flick from me to Ethan and back to me.

Before going anywhere, we stopped by her house to run it past her. If we're going to bring someone branded as a traitor back to this town, our boss needs to know about it. That way, we can try her North Shore style. She's pacing around in her kitchen, fuming at what we did.

"We found Jade and we're going to bring her back," Ethan explains calmly, again. He runs a hand through his black hair, then starts playing with his helix piercing.

"Not that," she hisses. "I meant *how* you found out where she is. You went to Xi's house. I told you guys he was out. We have a deal with NSC, and you went behind my back."

I smile brightly at her, the reassuring kind. "Kayla, we're not idiots. We knew Xi wants nothing to do with this life anymore and would be more than happy to give us the address."

"Don't give me your manipulative smile, Elliot," she says, her voice low. "It might work on others, but I've known you long enough to see when you're trying to fuck someone over. You took Caden with you when you know the two hate each other."

"Hey." Caden stops spreading mustard on the slice of bread in front of him. "I was good."

"I don't give a shit," she tells him. "Don't ever go behind my back again."

"Look," I say as I sit down at the kitchen table next to Caden, facing her. "The point is, you wanted to find Jade, and we know where she is. It's just under eight hours to get there. We can leave tonight, grab her in the morning, and come back right away. We'll be back here by tomorrow evening."

She looks straight into my eyes, strength and determination burning brightly in her gaze, trying to find anything that could give her an excuse to punish us. Unfortunately for her, she wants Jade back too. She wants the bitch to pay for what she did, and she's not going to say no to us. Knowing her, she will have conditions, though. I can see her scheming the moment she stops pacing and stares at me, revenge brewing in her genius brain.

"Okay," she finally relents, pushing out a heavy breath. "You're going to go get her, and you're going to bring her right back to me."

I let out a quiet laugh, my hand coming to graze the table, fingertips tapping on the surface. "That's if we don't kill her before we make it back."

"I get you two have your personal vendetta against her since she fucked the both of you, but the bitch owes me fifty thousand dollars. If you think you're killing her before she

3

JADE

Trouble - Adam Jensen

A noise in the ensuite bathroom wakes me up. Stan is shaving. I recognize the taps of the razor against the sink when he tries to get rid of the hair stuck in the blades. Every morning, he showers then shaves meticulously. He leaves the bedroom in nothing but a towel around his waist, showing his beautiful abs, and heads for his walk-in wardrobe. There, he chooses an expensive suit and slowly gets dressed. Then cufflinks. Then a tie. Finally come the shoes.

When he's done getting ready, he heads for the kitchen and makes himself an espresso.

It's only once he's fully awake and ready that he calls for me.

That's his routine. Every single day that he is here, that is. Sometimes he disappears for weeks at a time, and I get the house to myself. I'm not allowed to leave, but I appreciate the peace I get without him. He might be on work trips, or maybe on vacation. Probably in his main house with a wife and kids. I don't want to know.

I must have fallen back asleep, because the next thing that awakes me is a bell ringing from the kitchen. My cue to get out of bed.

I fucking hate that man.

After a quick shower, I go to his closet to check the outfit he chose for me today.

"Oh, come on," I grunt. I hate when he wants me to dress like this. It's not actual clothes. Never.

Yesterday was a skimpy schoolgirl uniform. Today is his favorite, and the one I hate the most.

I slip on the bright pink cotton panties and the knee-high white socks. Next comes the see-through pink lace bra. I dread the last item, but I know I'll end up wearing it anyway. Whether I choose to put it on myself, or he forces it on me after a harsh spanking.

With a sigh, I open my mouth, sliding the pacifier labeled *Daddy's Girl* between my lips. Grabbing the two straps, I wrap them around my head before buckling the gag tightly.

I make my way down the grand staircase and to the dining room. He's sitting at the end of a white marble table, the little bell in his hand and the espresso cup set in front of him. When he sees me, his eyes light up.

"Mm, my pretty girl," he says lowly. "Come here, baby." He slides the chair back and spreads his leg, snapping his fingers and pointing at the floor in front of him. Knowing my place, I get on my hands and knees and crawl to him. I settle between him and the table and look up.

"Good morning, puppet."

I nod to acknowledge him and suck dramatically on the pacifier to make sure he notices.

"Good girl." His hand comes to my cheek, and he caresses my skin. "My baby likes to suck, doesn't she?"

I nod again, doing my best to fake a plea with my eyes, pretending I'm desperate to suck on his dick.

I've spent two years being at this man's mercy. I know exactly what he wants, when, and how. There is nothing his body can hide from me. I know his deepest and darkest desires. I've experienced all of them. And I chose to stay.

First, it was for my mom. Because he was the one taking care of her. He paid for everything. He put her in the best hospitals with the best doctors. And when none of that worked, when the cancer got the best of her...I stayed because I had nothing else.

I have nothing. Nowhere to go, no one to call. I have no place to go back to. Stan stopped paying the rent on my mother's studio apartment as soon as she died. Not that I could go back to the North Shore. I have no money, because I can only use what he gives me, and he makes sure to drip feed it.

Leaving is something I stopped thinking about a while ago anyway because that's not what Stan wants. Stan wants me here. He wants the whore he saved from her poor town, and what he wants, he gets.

We fought once. The stupid kind. I still thought he'd listen to me back then. I wanted him to take me on a date. Anywhere but this house. When he said no, I left and slammed the door. Took one of his cars and drove.

I didn't even make it out of Long Island before one of his security guards brought me back, kicking and screaming. That's the day I learned he had security guards who didn't live with him, but who he could call whenever he wanted. That's also the day I learned Stanislav isn't just a filthy rich man. He's a filthy rich *Bratva* man. The Wolves, to be exact.

The same organization who owns the Kings. That's no surprise since I met him on the North Shore.

I pay you. I own you. Period. That's all he said when they brought me back and he tied me to his bed. Then he shoved a dildo so far down my throat, I couldn't talk for days.

Now I hate him, but everything has become a habit. Being Stan's whore is second nature to me. I live to please him, and in return, he feeds me, and gives me anything I want, as long as I don't ask for something outside of his property.

Stan, can we go to the movies?

There's a media room in this house. I'll buy whatever movie you want.

Can I go shopping?

I'll bring a stylist to you.

I would love to go to the restaurant with you. On a date.

The chef will cook you whatever you want.

At least I have the ocean. I just have to stay on his private beach. I haven't talked to someone else in so long; I don't even think I know how to hold a conversation anymore. No one who works for Stan is allowed to talk to me, and I'm not allowed to talk to them.

His phone beeping brings me back to reality. He looks under the table and sighs.

"I can't play with you this morning, Jade. I'm sorry, I just don't have time."

I nod. "Let me finish my breakfast and crawl with me to the door. Then you're free to go enjoy the pool without your outfit."

I count the minutes, kneeling between his legs as the chef brings him a breakfast that smells so good, I salivate. It pools down my chin, and I suck on the pacifier some more. When my stomach growls, I hear him chuckle above me. It seems like years before he finally gets up and I crawl after him to the front door.

"Be a good girl this morning. I'll be back at lunch."

I nod again and watch him leave. *Finally.*

I don't move for a few seconds after he leaves. I know he'll be watching this on his phone in the car, so I put my hands on the door, pretending to long for him. Then I slowly get up and take off everything he made me wear this morning.

It's only when I'm making my way to the lower level, where the interior pool is, that I hear something breaking upstairs. I freeze on the stairs, looking toward the upper levels. I can't see much from here, so I call for Stan's maid.

"Sylvie?" I don't know why I do that. She wouldn't answer me.

Climbing back up the stairs, I walk around the house until I see her from the corner of my eye. She's walking the hallway opposite me, not even looking my way. I retreat, aware that I'm completely naked and under strict orders not to wear anything. Reassured that it's just her, I head for the pool again.

I love swimming, and the warmth of a heated pool in the middle of winter is a luxury I never thought I'd experience when I was younger. It's just too bad it comes with being a stay-at-home escort.

But I don't dwell on it, because it's the life I chose, and it's better than being on the North Shore with my own crew wanting me dead. Instead, I decide to be good to Stan and do something that might grant me some pleasure when he comes back.

I swim to the deep end of the pool, which I know is facing the camera. Holding on to the edge with one arm, I look right at it as I slide my other hand to my pussy. It's underwater, but he'll still see it fine. I slowly play with my clit, taking my time until I feel it swell under the pads of my index and middle fingers. I imagine the last time Stan bent me over the bed and made me take it *like a good puppet*. I think of the ways he pounds into me so relentlessly.

When I slide one finger to my entrance and push in, his voice morphs into someone else's. His movements are different, and he puts his hands around my throat like Elliot used to do. That's when my wetness doubles. My mouth falls open and my eyes flutter shut as I press another finger inside me. I fuck myself, moaning loudly, even though Stan can't hear anything through the cameras. My heartbeat pulses in my ears, everything around me disappearing. It's not long before my breathing becomes shallow, and my moans are cut short by a soft whimper exploding out of me as I come on my fingers.

"That was quite a show."

My heart jumps out of my chest as I open my eyes, snapping around to face the edge of the pool. Two pairs of feet are right in my line of sight. I look up to find one of them squatting, and the other looking down, his arms crossed over his chest.

"Hello, Jade." Elliot, who crouches beside me, smiles brightly. That horrible fake smile he gives everyone he's about to fuck over.

He's here to kill me.

I know it.

4

JADE

toxic energy – blackbear, The Used

The equation is simple. Three years ago, I did something bad. Really bad. Something that would most certainly lead to Elliot Pearson wanting me dead. I had planned on taking that secret to my grave.

Two years ago, someone told him.

So I ran.

Plain and simple cowardice. I didn't wait to talk to him about it. I didn't take a second to even *think*. He knocked on my door, and I jumped out of the window.

The North Shore teaches you survival like nothing else, and I didn't want to die.

Now he's back to kill me.

Grabbing my wet hair, Elliot cuts short the blood-freezing scream bursting out of me as he pushes me underwater.

The moment he pulls me back up, I spit out the water I'm choking on.

"Miss us?" Elliot sneers as I suck in a breath. He lets go

of my hair, only to haul me up by the armpits and force me out of the pool. I roll on the wet tile and crawl away from them as he straightens.

I don't even wait for them to say anything else. Jumping to my feet, I take off in a sprint, practically falling on the slippery floor. I run to the door, calling out for Sylvie as if she's going to be able to do something about the two deadly men who came for me.

"There's nowhere to run anymore," Elliot taunts as I take the stairs two steps at a time.

They follow, of course. They came for me, why would they not?

"Sylvie, call Stan!" I scream as I run to the front door.

I don't know why I bother. She's probably dead at this point. I try to open the door, but it's locked. It's never locked.

"Fuck!" I panic as I look down. They broke the fucking lock.

I snap around, watching the two of them close in on me. "W-wait," I pant as I put my hands in front of me. "Stan... he'll kill you if you hurt me."

"Aw, no." Elliot fakes a pout. "Should we leave him a little note saying you ran away?"

"There are cameras everywhere," I babble. "You can't kill me."

"Kill you?" Ethan chuckles low. "We're not here to kill you."

Time slows as my eyes hop from one to the other on repeat.

Elliot's blond hair is longer than the last time I saw him, reaching mid-ear. It's falling into his eyes like it always used to do, and he flicks it to the side with a quick head movement. The smirk on his face tells me they have so much worse than death in store for me, and my legs shake at the idea.

Ethan takes a small step toward me, forcing me to flatten myself against the front door. His black eyes are as deep as the universe, his hair, the same length as Elliot's, the color of the darkest ink. He dyes it, which gives it that blue hue in the sun. I can't see that today because it's not sunny.

It's not been sunny in my life for a few years.

Ethan doesn't smile like his stepbrother. He's always been too sad on the inside, too *weird* as everyone called him. But when he makes it so close to me that I have to crane my neck to look into his eyes, he spares a deadly smirk for me.

"Why would we kill you when we can make you suffer?"

I shake my head, swallowing the fear, too aware of how naked I am with him so close to me. He's so fucking tall too. Both of them are well over six-foot, with Elliot being the tallest at six-foot-seven. I know it because everyone always asks him.

Damn, you're a giant. How tall are you?

He got sick of it real quick.

I cross my arms over my chest, hiding my boobs.

Ethan chuckles darkly. "Nothing any of us hasn't seen. I'm pretty sure you could walk naked around the North Shore and most of the guys there would be familiar with the view."

My nostrils flare at his insinuation.

"What do you want?" I push through clenched teeth.

I know what they want. Me in a coffin, six feet under. I'm surprised Elliot hasn't already put a bullet in my skull.

A hand pulls Ethan slightly away from me, and Elliot stands closer too, both of them cornering me. "You're coming home, baby," he says, tone softening but still as unnerving. "The list of what *we* want is too long to share. You can deal with Kay first. Then maybe Caden."

Sometimes in life, you're forced to assess a situation at the speed of light. Your instinct takes over, and you either follow it, or you die.

The reason I left the North Shore is not something I would ever want to say out loud. People think I did something bad, that I pissed off the wrong guy, but they have no idea just how bad it truly is. They think I ran because Caden King wanted me dead.

I look at Elliot, searching his gaze, the features on his face, the way he's holding himself. The fact that his gun is not against my forehead. That I'm still standing. Very much alive.

And it's clear to me...he *doesn't* know.

He doesn't fucking know.

In the span of a minute, I'm questioning every single decision I made in the past two years. I ran because I thought he knew the secret I'd been keeping from him. From both the brothers. When it turns out that they don't know what it is, or I would have taken my last breath a few minutes ago.

They're just here to...what? Bring me back to Caden? To Kay? He wants me dead. She's probably incensed because the Kings aren't the kind of crew you just *leave*. Blood in, blood out kind of thing.

I wonder how long I stay silent, attempting to keep my shock to myself. Still trying to process that Elliot Pearson has no idea about the real reason he should be mad at me.

"If you bring me back to the North Shore"—I swallow thickly—"I'm dead."

That's true no matter whether he knows or not.

Elliot lowers himself until he's facing me, the pretense

of pity softening his features. "Don't worry," he murmurs. "We won't let anyone kill you." He brings a hand to my still wet hair, pushing some messy curls behind my ear. "You'll be with us now. We're going to keep you and take *such* good care of you."

"Stop," I say desperately as I shrug his hand away.

It's dangerous to listen to Elliot. To his enchanting, deep voice, especially when he talks reassuringly. I know it's all a game to him. He's a manipulator, and I always promised myself not to fall for it.

My eyes cross with Ethan's as I try to avoid looking at his brother. "Isn't that what you've always wanted, Jade?" he snarls. "Attention from the both of us?"

I don't dare deny anything. I dated Ethan, then I fucked Elliot. While the latter didn't care, the former never forgave me.

They both take a step back, and Ethan pulls out a gun from the back of his jeans.

"Wait..." I panic, putting my hands in front of me again in a useless gesture that would never protect me.

Ethan doesn't pause. He aims.

And he shoots.

I shriek, jumping to the side and bringing my arms to cover my face. It makes them both laugh. Not the *I'm having an amazing time with my friends* kind. The subtle, humiliating kind that makes me want to curl up in a ball and die.

When I look up again, I realize he shot the lock, forcing the door to release open.

"Come on," Elliot tells me brightly. "Let's get you in the car. It's a long drive."

I pinch my lips, trying to calm my raging heart. I've been scared in my life. I've been through worse situations. Ethan and Elliot are the same boys I've always known, and I was never scared of them before. I raise my chin and square my shoulders, finding some of that old strength back. "Can I at least put some clothes on?"

"Come on." Elliot rolls his eyes. "Do you think we don't know you? You're going to run out the back and we'll never see you again."

"Come with me to the bedroom, then."

They eye each other for a second, not needing to talk out loud to communicate.

"That would be my absolute pleasure, baby." Elliot is more dangerous than a hunter. He always says the sweetest things until you're in his clutches. He lures people in until they're so close he can strangle them with both hands. "Come on." Snapping his fingers at me, he shows his lack of patience.

They both follow me to the bedroom, walking closely behind me until I reach the closet. Then they make me sit on the bed.

"I'll choose for you," Elliot says as he enters the walk-in wardrobe. Ethan leans on the wall, watching me like a hawk with his strong arms crossed over his chest.

"How's the music?" I ask, using the sheets to give myself a semblance of dignity.

He ignores me, bringing a hand in front of him and scratching some of the black nail-polish he's wearing. It's always chipped from playing the guitar.

"Have you composed any songs since I last saw you?" To say Ethan is a musical genius would be an understatement. He can play any instrument he touches, read music like one would read a book. He's beautiful when he plays. Not that I've seen it in a while.

Clearly finding my small talk unbearable, he knocks

on the wall the room shares with the closet. "Are you done in there?" he shouts at Elliot. His voice isn't as deep as his brother's. It's slightly higher and raspier. Fucking addictive.

Ethan and Elliot are technically *step*brothers, but they grew up together since they were six, so they started considering themselves brothers a long time ago. Elliot is only a year older than Ethan and me.

"Well, would you look at that," Elliot cheers as he walks back into the room. He's holding one of Stan's button-downs and a pair of silk sleeping shorts in one hand. In the other, he's got a basket of Stan's favorite toys.

My nostrils flare as my eyes narrow. "Put that shit away," I snap harder than I should. He'll know they're a weakness to me.

He chuckles, bright eyes meeting mine. "I don't think you're in any position to give orders, baby."

"Stop calling me baby."

"You want me to stop calling you baby?" His voice lowers, a few shades of darkness I know don't announce anything good. He slowly stalks toward me, purposely giving me time to regret my demand.

"What would you like me to call you instead?" With another slow step, his blue eyes dig into mine. "Traitor?"

I attempt to swallow the ball of nerves sticking at the back of my throat. The bastard doesn't stop until he's right in front of me, towering over me as I tighten the sheet around my body.

"Manipulative bitch?" he insists, letting me know what he really thinks of me.

"No." I do attempt to say it loudly, but it seems my body didn't get the memo and is trying to make itself small in front of the hunter.

He rips the sheet off, and my hands come to grab the edge of the mattress on either side of me. "Whore?"

I shake my head, my eyes darting to Ethan still leaning against the wall. He's watching us, completely unimpressed.

Elliot's excited stare goes to my legs, dragging it languidly along my thighs and stopping at my bare pussy. Pressing my thighs together doesn't help one bit. I feel watched, practically analyzed.

"Mm, Jade," he hums with appreciation. "I'm not ashamed to say I *am* one of those men who is a fan of what's between your legs. I bet...what did you say his name is? Stan? I bet he loves it too."

He puts the basket on the mattress and grabs a pair of black panties from inside. They're all lace apart from the crotch, which is thick cotton.

"What's that?" he questions out loud. He brings it in front of his face, inspecting it and sliding his finger inside the pocket in the crotch. His eyebrows furrow, and he looks back into the basket, grabbing the clitoral stimulator that goes in the pocket and the remote that controls it.

"Oh," he chuckles. "This is perfect."

"This isn't a fucking game," I hiss. "I'm coming with you. Now stop playing around and let me get dressed."

I try to reach the button-down he left on the side of the bed, but he grabs my arm before I can touch it. "Jade," he admonishes me in a tone he pretends is playful but is thick with a threat. "Put this on."

He shoves the panties in my hand.

"This isn't fucking funny. You're already bringing me back to the North Shore, where you know Caden will have my head. There's no need to humiliate me in the process."

"I think there's a need for whatever I want. And I want you to wear those. I'll only turn them on if you're a bad girl."

He cocks his head to the side, assessing me. "Do you think you can behave for me?"

Fuming silently and wanting to get this over with, I snap into a standing position and angrily put on the panties. Before he can stop me, I snatch the button-down and slide it on too.

"There," I say, practically stomping my foot in frustration. "Happy?"

He doesn't answer. Instead, he grabs me by the shirt, dragging me closer, and brings his hand to my pussy. I gasp when I feel the silicone object sliding into the panties and inside the pocket. As I attempt to squirm away from him, he takes his time rubbing me to make sure it's settled. I ignore the slight pleasure it brings me, and the way my body responds to not only his hand, but the excitement from the erotic toy Stan loves to use in the best way.

Elliot smiles down at me, his hand still inside my panties. It's warm against my pussy lips. If he was to spread them, he'd be able to feel how wet I'm getting by the second.

"God," he snorts. "I shouldn't even be surprised that you ran away from the North Shore by becoming someone's whore." I feel my face scrunch up at his accusation. Knowing it was never easy. Hearing it is worse. "How often does he use it on you?"

I gulp, choosing silence over telling him something that might anger him.

"Weekly? Daily?"

"It's not important."

"Answer."

I look into his eyes and away. "Multiple times a week."

"Mm, so you must be familiar with how it feels, huh?"

Looking up at him, I nod.

"Good." He takes the remote in his hand, presses it once, and turns it on to the maximum setting.

I gasp, falling back on the bed and folding in half. The vibration is way too intense for something directly touching my clit. With a hiss, I bring my hand to push the panties down. Elliot is quicker than me, though. He grabs it and pulls me back into a standing position.

"Be good and this stays off. Be a bad girl and I'll make you come enough times to pass out in the car. Seven hours is a long drive, baby. Clear?"

"Okay," I pant in a mix of pain and pleasure. "Okay, I get it. Just turn it *off*!"

He does so right away, leaving me feeling like I'm suspended in the air. I'm longing for more, yet hoping he never turns it on again.

Smiling, he puts the remote in his pocket. I look back at Ethan, who's still in the same position. His disgusted expression makes my cheeks heat. Most men would be turned on by seeing me wearing a sex toy. Ethan looks at me like he'd rather jump out the window.

"I think we can make our way now," Elliot says proudly, tapping his pocket where he put the controller. The complete opposite of his brother, he's not even ashamed of the hard-on tenting his jeans right now.

"The shorts," I say simply.

"Yeah, I decided against those in the end. Come on."

My hunch about Sylvie being dead is confirmed the second we step outside in the rain. Her body is on the front lawn, one bullet to the head, right between her eyebrows. She isn't the first corpse I've seen in my life, but it's been two years since I've been confronted with the criminal life, and it's a fucking slap in the face.

I only realize I stopped to look at her when Ethan's

creepy voice rings in my ears. "Could be you if you so much as *think* of escaping us again."

I let his cold words spread down my back in a shiver. If Ethan is a weirdo, I wonder what I am for always having loved that sick side of him. Something is seriously wrong with this man. That's the reason I fell in love with him. Back then, we were both creepy losers.

They're on either side of me, Elliot holding my upper arm tightly as they walk me to Ethan's matte green truck. It belongs to him, not Elliot, and I fucked the blond brother in there. The hot, gorgeous brother who's always had the girls, the reputation, the friends. Who's taller and stronger. Who was never bullied by anyone because they wouldn't dare. I fucked *him* in Ethan's truck just to rub it in his face. Just because he broke up with me and stomped on my heart. High school fucking drama seems ridiculous now that they both hate me.

I make sure to look back at the camera that points toward the driveway, showing a distressed face for when Stan will be looking at who took me.

I can't fucking wait for Ethan and Elliot to face his wrath. Who fucking cares that the Kings want me dead when I know Stan will do anything to keep me alive and by his side.

The brothers have no idea the mistake they just made by taking me away from someone who is part of the Wolves.

Someone who could destroy the Kings with a snap of his fingers.

Best thing is, I bet they have no idea who Stan really is.

It's not until we're in the car and on the highway that I realize the extent of what's happening. Not until Elliot, in the passenger seat, shows me a text that just popped up on my phone. The same phone where only one number can get through. Stan's.

> Stan: Puppet, something has come up with work. I won't be back for a few weeks. Sylvie will stay with you and cook for you. No clothes for the whole time. That's an order. I will be abroad and won't be able to be in touch too much. Make sure you stay good.

A few weeks?

A few *weeks*?

My breathing accelerates as my wild, panicked eyes go to Elliot.

"Uh oh," he says cheerily. "Looks like we have a while before your employer realizes you're gone."

No. This can't be possible.

It's not hard for Elliot to acknowledge the way he should answer Stan's message. I'm only allowed to reply to his texts with two words unless there's an emergency. He can see that from all the other times I've replied to him.

"Yes, Daddy," Elliot murmurs to himself as he types. "Sent." He looks back at me. "So, excited to go home?"

To go home?

To a place where I don't belong?

To a place where my own childhood best friends hate me and where people want me dead. I ran away. I made myself look guilty to the Kings.

I have absolutely nothing left in this life. All I've done for two years is become the puppet of a man who's never been refused anything since he's had power. But at least I was safe.

Ethan and Elliot are throwing me back into shark-infested waters, and they'll be all too happy to watch as I'm shredded by their sharp teeth.

"Elliot." Ethan's tone is annoyed, to say the least. "I don't like hearing her voice. Stop asking her questions."

Elliot smiles at me. "You made him grumpy."

Grumpy is a fucking understatement. Ethan hates my guts. He's so fucking sure he gets to do that when it's my heart he broke.

I observe Ethan as he drives. He's rolled up his sleeves, and his strong forearms tense, the veins swelling the harsher his grip become on the steering wheel.

Ethan didn't use to be strong and deadly good looking. He used to be the tall, skinny loser who dyed his hair and painted his nails black. Who listened to bands others found strange. He was odd looking, lithe, and strangely quiet. People would say he needed an exorcism. They'd make fun of him and beat him up, and he wasn't strong enough to fight back.

For three years of high school, that's what his life was. For two years and four months I dated him and fell in love despite everything everyone said about him. People thought I was ugly, and not worth giving me the time of day then. It was before what my friends like to call my *glow up*. Before everyone wanted to fuck me.

But I wasn't an outcast.

They only began including me in their hatred when I started dating Ethan.

Elliot didn't care as much as he does now. He only protected his little brother once in a while, when he'd show up to school. He had other shit going on at home, where they both needed more protection than at North Shore High. Elliot took care of things. He was already part of the Kings.

Then Elliot got Ethan to join. Ethan met Caden King, and everything changed. They became best friends. Ethan's appearance changed as he started exercising, lifting weights, building his body. Caden is a fucking psychopath who started turning my boyfriend into a man with no conscience. Ethan earned himself the reputation of being dangerous and deadly. He became *hot* by everyone's standard of physicality. He became *mysterious* rather than weird. And guess who got left behind?

The ugly girl who didn't fit his new reputation.

The girl who realized that if she never wanted to be left behind again, she had to do the same. Glow up, join the Kings, become fierce and fearless. Turn into a *real bitch* because I knew what I wanted, and I wasn't scared to go for it. I was never ignored again after that. All I had to do was live with my new reputation: a hot, heartless slut.

I did the same as Ethan. I was just labeled differently.

Having sex with Elliot was just the cherry on top.

And my ex-boyfriend dared hate me after that.

"You don't get to hate me, you know?" I tell Ethan. "You're the one who broke up with me."

Our eyes cross in the rearview mirror and he gives me a scathing look.

Because he refuses to carry on, I keep going. There's an advantage to having loved someone so strongly in the past. Their buttons are so easy to push.

Being out of that suffocating house for less than an hour already makes me feel more like myself. Maybe it's being near the brothers too. I know I don't have to endure anything they want to force on me. I can always fight back like I used to before Stan.

There's only one way to get inside the brothers' heads.

"You hate me because I fucked Elliot to make you

jealous after you broke up with me. Then you hated yourself because I fucked him again. And then again. And then regularly. You couldn't take that you threw away something really good."

"Jade," Elliot growls. "Shut the fuck up, will you?"

Only one way to destroy them from the inside and earn my freedom.

"I did things with him I would have never let you do to me," I snort.

And that's to turn them against each other.

But I guess my first attempt doesn't work exactly as planned when Ethan gives me a chilling smile. "The difference between you and me, Jade, is that I don't hold on to the past. We were seventeen. You're twenty now. Almost twenty-one. I know you took it hard, but it's time to move on. Why don't you fuck Elliot again to try to get over me? He seems to have a thing for cheap whores."

I feel my nostrils flare as his eyes flick to the mirror again and then back to the road. His little satisfied smirk makes me feel the exact same way as nails on chalkboard do.

I want to fucking kill him. I kick the back of his seat, which only makes him laugh.

Ethan presses play on the car screen and "*Welcome To Hell*" by Sum 41 comes on. That's Elliot's favorite band. I noticed he's wearing one of their shirts today.

The man hasn't changed one bit in two years. He still wears band t-shirts like an old dad who can't move on from the good old days. Except they fit him much better than they would an old dad. *So* much better. That's the only thing the brothers have in common. Their love for punk rock music. Everything else makes them polar opposites.

My eyes dart to the right, watching Elliot's sharp jaw and

dragging my gaze down to his strong shoulders, his muscly arms confined by his loose shirt. He's still holding my phone in his left hand, playing with it without a care in the world. He's just sliding it to one end, stopping it by pressing his thumb and forefinger to the edge, and then pushing the other end against his thigh to slide it again. My eyes are stuck on his thick fingers, remembering how close they were to my pussy earlier. The mere memory of knowing the things he can do with them has me squirming on the seat.

I scratch my throat and look out the window. Grabbing a thick, damp curl, I roll it around my index finger and tighten until I can feel the blood flow stopping.

Keep yourself grounded, girl. The last thing you need right now is a foggy mind.

5

JADE

Bad Bitch Energy – Damien Styles

By the time we reach Elliot and Ethan's house, I feel sick to my stomach. The road was long. I slept, trying to avoid reality the only way I know how. I've always been a heavy sleeper, easily falling into the darkness to forget the truth waiting for me in the land of the living.

But I woke myself up tonight. It's like nothing could stop reality from hitting me in the gut painfully. When my eyes open, we're already on the North Shore, already on their street, parking not far from their house.

Each booming note of the bass from the party going on inside their home is a hit to my heart.

Boom. Everyone here hates you.

Boom. You're on your own.

Boom. Kay is going to put your head on a spike for running away.

Everyone thinks I did them wrong. They're not even sure what. They just follow whatever the rumors say. No one believed me when I begged for help, but the second I'm the one accused, they're ready to burn me at the stake.

A witch hunt. That's what they're all on.

"Looks like you'll be back right in the swing of things, Jade," Elliot tells me.

"Did you throw me a welcome back party?" I snarl.

I just spent two years being a docile woman for Stan. I'm back home for less than a minute and my claws are back out. You can't let anyone see your weaknesses in this town, they'll eat you alive.

"It's just a Friday night, baby. Don't get ahead of yourself." Elliot opens the door, the night air freezing me.

There's a brief moment between when Elliot closes his door and opens mine. A few seconds when Ethan and I are the only ones in the car. It's long enough for our gazes to cross, for his eyes to grab ahold of my soul.

There's no hate in them, just longing. I don't think we've ever connected quietly so deeply. He can say anything he wants out loud, threaten me with death, but he missed me.

And I missed him too.

We're both startled when my door opens. "Come on," Elliot says with a sickly-sweet voice. "Let me walk you to your new home."

I'm surprised I don't vomit the snacks they fed me in the car on their doorstep. So many Kings are partying at their house right now, all I want is to run away as fast as I can. Left without a choice, I roll back my shoulders just before they open the door.

A wave of warmth hits me in the face. It smells of weed and alcohol. The windows are steamed, and the people are cramped in the living room.

Elliot and Ethan have one of the biggest houses around, but their bedrooms and basement have always been off limits. Everyone must stay in the small living room and kitchen. The parties used to be mainly at Sawyer's, but since he and I were deemed traitors, and he was killed...they seemed to have moved to the brothers' house.

"LIGHTS OUT" by Kxllswxtch is playing loud enough to burst my eardrums and my head spins the moment we walk through the crowd. Despite having Ethan and Elliot on either side of me, I'm shaking when the music lowers and heads turn toward me.

I have a feeling I look pale despite my dark skin complexion. Is this how I die?

The gangs of the North Shore are ruthless, violent. Traitors are treated the same as the opposite crew, if not worse. Individually, they don't all scare me. I could probably take a bitch or two in this room. All together? It's another problem.

It's an unconscious gesture to press myself closer to Elliot. Probably because he's the biggest in the room. Survival instincts and all.

I only realize my movement when he wraps a hand at the nape of my neck. And because all my senses are on high alert, I can't help but notice the way Ethan's hand twitches at his side.

He fucking missed me, I chant internally. It's all I can do not to let a smile eat up my whole face. There are more pressing concerns right now, after all.

"Nothing to see here," Elliot says with a kind voice. "Keep enjoying your night."

If Kay isn't here, then he's the one people listen to. He was already high up in our ranks, but when Kay's dad died and she took over, she wanted Elliot as her right-hand.

What kind of leader wouldn't want a six-foot-seven monster with the smile of an angel and the scheming brain of the devil as their right-hand man? She's smart enough to know you want Elliot by your side, as your ally. Never give him a chance to think he would be better anywhere else but with the Kings.

The music turns loud again, and people go back to their activities despite side-eyeing me. They part when the three of us walk through the crowd, not daring to make a move on me since Ethan and Elliot are right here.

But I hear the insults.

Whore. Traitor.

The threats.

You're dead. Wait till we get you alone.

Something feels even more off than I thought. I understand why Caden wants to kill me. I beat up his girlfriend. I set her up. But everyone else shouldn't even care about her. She's from the opposite crew.

So what is it they all have been saying behind my back?

The discomfort that they all know something I don't makes my skin crawl. I don't like this.

We're almost by the door to the hallway that leads to the bedrooms, when someone comes out of a group of girls and blocks our way.

My stomach twists, my chest tightening the moment I see Kay's best friend.

Vickie.

"Nothing to see, huh?"

My limbs tremble at the mere sound of her voice. The attitude in her tone makes me want to punch her. Her and I have gotten into enough fist fights that then got *me* in trouble. Because Kay would always take her side. Of course, they're best friends.

Vickie is the one who convinced me to keep my mouth shut in high school. When I got hurt and turned to her, she told me I was a liar and to not spread bullshit about Kings' men who were untouchable.

Don't make up a lie to bring attention to you, Jade.

Never bring this up again. I'll fucking kill you.

I shake my head. "Get out of the way," I hiss at her.

I don't even wait for anyone's reaction. Hesitation can get you killed in this town. I shove her in the chest, forcing her to take a step back.

"Here we fucking go," Elliot mutters. "The real Jade is back."

Yeah. Being a sweet little thing didn't last long.

I can't stand Vickie. The sight of her makes me absolutely feral. There's something about not being believed that kills your sanity. And the person who called you a liar is not just your worst enemy, they're a reminder of the nightmare that annihilated you.

Vickie reacts on reflex. She shoves my shoulders, rearing her arm back, but Elliot grabs her wrist before she can get to do anything else.

"Let me go," she snarls. "The bitch deserves everything coming her way." Her upper lip curls as she looks me up and down with disgust plastered on her face. Her upturned nose gives her another level of condescension. And to think high school me wanted to look *pretty* like her.

"You're going to give that money back, Jade. Trust me."

I pause, my brow furrowing. "Money? What money?"

Is that what they think I did? Stole money? That I would be that stupid?

"I can't wait for Kay to get her hands on the lying bitch."

I lose it.

"Shut up!" I shriek, throwing myself at her. I get a messy punch to her eyebrow—hurting my knuckles—before Ethan pulls me back.

His arms are around my waist, and he lifts me up easily. Five-foot my ass. My biggest regret in life is not getting those hours of sleep when my dad put me to bed as a kid. I might have been taller. It might have been harder for Ethan to pick me up like I weigh nothing and high enough that my feet don't touch the floor anymore.

"I'll fucking end you, Vickie," I shout as Ethan sidesteps her and pushes the door to the hallway to carry me to Elliot's bedroom. Elliot follows, closing the door behind us and cackling like he's having the time of his life.

"Fucking hell, you haven't changed one bit. Still angry at the world, are you? You're way too volatile for someone who owes everything to this crew."

"I owe *nothing* to the Kings," I spit. "Fuck you. Fuck all of you."

"Anytime you want, baby," Elliot chuckles as Ethan finally lets me go.

I stride away from him, angry enough to punch the wall and split my knuckles open. When I turn around, I'm breathing so hard my nostrils flare.

I wasn't always angry at everything and everyone. It only began when the world started being unfair to me. When, despite all my best efforts at doing things the right way, no one would hear me.

But since senior year, that's all people know me for. A furious woman. A real bitch who can't keep her fists to herself.

"You can stay in here while you calm down," Elliot says, taking a few steps toward me. "You don't want to be out there anyway, believe me."

I am a ball of burning rage, and Elliot makes it worse. "You've always been too quick to light up. You've got anger issues, Jade." The clinical way in which he says that is oil to a burning flame.

"I fucking know that!" I scream at him so fiercely my vocal cords sting.

Maybe if I'd ever felt listened to in my life, I wouldn't feel the need to shout.

But no one ever heard me.

No one ever cared.

So I get angry, and I scream, and I shout. And fuck them.

Ethan shakes his head. "Come on," he tells his brother, not acknowledging me. "We'll come back when Kay is here."

Ethan leaves, but Elliot stares at me, his scheming gaze roaming over my body.

"I have an offer for you, take it or leave it, but if you know what's good for you, you'll take it."

"Great," I huff. "You're famous for always having wonderful offers." I roll my eyes. "I fucking know you, Elliot."

"In case you didn't notice." He takes a step toward me. "You're in danger on the North Shore. You're smart enough to know that. I'm powerful, you're nothing. I'll give you protection."

My eyes narrow at him, hoping my look can kill. Knowing he would never offer something for nothing, I ask, "What do you want?"

His smirk sends a chill down my spine, but I keep my head held high. Even when he grabs my arm, flips me around, and wraps an arm around my waist to keep my back pressed to his stomach.

"You can guess what I want, can't you?" My breath hitches when I feel him growing hard against my lower back. "I want what we had. I want you to give me all of you. You know how I play."

I snort, grabbing his wrist and forcing his hand back down as he tries to reach my boobs. "Of course that's what you want. You're not any different from literally every single man I've ever encountered."

Tensing, his other hand grabs the back of my head, tangling his fingers in my hair. He pulls until my neck is taut, and I can see him looking down at me.

"I am *not* like the other guys, Jade." He presses his body harder against mine. "I made you come, I made you my slut, I broke down every single part of you and put them back exactly how I wanted them. And the worst is? You loved it. If you gave it to your rich fucker, you can give it back to me. So here we are. Protection, for you to become my little slut again. I find the bargain quite in your favor."

A small laugh escapes me, my back shaking against his stomach. "If you want it so badly, why don't you take it?"

His chest rumbles with a growl. "You know why."

I fake a pout. "Because you want *consent*? Because you love when women throw themselves at your feet, *begging* you to make them your whore?"

He thrusts his hard dick into the small of my back. "What do you think?"

Just to amuse myself, I push back against him, rubbing my ass against his body.

"I think you should go fuck yourself."

He brushes the rejection off with a laugh, letting me go. I turn around, scowling at him, even though it changes nothing.

"Okay." He nods. "Your funeral."

With one last look, he closes the door. It's indescribable. I couldn't say if it's pity, a warning...or something deeper. I

44

don't understand him, I never have. I understood Ethan because we had a connection. But Elliot was a fan of my body, not my mind.

Voices scream through my racing thoughts the moment he's gone. I don't want to be here. I know this house too well, the atrocities it can deliver. There are demons lurking everywhere. Ghosts that haunt my every waking moment. And at night, they crawl from under the bed, grabbing my bare ankles and dragging me down to hell with them.

Being here waiting for Kayla King, the ruthless leader of the Kings, feels like being in purgatory.

My sentence will fall soon.

6

JADE

dying on the inside - Nessa Barrett

I wonder in what fucking world Elliot Pearson thinks I'm going to listen to any order he gives me.

Less than fifteen minutes after he left, my strength came back. I just needed the brothers away from me to remember who the fuck I am.

I'm thirsty, I'm starving, and I don't give a shit about the people who want to beat me up.

I look around the room, looking for any weapon I could use to protect myself. I am *not* going to let Elliot put me in his bedroom like I'm some sort of kidnapping victim.

Not caring about anything that belongs to him, I turn his room upside down as I search. I might unnecessarily push some stuff off the shelves and break a framed picture of him and Ethan.

Oops.

I don't find a gun, which would have been nice, but I do find a knuckle duster with his boxer shorts.

"That's mine, you thief," I mumble to myself.

I know that because he'd gotten it for me, and it's got my name engraved on the inside.

I get rid of the panties he stole from Stan and the shirt. Instead, I put on one of his band t-shirts that reaches just above my knees and a pair of his boxers.

I can't help but glance in the mirror. It's a habit I don't think I'll ever be able to stop. I always need to know what I look like, obsessively checking my skin, my makeup, how my clothes fit.

I spent the entirety of my high school years terrified of everyone and what they thought of me. I used to walk through school hallways and hear people calling me ugly, stupid, and anorexic. People would mock my eyebrows for being thick and compare me to NBA player Anthony Davis.

I've been called pizza face, asked if I washed my skin with toilet water, and mocked so many times for my acne I would run home crying to my mom.

My jaw tightens when I see some of my acne scars along my cheek. I'm not wearing any makeup and my stomach twists.

Knowing I'm probably going to get in a fight with people doesn't stop me from going out, but the idea that they could make fun of my appearance terrifies me. I've not been ugly Jade for a long time. When I joined the Kings in senior year, I also transformed myself. I spent money on acne treatments, bought makeup, started waxing. Instead of changing my way of thinking and finding beauty in who I was, I let them win, and I changed how I looked.

I run my hands over my hair, my face. I press the pads of my fingers under my eyelashes to try to curl them.

I look ugly and I'm scared.

"You're not ugly," I murmur to myself. "Stop it. You're fine. You've always been fine. It was them, not you."

48

My stomach growls, refusing to let me stay in the room. I used to let myself starve for days, but I refuse to do that anymore.

I take a deep breath, curl my fingers around the knuckle duster, and walk out of the room.

The party is at its peak. People look at me, but don't really say anything. Just nasty glares sent my way. They're drunk, most of them probably high. I'm lucky enough to not see Elliot or Ethan as I head to the kitchen.

There are at least ten pizzas on the kitchen table, and my mouth waters right away. This is exactly what I needed.

Some guys look at me on the other side of the table as I grab a slice of pepperoni. They have cups in their hands and hazy looks in their eyes.

"Lost your pants, pretty girl?" one chuckles.

They don't know my name. They must be new enough to this crew that they never heard of me. Now that I take my time to study them, they don't appear older than high school age.

I take a bite, looking at the three of them with my best unimpressed expression. I take my time to swallow before answering.

"In case you didn't notice, that's a knuckle duster in my right hand. Let me enjoy my food and fuck off."

His two friends laugh at him. "Not your best flirting," one of them says.

"She's the one walking around half naked. If she didn't want to be hit on, maybe she should have put on some clothes."

"She was never very good at not being a slut."

Vickie.

She's behind me, probably entering the kitchen, but I

don't want to look back. I'm halfway through my slice when she settles right behind me.

"Are you stuffing your face so you can go puke it all up? Old habits die hard."

I almost choke on the bite, swallowing it with difficulty.

Just like that, my hunger is gone. I eye the pizza in my hand, feeling sick as my fingers weaken and I drop it on the table like it's a gift from the devil.

"Fuck you, Vickie." I try to say it with all the venom I keep in reserve for her while knowing perfectly her jab weakened my defenses.

"You like how she looks now, boys, but believe me, she wasn't always like this. This kind of skinny only comes from putting her fingers down her throat."

I'm shaking when I turn around to face her. "Are you seriously so petty you want to insult me for what I looked like three years ago?"

"Three years ago?" she snorts. "You're still ugly, Jade. No amount of jumping from dick to dick will ever make you pretty." She presses a finger on my cheek. "I can still see your zits. You really are disgusting without makeup on."

I blink as my vision narrows. At the back of my mind, I can hear the verbal abuse from my school peers. The words they'd use and the way I just ran to the bathroom to cry it out. And then I'd make myself sick.

"Hello-oh?" Vickie sing-songs. She waves a hand at me, refocusing my vision. "Holy shit, you're worse than before you ran away from us."

My grip on the knuckle duster tightens, and my anger at the world comes back tenfold.

Fist flying without another thought, I hit her eyebrow on purpose. I want something that will hurt like hell but that won't punch her lights out. I need her awake to suffer.

She crashes to the floor with a cry as the three guys cheer for us to fight. Fucking assholes. As I straddle her hips, people are already gathering around us. I hit her in the exact same spot. Blood is gushing from her face, but I'm ready for the third hit.

I rear my arm back just as someone's fingers grab me by the waist, pulling me back.

"She started it," I scream.

I shout to let me go, but there's nothing I can do when two arms wrap tightly around my waist. I know it's Ethan *again,* because I recognize the tattoo of a dismantled doll on his forearm, and the smile of a skull on the back of his hand. He seems set on not letting me get into a fight tonight.

He doesn't say anything to me as he drags me away, but when he puts me down, he turns back to Vickie.

"You. Out."

She tries to fight back on his order, whining like the little bitch she is as she holds a tissue to her face. "But Ethan—"

"Get out of this house, Vickie, before I kick you out myself."

I use the distraction to get away. My stomach is heavy, *aching,* I feel sick. I stride out of the kitchen, pushing through the small crowd that gathered, and through the living room.

The second I'm in the hallway, I run for the bathroom.

Don't do it. Please, please, don't do it.

I close the bathroom door behind me, whimpering when I see myself in the mirror.

An ugly fucking monster. That's what you are.

I wipe tears away from my face, throwing the knuckle duster to the side as I do it.

Taking in a scattered breath, I wash my hands. "Don't do it," I tell myself.

But there's a difference between what I say and what I do. It's an unstoppable force. It pulls from inside me. There's lead in my stomach, and it won't go away until I force it out.

I'm sweating by the time I kneel in front of the toilet. This room is my worst nightmare for so many reasons.

I stare at the white bowl, tears streaming down my face.

With a shake of my head, I press my fingers against my lips, still trying to convince the poisoned part of my soul not to do it.

It's a battle with myself. I *need* to do it, though something is screaming not to, keeping my mouth shut so I don't let my fingers in.

But I give up, hearing Vickie's comments again.

My lips are parting when the door bursts open.

Ethan is on the floor, gripping both my wrists right away. "Don't. Don't. Don't." His words are whispered so quickly I barely catch them.

A sob gets stuck in my throat as I shake my head. He leans back against the bathtub, spreading his legs so he can bring me to him. My back against his chest, he keeps hold of my wrists at the small of my back, and puts a hand on my forehead, pulling until I lean against his shoulders.

"You don't need to do this, Jade."

"I'm ugly," I whimper, my eyes squeezing at the admission.

"You're beautiful. You've always been beautiful."

I shake my head, sniffling. "Let me go."

"Say it. Tell me you're beautiful and I'll let you go. Promise me you won't try to make yourself sick and you won't have to deal with me anymore."

When I keep quiet, he brushes his cheek against mine. "All that Vickie wants is to get a reaction out of you. Don't give it to her."

"Is she gone?"

"She's gone. I kicked her out."

"Why?"

He hesitates for a few seconds and gives me what I know is only half the truth. "Because I can't stand the bitch." *Because she upset you,* he doesn't add.

In my vulnerable state, I say something I know I will regret. We just found each other again, now isn't the time to bring up our past. "Tell me you don't hate me, Ethan."

I feel his skin leaving mine and his head falls back against the edge of the tub.

"Tell me you're beautiful," he responds.

I sigh, knowing I'm not getting my answer. "I'm beautiful," I rasp.

"Promise me you won't make yourself sick."

"I won't make myself sick." My voice is robotic, but it seems to be enough for now.

Releasing my wrists, he helps me stand up.

He looks down at my face, shaking his head as he wipes my wet cheeks with his thumbs. "Don't tell Elliot about this. Not what you were going to do, and not that I was in here with you."

"Why?"

"Just do as you're told."

He's about to leave when I call out again. "How did you know?"

A tiny smile tips the corner of his mouth. "I know you by heart, Jade. You can put up a tough front for everyone else. Just not me."

He leaves, and I ignore my reflection in the mirror as I follow. It's calling for me to look, to show me how ugly I am.

Ethan is about to leave the hallway, and I'm just coming out of the bathroom when Elliot opens the door that leads to the living room, letting loud music in. We freeze on the spot.

Elliot's tongue pokes at his inner cheek. His eyes flick from Ethan to me and back to his brother. He closes the door, shutting us out of the party.

"What are you both doing here?" He says *both*, but he's asking Ethan, not me.

He cocks an eyebrow at him, waiting for a response.

"Nothing," Ethan mumbles, pushing past his brother and into the living room. The door closes again, and it's just me and Elliot.

He brings his inquisitive stare to me. "Was he with you?"

I shake my head, unsure why I'm doing what Ethan said. "I was in the bathroom. I just saw him come out of his room."

I'm not sure if he believes me. Elliot is smart, cunning. It's not easy to lie to him. But before he can keep going, I notice the object in his hands.

"No." My voice is firm. He is not putting those on me.

"Oh, yes. That's two interactions with the Kings, and two fights in one night. You clearly can't be trusted to roam around freely."

I take a step back. "Don't you fucking dare."

"Jade, baby. Don't confuse me with Ethan. He's weak for you. I'm not."

I shake my head so intensely I make myself dizzy. "It's because I didn't take your fucking deal, isn't it? You're such an asshole, Elliot."

"Ah, maybe I'm a little hurt." He shrugs. "Or maybe I think you just need more convincing."

He pounces on me, grabbing my arm and slamming me against the wall. "Fuck off," I shriek as he grabs both my wrists.

"That fucking mouth," he growls. "It's going to get you in serious trouble one day."

He wraps a cuff around my right wrist, then my left, my hands now safely secured behind my back.

"I hate you," I grit out, my cheek against the wall. "I swear I'm going to kill you in your sleep."

"With your hands cuffed behind your back?" he mocks me. "I don't think so. Come on now. Trot back to the living room and let's see if I can make you change your mind about that deal. Maybe a little time with your old crew will show you how much you need my protection."

When I don't move, he sighs. Like a parent who doesn't want to have a go at their kid, but who knows it's coming. "Go back to the living room, Jade."

"Don't tell me what to do," I snap back.

Damn, I really have no survival instincts.

He pulls me away from the wall, holding me by my upper arm as he drags me back to the party.

"Jade, baby, I think you'll be doing *exactly* what I tell you to do from now on."

7

ELLIOT

All the Things I Hate About You - Huddy

I wonder if Jade gave that man her consent to play with her however he wants.

Stan.

What did he do to keep her? Apart from helping her stay away from us. Was it a monthly payment? Or just whatever she wanted she'd get? Did he bring her to fancy restaurants? He's clearly a rich motherfucker who can afford anything. He probably bought her thousand-dollar dresses for the charity balls he took her to. And she'd do anything he wanted in the car on the way there. At the event. On the way back. At home.

My shoulders tense at the girl who keeps putting her hands on my chest while she talks. She's sitting right next to me on the sofa, but my eyes are on Jade kneeling on the floor in front of me. I can't look away from her glaring at me.

No one has done anything yet, just observing and daring each other to do something in the last five minutes I've put her there.

I just need one person to scare the shit out of her and she'll be begging me to offer that deal again.

"EAT SPIT!" By Slush Puppy is blasting through whatever speaker someone brought to our house. The walls are shaking, the floor feeling unstable.

The new Kings' girl next to me starts kissing my neck like she'll rise in our ranks if she makes me come.

She won't.

She won't make me come, and she won't rise in our ranks.

People think I'm the number one fuckboy in the Kings' crew—and God knows I've had my share of our girls—but no one gets my attention if Jade is around. No one else but her can get my dick hard if she's in the vicinity. And the cute blonde with blue eyes—the opposite of the girl kneeling before me—doesn't stand a fucking chance.

Bless her soul for trying, though.

I've done a lot of things to keep Jade close to me. To make her mine. Most I'm not exactly proud of, but I think the current plan takes the trophy.

I look at my brother, sitting in his armchair like an old man. It's a worn-down leather thing close to the corner of the room, looking out of the window at our street. No one is going near him. People still secretly think Ethan is a weirdo; he acts strange, hates to be touched, will stay silent until he explodes. But no one tells him it's weird. They're too scared now. They seem to not want to die a painful death.

He's bobbing his head to the song, his black-painted nails tapping the left arm of his chair, completely detached from the situation like he lives in a different reality from ours.

I huff and push the girl away from me.

"Go sit on Ethan's lap," I order her sweetly.

Her blue eyes widen, and she hesitates. She's so fucking new, her Kings tattoo is still in a plastic wrap. A crown on her collarbone. We all have one, proud to forever be a part of a dangerous gang that only has any importance in our broken town.

"But..."

I lean toward her. "But?"

"He's scary," she whispers, barely audibly above the music. "And everyone says not to touch him."

Jade snorts in front of me, mocking the girl. She doesn't understand she's the only person Ethan ever lets near him. That she's privileged when it comes to my brother.

"You stay quiet," I order without even looking.

Understanding the blonde's weakness in a split second, I decide to use it against her. "If you're scared of Ethan, sweet thing, maybe you shouldn't be with the Kings. There's much scarier than him out there."

I watch her throat work. "No, I know. It's just..." She eyes him. "I know what he did to those guys at the warehouse."

Licking my lips, I smile brightly at her. The warehouse is where we fight once a week. One cage, anyone can fight, NSC and Kings alike. Just like everything in our town, there are no laws inside the warehouse. Deaths are rare, but people leave changed.

Occasionally, Ethan fights there. When the lethal energy inside him needs an outlet and I forbid him to kill anyone. The last guy he fought lost his hand from the number of times my brother stomped on it. The one before lost an eye when he pressed his thumb in the socket.

Creepy boy he is. No one understands him. Not like I do.

"I promise he doesn't hurt the women he fucks." I chuckle to myself. "Well, not beyond repair. Go on, now." A lie if I've ever heard one. Ethan doesn't fuck anyone.

But not only does it get the blonde going, it also makes Jade's face fall. She doesn't like to hear about her ex with other girls.

I smile to myself as I relax on my sofa.

Because if Ethan is busy with a girl, he won't be busy thinking about someone else. If she pesters him all night, he won't give Jade any thought.

His eyes go to mine the second blondie approaches to get his attention. Narrowing his eyes at me, he waves her away no matter how much she tries to make conversation.

She puts a flat hand on his chest, and he grabs her wrist. I hear her whimper over the music. Then he's pushing her off, getting up from his armchair, and stalking to the hallway.

Good. I don't want him around for what's to come.

I watch the first guy who decides to try his chance. He steps next to Jade.

"So the traitor is back?" he asks me as he looks down at her kneeling form.

"I'm not a fucking traitor," she spits back at him. "And if you touch me, you're dead."

"Yeah?" he snorts. He kneels next to her, flipping a switchblade open and pressing it against her cheek.

I cluck my tongue at him. "No hurting beyond repair."

He nods at me, pulling the blade away and looking where to hurt her.

Her wide eyes go from his blade to me. "Are you seriously gonna let him do this?"

"Wanna rethink our deal?"

"Fuck you."

I nod at the guy, and he slams his blade down, making Jade shriek. The point lands in the carpet, right between her legs.

Her eyes flutter open, staring at the floor in front of her. The guy grabs her hair, pulling her head back. "You're going to suffer for what you did."

He releases her violently, and she looks up at me with all the hate she can muster.

This is going to be fun.

The next guy tries to put his hand under her shirt, but I shake my head at him. "Not if you want that hand to stay attached to your body."

Changing his mind, he drops his entire drink on her, making her gasp when the ice lands on her head.

"You're an asshole, Elliot," she seethes, pulling at her cuffs as if they're going to break because she wills them to.

"I can be worse."

As the night goes on, more hover around her. I dissuade them with a single look when they want to try something too harsh, so most end up throwing food at her or pouring their drinks on her. She gets a flew slaps to the face, and somehow ended up with a bloody nose. No one fails to call her a traitor. Her cheeks are red, eyes watery. No tears fall, though.

The girl can take it.

If anything, I'm the one who hates this fucking plan. Every time someone calls her a bitch, a traitor, or a whore, I'm ready to slam their heads against the floor. Every time they hurt her, I think of a thousand ways to kill them.

Someone lights a cigarette next to her and points the burning end at her arm.

She shakes her head, looking at me. "Elliot."

"If only you'd said yes to our deal."

"Don't let him..."

She tries to move away, but he holds her by the hair.

"Elliot," she whimpers. The burning embers are so close, ready to burn her skin and leave a scar.

"You want a taste of what it'd feel like to have my protection, baby?"

She nods frantically, eyeing the cigarette. "Fuck... fuck...*do something!*"

"Stop." My order is calm, but he stops anyway.

"Aw, man. Come on, it's fun."

"You know what else is fun?" I tell him. "A bullet in your head. Now fuck off."

Jade is panting when he lets her go. "Now why don't you think real hard about my offer?"

The party has died by the time Kay shows up. I stayed up all night, partying and drinking a little too much, but mainly keeping an eye on a desperate Jade. Kay turned twenty-five at the beginning of the month, and she's a mother of two little twins. Her girls are staying with her mom, away from the North Shore, but even without them here, partying isn't really her thing anymore. She prefers showing up in the early morning when everyone is either gone or passed out on the floor.

She walks in casually, every step calculated to not show her eagerness. She's with her boyfriend, Ivan. They met through the Wolves. He's a simple soldier for them, but important to the Kings. Being Kay's right-hand man, I do a lot of work with him and quickly understood why he's not worth anything to the Wolves. The guy is fucking useless, and I know she's only with him to have a direct contact with the Bratva.

Kay's pitch-black hair is tied in a low ponytail, two

strands falling on either side of her green eyes. She looks at the mess, and mainly the people on the floor.

She huffs, unimpressed, like a CEO realizing all her employees are scrolling on TikTok rather than sending important emails.

And that's pretty much what it is, except we do illegal shit rather than send correspondence.

She walks to the shelves on the other side of the room, picking up the baseball bat we keep against the wall, and whacks the first person she finds on the floor next to her. Not enough to break anything, just a nice bruise. Then she hits the metal against the next person.

"It's six a.m.," she shouts. "Does no one do any work in this fucking crew?"

When people start to realize who's waking them up, they hurry into standing positions, muttering *shit* and *sorry, boss* as they leave the house.

Once it's empty, she turns to me. "Wake the bitch up. I'll get Ethan."

Kay and Ivan disappear through the back, and I look at Jade.

She's sleeping on the floor by the sofa, her hair wet and sticky from the things that have been thrown at her, her—or rather my—t-shirt damp, and her hands still cuffed. Shouting wouldn't wake her up, though. Sleeping is her escape, I know that. Everyone used to tease her about how big of a sleeper she was, and I wonder what she's always trying to get away from.

I squat next to her, reaching out to grab her small breast through the shirt. It fits perfectly in my palm. Everything about Jade's body fits perfectly with mine. She's a small thing, barely reaching five feet. I'm big, huge, and I can wrap her and manipulate her body in any way I want. I can fucking swallow her in one bite.

Pulling my hand away and moving to her shoulder, I attempt to shake her awake, but there's nothing to do. When she's in deep sleep, she can't be woken up. Only Ethan and I know how, and we've never shared it with anyone. I press my palm against her mouth and pinch her nose. In a split second, her eyes snap open, and she thrashes under me, so I release her.

"Fuck," she pants. "Asshole."

"Kay's here to see you," I explain.

"What? Fuck." Panicked, she tries to get up, but I stop her with a palm on her chest.

I help her stand up only to force her to sit on the sofa as I stand in front of her. "Now is the time to accept my deal."

She snorts. "Let her fucking kill me."

She starts regretting her decision the second Kay walks back into the room with Ivan and Ethan. When she sees Kay, her green eyes annihilating her on the spot, she turns to me, silently begging to go back on her word. Our boss strides to her, ready to end her.

I think I'll let her learn her lesson before I make her a new offer.

"Kay..." Jade attempts to talk calmly, plastering herself to the sofa's overused cushions.

She fails to placate our boss. Kay grabs her by the back of the head, bringing Jade forward at the same time as she pulls her knee up and crashes it against her nose.

I grind my teeth. I wasn't ready to see that.

Fuck...I hate seeing her hurt, but this is a game of patience. One of us is going to break first, and it has to be her.

Jade's whimper is barely covered by Kay's deadly tone. "Welcome back to the North Shore, bitch."

She lets her go, and Jade falls against the sofa again. She throws her head back, her nose bleeding.

"Get her up," Kay seethes.

I pause for a second, my eyes stuck on Jade's bloody nose.

"Elliot," my boss snaps. "Today."

There's always been that strange feeling in my body when someone hurts Jade. She once got into a huge fist fight with Billie Scott, from NSC. Caden's now fiancée, Billie, is an MMA fighter. She kicked Jade's ass before we even showed up for help. Jade was hurt, unconscious on the floor, and I remember my heart dropping so low I thought my legs were going to give up. I could have killed Billie that day. I thought I was going to.

But there's a point to this madness. I need to remember that.

"If you're going to beat her up, at least let me uncuff her. Give the girl a chance to defend herself."

I pretend I don't care, but I don't wait for Kay's answer. As soon as I uncuff her, she brings her hands to her nose. Blood seeps through her fingers as she groans in pain.

Grabbing Jade by the upper arm, I drag her off the couch to face Kay. Ivan is standing a step back, letting his girlfriend thrive in her role.

"Here's how it's gonna go," she tells Jade. "The longer this lasts, the more it hurts. So let's get straight to the point. Where's my money?"

With one hand still pinching her nostrils, and blood dripping down her face and onto her lips, Jade turns to me, confused.

"What?"

"My. Money. Where is it?" Kay insists. She can stay so calm for someone desperate to get her hands on the fifty thousand dollars.

"What money?" Jade panics.

Kay's nostrils flare, her anger amping up. She hates liars. Especially those who were part of her crew.

"The money you and Sawyer stole from me."

I know Jade can take a beating. We're from the North Shore, we all can. But my chest tightens seeing her like this.

"I don't...I don't know what you're talking about."

When Kay hits her in the stomach, she drops to the floor.

I close my eyes, anger simmering in my veins, but I have to stay in character.

"Get up," Kay orders, her patience wavering.

"Jade," I interject, knowing nothing good can come from not listening to Kayla. "Get up."

She hides her face against the carpet that's turned gray over time, shaking her head. "I didn't steal anyt—"

"Get. *Up!*" our boss barks.

"Come on." My voice is softer than I want it to be, a reassurance more than another order. I grab her at the waist and force her to stand.

She's trembling in my arms, her face bloody and her breathing staggered.

"Elliot, I didn't—I don't understand."

"You little *bitch*." Kay is fuming now.

She grabs Jade by the hair, rears her arm back, but before she can strike again, Ethan's still voice resonates in the room.

"Kayla." I fucking knew he would lose it if he saw Jade hurt. He can put up a front all he likes, but he was deadly in love with her in the past. Feelings that strong don't just disappear. "My carpet," he adds. "Don't ruin it."

And while this might sound disinterested to anyone else's ear, I know my brother. I know that's his way of intervening. I know it the moment he stands up slowly from his chair, walks to a terrified Jade, and gives her a tissue.

She grabs it with a shaking hand, bringing it to her nose. Ethan observes her for a few seconds that seem infinite before plastering a look of disgust over his face and walking back to his seat.

"Kay," Jade tries to talk through the blood dripping from her nose and onto her lips. "I promise you, I didn't steal anything from you."

It's crazy how accustomed we get to being beaten up on the North Shore. It happens to us so often, everyone just keeps going along with their day when it does. I'm not surprised Jade keeps trying to resonate with Kay right now when anyone else from the South Bank would be running to the hospital.

"Sawyer *told* us you did. He might have been a coward, but at least he stopped lying when he knew he was close to dying. Why don't you learn to do the same? Because I swear to God, Jade, I will hurt you. *This*"—she points at Jade's wound—"is nothing. Don't fucking try me."

"Sawyer said I helped him steal money?"

"You helped him on some jobs, didn't you?" Kay asks.

"Yes, but—"

"I went away when my dad died to protect my daughters, and you two became real close, didn't you?"

Kayla and Caden's dad died in a fire NSC started in home. Kayla's toddlers almost died too. They would have if Caden hadn't gotten them out of the house in time. After that, Kayla, who should have taken over the Kings' crew

67

right away, had to leave town. She wanted her daughters away from the danger and brought them to her mom.

The whole time she was away, Sawyer assumed it was his right to be at the head of the Kings. Of course, Jade, in her eagerness to get to the top, sat on his dick the moment Sawyer took the power. But he was stupid, didn't think before he acted. His pride made him volatile in the war against NSC. Mainly, none of us knew he was stealing from the Kings to set himself up for life.

Jade hesitates. "We became close, but—"

"And you listened to whatever shit he said. You did his bidding, sucked his dick whenever he asked, spread your legs for him. *Didn't. You?*"

"Kayla, I didn't know—"

"You helped him pick up the money from Elliot's card cloning."

"I did, but we brought it back!"

"Oh, really? Where's the missing half, then? Thirty grand, to be precise."

"What?" Jade chokes. She coughs, spitting blood on the floor. "We brought it back to Sawyer's house."

"It's *not. There.*"

"But..."

"What about when you set up Billie, huh?"

Billie Scott used to do jobs for Caden. He didn't give her much of a choice. She moved guns for him and brought the money to us. Jade and Sawyer stole the money out of her car once, setting up Billie to believe it had been robbed by randoms. When she came to Sawyer's house to tell him, they beat her up. Sawyer wanted to do worse, but Jade stopped him.

"I set up Billie because she's NSC!" Jade defends. "Caden is one of us, and he was dating someone from our rival gang. You hate her too. I might have hurt her, but I didn't take the money that night."

"Yes, you did." Kayla's tone is much calmer than Jade's terrified one. "You took the twenty grand and probably hid it in the same place you hid the scam money. You better fucking tell me where that is before I cut your tongue off and make you guide me there in silence with a gun at the back of your head."

Ah, there's the Kayla we all know. So deliciously savage.

"I don't..." She looks around in utter panic. "I didn't steal anything, and if Sawyer did, then he didn't tell me about it."

Pausing, she looks at Ivan, Kay, and finally me. She bites her lower lip, and I know that's what she does when she doesn't want people to see it tremble. When she doesn't want us to know she's about to burst into tears. God forbid someone saw an ounce of emotion apart from her anger.

"Why won't any of you believe me?" she rasps. "Elliot...I promise I didn't know anything about this."

I look deep into her eyes, and I do something I'll regret in the future.

But if it keeps her here, scared, at my mercy, then I don't care.

I smile at her, knowing my next words are exactly what is going to be her downfall.

"If you didn't know about the stolen money...then why would you run away?"

And the way her face falls tells me everything I need to know.

She's hiding something else.

8

JADE

MakeDamnSure - Taking Back Sunday

I would rather Kay beat me to death than answer Elliot's question.

The day I ran, I thought I had a reason to.

Two years ago, I believed with all my might that Sawyer had told them my secret. The one he was blackmailing me with. The fucker had a good time making me do his bidding. He knew my secret for months, but only started using it against me when things got tough for him. When his hunger for power became starvation.

The bastard was good at tricking me into listening.

So when he got caught by Caden for what he and I did to Billie, I knew I was going down with him. When the brothers came to my house, saying Sawyer had spilled it all, I couldn't stay.

But now I know what he said was absolute shit. Stealing money, my ass. Sawyer didn't have a chance to spill my *real* secret, and it's coming with me to my grave. Even if it's earlier than I ever anticipated.

"Tell us, Jade," Kay sneers. "Tell us why you ran away if not because you stole money from us."

It's not really a lie if you tell a half truth, is it?

Still holding the tissue to my nose, I bring a hand to my ribs. They're going to bruise. I can barely fucking breathe right now.

"You know why I ran away. I set up Billie. I attacked her. I carved a fucking Kings' crown on her neck like I did to many of our enemies before. Caden killed Sawyer for what we did. I was next on the list. *That's* why I ran. Not because I stole some fucking money. I don't know where that is."

They all look at me, not one of them believing my excuse. It's so clear in their eyes.

The front door bursts open, but I'm not too surprised. Because when you speak of the fucking devil...Caden King shows his face.

Caden strides into the living room, his piercing green eyes on me, ready to annihilate.

"Like a fucking Christmas morning," he purrs as he puts a hand at the back of his jeans.

My eyes round when he pulls out a switchblade and clicks it open. And that's when I change my mind.

About everything I said until now.

About being strong.

About dying.

If I need Elliot to survive in this town. Fuck it. I'll do it.

I take a step back, standing right next to Elliot.

Kayla is talking to her brother, busy telling him he has no right being here, and while they're all focusing on that, I turn to Elliot.

"I'll take it."

He cocks an eyebrow at me, his smile already spreading.

"What's that, baby?"

"I'll take your fucking deal, Elliot," I grit. "Now fucking do something about your psychopath of a best friend."

"Jade." Caden shows me his sadistic smile, ignoring his sister. "How wonderful to have you back on the North Shore."

In two strides, he's in front of me, but in one, Elliot stands in his way.

Thank. Fuck.

"Cade," he warns. "We had a deal."

Like the maniac that he is, Caden throws his head back laughing. "No. We had a deal that I'd leave her alone while she was in town. Then she ran away. Then we learned she had stolen from us. Now it's off. Step aside, Elliot. I have a dying need to stab your girl in the heart."

"You're not stabbing anyone," Elliot growls back. "Behave yourself."

"Oh..." Caden nods to himself. "I see. So all the pretending to find her so she could pay for her crimes against the Kings was just a nice little talk until you got her back. What is it? You haven't gotten your dick wet yet so we can't kill her?"

"Caden," Kayla warns. "We don't have the money. No one kills her until I get my fucking bills."

"Are you that stupid?" He turns to his sister and tilts his head to the side. "She ran away with it, Kay. She probably spent all of it by now. It's been two years, you idiot."

I shake my head, hating the false accusation. "I didn't! I didn't steal any money."

I try to go past Elliot, but I feel a hand grab the back of my t-shirt and pull me back. Now I'm standing behind both Elliot and Ethan, who apparently deemed he doesn't want Caden to kill me either.

"This shit is too fucking funny," Caden laughs again.

"Look at all of you. She's got you two wrapped around her fucking finger." He points at Elliot and Ethan. "And you"—he points at Kay—"are clearly too fucking stupid to run a crew."

"Spare us the bullshit," Ethan says in a low voice. "You don't care about the money, and you don't care about her running away. You're not part of this, remember? You never wanted to be. You left the North Shore so you and your fiancée would never have to face any consequences. So be kind and *spare us.* The only reason you just drove I don't know how many fucking hours to come to a town you barely ever put a foot in anymore, the only reason you want her dead, is because she fucked up Billie. And we had a deal for that. You let *us* punish her for it."

Caden's smile grows bigger. Scarier. It's always bad news when he smiles. Everything is backwards in his brain.

He lets out a short breath. "So perceptive our Ethan, isn't he?" Taking half a step back, he runs his hand through his messy black hair. "As you said...she touched Billie." He chuckles to himself. "She *fucking touched her!*"

With a roar, he jumps on his friends, attempting to push them aside as he tries to grab me. He still manages to cut my arm, and I cry out, more from the shock than the pain, pulling away but quickly blocked by the wall behind me.

It only takes Elliot to hold him back. The rage inside Caden might be strong, but Elliot is a beast. And if he doesn't want anyone to touch me, they won't.

Accepting his deal might be the best fucking decision I ever made.

The door opens again, and Billie Scott runs inside panting.

"Caden!" she shouts. "Stop." She mumbles *for fuck's sake*

to herself, like this happens way too often. "Stop, you maniac."

"You're fucking dead, Jade. Wait until I get you alone."

"Caden, enough," his fiancée orders. She sounds like the kind of pitbull owners who can never get their dogs under control.

"Little bee," Caden says to her softly, but his lethal eyes are on me. "Let me do this, and then we go home."

"You just had me chase you across the entire North Shore, you lunatic. Don't *little bee* me."

Billie settles beside Caden, and Elliot lets him go. Now that the woman who owns him is here, he doesn't seem as scared that he's going to do something irrational. I am.

"Jade," Billie says sternly as a hello.

I nod at her, my eyes automatically going to the scar I left on her a little over two years ago. The Kings' crown carved into the side of her neck.

Billie and I hate each other. There is no other way to put it. She's NSC. I'm Kings. Or at least, I was. I didn't need a reason to hate her. Our gangs were at war. But when Caden started becoming obsessed with her, Sawyer's hatred for Billie became irrational. In his eyes, we were all doing our parts to keep the city in our hands except Caden.

And guess who Sawyer chose to go after Billie?

The only woman who couldn't say no to him.

Me.

So I tried to beat her up with a few friends of mine, thinking that would appease Sawyer and his need for blood.

But Billie was a semi-professional MMA fighter back then. She humbled us real quick.

NSC has a scar they leave on their enemies. The pathway for tears. That's what Billie did to me that day. She pinned me to the ground once I was beaten up, grabbed her knife, and cut me. I can't admit out loud that I deserved it, but I know it. Now I have a scar from the corner of my left eye, across my temple, and all the way to my hairline. Ethan and Elliot saved me that day. It's not something they would do again now.

Billie and I are quite alike when it comes to size. We're on the smaller side, barely five-foot tiny girls who think ourselves bigger than we are. She has that innocent look about her, with big brown eyes that always seem surprised. Whereas I have the catty look, with almond eyes and high cheekbones that make me look like I'm always judging someone.

Now we even share scars we gave to each other. My stomach twists when I see the thick scar today. I regret everything I did for the Kings to keep the North Shore in our hands, but even more, the things Sawyer made me do.

We become inhuman for a slice of power in our corner of Silver Falls. As if any of this matters.

Now I bear Billie's scar and she bears mine.

"Caden," Kay snaps, fury powerful in her voice. "The reminder of you not being part of this crew anymore should be enough for you to step the fuck back."

His jaw works from side to side, grinding his teeth, and his lethal eyes are still on me. He's swallowing me whole without a single movement. Kay ignores him and steps in his line of sight, allowing me to breathe again.

"Don't worry about him." Elliot's voice startles me. I hadn't realized he was so close. I was too focused on Caden. "You're going to be with us, anyway."

The ominous tone doesn't help in the slightest. My heart is going to explode from the anxiety freezing me right now. The pressure on my bones threatens to break me.

"Jade." Kay brings my attention back to her. I'm backed against the wall, with Elliot and Ethan on either side, and she's towering over me. "You're stuck with me until I get every single cent back from the money you stole."

I startle when she puts a hand on my shoulder, and it makes her smile. I thought she was going to hurt me, and she loves that I'm scared of her.

"Kayla." I lick my dry lips. They taste like blood. "I don't have your money. I promise you."

"That's okay." Her smile is terrifying. Caden doesn't get his craziness from nowhere. The whole family is fucked up. Their dad was the worst of the three. "You're going to work for me until you've paid me back. You remember how that works, right? I give you something to do, and you execute like a good little soldier, huh? Except now, if you don't, I'll be putting your body on your father's grave, and your head on your mother's. That way, you can be with both of them even in death."

A shiver runs past me. She has no pity, no fucking heart. I know how that feels because I used to be the same. The Kings had made me that way.

Being away for so long has weakened me. I might still be angry and look tough, but I know my skin is not as thick as it used to be because my heart fissures at the mention of my parents. It reminds me that I truly have no one anymore.

My dad killed himself when I was a senior in high school. He couldn't take the situation we were in anymore. The debts were too high, the money coming in too low. He lost his job, and that was the end of him. He apologized that he couldn't take care of us anymore right before he went to his bedroom and hung himself. Never in a million years did we think that's what he was about to do when he apologized.

Nine dollars and ninety-seven cents. That's how much money was in his bank account when he pushed off the stool that was holding his weight. The credit card was well below the zero line, but going under the ten-dollar line on his main bank account tipped the balance. Three cents.

Nine dollars and ninety-seven cents. Why? Why not five?

Why not zero? If he had just waited for zero, I might have realized something was up. But he was always taking care of us. We had a place to live, no matter how small. We had food on the table. I had clothes on my back. He gave me lunch money for school.

If only he'd said something to me. If only he'd just opened up and told me that we had nothing. I was already with the Kings. He knew that. I would have asked for a loan, worked harder, done anything.

I still can't sleep at night knowing I could have easily asked for a thousand dollars from Kay. We were friends. She was important and would have given it to me if only to pay for the rent.

"Do you even know where your mother's grave is, Jade?"

My gaze drops, throat tightening.

Talking about my parents is more than I can take right now.

"Of course you don't," she snorts. "You weren't here for the funeral."

My ears start ringing. I'm choking on tears I refuse to let reach my eyes.

"I was there," she tells me. "I paid for it because I thought you'd show up. I'll be adding that to your bill."

I throw my head back, swallowing the sob that threatens to explode out of me. "Stop."

"Why didn't your sugar daddy pay for it?" she insists.

I don't know. He didn't tell me she was dead until months later. He wanted to hold over my head the fact that he was paying for her medical bills. A way to make sure I wasn't going anywhere.

"Fucking hell," Kay mocks me. "We all knew you were a heartless bitch, but not attending your mother's funeral is a new level of selfish."

I look back at her, slightly up since she's taller than me. "I didn't know," I force out between clenched teeth.

I see Ethan shift next to me. He looks down at me, brow furrowed like he can hardly believe it, and yet...he still does.

"Well, don't worry," Kay says, tightening her grip on my shoulder. "You'll join her soon if you don't do what you're told."

I shrug her off. "I'll do your fucking jobs. I'll get your money back."

Fifty grand? I might as well ask her to kill me now. I'll die of old age before she gives me enough jobs to call us even.

"Yeah. You will," she confirms with a confidence I yearn for.

"The brothers can keep an eye on you while you do my jobs. You'll stay here with them since you're homeless."

Another jab. Another hit I take by grinding my teeth.

"Do I get to kill her once she's paid you back?" Caden sneers behind his sister.

Kay moves to the side, but it's Billie who comes forward.

"No." Her eyes are on me, and the pity in them makes me want to puke. My own worst enemy thinks I've fallen so low she feels sorry for me.

"Jade," she says to me. "I forgive you for what you did. I'm alive and well. You stopped Sawyer from raping me."

My eyes widen. She remembers?

And I must look truly vulnerable right now because she reads me like an open book. "Of course I remember."

"I set you up," I admit out loud, like confessing to a priest.

"Yeah. And I bullied you and beat you up in high school, just 'cause we were from different gangs."

"You could have died," I insist.

"And I could have been raped. But you stopped that."

Yeah. I wouldn't wish being sexually assaulted by any of the Kings men on anyone. Clearly, not even on my worst enemy.

She turns to Caden. "I told you a million times that I have nothing against her anymore. Move on, Caden. I'm serious."

His eyes narrow on me, practically growling at me like the fucking guard dog he is.

"We're going home," he finally says.

"We are?" Billie can't believe she actually got through to him.

"Yes, little bee. I must punish that ass of yours for ordering me around, don't I?"

We're not privy to the rest of their conversation. Jealousy rips me inside as I watch them leave the house. He's so in love with her. My gaze flicks to Ethan. We used to be in love. What happened to us?

Kay throws something at me, and I catch it before it hits my aching ribs.

"I call, you come. Any time of day or night. Anything the brothers need, you're on that too." She takes a few steps back, smiling at me. "Welcome back to the North Shore, Jade. We missed you."

9

JADE

Roses red – Jeris Johnson

Kay and Ivan are gone, leaving me with only Elliot and Ethan who have been so silent I forgot they were here. They did that on purpose, of course. Making sure to observe my every reaction.

Without saying a word, Ethan leaves for his bedroom. I know exactly where it is. I know where every single room is in this house. Ethan's, Elliot's, their parents' room. The kitchen, the garage, the basement where they kidnap and torture people for the Kings.

"What a gift," Elliot says in that horribly soft voice of his that announces the worst. He puts a hand at the small of my back. "We get you to ourselves until you pay back Kay."

The tight ball in my throat keeps swelling, reality hitting me harshly. A slap in the fucking face.

No parents. No home. No money. Now I know why all the Kings hate me and want me dead. They think I stole fifty grand from them. I have a debt that was never mine to pay in the first place.

All I have are the two men in this house.

One who loathes me.

One who never saw me as anything but a plaything.

Biting my trembling lower lip, I square my shoulders and look at Elliot. "Lucky you."

I take my time walking past him toward the back of the house, doing my best to pretend I'm not affected by any of this. Like most houses on their street, they have a single-story ranch-style home. The outside has panels falling all over the place, but they've managed to keep the inside liveable, especially since it's just the two of them. Their house is a little bigger than most around here. They have three bedrooms, and their backyard is wider than others.

I step along the hallway that leads to the back, past Ethan's bedroom, and turn left into the bathroom right next to his door. Closing it calmly, I lock it and push my back against it. I slowly slide to the floor and take a deep breath.

Then I explode into tears.

Fuck.

I can't believe I agreed to Elliot's deal. Only he would manipulate me into whatever he wants me to be. That's the way he is. He wants someone completely at his mercy, who would do exactly what he says. As long as a woman is his good girl he can praise, he doesn't care what happens to her.

I let my heart bleed on the floor of their bathroom, knowing there's nowhere else I can do this. I'm fucking stuck here, and I let the pain tear me apart.

Should I even care what happens to me? I'm the woman who ran away and left her sick mother behind. This is my punishment for not even knowing her resting place.

Fat tears fall down my cheeks, and I choke on a sob. I missed her when she was alive and I was away, but I could deal with the fact that being with Stan kept her alive. What now? What would she think of me if she knew the things I did with that man? That her daughter sold her body like it was worth nothing. She's better off dead, because she couldn't take the disappointment of what I've become.

And all for what? I'm back to square one, except way worse.

My eyes lock on the chipped bathroom sink as I attempt to take a breath and it gets cut short. I swallow it back, coughing as I choke. My chest tightens, the muscles straining and cutting off my breathing. I squeeze my eyes shut, but when I open them again, and my gaze goes higher, to the vanity mirror above the sink, I jerk my head back, hitting the door behind me.

I was too focused on my own misery yesterday to let the memories of this bathroom take over me, but they hold me in a tight grip today.

I spent a lot of time in this house as a teenager. Everywhere Ethan was, I followed. His attention meant everything to me, and I wanted to be by his side when he felt unwell, too sad. I wanted to hold his hand and tell him how much I loved him when he thought it was the end. When darkness engulfed him, I was there, bringing him back to the light. After we broke up, I was here for Elliot. The sex was wild, cathartic, and he wanted to see me all the time. I came and went in this house like it was my own place.

But being around this family came with consequences.

It's so easy to surprise a young girl while she washes her hands. To press her head against the mirror. To scare her into silence.

My gaze is stuck on the white sink. The same one from years ago.

I just want to be away for a second. Take a break from the situation. That's all I need. Then I'll be able to think straight.

Lying down on the cold tiles, I avoid the broken ones and press my burning cheek to them. I'm just going to rest here. Leave reality for a little while.

It's the feeling of losing balance that wakes me up. I recognize Elliot simply because of his smell. His cologne tickles my nose, a strong scent of fresh citrus. He's always smelled like a chill spring afternoon, resting in the shade of an orange tree, surrounded by the spice of life. Somewhere far from a city in a lush, green field.

Of course, once you know him, you know that field is a lure that leads innocent souls straight to hell. I only ever survived him because I'm not innocent.

"Jade," he sighs. He carefully puts me in his bed. It smells like him too.

The room is a dark blue from that time Ethan, him, and I painted it in high school. The paint is chipped in many areas now, but I can't see much else. It's probably still early morning, according to the deep blue sky outside.

He's got no nightstand, no alarm clock anywhere. Just a bed and an old chest of drawers that still has Pokémon stickers from when he was a kid.

Elliot slides in next to me. It's only when he pulls the covers up our bodies that I notice he's in nothing but boxers. I have a split second to catch the ridges of his abs, his strong chest, the scars on it. White and thick.

"Jade," he repeats softly. His hand comes to my cheek. He rubs his thumb under my left eye, then traces the scar I have at the corner, grazing it all the way to my hairline. "You cried."

He doesn't care, I have to remind myself. He just wants to see it.

When I don't say anything, his hand lowers, grabbing my cheeks and pouting my lips. He turns me to face him, his blue eyes the only light in the darkness. "You cried without me?"

I want to retort something, but he tightens his grip on me. "You didn't think I'd want to see that? Baby, you know how much I love to see you cry. How could you do this to me?"

My body is still heavy from sleep, my limbs paralyzed from the kind of tiredness I can't control.

"Elliot," I grunt, but the consonants are barely audible.

Grabbing my hand, he presses it against his hard-on. All that separates his silky skin from mine are his boxers.

"Just the thought of it," he whispers, his voice gravelly. "I know you'd never cry in front of us. You're too strong and stubborn for that. You wouldn't want anyone to see you as anything but the heartless bitch you pretend to be."

I twist, attempting to retreat, but something stops me.

My body.

My desires.

The memories of the things we used to do.

It's the way he makes me feel. That tingling sensation of electricity coursing through my body. The dampness I can feel in the boxers I'm wearing. His.

"But for me...you'd do it for me, right? You'll do anything for me now."

I take in a ragged breath.

"Do you understand your situation, Jade? You're mine now."

In a small but strong gesture, he brings me closer to him, his lips against my ear.

"Say it," he rasps.

I'd love to fight back, but I'm exhausted. Everything feels wrong. I'm still dirty and sticky from last night. I just want to sleep and forget.

"I'm yours."

"Now give it to me."

He senses my confusion. I know he does because I feel his smile against my ear. "Consent. To play with you however I want. Even when you're in states where you can't fight back. Even when you're sleeping. You wanted the deal, and it comes with all of that. So say it."

The hand holding mine against his dick closes into a fist, forcing my fingers to grab his thickness.

"Fuck," I sigh.

The mere fact of holding him, without him touching me anywhere near my pussy, makes me need him. If he wasn't keeping my cheeks hostage, I would probably already be panting for him. It's an unfair advantage he has that I know the sort of heaven a devil like him can take me to.

I shake my head, or at least I try.

"No, no," he whispers, his lips now brushing the skin below my earlobe. Tickles of pleasure bring goosebumps to my skin. "Think before you answer," he continues, as he keeps my head in place to make sure I can't shake *no*. "Remember what you accepted. I just saved you from Cade."

Keeping his grip on my hand, he thrusts slowly into my fist.

I have to force myself to swallow a moan. He's pleasuring himself, but it goes straight to my pussy.

"Think real hard about Vickie, who's only waiting for you to be alone before she strikes," he says softly.

He pulls away in the slightest to look into my eyes.

The room is only illuminated by the light of the moon, but I know he wants to check how I'm doing. Because Elliot is a lot of things—a playboy, a manipulator, a sex addict—but he isn't a rapist. He would lose all sorts of pleasure if I wasn't into this, and his pleasure is everything.

When he's happy I'm not unwell, he smiles with pride, knowing he's practically got me exactly where he wants me.

"I'm not even counting the other Kings who want to hurt you. I will make it go away. All of it."

Is it really worth fighting him? When I know I already agreed in the living room? Everything just feels so real now. It's the only thing that will give me a semblance of normality and happiness in this fucked-up situation. Going back to being Elliot Pearson's toy is the only thing that will feel like nothing has changed.

His lips graze mine, his tongue darting to lick my bottom one.

"Mm, baby."

I'm seriously panting as he keeps using my hand to fuck himself through his boxers. I need him to touch me too. Just a bit of pressure.

A small whimper escapes me as he bites my bottom lip, then sucks on it to make it all better.

"Say yes," he rasps. "Say, 'Elliot, I consent to being your good little fuck toy again. Any time of day and night, any state I'm in.'"

His knee slides up against the sheet, against my thigh, and he slowly spreads my legs.

"Oh God," I moan. He's not touched me where I need him yet. He's not put pressure where I need him the *most*.

"Go on," he taunts me, his breath against my wet bottom lip.

He relaxes his hold on my cheeks, enough for me to be able to move, but I'm not going anywhere.

"Elliot," I pant. "Just do it."

"That's not what I want to hear," he growls. "And you know I hate bad girls who can't listen to what I ask for."

I take a deep breath, grounding myself. "Elliot..."

"Yes?" I can feel the way he's already tasting victory on his tongue, and I hate him for it, but I give in anyway.

"I'll be your fuck toy again. Any time you want."

"Now that's the good girl I missed."

He lets go of me and turns around, leaving me desperate for more.

Of course he would. That's how he plays his games.

When I think he's asleep, I slide my hand under the covers. I slither my way under the boxers, ready to feed the hunger he's started inside me.

I startle when he grabs my wrist through the sheets before I can press against my throbbing clit.

"Don't make me cuff you," he says in a groggy voice. "The only way you'll get pleasure is through me. Now take that pretty little hand away from my pussy."

I want to roll my eyes at the way he thinks my pussy is his, but I do it.

He grabs my hand, keeping it in his as he brings it to his chest.

I fall asleep feeling his steady heartbeat against my skin.

10

JADE

Fool & The Thief – THE HARA

I think it's after twelve when something wakes me up.

Pleasure.

I moan, feeling the flick of his tongue repeatedly against my clit. My hand slides under the covers, grabbing his hair.

I can feel how wet I am, and the way he laps it up.

"Elliot," I gasp when his teeth graze my clit.

I press harder against his face, feeling so close to the edge. Let there at least be one good thing about this deal. I get to have sex with Elliot Pearson again.

That's until he pulls away, his face appearing from under the cover.

"Good afternoon, my love."

I throw my head back, tense from the need to orgasm.

"Don't leave me like this," I huff.

"I am absolutely leaving you like this."

"Elliot," I whine. "Isn't this deal meant to be fun?"

"For me. And my fun is watching you become more and

more desperate for me. That's when you become really interesting to play with."

The few hours I slept were the worst sleep I've had in a long time. At least Stan would always feed the undying need for sex inside me. He would attempt to satiate the both of us to no end. Elliot prefers torturing me just because he can.

"You should go shower," he says. "Then I'll make you something to eat."

When I'm showered, Elliot gives me yet another of his band t-shirts. My Chemical Romance this time, and I know he got inspired by the album his brother is currently listening to on repeat in his bedroom. I slide on a clean pair of boxers and walk to the kitchen with him.

"I'm loving seeing you dressed in my shirts," he says casually. "I think this should become a rule."

"You're making rules now?" I roll my eyes as I open the kitchen door. Ethan comes out at the same time, bumping me with his shoulder and not sparing a word as he keeps walking toward the hallway. Turns out, he wasn't in his bedroom.

His black hair is disheveled, like he ran his hand through it many times, strands falling in his eyes. He's wearing black jeans with a chain hanging from the front pocket to the back belt hoop.

And no shirt.

My mouth waters, catching a glimpse of his hard abs and the myriad of tattoos spread all over his torso. Unlike Elliot, who's on the bulkier side and whose body has always been thick, Ethan is skinnier. He clearly has to work twice as hard as his brother to develop his muscles and put on weight. He's lean, the hard ridges of his abs prominent.

He didn't look like that when we were together. He was a skinny boy with long hair to his mid-neck. He didn't care what he looked like. I didn't care either. There's something special in Ethan's mind. He's a creative genius. Life takes a different meaning through his eyes. He turns ugly things beautiful. He turned *me* beautiful through him.

"He's making music," I mumble toward Elliot, surprised I can see it so clearly after so many years.

I can see it because the plate he's holding indicates he'll be eating in his room, yet the simple slice of buttered toast means he's not really eating much. I also know because he's not wearing a shirt. Because his hair is greasy and messy. There are moon-shaped nail marks on his biceps because he presses them into his skin when he can't get it right. He needs pain to function, needs things around him to break and bend to his will, or else he gets frustrated.

"You need to eat more than that," Elliot throws his way.

He ignores us, of course. We hear his door slam, and the deafening music carries on.

Yet another clue. Back then, he would put an album on for everyone to hear, and then he'd pick up his headphones, plug them into his amp, and create magic.

"He hasn't made music in months," Elliot says to himself, but I'm here to witness it anyway.

Unlike Ethan, Elliot and I eat eggs and bacon like we've been starving for days.

I just hope there're no regrets afterward. That I don't feel sick from it.

I decide to not look at myself in the mirror when I brush my teeth, turning my back. I ignore the way my eyes are desperate to go to the reflection and find something wrong with me.

There's a knock on the front door as I finish, and I walk back toward the main bit of the house in time to see Elliot open for Kay.

Shit.

She's back already? It hasn't even been twenty-four hours.

"Where is she?" is the first thing she says. There's no avoiding her, so I make my way to the living room.

Her smirk makes me want to punch her in the face. "Nice bruises." My cheek feels swollen from her hits, and the skin around my left eye feels tender. I wouldn't be surprised if I have a nice black eye. I'm glad she can't see my bruised ribs.

"I got a job for you."

"Couldn't tell me over the phone?" I snarl.

She throws a plastic bag at me, and I catch it, opening it as she talks. "Not unless you want to work for me in Elliot's boxers."

There's a pair of jeans in there, a bottle of apple-scented shampoo, and a makeup pouch. I open it, finding eyeliner, some mascara, and red lipstick. There're also some skincare products.

My eyebrows lift when I realize she remembers every single product I used to buy. The kind of stuff that's expensive and that I still would spend my hard-earned money on because I wanted to be *beautiful*. Because I never wanted anyone to make fun of me again.

She must see my surprise because she says, "Elliot sent me a list. So if you think I'm a weirdo for knowing your products by heart, he's the weirdo."

My gaze flicks to him, but he's not ashamed in the slightest. He's got a huge, proud smile on his face.

"That's weird, Elliot," I tell him.

"I don't think it is."

"Why do you know all that?"

He shrugs. "Call me obsessed."

But I know that's not true, because he was never obsessed with me. He just loved the things I let him do to my body.

I put the jeans on and look back at Kay. "What's the job?"

Kay glances around. "Where's Ethan?"

I don't miss the surprise on Elliot's face. "We're about to go get Stephen—"

"Who's Stephen?" I interject.

"None of your business." Kay stays calm, but her words cut deep anyway. I'm not sure I needed the reminder that I'm not trusted in this crew anymore.

"I'll go get Ethan."

My eyes follow Elliot as he leaves the room because I can't get myself to look at Kayla while being alone with her. She sits on their sofa, and I walk to Ethan's chair, the one he keeps by the window.

"You know why he always sits there?" my old boss asks.

I keep my eyes on the road in front of the window, making sure I avoid her gaze. I can still feel her drilling holes into the side of my face.

Since I don't answer, she carries on. "He told Caden that every day he looked to see if you came."

"He knew I wasn't coming back." If only she knew I'm not the only one who can't be trusted in her crew.

"Not while you were hiding from us," she clarifies. "It was after he broke up with you in high school. He grabbed that armchair, faced it toward the window, and every day he watched if you came to his house to fuck his brother."

I turn to her, narrowing my gaze. "You're making it

sound like I fucked him over. But I think you're forgetting who broke up with who."

Kay looks me up and down, unimpressed. "He made a mistake back then. You didn't have to rub it in his face for months afterward."

It's exhausting having to justify myself constantly. I've had to spend my life proving I'm not a manipulative liar. Like the sky having to prove it's meant to be blue on a rainy day. No one has the patience to wait and see. They only believe what's right in front of them. Who cares about what's behind a façade when you could just jump on a reason to hate someone.

Ethan used to say we're a doomed race. He was right. We humans don't deserve the place we hold on this planet.

"You know," I say simply, my eyes going back to the road. The view shows exactly the side of the street I would come from, up to the doorstep. "There's one person he never told he made a mistake. Me. He only had *anger* toward me." I close my eyes, tired of existing right now. "Like I deserved it."

I open my eyes again when I hear footsteps approaching.

"So." Elliot claps his hands. "Can you make this quick?"

My eyes are drawn to Ethan, standing right next to his brother. He is so beautiful in his own way. Everything about him makes my heart light on fire until it burns to ashes.

"I've got a job," she says while still looking at me, doubt clouding her eyes. "It's for the four of us. And if we get it right, Jade's debt will be paid in full."

"What?" My mouth drops open. Just like that?

I feel like I'm in one of those online videos, where someone just approaches you on the street to give you a thousand dollars. People look around, searching for the catch, for the trap. And I know it's coming.

Ethan takes a blind step to sit in his armchair, his brow furrowing when he sees I'm sitting in it. I struggle to take my next breath. Everything in me is screaming to get up and apologize, but I consciously decide not to. Ethan will eat me alive if he senses weakness.

When I don't give up my seat, he ignores me and turns to Kay instead.

How can he just ignore me after helping me in the bathroom yesterday?

"Us?" His voice is so different from any other man I know. Nothing too deep, a rasp and some higher notes than the usual male. Every time he opens his mouth, my pounding heart nears explosion.

"Yeah. The four of us."

My pulse accelerates, a beat that makes me bite my lower lip and tap my fingers against the arms of the chair. There's a mix of anticipation and fear bubbling in my belly.

Regardless of what this is, does it mean I get to leave faster or die sooner?

Whereas Ethan isn't doing anything about where I'm sitting, Elliot doesn't hesitate before grabbing my wrist and forcing me up. He takes two steps back, sits down, and pulls me onto his lap before wrapping a strong arm around my waist.

"Alright, I didn't know you wanted to do this so quickly. But let's do it. Share your plan with the room," he says as Kay crosses her arms over her chest. He doesn't need to speak any more for me to understand he's well aware of her plan. She would have run it past her right-hand man before seriously organizing something big.

There's a tight smile at the corner of Kay's lips, and I know nothing good is about to come out of her mouth.

"We're going to rob a bank."

11

JADE

CODE MISTAKE – CORPSE, Bring Me The Horizon

"Do you think this is Ocean's Eleven?" All heads turn to my way, but no one acknowledges me.

Elliot laughs like this is a joke. His breath tickles the back of my neck, and for a split second, I feel him inhale the smell of my hair.

But there's nothing humorous on Kay's face.

Ethan's approach is more serious. "Kay, you're the head of the Kings. You can't do dangerous jobs like this." He plays with his helix piercing, distracting me.

"We need money. And we need it fast. Now that NSC is backed by the Cosa Nostra and got their own police protection, we have little advantages on them. *Money* is something they don't have."

"Can't the Wolves give us an advance?" Ethan insists. This is the most I've heard him talk since I've been back.

Elliot relaxes in his seat—like Kay hasn't just

announced the craziest shit ever—and he brings me closer to him, my back against his chest.

"No." Kay's eyes dart to me briefly. I wouldn't have noticed it if I wasn't staring at her. She has issues with the Wolves. I can tell.

Ethan narrows his gaze on Elliot, silently telling him to do something about the current situation.

Elliot shrugs. "We've planned the fuck out of it."

"You guys are my perfect team for this. I need someone who can carry heavy bags." She nods toward Ethan. "A sweet charmer," her eyes go to Elliot. "And a great driver." She finishes on me.

"What?" I snap. It seems it's the only word that can come out of my mouth today. "That's the riskiest job. The cops are more likely to show up once you have the money. I'll be waiting like a sitting duck. This is death waiting to happen."

"Yeah." She nods, not even bothering to pretend she feels bad for me. "That's unfortunate as fuck for you. Especially since you're the only one who doesn't have a choice."

I've been a racer since I was seventeen. Before I was a traitor, I was the car specialist in the Kings' crew. I got my 1993 Mazda RX-7 with my first payment from the Kings. One thousand and five hundred dollars of pure junk. I worked day and night to buy the crap car that it was back then. The only car I didn't steal in my life. I raced with stolen cars while I tuned my baby, and at eighteen, I finally raced with my own. I won, of course. I never lose. And Kay knows that.

"We're not talking about walking into the bank, shouting at people to get on the floor, and leaving all guns blazing kind of robbery," Elliot explains. "More of a George

Clooney planned the whole thing and no one will ever know it was us."

"Did you just compare yourself to George Clooney?" I mumble, my lips numb from the insanity of their plan.

"What? We're both handsome and we both planned to rob a bank."

"Casinos, Elliot." I roll my eyes.

"Oh," he laughs to himself. "I didn't actually see the movie–"

"Guns blazing will depend on if we get caught," Kayla cuts back in. "But if it all goes well, no one should know."

"Where did you get this stupid idea from?" Ethan snaps. My eyes roam over his abs. He's still standing, shirtless, and when he talks, the Kings' crown just below his pec trembles.

I force myself to look away and out of the window before he notices me drooling.

"I have from trusted sources that the Bank of Silver Falls is getting some major renovations done in May. And it just so happens that the CCTV will be cut off from seven-thirty to nine-thirty on the morning of May thirteenth."

"Bank of Silver Falls has a good few million dollars in its vault," Elliot backs her, his hand splaying on my stomach, keeping me close to him.

"That's right. If we get in there, we'll have access to a hundred million dollars."

"We'll never be able to carry all of that." Ethan's telling her like he knows she's got something else in mind, which she proves right away.

"But we can carry ten million."

"You're going to need to explain to me how the hell we're going to do that."

"Sure will." She uncrosses her arms and takes a five-dollar bill out of her pocket. "Did you guys know the

Bureau of Engraving and Printing has set the specification that every dollar bill of any denomination has to weigh one gram." She waves the bill in the air. "And the Bank of Silver Falls only has hundred-dollar bills in their vault."

My eyes follow the five dollars in her hand. This girl has always been good at math and even better at scheming.

"They keep them in bricks." She turns to me. "You know what a brick is. You've picked those up for me before. Tell the class."

I glare at her as I answer. "Ten grand in hundred-dollar bills."

"You really are aware when it comes to money," she mocks me openly. "To make it simple, a brick weighs a hundred grams."

"What's that in pounds?" Ethan asks.

"About 0.22 pounds for a brick. Anyone can easily carry a hundred bricks each, that's 22 pounds. Or to put it in your guys' language, anyone can carry a million dollars."

"But you want ten million. So who's carrying a thousand bricks? In how long? One can carry 22 pounds, but it's a bit harder to move 220 pounds."

"You," she simply says. "Jade will be in the car, and Elliot has his own task to do. I'll be watching the back door. You are going to use those muscles you work so hard on to do ten trips of a hundred bricks. You're capable of that, aren't you?"

She hit him right in his pride, and a man's pride is a dangerous thing. It makes them do stupid shit like agree to rob a bank. Never again will Ethan accept to be called skinny or weak, and Kay knows exactly what she's doing.

"I am," he says cooly. "I can easily carry 44 pounds. I could do it in five trips and we'll be out of there much quicker."

"No," she answers firmly. "Because this isn't a gym contest, this is a bank robbery. So you will carry two bags each trip. Each bag will have fifty bricks, or five hundred fucking dollars. Put it how you want."

"Why would I do that?"

"Because if everything goes to shit, and let's say you have to drop a bag, I would rather you drop five hundred grands than a million."

"Yeah, but if I move more money at the same time, then we're getting out of the bank quicker. What if we get caught in the middle of it? Wouldn't you rather already have more money out of the safe?"

"If we get *caught,* we get nothing. Lighter bags are an advantage. If we have to abandon the van and all run with a bag, it'll make things easier. Personally, I would rather run with a lighter bag of five hundred thousand dollars than be slowed down by a heavy bag, get caught, and lose everything. Including my freedom."

Fuck. She really thought of everything.

"So you carry however many bags you want, in however many trips you want, but each bag will have fifty bricks. Clear?"

Ethan crosses his arms, slowly nodding.

There's a long pause as we all process what she just said. And fuck, there's a lot to process.

"If we end up with ten million split in four, that's 2.5 million each. That's way more than what I owe you," I finally say. I try to sound like I mean business, but I know they all hear the weakness in my voice.

Kay takes advantage of it, pinning me with a stare. "Oh, how cute. You...you get nothing. Your debt will be waived, and I don't care what you become after this, as long as you never set foot in my town again."

"That's not fucking fair," I rage. "I didn't even steal that money from you."

"You did, and then you ran away. Now your punishment is to drive that van and shut the fuck up."

"What van?" I insist. This drip-feeding of information is getting on my nerves, but the second Elliot feels me tense, he tightens his hold. Slipping his thumb under the shirt I'm wearing, he caresses my lower stomach.

I shift on his lap, but it doesn't seem to bother him.

"The van you're going to tune for us. I don't want some slow van that's going to get us caught. I want one fast enough to lose the cops should we need."

"If we start driving like crazy, it'll bring attention to us," I retort. Why am I talking like I've agreed to this?

Probably because I don't have a choice.

She leans over, lowering her face to mine. "It's a worst-case scenario kind of van. We are robbing a bank after all."

I throw my head back. "You're fucking insane. It'll look suspicious as fuck to have a nondescript van waiting in front of the bank."

"You'll be parked a three-minute drive away from the bank." I feel my brow furrow, knowing she's coming with more. "I'll need you to make that drive in fifty-nine seconds."

"What?" I hiss.

"You're a racer," she says deadpan.

"Yeah, not a fucking *magician*."

"Okay." She chuckles to herself, takes a couple of steps back, and before I realize what she's doing, she's aiming a gun at my face.

"Kay," Elliot barks at the same time he pushes me to the side and over the sofa. I land on the floor next to the sofa, and the gun ends up being pointed at him. "Put that shit away, will you?"

"This will be my last warning, Jade. Get on board with your new situation as the Kings' little bitch, or you're out. For good this time."

I grab the arm of the sofa to stand back up, my heart beating furiously in my chest. "Fine. I'll drive your fucking van."

"Yeah, you will. We parked it in the brothers' garage. I want you to show me something by the end of March. I want something fast."

"You're giving me barely over a month. That's delusional."

She doesn't even deign me a response, talking to the two men instead. "Ethan." Her voice is softer this time. "I need you to get on board. I need someone I can trust on this. All you'll have to do is carry the bags. Elliot can run you through the exact plan."

I can read Ethan like an open book. That's what happens when you've shared so much with someone. The way he looks at his brother right now tells me he feels betrayed he hasn't been made aware of this sooner.

Kay is already on the phone with someone else, heading for the door. Ethan is walking to his room, ignoring me. Elliot stands up, towering over me, too close for comfort. He puts a strand of wild curls behind my ear.

"Should I show you to your workshop for the next few months?" He keeps his hand in my hair, his dazzling eyes searching for something on my face.

I hope he can read the anger. That this job is fucked up and we could all die.

"I know where your garage is." I shrug him off and

storm off to the kitchen, slamming the door to the garage behind me.

Just like Kay promised, there's a van here. A GMC Vandura that I'm assuming is supposed to be white but looks gray from the dirt and dust caked on it.

We look like we're going to kidnap children with this. Or rob a bank.

The driver's door squeaks when I open it to pop the hood. When I walk back to the front and lift the metal, my eyes practically bulge out of my head.

It's a shitshow in here and she wants me to give her something that drives before the end of March?

I spend a few hours checking everything, dirtying Elliot's shirt and trying to judge the kind of work I'm going to have to do.

When I'm done, I take the phone Kay got me and message her.

> Jade: I need money to fix this shit van and tune it. At least ten grand.

> Kay: Your problem.

"Fucking bitch," I mutter.

I spend the rest of the day stripping the van of everything it doesn't need. The lighter it is, the faster we'll go. The engine stands no chance against anything, so I make sure to take that out too.

There's only one way I know how to get money.

Race.

12

JADE

deathwish - Stand Atlantic, nothing.nowhere.

It takes me almost an hour to walk to my destination. I'm taking huge risks going into NSC territories.

I walk into the tiny reception room with a worn-down blue carpet and one chair. There's a small counter with a plexiglass window and a hole at the bottom for people to pay. Another window gives a view of the shop floor where a few cars are parked. One is lifted high so they can walk under it for repairs.

"You..." someone says gruffly. "I thought you were fucking dead." And by that, he means he *wishes* I was fucking dead.

Logan and I don't have the best relationship, starting with the fact we're opposite gangs. It was at its lowest when Caden, Elliot, Ethan, and I kidnapped him and his friends to make them dig their own grave and use them as leverage to talk to his boss. Just casual North Shore evenings, really.

"Water under the bridge, Logan." I offer him a big smile, telling him I know we're thinking of the same event.

"Not enough water under that bridge."

Clearly, he didn't get over that night. Luckily, while this garage belongs to him, I'm not here to see him.

"Racer," I say loud enough for the person I'm really here for to hear. "Where is he?"

The man everyone calls Racer walks into the reception room just before he throws his head back. "Fuck."

"Where is she?" I don't see my car, and my blood is starting to boil.

Racer rolls his eyes. "Hi, welcome. Oh, nice to know where you've been and the reason you're back." He tries to sound annoyed, but he's the least threatening being I've ever met.

"You know where I've been." I push past him and through the door that leads into the workshop.

"No, I don't," he calls after me as he follows. "I never read that piece of paper."

I stop and slowly turn around. "Don't bullshit me, Racer. I can excuse you being a traitor because I never trusted you in the first place, but being a liar when confronted is something entirely different. The brothers found me, and you were the only one with a little note that said exactly where I was. Ethan and Elliot are smart, but they're no fucking wizards. They couldn't have found me without you opening your mouth."

"He never read it," Logan adds.

"Supportive of your boyfriend's lie," I say with all the fake sweetness I can muster. "True love. Where's my car?"

"It's true," Racer insists in that small voice of his. The guy is as shy as they come and ended up with his complete opposite. "I didn't read it. I didn't want that kind of information. The entire Kings' crew was after you. Imagine the kind of torture they'd have put me through." He scoffs. "Fuck that. I gave it to Xi."

My heartbeat races, my ears ringing. "You gave it to…" Three steps and I'm in his face. "*Motherfucker*," I hiss.

The asshole gave my address to his boss. The same man who hates me, who hates the Kings more than anyone I know. Caden fucking stabbed him and left him for dead. And guess who was there that night? Yours truly.

"Hey." I feel Logan's hand on my shoulder as he pulls me away. "Fucking relax."

"You owed me!" I shrug Logan off and point an accusing finger at Racer.

He's smaller than his boyfriend, skinnier. He could have been a sweet man if he hadn't been born on the North Shore.

"You lost that race against me. I could have taken your car, your livelihood. I could have let you get killed, but I didn't."

Racing is in my blood. Illegal races are my favorite playground. It's in Racer's blood too, hence the nickname. We bet our cars, and I won fair and square that night. No one from our crews was there. It was accidental that we bumped into each other at a race so far from the North Shore.

It's a customer's car, he said, panic dancing in his eyes like wildfire. *I took it from the repair shop. He'll kill me. I can't lose it.*

He was so vulnerable.

I'll do anything, Jade. Please.

His despair was stark compared to the confidence he had before I crossed the finish line.

I'll owe you.

And that sparked my interest, because it's always an

advantage to have someone from NSC owing someone from the Kings. I didn't think I'd use that favor so quickly.

I let him leave with his car that night, knowing I'd call him whenever I needed.

A week later, I drove to his and Logan's repair shop in a panic.

I'm leaving. You have to take my car.

He knew what was happening already. *Leaving? You're not fucking leaving. You're running! I can't keep this for you. If the Kings see it, they'll burn this place down.*

But he was stuck because owing someone on the North Shore means everything. A favor is a favor. It doesn't matter who, where, when.

You owe me, Racer. I saved your ass. Keep it for me. Hide it. Here's my new address. I remember folding the small piece of paper and snapping it away before he could grab it. *Do not give this to anyone. When things calm down, drive it to me. Don't let anyone see you.*

Then I let him take it. He didn't unfold it in front of me. He stayed in place when I shoved the keys in his hand.

You're a traitor. You betrayed your crew. The shock kept him from saying anything else.

It didn't stop me. *I didn't betray my crew*, I hissed. *I would never.*

He didn't believe me. I didn't care. I was too worried about getting caught, and Stan was going to pick me up. I left it with him because I had no one else and no time to find a better solution. I gave him the address because he was supposed to drive it to me.

"Instead of bringing it to me, you gave my address to Xi."

"You said to not let anyone see me," he fights back weakly. "Do you really think I can drive a pink Mazda RX-7 across the North Shore? One that has an exhaust we can hear across town. I kept the car hidden. I did my part."

"You sold me out to the Kings by giving it to Xi. You signed my death warrant."

"Xi would be the last person to give your address to the brothers. Why would he want them to find you? Whatever Elliot and Ethan want, Xi wants the exact opposite. He had some leverage against them, and I was free of the weight of your location."

Blood boiling, I talk in his face again, hissing through clenched teeth. "And yet here we *fucking* are. They found me. Why would he tell them?"

"Because he fell in love and that clearly fucked with his brain." Logan grabs me again as he says that. He's a little less delicate this time, shoving me away from his boyfriend. "Now let me remind you that you're on NSC territory and that we have no obligation to be kind to you. Don't piss me off and take a few seconds to calm down."

I'm panting with anger as I stumble back. Taking his advice, I walk toward the towers of tires and press the nail of my thumb against the wear bars, playing with the ridges. When I feel my heartbeat settle, I turn around. They're both facing me, next to the other.

"Okay." I nod. "Where is it? Give it back to me and we're done."

Racer's eyes are still looking guilty as he goes to the back of the shop, but Logan stares daggers at me like I ran over his puppy. Maybe one day I'll have someone protective over me like that.

Who am I kidding? The only person offering me protection is taking my body in exchange.

Racer comes back with a set of keys for a Mercedes and I'm about to lose my shit when he puts a hand up. "I took the main key out of yours and put this Mercedes plastic cover on it. I didn't want anyone to see I had a Mazda key."

Logan is currently reversing one of the many cars parked in here. It reveals a car protected by a beige cover. I'd recognize the shape of my baby anywhere.

"Fuck yes." I smile.

"Um, there's something else..." Racer hesitates.

My eyes narrow on him and his dart to Logan just as he uncovers a black Mazda RX-7.

"Racer!" I shout with frustration.

"Do you think it's easy to hide a *pink fucking car*?"

"You had a cover on it! Why paint it black?"

"No risks," he repeats. "I made that decision the day after they destroyed the fucking garage. Do you know the kind of shit they did to find you?"

Everything is gone. The pink, the stickers. The... "You took out my wing," I gasp.

"So it wouldn't bring attention. I'll put it back." He sighs. "I took care of your baby, Jade. I made sure to change the battery. Once I painted it, I took it for a drive once in a while."

"In that case, you could have driven it back to me."

He shakes his head. "I didn't want to know where you lived. What's the point in you saving my ass if you throw me back to the wolves?"

"Take it and leave us out of this," Logan says with a violence that tells me he's done with me today.

I bite my lower lip, looking at both of them, and concede. "Put the wing back and you won't hear from me again."

Nodding, they both get to work, but I stop them the moment they bring a spoiler out.

"That's not mine. I want my wing."

"Fucking hell, you're a piece of work, woman," Logan snaps.

"Why? Because I know what I want? Because you're putting a wing that isn't mine back on *my* car? I had a GT2 high wing carbon mount. What am I going to do with your fucking BA Trunk mount wing?"

"It's a really good piece," Racer mutters to himself.

"It's good," I agree. "But it's not my wing. Mine is Japanese quality for a Japanese car. Mine is what gives me so much stability and grip, and the reason why I go so fast around turns. My wing is the reason, among many others, why I won that race, and you ended up owing me." I narrow my eyes at them. "So put it back and keep your comments to yourselves."

They exchange a look, and Logan shrugs before Racer walks to the back of the shop. Half an hour later, I'm leaving with my car again. It's black, and since he took out my loud exhaust too, it's discreet compared to the beauty I had brought here two years ago, but at least I have it.

As I drive out of their front parking lot, another car comes in. It's too early for a customer, and I cross gazes with a small woman, probably only a few years older than me. Her eyes widening is a good indication that she knows who I am and didn't expect to see me here, especially when she looks away as quickly as our gazes crossed. I keep an eye on her in my rearview mirror as I drive away.

I quickly come to a crossroads that I know could change my life, yet I don't hesitate. If I turn left, I could leave the North Shore by the highway and drive right back to Stan. I don't know how to get there, and it's not like I have a GPS, but I can follow the signs to New York City and then the Hamptons.

But I turn right instead. There are a lot of reasons for

that. I'm a vengeful person; I grew up surrounded by violence until I soaked in it myself. I'm stubborn. I make terrible decisions.

But mainly? I loathe Xi, and I have a raging need to get back at him for selling me out.

So I drive to where I know his house is, the motor of my baby purring softly under my foot.

NSC territories are much smaller than they used to be. When I was in high school, they owned our town, and us, the Kings, were tiny little insects they could crush under their boots.

Back then, they were supported by the Cosa Nostra, the Bianco family, to be precise. That made them invincible. But then Bianco went down. His power disappeared, and after a fight in the Death Cage, where we decide the fate of our town, the Kings took back power. Kayla and her dad got support from the Bratva Wolves, and we—the Kings of the North Shore—became the Kings of the world. At least in *our* version of the world.

We took over the North Shore Crew, over the entire town. Their territories were ours, so their crew members started dying or joining us. We had suppliers where they didn't. We stole their best dealing spots, their clients, *everything*. We didn't need to kill their boss, Emma Scott, and her family; we could just slowly take everything away from them. And we did.

They kept fighting back, of course. Whoever stayed loyal to NSC were as devoted as they come. And no one is more devoted to NSC than Xi Benhaim. He led their drug operations. A small-town dealer who turned into a full-on businessman. CEO of feeding the rich kids from the South Bank and Stoneview their weekly cocaine.

No one can take Xi's business away from him. Not only

is money too important to everyone on the North Shore, but protecting those he loves is the essence of who he is. NSC has always had their own version of an enforcer in him, not because they paid him, but because that's who he is deep inside. Taking the responsibility of everyone's lives makes him irreplaceable.

I look up at the house and pause, blinking at what's in front of me. What used to be a rundown house—scratch that. What used to look like an official waste dump has turned into the kind of house you would usually see on the South Bank. A smaller version.

It's been repainted a clean white, slates repaired and put back together. The front lawn is green, freshly cut, his property lined with edges of pink peonies, and even his door is painted a bright pink.

"What the actual fuck," I mutter to myself.

The guy is a lethal gang-member. Is he alright?

I reach over the central console, grabbing the crowbar I keep under the passenger seat.

"Fucking peonies," I say to the wind as I walk past them. Just because he pissed me off, I destroy a large chunk of the edge before striding up the small pathway bordered by flowerpots. It leads right to his pink door. There's a matt on the floor that says *welcome home* and my entire body cringes.

Maybe he moved? He wouldn't, though. Everyone knows this house is where his father died, and he was so close to him, he would never stop renting it.

There's a small window next to the front door, and I roll my eyes. The guy forgot he lives on the North Shore.

Using the crowbar, I break the rectangular window, clear the frame of the shards, and slide my hand inside to unlock it.

I'd never been inside, but it's not what I would have

imagined in a million years. It smells good, a flowery scent I don't recognize, and as I reluctantly enjoy the sweet fragrance, I advance on the plush carpet. Walls are painted a beautiful pastel green, the carpet a clean cream color. I stand in the middle of the living room, spinning on the spot and looking around like I just walked inside a Pinterest board.

"What in the fucking Barbie-house happened in here?" I walk to white shelves built into the far wall and look at the pictures resting there.

Everything becomes clear when I realize that what happened is a literal Barbie walked into Xi's life.

"No fucking way." The North Shore playboy actually settled down. Pictures of them near the falls, another standing on the front lawn of this very house...with two bunnies in their hands.

Two. Pet. Bunnies.

They're smiling brightly, the girl looking at the bunnies, and Xi looking at her with half-lidded loving eyes. Xi is pretty gigantic, and she looks like she barely reaches his chest. I know I don't even reach his chest, hence why the crowbar could be awfully useful today. But even better if he's not here.

Another smell hits me, and I look around, confused. It smells of paint, and now that I think of it, everything looks awfully shiny.

They've just redone the house. I press a hand against the green wall and while it's not wet, I can feel how fresh the paint is.

Oh. How lucky. The guy wants to mess with my freedom? Why don't I mess with his new shiny house.

Flipping around, I hit the crowbar against the shelves, a smile spreading on my lips.

Fucking asshole selling me out like he has the right.

I'm a tornado. The walls, the frames, the artwork they hung. Then the sofa, destroying it and sending foam flying into the room.

"Asshole!" I scream into the mess I caused. The kitchen door is next, destroying the freshly painted wood.

I'm about to hit again when a gasp stops me. I snap around, holding the crowbar far back and ready to hit, but I'm met with wide hazel eyes on a shocked face.

We could not be more opposites if we tried. She's got pale skin, average height, dirty blonde hair, round eyes, curvy.

Me? Brown skin, dark brown hair, tiny frame, and eyes so sharp I could probably kill her with a look. I narrow my gaze at her, knowing the impression I give is usually enough for people to run away.

She opens her mouth, taking in a breath, and I shake my head. "Tsk, tsk," I tut her. "Crowbars in the face are painful, Barbie. Don't scream."

Her entire body freezes, bar her hands trembling at her side. "Xi and I have had a little misunderstanding, but I can leave without hurting you."

I'm pretty sure I got to her, so I take a step to the side, ready to leave. "Do tell him that the brothers found Jade, and as long as I'm alive and in this town, I'll be making his life as shit as mine is."

"Y-you're Jade?" she murmurs, clearly terrified of someone half her size. I tend to have that effect on people. It's the craziness in my mind that scares them, not the physicality.

I roll the crowbar in my hand. "I wonder what he could have possibly told you."

Her eyes go to my inner wrist, where I bear the tattoo of the Kings' crew. A crown, of course.

"That I'm part of the Kings," I say for her.

Her gaze flips up, looking at the scar on my temple. "And my past with Billie," I add.

Xi used to be in love with his stepsister. I'm surprised to see he actually managed to move on with someone else.

She gulps. "Xi isn't part of NSC anymore," she says in a rush of breath. "He has an agreement with Emma and Kay."

It's my turn to turn mute from shock.

Oh.

This isn't good. Not good at all. If I'm currently stomping on a peace treaty between life-long enemies Kay and Emma, Kayla will have my fucking ass. As if she doesn't have enough reasons to chop my head off.

"He's not part of NSC anymore." That would explain the cute little *I'm not part of a gang* lifestyle. "He's not part of NSC anymore," I repeat slowly, attempting to process the information.

"But he can still kill a bitch for destroying his house."

My heart stops, slowly sinking to my stomach.

That wasn't Barbie. That was a deep male voice. A deep, *extremely pissed*, male voice coming from right behind me.

13

JADE

HELL REPLIED - Grey

I slowly turn around, dragging my eyes along his hard body until I tilt my head back and meet his deadly stare.

"Especially knowing the Kings don't claim her anymore."

I barely have time to notice the smudge of pink on his knuckles as his fist comes at me.

Thankfully, while not being the strongest girl around, my speed is a great asset. I duck, avoiding him and sidestepping when he throws another one.

"Xi!" Barbie calls out. "Don't hurt her."

He stops, a fist in the air, and I step back, hitting a wall. This one was still wet, and I can feel the stickiness right away. I lift the crowbar, ready to hit him, but he grabs it, twisting it and throwing it down the hallway.

"Cupcake," he says low. "You're too good." His hand is around my throat right away. "You seem to be in trouble, Jade," he growls. "And you seem to be wanting to bring that trouble to my house. That's a big fucking mistake."

I hit his forearm and go on my toes to try to match the height he's imposing on my body. "You gave them my address," I rasp, feeling my airways tightening.

His brown eyes darken, and I think that was the wrong choice of words. Fuck. I'm hot, dizzy, and this is not going in my favor right now.

"I have no loyalty to you. You're Kings' crew. You're a traitor. You mean absolutely fuck all to me."

"You led them to me. I at least get to fuck up your house," I grit back, coughing, feeling the air thinning to a dangerous level.

"Not even gonna beg me to keep you alive? That stubborn, huh?"

"If you wanted me dead, I'd be dead."

A smirk spreads on his face, so slow and evil. I hear tires screeching outside, and he hears it too because he lets go of me.

I cough and wipe the tears of pain in my eyes, hunched over and talking to the fucking carpet. "Motherfucker," I pant. I straighten up and stare right at him. "Do you have them on speed dial? Are there hearts next to their names too?"

His hand comes to rest on the back of Barbie's neck. He watches me with a bored gaze as I notice two shadows coming into the house from my peripheral.

I let out a dramatic huff and turn to Ethan and Elliot, walking in like two angels of death coming to rip out my soul from my body. Said body is already thrumming from being in Elliot's vicinity after yesterday. Fucker.

"Xi," Elliot calls out merrily. "I see you found our stray. Thank you for letting us know."

"Get her out of here," he growls in return. "You guys got the worst fucking crew."

"She's not one of us anymore," Ethan spits out like I'm a curse.

I roll my eyes at him. "So fucking dramatic."

Narrowing his deep beautiful black eyes at me, Ethan looks at me from head to toe and back up.

"Jade." Elliot snaps his fingers at me, like I'm a fucking dog, and I'm ready to bite him like one. "Let's go, baby."

I look around the destroyed living room, and anger runs through me when I catch the pity in Barbie's eyes.

"We'll send someone to fix this." Ethan's voice is barely audible as his gaze darts around the room. It's a fucking carnage, but Xi shakes his head.

"Not in this fucking lifetime, no. That's enough Kings in my house forever."

"We just finished this morning," Barbie sighs sadly. Her voice is high and light, like a real fucking angel surrounded by demons. I sound like an evil fiend next to her, with my unbothered, barely formed syllables.

"Don't worry, cupcake. I'll fix it all."

She nods, hugging herself closer to her boyfriend. Would you look at that, another joyous couple rubbing their happiness on everything they touch.

I'm the first one out of the house, the brothers right behind me, close enough to grab me should I want to run.

I could have run. Less than an hour ago, I had a car and a left turn to take. But I'm too dumb for that.

Making a beeline for my car, I unlock it, ready to hide in there just as someone grabs my arm. Elliot lazily takes the keys out of my hand and pushes me to the side, right into his brother's arms. Ethan doesn't hold me the same way. It's at arm's length, more like a trash bag than something he wants to keep close.

"If you think you're getting into a car on your own, think

again," Elliot says as he sits down in my seat and slides his palms against the steering wheel. "I'll be bringing this pretty girl home." He looks up, smiling brightly at me. "I've always wanted to drive your car."

"No one but me drives my car. You can sit in the passenger seat, and I'll drive to your house, but not in your wildest dreams will you drive her."

Elliot's snort is louder than Ethan's low chuckle, but they're both equally mocking me.

"Jade, my love," Elliot drawls. His beautiful, low voice resonates deeply inside me. "The times where you made the decisions are over. Forget independence and forget demanding anything. We own your ass now. So if you don't want it spanked until you cry, I suggest you take the mercy we're currently giving and just let us take you home. Now go to Ethan's truck and keep your mouth shut. Because that's what good apologetic girls do."

I grit not only at his words, but at the reaction I feel from this. Does he have to make everything sound so fucking suggestive?

Crossing my arms over my chest in the only act of rebellion I can afford, I shrug off Ethan and follow him to his truck.

"One scratch," I mutter. "One and I'll bury him alive."

Ethan ignores me as he drives away, but I'm not about to let him get away with not talking to me and pretending he hates me when he clearly cared yesterday.

"Are we going to ignore the fact that you took care of me and haven't talked to me since?"

Ethan is as antisocial as they come. His entire behavior screams to leave him alone, but he's the one who decided to follow me to that bathroom and help me when I was about to make a stupid mistake.

He's the one who caressed my hair with the palm of his hand, murmuring that I was beautiful.

The same person who hates being touched pulled my body against his.

"Ethan," I snap. "You can't just keep ignoring me. I'm going to be here until we rob that bank. Until May thirteenth, to be precise. Are you just going to pretend I don't exist till then? You're the one who fucking took care of me. I didn't ask for anything."

My nostrils flare when he just looks ahead and doesn't react.

"You drive me fucking insane. You love to tell everyone you hate me because I slept with your brother *after* you broke up with me. Because I dared to sleep around when I was single. But then *you* came to me behind everyone's back when I didn't ask for anything." I huff. "Three months with you is going to be a nightmare."

"Just keep doing exactly what Elliot tells you, and you'll be fine."

That's all he says during the whole ride. That simple sentence with an undertone of rage.

I wish Ethan hated me loudly. Like I do. I wish he'd scream and shout and give me a reason to fight.

The silence is just too painful.

Ethan slams the front door behind us the moment we cross it. Elliot is already here since I saw my car parked in front of their house. His brother strides to the hallway, and I hear the slamming of his bedroom door before a song from My Chemical Romance starts resonating within his walls.

"What did you do?" Elliot's voice comes from the

kitchen. He appears in the doorframe and crosses his arms over his broad chest.

"He's a drama queen. And a hypocrite." I look Elliot up and down. He's dressed so simply in black jeans and a blink-182 t-shirt. It's weird how good these things look on him. "I want the keys to my car."

He cocks an eyebrow at me. "Go shower." Him ignoring my request makes me want to do anything but listen to him.

"My keys," I insist, holding out my hand in front of him as I walk all the way to the kitchen door.

"You want the keys to something that'd help you run away from us? Think before you make ludicrous demands."

"I won't go anywhere," I fight back. "I could have done that this morning and I didn't. I'll work for Kay, I'll do what you want, but I want my car in return. I need money for the van and I'm going to race."

"You're absolutely not fucking racing under any condition."

"What? You can't forbid me to race!"

"Would you look at that? I just did. You might not have noticed the Kings who saw you walk around the North Shore earlier, but I sure as shit was notified. And guess why you're still alive? Come on. Take a wild guess."

My jaw clenches. Will he be mad if I spit in his face? 'Cause I'm really tempted right now.

"Nothing?" he sneers. "Let me help. It's because I told all of them if they touch you, they're going to have to deal with me. And no one wants to deal with me. That's called holding my end of the deal. Now, why don't you be a good girl and hold *your* end by doing what you're told. No car keys. No racing. No leaving the house without my explicit authorization. And watch your mouth when you talk to me."

It takes all of me not to explode in an uncontrollable fit of rage. My hands tighten into fists, my teeth near fissuring from the way I grind them.

He waits a minute or so, silently daring me to fight back. And then he smiles. So fucking proud of himself. "Go shower, Jade. Your punishment awaits."

I shove his chest, where I know his scars are. They were put there by the same man who created mine. Except his are on the outside, so people believed him. Mine are hidden, so I was labeled a liar when I spoke out.

"Asshole," I throw back as I make my way to the bathroom.

He's in his bedroom when I walk in with a towel wrapped around me. I don't know where I'm meant to stay, so I assumed his bedroom will be my base since he brought me here yesterday.

"I know you can be a good girl when you want to, my love," he says softly, sitting on the end of his bed and resting back on his hands.

That's what's always so hard with Elliot. Anyone who snaps at him sounds crazy, because he pisses you off with a calm tone and a huge smile on his angelic face. Manipulative bastard.

Ignoring him, I walk to his drawers and grab a clean pair of boxers and a t-shirt.

"Don't bother putting those on."

I slowly turn around, already feeling a jolt of electricity zapping all the way to my lower belly. "Excuse me?"

"Your punishment, baby. You're not getting your way out of it."

"I didn't run away."

He pushes some blond strands away from his forehead.

The boyish innocence on his face could almost make me believe he's not a dangerous criminal.

"You sneaked out of the house. You went to an old NSC member and destroyed his house, putting an agreement Kay has with Emma at risk."

Giving me a bright smile, he adds, "We could let Kay decide what kind of punishment that deserves." The moment he sees my lips parting to retort, he cuts me off. "Or you could just deal with me. Xi is not the kind to go complain to Emma. Kay won't know unless we tell her. It could just be our little secret."

I lick my lips, trying to control my body temperature. It keeps rising.

When I don't say anything, he straightens on the bed and leans forward. "Drop the towel, baby."

My heart is beating too fast already. I fell asleep with the need to be touched, then I woke up being teased some more, and he just brought it all back to life.

Fucking dangerous memories. That's what it is. Knowing all the pleasures Elliot is capable of bringing me.

I lift my chin, trying to keep an ounce of pride as I drop the towel.

He takes a slow inhale through his nose. "Fuck," he breathes out. "Sit in the armchair."

There's an armchair with a few clothes on the back, and I sit down on it before my shaking legs give up.

Elliot won't hurt me. His punishment will be worse than physical pain, I know it.

He stands up and comes to me, putting a hand on each of the arms, blocking me in and looking down.

"Why are you so docile, Jade?" he murmurs. "Do you think you're going to enjoy being punished? Like you used to?" He clicks his tongue. "That's not how it works."

I retreat as much as I can into the chair, looking up at him through my lashes. His fingers grip my chin and hold me that way, making sure there's nothing else but him in my field of vision.

"Spread your legs."

When I don't, the corner of his lips tips up. "Don't anger me, Jade."

I narrow my gaze at him, slowly spreading my legs. "You're so addicted to me it's ridiculous," I rasp.

"Baby," he chuckles. "This is nothing, believe me."

He walks backward until he can sit on the end of the bed again. "Put your feet on the edge of the chair. Keep your legs spread."

I do it, knowing there's nothing I don't enjoy about this.

I don't have to wonder what he's up to for long. He takes off his shirt, then slowly undoes his jeans and lowers them and his boxers. His dick is already hard. It's thick, veiny, and I close my eyes when I'm hit with memories of him and I. Entire nights in his bed, sweating bodies, the burning heat of skin against skin.

My eyes flutter open, and I know from the look on his face that I can't hide my thoughts from him. His hand wraps around his cock, and I lick my lips. That makes him smile, of course.

"Your simple existence is better than any porn I could watch, baby."

"You're disgusting," I snarl, my lower belly tightening.

"If only you didn't love that so much."

I'm transfixed as he starts touching himself, choking his cock with his fist, and rubbing up and down. It takes less than a minute for his torturous smile to spread. "I can see it, my love. Your wetness."

I look away, but he calls me back. "Keep your eyes on me, Jade."

I'm panting when he gets up and kicks his jeans aside. He walks closer, smirking, and stops right in front of me. I can see it perfectly, the curve of his dick. That magic fucking curve that means he hits the best spot every time.

Elliot never needs to chase after girls; they all run back to him once they've had a taste of what he can provide. With that curve, it's practically impossible for him to not hit a woman's G-spot when he fucks her. It's like God decided to create him with the purpose of being an orgasm machine.

Leaning over, his hand finds the back of the chair and his face hovers right above mine. I can feel his breath, see his smirk from up close. I don't think I realize my hand has moved toward my pussy until he grabs my wrist.

He tuts me, shaking his head slightly. "I think you're starting to understand your punishment."

I groan when he pushes my hand away and goes back to touching his dick. It's so close to me, the silky tip near my wet entrance.

"Do you remember our times together?"

A breathy moan escapes me. I can't take my eyes away from his beautiful dick.

"Do you remember the orgasms, baby? When you're a good girl, I give you anything you want."

I inhale a sharp breath. This isn't helping. Fuck.

"All I need is for you to beg, and I'll get on my knees right here. I'll bury myself in your pussy. I'll taste you, and tease you, and lick you until you're nothing but a crying mess on this chair."

"Fuck," I exhale. "Don't...don't do this to me."

"What? Punish you?"

"Elliot..."

"Beg."

I shake my head, refusing to give him what he wants, but this is torture. I need him inside me. I need to feel his entire body shuddering against mine.

"Beg, Jade, and I'll give you the world."

I'm panting as I look into his eyes. I lick my lips, ready to give in.

"Fuck you," I grit.

I will never beg this man for anything.

He straightens up, and his movement accelerates. With a grunt, he locks his eyes with mine, and I feel the spurt of thickness on my belly.

"Elliot!" I rage. "Fuck you!" I'm about to stand up when he presses on my shoulders and pushes me back down.

"Stay down. Feet on the edge of the chair."

My glare feels powerful, but I know it does nothing to him.

"You're so wet right now, my love. You're lucky I don't make you lick your stain from the cushion."

My gulp is loud. He can hear it and that makes him smile wider. Sitting down on the bed, his cock softens only in the slightest bit. The fucker is still hard, and he sees the moment I get it.

"No." I shake my head.

"Yes."

His hand is back on his cock, caressing it until it becomes fully rigid again.

I can't go through this. I'll break. I'll beg him to fuck me, and it'll make me look weak.

But it's not like I have much of a choice, is it?

He does it two more times like the monster he is. I

writhe and moan as he comes on me, his thick cum running down my tits and to my navel.

"I hate you," I grit out.

He brings his lips to my cheek, and I feel him smile against my skin. "You look delicious covered in my cum, my love."

"Go fuck yourself."

"That's what I just did," he laughs. "Thank you for being such a pretty canvas."

He steps away from me and grabs some tissues, wiping his hands and cock before putting his clothes back on. "I've got some work to do. When your punishment is over, you can go back to working on the van."

"What do you mean *over*?"

"You can move from this chair once my cum has dried." He leans down and, against all odds, captures my lips in a violent kiss.

Elliot is not a kisser.

Elliot fucks, and punishes, and rewards. But he doesn't *kiss*.

A breathless moan slips out of me, my entire body lighting up again. He bites my lower lip, sucking on it until I feel it swell between his teeth. I groan for him to let go, even though it's the best feeling I've had in a while. It hurts when he sucks on the cut from Kay's punches, and I whimper when I feel it split open again.

"Elliot," I mumble against his lips.

When he releases me, my lower lip feels twice its size. It burns deliciously, like a scalding hot shower on a winter day. That's what Elliot feels like. He's too hot to be bearable, and yet I want nothing but for him to burn me alive.

There's an inner battle inside me the second he leaves his bedroom. For a minute, I'm sure there's no way in hell I will stay still. I feel disgusting, used. He did it on purpose, to make me feel like I am worth nothing more than what he comes on. It starts a fury inside me that I'm not sure I can control until I decide to pick my battles.

He wanted me to beg, and I didn't. I kept strong. I'll take his fucking punishment and show him that there's nothing he can do to make me break.

Doesn't he know who he's facing?

14

ELLIOT

Red Flags - Gomey, Xuitcasecity

"What a heavy motherfucker," I grunt as I carry Steven's unconscious body down the stairs to our basement.

"Save your strength and shut the fuck up." Ethan tightens his grip on his ankles and huffs.

We throw him on the floor the second we get to the basement. It takes me less than a minute to lock a metal cuff around his ankle and check that the chain it's attached to is properly bolted to the floor.

"Alright," I huff, shoving my hair away from my face as I straighten up. "Dinner?"

"I'm not hungry. I'll wait for him to wake up and let him know what he's here for."

The reason being that he's been the man Emma Scott uses as her link between her crew and the Luciano family. Emma finally struck a deal for NSC with the Cosa Nostra, and they're about to get as much power as we get from the Bratva Wolves. This is not good for us, and we need to cut it off at the root.

We can't kill Emma, or all hell will break loose. But we can kill whoever she uses to communicate with the Lucianos. Not before we get as much info from him as we can, though.

"The guy knows what he's here for, Ethan, and you need to eat."

"I'm not hungry," he repeats.

"You need some meat to keep those muscles alive, brother. Protein, exercise, weights." My lips spread into a smile. "Sex?"

If only he'd fucking have sex. That way, he'd stop obsessing about the woman upstairs.

"Shut up," he growls. "I know what I need. I won't go back to being the weak, skinny fucker you have to defend from bullies just because I skip a few meals. Don't worry."

"I never said that. You're the one obsessed with that weak, skinny fucker."

"I'm not feeling chatty, Elliot. Drop it."

Of course, I don't. I know my brother. It's important he talks things out. When he bottles it up, people die.

"Are you going to go on a hunger strike because I didn't tell you about the bank? Grow up, will you? I'm higher in ranks than you when it comes to the Kings. You have to understand I can't share everything over dinner like I'm your fucking dad."

"Boundaries, Elliot," he insists as he turns his gaze away from Unconscious Stephen and to me. "Don't push them."

"Or are you mad because of her? Because of what I told you?"

"Stop it," he bites out.

My brother is so good when it comes to me. Too good. That's the reason I've always eaten him alive, and he just takes it. He takes and takes...and fucking takes.

I hope my smile is as conceited as I feel. "Just keep your word, and we're good, Ethan." I shrug, lazily making my way up the stairs. "I'm going to go check on Jade. You know...because I can."

He turns his back to me, ignoring the facts I throw in his face.

This girl has got some sort of death wish. She wasn't in the fucking bedroom or garage. I've just stepped into the kitchen, looking for her everywhere, when the front door slams and a tiny tornado of dark hair strides into the house. I meet her in the living room, waiting to hear what the show is all about.

"You went out?" I scold her. "Are you dying for me to turn your ass red?"

"Did you write this?" she hisses, shoving a piece of paper against my chest.

I cock an eyebrow, calmly grabbing the crumbled note, but I don't open it.

"Why were you out, Jade?" She's holding the keys to her car, which she probably found in my bedroom, and I think tonight is the night I make her choke on my cock to teach her a lesson.

"I was looking at what's under my hood. I didn't go anywhere, okay? It was for the van."

Her hands are covered in oil, a trace of it on her forehead like she wiped some sweat with her dirty hands.

She didn't go anywhere.

"I answered your question. Now answer mine."

Sounds fair. I unfold the note to read it.

You should have stayed away. Your days are numbered. Tick Tock.

A laugh bubbles in my throat, causing her brow to furrow, and her eyes narrow in fury. Oh, the bitch is good.

"Sending death threats to yourself, baby? Don't you think it's a bit much?"

"This isn't funny, Elliot! That was on my car, and you're the last one who drove it." She comes closer to me, her chest practically touching my stomach. Fuck, she's so ridiculously small. "Don't fuck with me."

"Stop always shouting and getting angry, Jade."

"Why? I'm *fucking* angry."

If her eyes weren't so feline-like, she would probably resemble a yapping Chihuahua with the way she gets furious and yet has no effect on me whatsoever.

Except one.

"Because I could fuck you when you're fuming like this. It does something to me, I swear."

"I could fuck you up."

"Why are you creating more problems for yourself?"

"Me?" She's almost on her toes now, smelling of apples like she always has, and I'm assuming it's from the shampoo I had Kay bring her. Or maybe that gum she's chewing. She must have found one of the packs I keep in the house. I used to always have them around for her, and it's been a habit to keep buying them.

She wouldn't be caught dead eating the fruit, but she's always been addicted to any candy that has that fake green apple taste.

It's weird that after two years, what feels the most like her is her smell. She hasn't changed much physically, but everything is different on the inside. She's weaker, yet angrier. Still angry. She's always been angry.

She lost some of her stubbornness, and she used to talk all day long about songs we should listen to.

Her, Ethan, and I listen to the same kind of music. They were already friends as kids, but they really bonded when they started texting late at night about their favorite punk rock bands. I didn't know what she saw in him back then. I'm still unsure.

I like those bands too.

I cared about her too.

And unlike him, women wanted me.

So why him? Why not me?

I guess what changed the most is that we were close, and we aren't anymore. It doesn't matter if it was physical or more. The scent of apples followed me everywhere I went. Having it shoved in my face after two years feels strange. Not the good kind. It's a dangerous force.

Lose-your-mind kind of dangerous.

"Did you, or did you not, put this note on my car, Elliot?" Her attempts at pinning me with a stare loses its strength when she has to strain her neck to look me in the eye.

"I didn't, Jade." I could yawn. Her games are getting old.

"What?" She falls flat on her feet again. "Then...who did?"

"Pretty sure you're the one who wrote it. Your games aren't that fun. No one feels any pity toward you. At least not the kind that would make us care. It's more like a someone-should-put-this-dog-down sort of pity."

She ignores my jab, paling. "Someone wants me dead."

She's pissing me off, and I get horny when I'm pissed off.

Or when I'm happy, tired. I get horny when Jade is in the vicinity, period. It's exhausting.

"Many people want you dead, baby. None who would put a fucking note on your car, though, so drop the act."

Her face falls, and a rush of air leaves her as she takes a step back. "You don't believe me."

"I would have to be an idiot to believe a liar like you." I smirk at her, twisting the knife. This is fun. "A traitor."

I notice every single movement her body makes. Her nostrils flaring, her eyes narrowing, the daggers sharp. It's always been a fascination of mine to watch Jade *exist*. Her jaw tightens and twists from side to side. Her hand goes to the pocket of the hoodie she took from me. It's too big, falling just above her knees.

She shoves me with her shoulder as she walks past me. Except she has nowhere to go. That's her problem, isn't it? So when she strides to *my* bedroom and slams *my* door, I'm right after her.

She's facing the far wall, her hands in her hair, grabbing the roots.

"Lose the attitude," I threaten low.

She swings around, furious. When is this woman not furious? She was born like this. "Fuck you!"

Two steps for me. One step backward from her.

"You don't believe me," she repeats, a desperate rasp breaking her voice. "Of course you don't."

"When have you ever proven you should be believed?"

"Why do I *always* have to prove things? Why am I the one who has to show I was wronged, when I call out for help?"

"What a fucking drama queen," I huff. "You're a lying little bitch who plays everyone. As long as you get out on top, you don't care who you betray. *That's* why."

"Shut up!" she screams. "I'm not a liar!"

I take another step. "Someone needs to show you screaming and hurling insults like a crazy little thing isn't how you should behave."

"Don't come anywhere near me. I swear to God, Elliot, I will *fuck. You. Up.*"

It's not even the words that make me grab her, flip her around, and slam her against the wall. It's the certainty in her eyes that she's capable of making me do anything.

She grunts when her cheek hits the wall. It's her left one, where she already bears the bruises from Kay. I grab her wrists, pressing them against her lower back with one hand.

"Behave."

My voice leaves her no choice, yet she still pushes back against me. I wrap a hand around her jaw, grabbing her cheeks and making her pout as I pull her head toward me. The angle is uncomfortable for her, and she winces when my fingers press against her bruised cheek.

"*Behave*, Jade."

She only struggles for a few more seconds before giving up entirely. "Let me go," she tries to say through her pouted lips. It's a dejected whisper.

I push my hips into her back and watch her shiver. "Baby, you know it turns me on when you finally bend to my will."

"Anything on two legs turns you on, Elliot," she hisses back.

"I don't know. I get pretty hard when you're on all fours."

She huffs in frustration, and I nuzzle my nose in her neck as my hand slides against her front, cupping her pussy through her jeans.

"Fuck." She trembles under my hand, and I chuckle against her ear.

I undo her jeans, shoving them down in one harsh movement. Leaving them just under her ass, I pull her hips back.

"It seems we only get along for one thing. Even you can't disagree."

She shakes her head, denying the truth before she licks her lips. I press harder and her eyes flutter closed.

"Do you see now why I know you're a liar?"

"Stop," she whispers. The kind that screams not to stop. It's the same tone as when Ethan is dying to talk about something and says *drop it*.

"I think you meant to beg me to push my fingers through your wetness. I think you meant to ask me to fuck this beautiful pussy and make you scream my name."

"Elliot," she pants as I start pushing two fingers inside her.

"Do you want me to make you come?"

She moans softly against the wall, and my hard dick presses against my jeans as I drive my fingers deeper into her.

"Shit...Elliot..."

Jade is the most sexual woman I know. It oozes out of her. She is an inextinguishable fire of lust. She spent the last two years being fucked all day, every day, and I've not let her orgasm since she's been back.

I know how desperate she is.

"I'll let you come," I rasp in her ear. My own need to explode is beyond reality. "Just beg."

I graze her lips with mine, but instead of giving her a kiss, I take her lower lip between my teeth and suck. Fuck, I love the feeling of her lip swelling in my mouth, of seeing it redden when I let it go.

"Say it, baby. Say *please, Elliot, I'm begging you to make me come.*"

Her lips part, ready to give me what I want. "Pl—"

My door bursting open startles the both of us. Ethan stands tall in the doorway, his eyes on us.

"Ethan," Jade gasps when she sees him. She struggles for me to let her go again, and I do this time.

She's quick to pull up her jeans, her cheeks flushed and a look of guilt on her face.

As if she owes him anything.

There's a short pause during which I wonder if my brother is going to lose his shit and claim back his ex like he's always wanted to.

His jaw tightens, eyes darkening, and I notice his hands turning into fists before he relaxes again.

"Stephen is awake. Let's get to work."

I thread my fingers through my blond hair, pulling it all back.

Jade takes a step toward him. "Ethan—"

"You stay here," I tell Jade. Her back is against the wall now, her eyes stuck on Ethan.

She better be in this room when I come back. I was so fucking close.

15

JADE

ALL ABOUT ME - Lilyisthatyou

I'm going to go insane in this place. As if I wasn't already crazy enough, Elliot insists on annihilating my brain. I take a step to the side to look out of his bedroom window, letting my forehead drop onto it. I can't stay in here while they're torturing someone in their basement of horrors.

I wonder who it is they have down there. Probably some poor NSC guy who refused to betray Emma Scott for the Kings. There was a wave of betrayals when we took over the town. Elliot and Ethan would torture enough people to scare the others into changing sides.

And they tell you loyalty is everything.

Deciding that listening to Elliot is the last thing I ever want to do, I go grab some tools from the garage. I'm going to do a bit of work on my car and take it for a test drive.

I'm going to race whether he wants it or not.

It doesn't take me long to check the battery, oil, the tires, and the brakes. That's the minimum I need to make sure I don't crash into a wall driving at high speed through our town.

The engine purrs beneath me, sending currents of satisfaction through me. As much as I hate Racer for giving my address to Xi and never bringing me my car, he didn't lie; he took great care of her while I was away. Probably because she's so amazing to drive.

I leave the street driving slowly. The moment I'm far enough away, I send it. I start with accelerating in a straight line to see how her zero to sixty is doing. And when I find myself on an empty main road, I push it to a hundred.

"You're doing so well, baby," I beam with excitement.

I fucking love this car. I spent so much time and money putting her all together that it almost killed me to leave her behind. I pull over to tighten the straps around my body, shifting left and right to make sure I'm not going to go through the window the moment I start drifting corners.

And then I have fun.

I make my way through town, screeching tires at intersections, sending smoke behind me as I overtake people down the streets. I brake hard at a traffic light, realizing I'm panting, but most of all...

I'm smiling.

Excitement prickles from my chest, down to my belly, and I squeeze my thighs. The electric happiness is giving me a lightheaded buzz, and a soft giggle slips out of my mouth.

"Oh shit. I missed this."

There's nothing that feels more like freedom than driving crazily around town. As long as I don't get caught.

I take a minute to let crazy ideas run through my head before I decide to act on them. There's nothing wrong with checking if there's a race tonight. My car is clearly just as special as it used to be, probably thanks to Racer. He's even added a roll cage for protection, which makes me think he was planning on racing with it. Fucker.

I make my way across the bridge that links the North Shore to the South Bank. The difference is stark. Our rundown streets don't compare to the middle-class side of town, and I observe their privilege on the long drive to the abandoned development where we race.

I used to be told about those every month. People waited for me to show up at the races in the hope of finally winning the beauty I worked so hard on.

My heartbeat accelerates when I reach the end of their side of town and find a crowd of eager drivers, supporters, and half a dozen tuned-up cars.

I'm in fucking heaven.

The gigantic development that was meant to be a mall, residences, and a new school was never finished. It's near the highway, at the point where the North Shore and the South Bank almost touch. They wanted to open something that linked both sides of town, but they lost their funding halfway through. The North didn't want to be gentrified and the South refused to mix with us. They thought the quality of the school would lower, and we thought the shops would be too expensive for us. So many points were raised on both sides that investors pulled out, and it was left with empty, half-finished buildings.

A ghost town. That's what it is. The amazing thing for us is that the road was completed, and enough buildings' skeletons surround us to use as corners.

I rev my engine for the crowd to split and let me drive through. I can't believe the number of people here. When we started racing, there were less than ten of us. Over the years, after some racers started posting on their socials, other drivers joined and brought an audience with them.

This is the one and only illegal race in Silver Falls and its surrounding areas. Because we always do it on a different date, we've never been caught. The police can't keep a constant eye on the area. We've been busted many times, but I've always managed to escape the cops on time.

Heads turn to my car, but no one recognizes me. I used to have a bright pink car no one could confuse with any other. Now I'm showing up in black, boring exterior. Thankfully, what's under the hood is still the best in town.

I leave the engine running so it doesn't get cold and get out of the car.

"So." I smile as silence falls over the crowd. "What's the buy-in?"

"No. Way. She's *back*!" someone shouts to my right.

A tall, lithe woman appears from behind some people and smiles at me.

"Fasten your belts and drive home, boys. Your odds have changed."

"Faith." She's still here. Still running the bets and ruling the races.

I run to her, and she wraps me in her arms.

Looking up at her tall form, she still has the same bright blue hair, cut to her chin. It matches her eyes.

"I fucking missed you," I say breathlessly. A wave of emotions crashes into me.

Faith is the only friend I've ever had outside of the Kings. We're not best friends, and we only ever saw each other at the races she runs, but it's good to see her again.

"Where the fuck have you been?" She fakes a pout, but the real hurt lingers in her eyes. "Two years, tiny. That's a bit long to not give news."

"Away," I admit. "It's a long story."

"Are you okay?" she asks seriously.

It takes me a second to make sure I don't burst into tears. I swallow and give her a tight-lipped smile. "Course. So, are we racing or what?"

She eyes me those extra few seconds that show she actually cares before moving on. "Same as before," she reminds me. "Buy-in is two grand or your car." Her mouth twists because she already knows my answer.

"Car it is," I nod. "She's still the best, don't worry."

Smiling, she points with her thumb at a car behind her. "That guy is new, and I think he'd love a little humbling."

I laugh as I look at him. Brand-new car, clearly bought with the modifications already fitted in. Latest model. The guy inside has a smirk on his face, and he winks at me.

"Rich kid from the South Bank?" I suggest, my fingers already tingling from the need to hold my steering wheel.

"They're easy to spot, aren't they?" she snorts. "Plus, he bet money, so you're leaving with a nice eighteen hundred after this." Of course, she has to take her cut as the organizer.

I nod, licking my lips with anticipation. I'm going to eat him alive. "Perfect way to get back into the competition," I agree.

"He's all yours." She whistles and waves a hand in the air. "Rocco, you're out. Jade is racing."

"Aw, man." He looks at me and smiles. "I'll give you the easy win. Welcome back." Rocco is another veteran in this race like me.

Two of his friends part the crowd to allow him to turn his car around and settle to the side again. A hint of jealousy pinches my heart. I used to have Ethan, Elliot, and

Caden supporting me through races. I'd call them my cheerleaders, but really, they were my bodyguards.

Even if Ethan loved to remind me how much he hated me, he would always show up. And he would nod when I gave them my sign that I was okay; the tip of my thumb meeting the tip of my forefinger like the universal ring sign. And then I shaped half of a heart with one hand.

I'm okay. Love you, guys.

Fuck, I feel so stupid right now, wishing the three of them were here supporting me. I'm still bruised from Kay, terrified of Caden, ashamed of the way I let Elliot play with me, and Ethan...I don't even want to think of Ethan right now.

I put on *"Na, Na, Na"* by My Chemical Romance, nod to Faith, and rev my engine, showing her I'm ready. I look to the side at the other driver, and he scoffs.

"Really? How old are you? Can you even reach the pedals?"

Taking my time, I pop two pieces of apple gum in my mouth. I found it at the brothers' house. There are packs everywhere. Elliot used to buy them for me and keep them around, and it makes me feel all kinds of ways to see he still does it.

I fake a pout at my opponent and shake my head. Nothing is funnier than playing with entitled men. "Please, be nice. I still struggle to shift gears."

"Let's add to the bet. I'll throw in another grand. You throw your car and a ride in mine with my cock down your throat."

"An extra grand? Is that what you think my blow jobs are worth? Come on, give me more credit than that." I trace my tongue along my upper lip suggestively and wink at him.

146

This is fun. It'll be even funnier when I leave with the money.

"Alright, five grand in total," he agrees.

"THREE," Faith starts shouting, pointing a scarf at me with her right hand. She's standing in front of our two cars, right in between us. I nod at her.

"That's a big boy," I tell him in a sickly-sweet voice.

"TWO," Faith continues, pointing another scarf with her left hand at the guy next to me. He nods at her.

"I can't wait to drive your car away from this place." He smirks.

"ONE..." She lifts the scarfs above her head, extending her arms to the sky, and I press the gas pedal at the same time as I slowly release the pressure from my clutch. I rev my engine, ready to speed away.

"Oh, sweetie," I chuckle. "You wouldn't know what to do with my car."

"Race!" The moment Faith brings the scarfs down, I release my clutch and we're both gone in a split second.

His car is brand new, so it picks up speed quicker than mine. I do need to rework the engine if I want to keep up with everything that was made in the last two years. But his is premade. Low quality for an expensive price. At the first corner, I go on the inside and overtake. He doesn't hold as well, and he loses too much speed when I accelerate again.

On the next corner, he's scared and brakes too early, throwing his chance of getting back in front of me. I brake at the last second, drifting around a building and sending smoke behind me.

We're on the last straight line, his nose on my ass, but I'm not worried. There's enough of the race left for me to put more distance between us.

There is nothing like the last few seconds of a race.

When I see the crowd getting closer, the finish line just out of reach, my brain lets go of everything that worries me to focus on nothing else but the win. That's when my heart stops beating in preparation for the excitement.

Freedom at the tips of my fingers.

I cross the imaginary line with at least two seconds on him. He didn't stand a chance.

I'm laughing when I stumble out of the car, drunk on adrenaline, with My Chemical Romance still screaming. My head is light, and I can't feel my body. Butterflies swarm my stomach as the crowd heads my way and Faith takes me in her arms.

First night back, first win in two years.

And yet nothing feels the same. Elliot isn't here to grab me in his arms. I don't get an impressed look from Caden or a mumbled *well done* from Ethan that means everything.

Taking the five grand from the sulking rich kid, I slap his shoulder. "Well tried." I pop a bubble as he waits for my next words. "But you're a shit driver with too much money."

Faith wraps her arms around my shoulders and drags me toward the trunk of her car. She's got bottles of beer, and she's right next to the car blaring a rock song much louder than mine.

"Welcome back," she laughs as I give her her share. "I'm glad you kept up with the expectations."

"Muscle memory, am I right?"

She nods, taking a sip of a beer. "That's right." She checks the time and takes another swig. "I have to get ready for the next guys. Stay as long as you want, help yourself to anything. I'll catch you after."

As soon as she's off, I check the burner phone Kay gave me. There are three missed calls from Elliot and one text.

16

ETHAN

Prescription Kid - KIND BRUNSWICK

"One, two, three, four, five," I sing-song. "You're not leaving here alive."

The knife digs into his shoulder, blood spurting. His cries of pain feed a hunger deep inside me. I can't wait to hear more.

"Six, seven, eight, nine, ten, no more blood through your veins." I drag the knife from his shoulder all the way to his wrist. "This one doesn't really rhyme, does it?"

"Please," he whimpers. "Please, please..."

I keep whistling to myself, bobbing my head. "One, two, three. There's no need to plea."

This time, I stab the knife in his chest. "Four, five, six. Love how your blood drips."

He tries to grab my wrist, and it takes all of me not to scream. I calmly say, "Don't touch me."

But then I lose it. Because why would he touch me?

I stab him in the throat. "Don't." *Again*. "Fucking." *Again*. "Touch." *And again*. "Me."

He bleeds to death quickly. Too quickly.

"You ruined the game," I sigh, unimpressed by the corpse in front of me. "You're not even fun."

17

JADE

RUN UP! - *iamjakehill, Josh A*

> Elliot: I'm going to find you, and I'm going
> to put you on a leash, baby. That's what you
> deserve.

My lip curls in annoyance. Can't a girl enjoy her win in peace? I make my way to my car, only to be stopped by a wave of bright pink and blonde hair.

"Jade!" Oh, that sweet as fuck voice is annoying. "You were amazing out there."

I stare at Xi's girlfriend with a cocked eyebrow. I look around for him, sure that he's going to jump me anytime.

A poised smile settles on her lips. "He's not here. I'm with a friend."

"Your boyfriend approved of you coming to an illegal race?"

"God no," she snorts. "I'd be in serious trouble if he knew I was here." She extends her hand. "My name is Alex, by the way. I didn't get to introduce myself when we met."

Shaking my head, I ignore her hand. "Go home, Barbie."

I walk past her, but she walks with me. "I just wanted...I wanted to check that you're okay after what happened at our house."

I stop and slowly turn to her. "Are you? No one broke into my house and threatened me."

Her mouth twists in a sorry smile. "No, but Xi told me everything. You ran away from the North Shore, and now they brought you back. It can't be good."

I narrow my eyes at her. "Why do you care? I don't need your pity."

"'Cause she's naïve like that," another voice says.

I know this girl. I've seen her places before, I'm sure of it. Crazy tall, eyes the color of a night sky, long ink-black hair. She's got the same kind of eyes as me, an almond shape that makes her look like a cat about to hiss in your face.

She's wearing a leather jacket on top of a gray hoodie and some black skinny jeans. The complete opposite of Barbie's pink, flowery dress.

They don't look like they should be friends.

The other girl steps in front of Barbie, tall enough to hide her.

"A sweet girl is asking how you are. Is there a reason you're being a dick about it, Jade?"

"Rose," Barbie groans, sidestepping to reappear in my field of vision. "No need to get defensive."

"Funny how you all know my name and give a shit about me, when I have no idea who any of you are." The corner of my lips lift in amusement. "Fans, maybe?"

Rose chuckles. "Yeah, we want to be front row when the Kings finally get rid of you." It feels like a mocking statement about my situation rather than something she really wants.

"I don't," Barbie fights back. "I just wanted to know if you're okay, and also tell you that you're an amazing racer."

"And I just want to state I don't give a shit if you're okay or not, but you are, in fact, an amazing racer."

I shrug. "Thanks." I look deep into Barbie's hazel eyes. "You're nice." When she smiles brightly, I add, "In a creepy way."

"Oh." Her smile drops.

"Where do I know you from?" I ask Rose.

"Lik. I'm his girlfriend."

"Right. Your boyfriends are brothers." I shake my head, barely believing what I'm about to say. "You two are basically NSC and you've been the nicest people to me this week."

"Xi left NSC," Barbie reminds me quickly. Like it's the proudest thing she could say tonight.

I nod. "The pink door."

"So cute, right?" she giggles.

Rose and I exchange a look. "Yeah, Alex is cute like that. Right, puppy?" Rose says, messing Alex's hair.

"Oh, shut up," she laughs.

A small smile creeps onto my face. These two are way too different to get along, and weirdly, it makes me feel like I can get along with them too.

My phone buzzes, and Elliot's name appears on the screen again. "I have to go," I mumble. "Gotta get in a fight with Elliot."

Alex nods. "Hey, take my number."

"Your number?"

I can see she thinks twice about what to say next. Instead of saying that we should hang out, which she seems to understand would push me away, she just says, "Yeah, so you can let us know when you race next. I'm your biggest fan now."

I don't make friends anymore. I don't trust people who say they have your best interest in mind and then let you down when you come for help. When you tell them your secret, your fear, what truly happened to you, and they call you a liar for it.

But I like to believe she just wants to be there for my next race.

"Here," I say, grabbing her phone and putting my number in it.

I eye Rose, silently asking if she's going to give me her phone number too.

"Don't make this awkward for the both of us," she chuckles.

"Agreed," I answer as I walk away.

"I'll create a group chat," I hear Alex cheer to Rose as I get near my car again.

I'm about to open the door, when someone slams their hand on it, forcing it shut. I whip around, ready to punch them in the face.

My mouth falls open instead.

His black eyes have always looked light in the night. Like a creature who belongs to the darkness. And I know he does.

Ethan blocks me, one hand on the car window, just above my shoulder, and the other grabbing my waist tightly.

"What are you doing?" I can barely control the trembling in my voice. It's not fear or lust. It's just the general effect my ex-boyfriend has always had on me.

I could spend hours in his room, talking and having fun, but the moment he dug his eyes into mine, I would lose all sense of composure.

There was no closure with Ethan.

I never got an explanation about why I wasn't good enough for him anymore.

His interest for me died when he joined the Kings.

His love simply vanished.

"I left the house to race. I wasn't going anywhere else. Kay said I need to sort out the money for the van myself. It needs a new engine, better...better...um..."

My voice dies in my throat when his hand tightens on my waist, his thumb caressing my hip. I'm wearing a hoodie. This shouldn't feel so good. It shouldn't raise goosebumps to my skin when I can't even feel his.

His features harden, like he's battling with his thoughts.

"Ethan..." I'm already giving up, my defenses falling easily in front of the man who broke my heart. "What do you want?"

I notice something on his cheek and bring my hand to it. His skin is warm compared to my cold fingers. They shake because no one ever knows how Ethan will react when he's touched. There was never an explanation for it; it's simply who he is. That's what he told me when he let me touch him for the first time.

Some things you're just born with. It's not because anything happened to me. It's because of how everything around me makes me feel. Noises, materials, people. They make me feel weird.

The whole world makes me feel uncomfortable, Jade. The whole world but you.

For a second, I think he's going to shrug me off, but he silently allows me to touch him, letting me wipe the blood with my thumb.

"What did you do?" I rasp.

His violent tendencies started early. Being treated like shit without being able to defend himself kicked off a cycle of gory imagination. He described to me the things he'd like to do to the people who bullied him and hurt us.

But he never put it into action. Not that I know of.

Our gazes lock, and it only takes him a few seconds to come back to reality. He slaps my arm away before grabbing me again.

His grip on my waist is tighter this time, pinching me. I shift, though not able to go anywhere. I'm not sure I want to. It doesn't feel good, but it's his hand on my body, and I want that.

I wince when he presses harder into my skin, and his eyes light up. The stars are suddenly bright in the black holes that are his eyes. He brings his other hand to my shoulder and presses down. My knees buckle, but I resist.

Eyes narrowing at me, he shakes his head, silently telling me not to resist.

"Ethan—" He pinches harder, making me grunt from the pain. His hand on my shoulder persists until I fall to my knees in front of him.

I'm stuck between his legs and the car, suddenly feeling claustrophobic.

His hand is on my jaw next, the tip of his fingers by my ear, his thumb skimming my lips. He traces the outline of my mouth. His chest is rising and falling slowly, breaths deeper and deeper with every new intake of air. Like he needs it to ground himself.

His attempts at self-control fail when he presses his thumb against my lips.

Clenching my teeth, I refuse him entry. "Stop," I grit out. As I try to turn my head to the side, he tightens his grip on my jaw, now grabbing my chin to keep me facing him.

He doesn't lose patience. He tries to push his thumb in my mouth twice again before I give in.

I don't want to know why I do.

Let me believe I'm a scared woman in the dark. Stuck on her knees between a man I know is dangerous and my car.

Let me fool myself that it's nighttime, and I'm vulnerable since I've been back in this town.

Anything to not face the fact that this man can get whatever he wants out of me.

His thumb slides against my tongue, pressing on it before he pulls it out and traces my lips with my saliva.

There's a low growl in his chest as he pushes in again. Instead of wrapping my lips around his finger, I tighten my teeth, biting him gently.

His smile is carnal. I'd never seen it that way. So dark and lustful. A promise that I can't take him. I can't win his games, whatever they may be.

Instead of pulling out, he pushes his thumb farther in, his skin against my teeth, until he presses so far, it makes me gag, and I'm forced to relax.

Tears spring in my eyes, but I still don't miss his other hand unbuckling his belt and opening his black jeans.

I shake my head.

Fuck.

He's really doing this.

My heart beats frantically for so many reasons. I'm scared Ethan is going to hurt me. I'm excited to feel him inside me again after so many years.

But the worst? Probably the remnants of our love I can feel zapping through me.

I should not let my ex use me however he wants without even a word.

When he pulls out his dick, my mouth falls open. He didn't use to have a piercing...there. He's got a silver piece pierced through his tip vertically from top to bottom with two little balls on both sides.

My heart is going to give up. He looks magnificent. He's so hard for me. Just seeing me on my knees for him has him leaking precum. He chuckles mockingly when I lick my lips, and I look up.

Say something, Ethan.

Talk to me, tell me you want this and me. That you missed me.

Ignoring the plea in my eyes, he grabs me by the hair at the top of my head.

The piercing clunks against my teeth as he pushes in, and he pulls at my hair to force my mouth wide open.

I do it. I open and lick his precum. I taste the metal of his piercing against my tongue and let him push deeper until he hits the back of my throat. Then he pulls out, taps my lips with his tip as a warning, and pushes back in.

I do my best to relax my throat, but I tighten again when I feel the piercing. It's foreign, making me feel unsafe.

His grip on my hair tightens, making me whimper from the force he's using. He comes back out, taps my lips, and pushes back in.

"Wait—" I choke on his length when he ignores my gargled plea.

This time he gets farther. My throat is clenched, but he pushes through, groaning in pleasure when he feels the tightness inside me. Saliva pools at the corner of my lips, and when he pulls out again, it spills down my chin.

I gulp air in just as he taps my lips again. The warning that he's about to push back in. He's harsher this time, less patient. He presses hard enough that my head hits the car, stuck between his crotch and the driver's door.

I'm choking on his length when my nose finally touches

his pubis. He stays there for several seconds, unmoving, his hand in my hair, his dick down my throat.

I panic, and it's only now that I realize I haven't tried to stop him until this moment. My hands have been by my sides, my fingertips skimming the freezing ground.

I bring them to his hips, trying to push him off, but he's immovable. A desperate whimper pours out of me, and he finally pulls out in the slightest, only giving me a millisecond to breathe before he pushes back in. His movements accelerate, becoming more violent. Within a few seconds, he's fucking my throat mercilessly, the back of my head hitting the car.

I feel one of his hands moving, sliding to the back of my head. He's not grabbing me, just keeping it flat against the car. When I realize why, I want to burst into tears. He's making sure I don't hit my head harshly against the metal. That I don't hurt myself while he uses me like a whore.

I've got saliva dripping all the way down my throat, and my hands push at his hips uselessly.

What I hate the most is the pressure between my legs. The way I want to bring my hand to my clit instead of his hips. I hate that I want to let him use me, and then beg him to push that exact same way into my wet pussy.

He stops abruptly, pulling out and only leaving the tip of his dick in my mouth as he explodes. His hips flex, his thighs tensing. Cum lands thickly on my tongue, and as soon as he pulls out completely, I'm ready to spit.

But I don't have time to. He slams a hand on my closed mouth and pinches my nose with his other. I thrash in his hold as he presses me against the car, his dark eyes looking down at me, and a devilish smirk on his face.

I hate you, Ethan Torres, my glare screams as he forces me to swallow his cum.

The second he sees my throat working, he lets me go and takes a step back, redoing his jeans and belt. I struggle to get on my feet, helping myself with a flat hand on my door.

I'm panting, my underwear soaking, and anger coursing through my veins.

"Fuck you," I rasp. Shit. It hurts to talk. I feel like I've swallowed a bee.

He looks at me calmly, perfectly composed, and ignores my insult. He simply turns to walk away. But he doesn't get to do that and just leave me here.

"You never told them, did you, Ethan?" I call after him.

Turning back, his brow furrows in question.

"That you're the one who helped the traitor run away."

His jaw tightens, but I still don't get anything out of him. He casually ignores me and is back on his way.

My hand is trembling when I open my door. It's only once inside my car that I notice the note left on my passenger seat. I hurry to unfold it and another wave of anger crashes over me.

How long do you think you have left? Tick Tock, dead girl.

I jump back out of my car and look around. Ethan is gone. The fucking asshole. It's him.

He's threatening me. Because he hates me, because he hates that I'm back.

Because I know his secret.

My mind only starts to clear when I park across from the brothers' house. It's going to be another battle in there, but surely the fact that I'm coming back will show I don't plan on running away. I grab the roll of money on the passenger seat and the note.

Dead girl, I read again.

My jaw tightens. If Ethan wants me dead, he can come say it to my face instead of being a silent dick who doesn't speak more than two words to me. Get in fucking line. The euphoria from the race is long gone now that I know Ethan is after me.

One note might have been a little game. Following me to a race to leave another is no coincidence.

And I know it's him. It can't be anyone else.

The Kings are clear about wanting me dead for the supposed betrayal. They don't need to scare me with petty notes.

I'm not important enough to be a threat to NSC anymore. Plus, they'd just strike. Vague threats really aren't like them.

Caden hates my guts, but he would just casually stab me in front of everyone without any remorse. And his girl holds him on a leash.

Unless Billie didn't really forgive me. I wouldn't blame her; I never forgave her for the things she did to me in high school.

But Billie has bigger, better things to worry about now.

So I know it's him.

My ex-boyfriend is planning to murder me, and he wants to play with me first.

I step out of my car and make sure it's properly locked. Because I parked on the other side of the road, I'm not on the sidewalk as I lock up.

I hear an engine coming down the street, but I assume it's far since I can't see any headlights.

But when I turn around and look up as I start to cross, it's already too late. Headlights turn on suddenly, piercing through the night. It blinds me, stopping me from seeing anything as I freeze on the spot.

Move, you fucking idiot!

All I register is the violence of the vehicle hitting me.

18

ELLIOT

Young God - Halsey

"I told you," she rasps as her eyes flutter open. "I fucking told you and you didn't believe me."

"Shut up," I grit out, holding her body close to mine, carrying her inside the house.

I heard the scream, and I ran outside.

All I saw was the way she rolled off the car and landed on the concrete. I didn't even see the car, too focused on her limp body on the ground.

I can't believe she's still conscious, and I can't believe she's not screaming to death right now.

She's too fucking stubborn to show she's hurt. She would rather tell me *I told you so.*

I'm inside the house when the front door bursts open, and Ethan runs in, sweat rolling down his forehead.

"What the hell was that?" He fails to stop the rush of his words.

He's striding toward me, his hands on Jade the second he can reach her. He presses a palm on her cheek.

"Hit and run. I didn't see the car properly."

"I told you," she repeats, her entire face scrunching at the pain she must feel when she talks.

"I told you to shut up."

She attempts to take a deep breath, stopping short when she hisses.

"I was right."

"You're in pain. Stop talking," Ethan growls.

This isn't good. I'm worried about her. It grips my gut, feels thick in my veins. One glance at my brother is all I need to know he's feeling the same way.

"Fuckers," she lets out on a shallow breath.

"You're so fucking stubborn." I don't control the way my arms tighten around her, keeping her head against my chest.

"Put her on my bed."

"Why yours?" I snap.

There's a pause. A short beat when his eyes cross with mine.

Oh. This isn't good at all.

"Because you're only good at attempting, yet failing miserably, to fuck her. I'm going to take care of her."

"Because you're not tempted to fuck her," I scoff. "Of course."

His jaw works from side to side as he combs his hair back. It brings my attention to the thick black strands. They look damp and his cheeks are red. Like he's been in the cold.

"Where have you been?" I ask seriously.

He disappeared earlier tonight while I was torturing Stephen for info, but I didn't realize he'd gone out. I thought he was locked in his room. The music is still playing in there, *"Misfits"* by Magnolia Park and Taylor Acorn. He clearly wanted me to think he was home.

Ignoring my question, he takes off his shirt, plenty of his tattoos on display on his golden skin, and uses it to dab the blood spilling from her eyebrow.

"Elliot," he insists. "Put her on my bed."

Broody, muscly, tortured artist. He is Jade's walking wet dream right now. She's always loved him for his broken soul, a stark contrast to my manipulative, sharp mind. My brother and I are complete opposites. I know him by heart. If he starts caring for her...we're done. She'll fall back in his clutches, and I don't want that at all.

"No."

That's all I say before I sidestep him and start walking to my bedroom.

"Elliot," he barks after me, trying to grab my arm.

I shrug him off easily. "I can kick your skinny ass while holding her," I hiss. "Don't fucking try me."

He takes a step back, shocked by my words. He's not skinny. Not anymore. He's a fucking hard dude who could punch the lights out of me. But it's all about knowing someone's brain and what makes them tick. What makes them *weak*.

Ethan has no confidence in his physical abilities. That's why he feels the need to get into fights and break people's bones. That's why he kills people. So he can keep proving to himself he's not the poor bullied boy from high school anymore. I can crush that confidence easily.

He leaves me alone when I walk to my room again, but it's Jade's voice that stops me this time.

"Ethan."

"Wrong brother, my love."

"It was Ethan."

. . .

She groans when she comes to her senses.

"Shit," she gasps as she tries to shift in bed.

She hasn't noticed me yet. I'm watching her from my bedroom doorway, leaning against the frame with my arms crossed over my chest.

Her head is propped on two pillows, but she's not aware of much. She winces when she tries to sit up, and it takes everything in me to not help her.

We have something to settle first.

I notice the exact moment she feels the band of leather around her throat. Her brows furrow in confusion, her hands going to touch it, even if it means she hisses in pain. Her eyes widen when she finally manages to bring two hands to her throat, feeling for the collar around her neck.

"What..." she rasps.

She jerks into a sitting position, whimpering from the pain. The second she attempts to move forward, she's brought back.

"What the fuck." An enraged panic settles on her face when she turns around and looks at the chain bolted to the wall...and leading right to her neck. "Elliot!" she shouts, then winces right away. "What the fuck is that?"

"A chain," I reply casually.

She startles, realizing I'm right there in the dark, observing her.

"I can see it's a fucking chain," she hisses.

"Linked to your collar." I shrug and finally walk into my room.

"Linked to my—Take that shit off right now!"

She brings her arms up, looking for a way to unbuckle the leather from her neck before she gasps. Either from pain or from the padlock she must have found, and that makes it impossible for her to unbuckle the collar.

"Shit," she pants. "My ribs…"

"You were fucking lucky. That hit was a warning. They didn't want to kill you. I think one of your right floating ribs might be fractured," I explain. "I iced it, but you shouldn't make any sudden movements."

"Maybe not being chained to a fucking wall would help," she bites out.

"I think I already told you, you'd be put on a leash for leaving the house without asking."

"I needed money for the van. I went to a race…I won." Her explanation doesn't mean shit to me. Not now that someone tried to hurt her. *Succeeded.*

"You got ran over," I hiss in fury. "If there's one thing I hate, Jade, it's my belongings being damaged. We brought you back. We make the decisions about you. Not you. Not Kay. *Us.*" I take a threatening step toward her, blood boiling.

Someone is playing with her life.

Trying to take her away from me.

"You can't *force* me to stay here."

"Well, why don't you try to leave now that you're chained to the wall? Let me know how that goes."

"You're an asshole, Elliot."

"And you're a fucking annoying brat who gets angrier at life every day. You're incapable of doing anything you're told, and you will be the end of me."

"What did you think? That I was a good girl underneath? Just waiting for the right man to make me behave? Think again."

I pause, licking my lips. "Isn't that what you did with Stan? I might not have the money, but I have other means to *make you* behave."

"Is that what you want, Elliot?" she insists, making sure to piss me all the way off. "A good girl?"

My smile makes her shiver. Probably because it's sick and twisted.

"No. I don't want a good girl. I want a bad girl I'll turn good through punishments."

I'm pretty sure she stops breathing for a few seconds, so I take a step forward to drive home my point.

"How many times do I have to say you're not leaving the house unless I let you before it sticks to your bratty brain? You do what you're told, because I get to call the shots." Another step, and I point a finger at her throat. "You wear my collar, because I get to punish you." I stop by the bed, grabbing her jaw and pulling her up as I lean down and talk in her ear. "I. *Fucking*. Own. You."

I put a knee on the bed and grab her hips. She shrieks when I flip her around, and I know she must be in pain. It's probably unbearable.

But I have a point to make.

She needs to fucking learn to listen, because I can't risk her getting hurt again.

Grabbing the boxers I put on her earlier, I slide them down as she kicks her legs at me.

"Fuck you!" she screams, but the next time she tries to take a breath, she whimpers.

There is nothing I hate more in this world than seeing Jade in pain.

I hate when anyone hurts her, and even less when it's me.

But I can't for one second let her know the kind of power she's always had over me. How *fucking worried* I am when she's not somewhere I have eyes on her.

I slap her ass harshly because it's that or admitting the whole truth.

That I've always been jealous of Ethan for having her in

a way I never could.

"Don't try to play smart with me," I hiss.

Another slap because it's that or divulging I'm the fucked-up one who fell in love with his brother's girlfriend so long ago; I can't even remember what my life was like when I *wasn't* in love with Jade.

I wore a mask in front of everyone. Back then, I told my friends I was just playing around with her.

Only Ethan knew the truth, and I can't have Jade know it too.

I pull her up, spread her ass cheeks, and spit on her pussy. "Jade," I growl. "You've been bad again."

My slap this time lands on her pussy lips because it's that or conceding to myself, I am utterly obsessed with Jade Alva, and the thought of knowing someone is trying to hurt her drives me fucking insane. Her shrieks turn into moans, and I do it again.

"Fuck..." she pants.

"Beg. Beg me to make you come because who knows what I'll do to you when I stop holding myself back." I'm dying to spread her lips and push my fingers inside her tight pussy. But I want—I need—her to say she's dying for it too.

I can see the signs; the wetness, the panting, but I want more. I want her to admit it. All I've ever wanted was for her to tell me she wanted *me*. Not Ethan, not fucking Sawyer...*me*.

"I'll take the pain away, my love. I'll put you to sleep again. Give you the orgasms you need. And no one will hurt you ever again."

"Please," she pants. "I want it all, please." Her first admission makes me push past her wet lips, teasing her entrance.

"What is that?"

"Everything you can give. Any—ah!" My middle finger presses in a little more. "Fuck, Elliot. Anything you want. Just make me feel good."

"You want to be my little slut?"

"Yes…"

I push in. Slowly, feeling her tightness and wetness enveloping my finger, I go farther.

"My whore I can use whenever I want?"

"Yes…please…*I'm begging you.*"

"Finally," I growl as I lay on top of her, my hand against the mattress to prop myself above her back. "Fucking *finally*," I repeat in her ear.

Pushing two fingers inside her, I force past her tightness. "You're going to be such a good girl. The best girl."

I play with her, moving in and out so slowly I feel her twist and chase for more. Grabbing the chain linking to her collar, I pull at it until I hear her whimper.

"Stay still, baby. I'll be taking care of you now."

I take my time teasing her. I lose count of how many times I rub her G-spot, only to pull out and push back in. I don't touch her clit once, showing her how unattainable her orgasm is, unless I decide so.

She fists the sheets, buries her head in the pillow, and cries out, "Elliot…*fuck.* Let me come."

I tsk her, shaking my head as I chuckle. "Patience is a virtue good girls like you should have. Show me your patience, my love."

"I c-can't…I just want to come. Just let me…"

My slap on her ass is so loud it resonates in the entire room.

"If you're bad, you'll get nothing. So I suggest you learn to behave."

When I stop moving entirely, she nods. "Okay. I'm sorry."

She stays still, and I smile to myself. Jade Alva's body is mine to play with and torture however I want.

"Atta girl."

I don't know how long I keep her like this. Torturing her sweet little pussy with the promise of an orgasm, but I'm so hard, I could fucking explode.

"Tell me," I purr. "Tell me how badly you want to come."

"Please..." she whimpers. "I need to. Make me come."

"What's my name?" And as I ask, I accelerate, giving her what she needs as I press my thumb against her clit at the same time.

"Elliot," she whimpers.

"Louder."

"Elliot. Fuck...*Elliot!*" she screams as she explodes on me. Her wetness leaks onto her thighs and the sheets, as she grinds against me frantically, riding the pleasure.

"That's right. That's the man who makes you come now, baby."

I let go, undoing my jeans and sitting back on my haunches. I pull her hips harder toward me until she's on all fours, the chain taut between her neck and the wall.

Lining my cock with her entrance, I take a second to register the situation. She's mine. Finally *all. Mine.*

She's not allowed to leave this house. She's not safe anywhere but near me. When Jade realizes she needs me to survive, that she has no one else but me, she'll understand how utterly mine she is.

I smile to myself as I push into her in one violent thrust. Her moan is practically a shriek, her pussy soaked and swollen.

I took my time making her come, but I don't have that

patience for myself right now. I just want to punish her for making me wait so long to give herself to me again.

"Two years, huh?" I grunt, my hands marking her hips from the strength of my hold. I'm relentless, pushing in and out of her. "You think you can run away from me for two. Fucking. Years." I punctuate my words with rough, powerful thrusts until her arms give up and she falls onto the bed.

"Kay might let you go after the robbery." Her pants are desperate, the small noises she makes completely addictive. "But you are never getting away from me again, Jade. Welcome to your new world. The one where you belong to *me*." I'm out of breath when I explode inside her with a roar, not a care about whether she's on contraception, or whoever she fucked while she was away. I need to feel her, to feel the way she comes again, contracting around my dick at the same time as I spill deep inside her.

She slumps against the mattress when I let her go, panting like she ran a fucking marathon. Her eyes flutter shut, and I bring my hand to her hair, pushing the strands sticking to her sweaty forehead with my thumb.

People who know me say I'm an addict. Not drugs and alcohol. That's never really been my thing.

No, it's power, sex, money, controlling people. But that's all superficial. The kind of dopamine I was using just to replace the best drug of all time.

Nothing is as addictive as Jade.

I can already feel the need for my next high as I watch my cum run out of her. I press two fingers against her entrance, listening to her whimper as I push it back inside. It's so fucking satisfying to see me in her. To know she took it all for me.

"How are you feeling?" I ask softly, pulling my hand away.

Her breathing calms, and she lets out a long sigh, like finally realizing what she's done.

"You have to protect me," she murmurs. "I don't want to die."

I help her on her back and lift my The Offspring t-shirt I put on her earlier. Her stomach and ribs are bruised. They're a deep purple, practically black. I can't imagine the pain she must feel right now.

Something twists in my stomach. I can't look at this. I can't look at her when she's in pain.

"Promise you'll protect me." Her eyes keep fluttering shut and back open, clearly struggling to stay awake.

"I promise," I murmur. "We have a deal."

"From Ethan too."

My brows furrow. I thought she was confused earlier when she said it was Ethan. It makes no sense whatsoever. Why would he try to kill her? I kiss her forehead, feeling the need to have my lips against her skin again.

"It wasn't Ethan, my love."

"You don't know that."

"I can promise you I know him well enough to tell you he wouldn't hurt you."

But still, if she feels that way, she has a reason.

I need to talk to my brother.

19

ETHAN

Loser - Sueco

I know my moment of peace is over the second Elliot knocks on my door and opens it before I can even allow him to come in or not.

If he was a normal person, and not a motherfucking extreme manipulator, he would have let his anger out, burst through the doors, and punched me in the face. We would have beaten each other up like Kings do and put the issue to rest.

Although I don't think our specific four-year-and-counting issue can just be *put to rest.*

My music is off, and I don't need to lie to him. He knows it's because I was eavesdropping.

That's why he made her scream his name.

I stay sitting at my desk chair. It's full of music sheets, some I just started, some crumbled, some ripped to pieces. My amp is right next to my chair, my guitar and headphones plugged into it. I have a mini keyboard on my desk, right next to my shitty laptop I use to edit my music.

Elliot looks around, observing calmly, like he'll learn something about me. The room is a fucking mess, but he forgets because he never comes in here. Clothes are scattered everywhere on the floor, my bed unmade. I've stopped counting the glasses I need to bring back to the kitchen. He closes the door behind him and uses his cheery voice when he talks to me. Like a pitbull pretending to be a golden retriever.

"You seriously need to tidy your room, brother. Maybe then you'll feel more at ease to bring girls here."

He stops by my old stereo. His dad had gifted it to me when I joined the Kings. I remember how fucking happy I felt. I spent all my money on CDs I could blast.

For the first time in my life, the voices in my head decided to shut up. They're not always clear, just calling me to do bad things. When the music screams around me, it stops the screeching in my head.

I thought the gift was for me. It wasn't. The reality was that it wasn't to quiet my inner cries. It was so I couldn't hear Elliot's screams in the basement when his dad would beat the shit out of him.

Many kids who have to live around unpredictable parents learn to manipulate behaviors. And God fucking knows how unpredictable Elliot's dad was. No wonder the man has no pity for others' souls. It's safer for him to create the personalities he wants around him, rather than take the risk of them being a disappointment. Or worse, a danger.

Elliot Pearson only feels safe when he can control everything around him. He enjoys playing with people's minds the same way I enjoy playing the guitar. His calculating behaviors don't stop for the ones he loves. One doesn't just let go of a passion; they keep falling more into the addiction every time.

And as much as I would like it to be, I'm no fucking exception.

As long as Elliot keeps control over me, he'll feel safe. No one wants to be around when he doesn't feel safe anymore.

He presses the ON button with the tip of his index finger. The plastic makes a strange noise before music blasts out of the speakers. *"KULT"* by grandson inundates the room, bouncing against the wall and making my desk shake.

Still, he turns it up, smiling at me innocently.

The way my jaw tightens nearly gives me a headache. At least I can focus. I've been sitting in a silent room for hours, waiting for Jade to wake up, listening to my brother drilling into my ex-girlfriend's mind that she's his fuck toy again. Listening to her moan his name.

The screaming in my head only had one word for me: *kill. Kill. Kill.* On repeat, like a prayer from the devil.

I didn't, because unlike what he thinks, I have more control over myself than he does.

Elliot leans with his thigh against the edge of my desk, facing me closer than I'd like him to. He knows that. That I hate people in my personal space, and still, he does it just to get me on edge.

I pull away, rolling my chair back and tilting my head up to look at him. I don't need to stand up, shouldn't let him think I feel intimidated and need to level myself with him. Even when I was skinny, I was tall, lanky, but no one is as fucking tall as Ethan. Standing up would only highlight that.

My brother smiles down at me, glancing at the black marker pen I'm tapping against the desk. I stop right away, knowing that's what's betraying my nerves.

Too late. His smile is wider when his gaze crosses mine this time.

"Why did you follow Jade to her race?" he asks with a lightness that could fool me into thinking he asked me what I wanted for dinner.

"I didn't hit her with my car, Elliot. I don't know why she thinks that."

The walls are thin. I heard her accuse me of being the one to attempt to kill her. She said it twice, so sure of herself. Jade and I have had our differences in the past, but I would never hurt her. Not like that.

"I know that," he replies with ease.

"I'm sure you've done your homework."

"You own a fucking Ford Ranger. She wouldn't have survived that. There are no marks of any hit on your truck, I checked. Plus, what would you have done? Hit her, go park down the road, and run back inside the house? Let's try to keep making sense here, shall we?"

I open my mouth to talk, but he puts a finger in the air. "But of course, let's not forget the main point. You would never hurt Jade." He shrugs. "I didn't ask if you tried to kill her, Ethan. I asked why you followed her to her race all the way to the South Bank when you know that's not something you're allowed to do."

My jaw tightens. I could break my teeth every time he tells me what I can and can't do. It's exhausting to live with a man who calculates every single move he's ever going to make.

Elliot is always five moves ahead, no wonder I'm fucking crazy after having grown up with him.

"Shouldn't you worry about who's trying to kill your girlfriend, rather than why I keep an eye on her?"

He pauses, looking away and smiling like a fool. "My

girlfriend." He experiments with the words on his lips before licking them, seemingly loving the taste. "I like that. Is that how you felt when *you* got to say that? All warm and fuzzy."

I could grab the gun in my drawer, kill him, cut his body in pieces, burn them to ashes, and throw them in a dumpster...It still wouldn't help with how much I loathe him right now.

"Don't." I try to say it coolly, try to take a page out of his book and go for the casual front. It never seems to work on me. "Don't mention my past with her. Just enjoy your prize and leave me alone."

"Yeah, I'm trying to." Something changes in his voice. It's dishonestly relaxed, but it now gives the impression of a still lake with monsters hiding underneath the surface. "I'm trying to, but it seems my brother keeps forgetting *my* girl isn't his anymore. Following her around like a lost puppy and shit."

I look at the sheet on my desk. Music notes in black marker. Messy, the ink so deep in some parts that it's torn through the paper. That's the music Jade makes when my brother makes her come.

It's desperate, like *"Comptine D'un Autre Été"* by Yann Tiersen. She kept wanting more and more. I could hear it in her moans, just short of obtaining exactly what she wanted and begging for him to give her everything she needed. And he did.

A beautiful melody. One I should have made her sing myself.

I uncap the marker and write some more. "I get your point, Elliot. You can leave." I try not to make it sound dejected, but how else am I meant to feel when the woman who had always been mine is only a distant dream now?

A hand lands on my sheet firmly. "I want you to answer my question. What were you doing at the race?"

Slowly, feeling the violence inside me wanting to spill out, I tilt my head and look up.

"Do you know the kind of things men say to Jade?" I feel my upper lip curl as I think of that rich boy and the offer he made her. "Do you know the way they look at her?"

"Yes, Ethan," he says lazily. "I was the one fucking her when people started opening their eyes and realizing how beautiful she is. I know how much men desire her."

"Then why don't you do anything about it?" I snap. The marker tears through the page, slipping on my desk, and practically ripping the paper in half.

His eyes focus on my hand, the line I just drew on my desk, and my white knuckles around the pen.

"If you want her so much, why don't you make sure no one ever talks or looks at her the way that man at the race did." My words barely make it past my gritted teeth.

He straightens up, and I watch as he slowly understands what I did on the South Bank tonight. He throws his head back. "Ah, fuck," he grounds out.

"The things he said to her..."

"Where's the body?"

"She bet her car, and he just *had* to add a blow job, huh? More money to get her in *his* car."

"Where is the body, Ethan?" he insists, anger clear on his features.

There are only a handful of things that will show on my brother's face. Anger at me for leaving bodies all over town is one of them. The others are Jade sleeping with other men, or the mention of his father.

Never talk to Elliot about his father.

"Ethan," he snaps. "Where?"

"In the abandoned mall. The one where they race."

"Is that the whole thing? Or am I going to find the head in a toy shop and the body in the food court?"

I look at my sheet again. Jade's moans are so beautiful. They could be a symphony to themselves. I push her sheet to the side and look at the one underneath. I called it *"Murderer on the Loose."* It hurts my ears to simply read it. The same way that guy's screams pierced my eardrums.

"It's the whole body." I nod to myself before looking at him. "In the underground parking lot."

"You're a fucking idiot." He's annoyed, but he doesn't raise his voice. "A fucking shithead serial killer who is going to bring the cops to our house because he can't fucking control his urges for blood."

"It's the way he talked to her," I justify, my voice now completely even.

"North Shore, Ethan. You promised to keep it to *our* side of town. I can hide bodies on the *North Shore*. I can't hide the bodies of rich kids on the South Bank, you fucking..." He takes a deep breath, his eyes fluttering shut.

When he opens them again, he smiles at me, his madness under control again. His violence is hidden by his golden-boy face. "I'll take care of it, okay? I just want you to remember one thing for me."

"What?" I mumble, drawing a semi-quaver on my sheet.

"The reason you're part of the Kings," he says, his voice low and meaningful. "And why they don't know what you've done *yet*." The threat is so clear he might as well have written it black on white and shoved it in my face.

"Tell me you remember, brother, and I can go and clean your mess."

I bite my tongue to the point I taste blood in my mouth.

"I remember." My tone is flat, my body tense, but I gave him what he needs.

"Good. Stay away from her, then."

He leaves my room the same way he entered. As composed as a politician about to lie through their teeth to the entire population.

He'll be gone for a while. By the time he goes all the way to the South Bank, finds the body, and gets rid of it. I have a good couple of hours to myself.

All the time I want to play with the woman he tells me to stay away from.

20

JADE

pretty poison - Nessa Barett

I startle. Couldn't he just let me fucking sleep and forget for a little while? He uses that stupid technique too, where he stops me from breathing so I wake up.

"Elliot," I groan against his hand. "St—"

He hooks his fingers under the collar he put on me earlier and pulls until I'm forced to lift off the bed slightly, then lets go. My head falls back and reality hits me right in the face.

I keep my eyes closed while I register the pain. Holy fucking shit, it hurts.

Grumbling low in my throat, I come to my senses, the first thing I feel being the ache in my ribs.

It all comes back so easily. I wish my brain had given me more time with ignorant bliss.

I got run over. By Ethan. My ex-boyfriend hit me with his truck.

I feel a hand at my thigh. Elliot.

Elliot chained me to his fucking bed and...what have I done?

This is the moment when I need to make a decision. Do I lie to myself, or do I admit that giving my consent back to Elliot is the best decision I made since being back in this town?

Nothing feels better than the pleasure he brings. It's so natural, like everything falls into place when he touches me. I don't know if it's the memories or an entirely new feeling, but having him close to me, feeling me, pleasuring me...it's like I've been waiting my entire life to be completed that way.

But I know what it entails. It means being utterly his. It means he gets to do whatever he wants with my body now. And Elliot takes that statement seriously. Once you give him yourself, there's no going back.

His hands slide up my thighs, and I tense. His fingertips are calloused. They're rough, like someone who...

I gasp as I open my eyes. I'm surprised I didn't recognize Ethan's touch sooner. I've learned his fingertips by heart. They're the ones of a man who plays the guitar all day long. Who spends hours honing his craft.

"What are you doing!"

I'm wheezing as I sit up, bringing a hand to my ribs and one flat on the mattress so I don't fall back. I feel dizzy from the sudden pain, but that orgasm from earlier knocked me out, and I'm rested and wide awake now.

He stays completely silent as he grabs my thighs in a deadly grip and spreads them wide.

"Ethan." I try to bring my legs back and push him off, but he simply looks up at me.

His eyes are darker than any fear ever known to man. In this moment, he doesn't care what he takes or who he hurts.

Nothing is as important as what he *wants*.

His fingers press harder into my skin, and my heart skips a beat. "Be careful," I hiss. I take breaths as deep as I can, but it's not much. "Ethan, don't." Keeping my voice steady, I do my best not to trigger the dangerous man I know he is. The same one who hit me with a fucking truck.

How? How could he go from caring for me to wanting to kill me?

"You don't have to hurt me," I insist, my heart pounding in my ears. "I won't tell anyone you helped me run away." I'm stuck on this bed, collared and chained to the fucking wall. And I've got a man who tried to murder me holding my legs wide open.

What am I meant to do but placate him?

His eyes soften, and he brings his face to mine. Patchouli, cedar, and bergamot.

So deeply him, my heart stutters once more.

I don't actually know what those three things smell like, but I remember googling and learning about his cologne back in high school. Anything that would bring me closer to him.

Just one of those things that led to me breaking my own heart. Too involved, too obsessed.

He moves the collar slightly, showing my skin underneath. It drives me insane that this thing pisses me off as much as it turns me on. My brain isn't wired for such contradictions. I'm a woman who knows what she wants, not one who is confused about what she feels.

His lips brush the skin he revealed under the collar, and his teeth raise goosebumps to the back of my neck.

He nibbles at it, sucking in. I feel a rush of blood and my stomach twists. He stays longer than comfortable, undoubtedly bringing a mark to the spot.

I moan when he lets go, like I'd been holding it all along. "I would never hurt you, Jade," he whispers in my ear.

A rasp of a promise.

A lie I shouldn't believe.

But my heart...it aches to hear more of his voice when it's not spurting insults at me.

My body...it vibrates to the notes that resonate when he speaks.

My beautiful Ethan. Life never loved him, so he loves *nothing* in return.

His calloused fingers drag up my thigh, his thumb coming to rest on my slit.

Before I even register what my reaction should be, he rests back on his haunches, keeping his thumb in place. With his other hand, he brushes my tits above my clothes and keeps going up until he can trace the outline of my lips.

"Beautiful," he murmurs to himself.

That word on his lips means everything. Because he said it before everyone else. He said it, whispered it, moaned it when the rest of the world threw insults in my face about how ugly I was.

I wasn't ugly. I was myself. I was growing up. I was a teenager finding herself.

Something I apparently wasn't allowed to do. Someone cut it short. They spat on my teen years and forced adulthood into my body. Into my state of mind.

They made me a monster.

Ethan...Ethan kept my soul alive. That's why he was the only one capable of destroying it.

His thumb presses against my slit, parting my lips, and he easily finds my clit, like the blueprint of my body is still on his mind.

Like he knows me inside out.

"You gave in," he whispers.

I know he's talking about Elliot, but I don't understand why he sounds so disappointed about it.

"Talk to me." I bring a hand to his face at the same time my hips lift to meet his strokes against my clit.

He's so soft.

So caring.

So him.

And yet the complete opposite of what he wants to do. I know that.

He slaps my hand away from his face and brings his finger back to my mouth, all the while still playing with my clit so carefully; I become the same as the instruments he's learned to master.

"Say something," I say against his thumb, the tension building inside my body. "How you feel. What you want. The truth. Anything, Ethan. Anything but the pretense of hate you have toward me."

Instead of doing just that, he shoves two fingers into my mouth and picks up his pace.

"You want to let him touch you?"

I moan when he pinches my clit. "You want to become a whore for Elliot? Is that it?"

Instead of pushing him away, I press harder into him. He lets go of my clit to coat his fingers in my wetness and pushes one in, then another.

"If you knew the things he did to get you."

I moan around his fingers. I want to ask him to explain everything, to stop the games.

I'm too busy panting as he fucks me insane. Too focused on the pleasure and the overwhelming love I can't help but feel around him.

Love me, Ethan.

Fucking. Love. Me.

"Do you have any idea what he'll do to you?"

I shake my head, and his fingers press deeper into my mouth, making me gag when he hits the back of my throat.

"He'll strip you of everything you are. And then he'll build you back just how he wants. And you'll be nothing, *nothing*, but the slut he wants you to be."

This isn't helping. This is making me hotter, needier, *wetter*.

"When *I* wanted to do that to you, you said no."

He curls his fingers inside me, rubs my G-spot, and pulls out. I cry out for him, and he pushes back in, deeply, almost painfully if there wasn't so much pleasure coursing through my body.

"When *I* talked to you about the depraved things I wanted to do, you said *no*."

We were young.

Inexperienced.

I was scared.

I didn't know my body like I know it now.

I would go to hell and back, shake hands with the devil, and sell him my soul if it meant Ethan Torres would take me back and do all the depraved things he once wanted to do to me.

And you know what they say, right?

Be careful what you wish for.

He presses his fingers on my tongue and smirks. Looking down at me with so much power radiating from him, it could burn the both of us to ashes.

"Elliot is a busy man. You'll come to understand how important he is to Kay. How often he *isn't* home. And guess who will be here? Me."

I'm near an internal explosion when he curls his fingers inside me again. "Everything you let him do to you, I'll do worse. Everything you give him, I'll take from you. There was meant to be no other man but me in your life, Jade. So believe me when I say, if he replaces me, I'll make sure you give me twice what you give him."

My moans are out of control when I explode. "You want to scream his name?" he grunts. "You'll be crying mine." I thrash on the bed as he keeps stimulating my clit while I'm already coming. "Won't you, baby?"

I nod, but my *yes* was a clear scream anyway.

Ethan doesn't have to take from me. I'll gladly offer anything he wants. My heart, for example.

When he finally stops torturing my clit, he pulls his fingers out of my mouth to replace them with the ones coated in my wetness. I lick them, then suck them eagerly, making sure to clean him of everything he got out of me. Too bad I can't claim my sanity back.

"You won't tell him anything," he says with a certainty that makes my heart skip a beat. "You'll be good and keep our secret. Right, Jade?"

When I don't respond, he gives me a soft slap on the cheek with his damp fingers. "Say it. You won't tell Elliot anything."

I don't understand why, but I agree. I'd say yes to anything when it comes to this man. "I won't tell Elliot anything," I rasp, my throat hurting from the way he presses down with his fingers.

Unlike his brother, Ethan isn't very good at giving praise. He takes and has nothing to give in return. Nothing but humiliation.

Just when I think he's done, he spits on my mouth, making me gasp from shock. "Lick it."

I should be much more hesitant. I should control my body better. Not just let my tongue dart out and lick my lips clean of his spit.

"Slut." Not an insult. Not a compliment either. A lustful discovery to him.

It's as if he's been waiting his entire life for me to show him my depraved side.

He gets out of bed. I'm too shocked to say anything else, even to wonder why he hides something from his brother.

Ethan is the one who pushed me away. I shouldn't mean much to him.

And yet he's here, made me come, saying there should be no other man in my life.

This type of behavior gives me hope. Dangerous, traitorous hope. I don't want to become the girl who waits for Ethan to give her a scrap of attention again. The hardest thing to do in my life was move on from him. I guess that's why I never really did.

"Ethan," I rasp as I watch him get off the bed. "Can you undo this thing, please?"

He looks at the leather around my neck and shakes his head. "I don't want him to know I've been in his room, made his girl come."

"I'm not Elliot's girl."

He snorts, running a hand through his black hair. "To him, you are, believe me. You've always been." Pausing, he observes me as he stands by the door. "Even when you were with me."

"Please. Please, undo it."

He smirks. "Maybe I like you like this. At our mercy. Unable to defend yourself from anything we want to do to you."

I narrow my eyes at him, spitting my insult with all my might. "You're a monster."

"If I'm a monster, you made me that way, Mi Cielo."

My lips part when he uses the nickname he had for me in high school.

He's not allowed to do that. He's not allowed because only my boyfriend called me that.

21

JADE

american jesus - Nessa Barrett

It takes almost a week and many painkillers before I can start walking without feeling like someone is crushing my lungs. Elliot kept me in his bed under the pretense of taking care of me. He only let me out to use the bathroom.

Clearly, none of my ribs were fractured because I feel much better. But Elliot still wouldn't let me out.

He fed me here, hugged me, covered my side in bruise cream, but at no point did he fuck me or ask anything of me. The collar is still on, the chain still attached to the wall, and I think I'll go insane if I don't get to leave this house very soon.

Ethan hasn't visited me again, and I need to know what the hell he meant the last time he was here.

"I really need to start working on the van if I don't want Kay to chop my head off."

Elliot stops mid-movement, then slowly finishes sliding his jeans on. His hard-on is still visible when he turns to me. He's spent the last week pretty much like this when he's in my vicinity. I don't understand how he does it. The simple knowledge of knowing he's hard makes me desperate for him.

His body was built for mine. The way he encircles my waist with one arm, or how he can practically wrap his huge hand around my thigh. How I fit perfectly within him and him within me.

So how the hell is he capable of not touching me when I've been half-naked in his bed for a week? My skin is burning with the need to feel him against me.

"Will you undo this thing?" He knows what I mean; I don't need to point at it or call it by its name.

Apparently, he loves to. "Your collar? No."

"Elliot, you're such an asshole." I huff. "We have a job to do. One you were very much aware of when you came to get me in New York. You can't keep me *chained* to a wall."

"I know." He smiles. "I'll undo the chain, but I won't take the collar off."

He never saw the mark Ethan left on me. It was perfectly hidden by the leather around my neck. It's gone now, and I miss it.

I still haven't said anything to Elliot. I don't know if I'm protecting Ethan or me.

The blond brother walks back to the bed and pulls the covers down. I'm not wearing anything, and my hands come to cover my stomach right away.

"Really?" he chuckles. "That's what you're hiding when you're fully naked?"

I bite my inner cheek, my gaze dropping. My fingers dig into my stomach painfully, hating the softness I feel there.

"Not moving much for five days has already made me put on weight."

His eyebrows shoot to his hairline. "Excuse me?"

"Stop," I scoff, looking away. "You're not blind, you can see it."

"Jade, there's nothing to see. You're perfect."

"Shut up."

He grabs my hands, pulling them away harshly. "Okay, first of all, you don't hide *anything* from me. Remember who owns this body now."

His hold softens, and he threads his fingers through mine. "Secondly, you are the most beautiful woman who's ever graced this planet. You didn't gain anything in these last few days, but putting on or losing weight wouldn't change whether you're beautiful or not."

"Right. Because you don't only date Kings' girls who look like runway models."

"God knows any runway model would beg for my dick." He smiles at me, white teeth, beautiful lips. A cocky grin like only he does. "But those girls got nothing on you, baby."

Dropping one of my hands, his knuckles graze the leather at my throat, down to my collarbone, my boobs, all the way to my lower stomach. I breathe in, sucking my stomach as a reflex.

"Stop that. I like the real you, Jade."

He splays his fingers on my skin, and despite the warmth of his hand, I shiver under his touch.

"If the saying goes cold hands, warm heart. Does it work the other way around too?" I ask softly.

When he crooks an eyebrow at me, I add, "Your hands are always warm." I don't say the rest, he can guess easily.

He snorts and his hand trails north again, gently cupping my jaw so he can tilt my head up. I look right into his eyes. "My heart isn't cold, my love."

I can't stand the proximity right now. The moment we're sharing. So I put a stop to it.

"Yeah, I guess one must have a heart for it to be of any temperature."

Ignoring my jab, he rolls his eyes playfully. "The leash is coming off. No need to be so dramatic."

My eyes flicker to the scars on his chest. Thick white lines. I count them slowly in my head like I have many times before.

One, two, three, four, five and all the way to twelve.

There's a thirteenth one where his abs begin. His father missed.

It's no wonder his heart doesn't function like us normal, able-feeling humans. Those scars must go deep. The ones on the left side must have cut through the skin, the muscles, shattered the bones, and pierced his heart. Now it's like an expensive clock missing one tiny but essential screw. It can never tick again.

Ethan's mom and Elliot's dad left when we were in high school. It was a casual morning when they both pretended to go to work and never came back. They abandoned their children. They left the dead weight that was Ethan and Elliot behind and found a better life. At least that's what everyone says, including the brothers. I wasn't at school that day, but the moment I came back, I knew how affected Ethan was. They had barely left, but he already knew they were never coming back. Elliot never liked his dad. He was a violent and volatile man. A good friend of Caden King's dad, both feared for their brutality.

Elliot became free when his father left. Ethan died a little more inside to lose his mother.

"Do you miss him?"

My eyes widen when I realize what slipped out of my mouth.

Never talk to Elliot about his father.

His brow furrows as he looks down at me, his hand on my jaw tightening.

"Th-that just came out," I stutter. "I don't know how." I try to shift slightly away from him, but his grip doesn't relent.

The violence in his blue gaze makes me tremble. He puts a knee on the bed, leaning closer to me, and...smiles. He's back under control. Just like that.

"Do you know what happens to bad girls who can't keep their mouths shut, my love?"

I gulp, shaking my head. Not death, I hope.

"They get gagged. How unfortunate would that be for you just before breakfast?"

"I'm sorry," I whisper, my gaze still fixed on his scars.

"Maybe if you were less focused on my scars and a little more on how to please me, you wouldn't spurt out ridiculous questions."

When I don't answer, he drags my face to his. "Isn't that right, Jade?"

My hands are forced to land on said scars, so I don't crash into him. "Yes."

"I'm going to undo the leash," he says against my mouth, his low voice vibrating against my lips. "What's the lesson you learned?"

My heart accelerates. Like when a teacher used to surprise me with a question at school. I wasn't good, never listened. Then they'd just drop some stupid question, and everyone would turn to me, expecting something.

I thought ugly people were smart.

Squeezing my eyes shut, I push away the remark I remember so well.

I know the answer to his question. It's just too humiliating to voice it.

"Jade." His free hand grabs the chain connected to the collar, and he pulls harshly. I'm forced a little closer to him, our lips practically touching.

"Fuck," I gasp.

"What's the lesson you learned?" he repeats.

"Not to leave the house," I squeak. "Shit, I can't breathe."

"You can breathe just fine, or you wouldn't be able to talk. Say it again."

"I shouldn't leave the house without you."

"That's right." His condescending smile accompanies his tone perfectly. "Someone wants you dead. I want you alive. Easy."

I nod frantically, and his hand caresses my hairline, down my curls, and all the way to the deep brown tips.

Wrapping the ends around his fist, he pulls my head back, and his lips crash onto mine. He only kisses me for a split second, barely enough time for me to register the stroke of his tongue against my lips. Then he focuses on my lower lip. He bites it, sucking it like he loves doing. My body buzzes as I feel it swelling. He keeps going long enough to hurt.

I whimper against him, and he only pulls away when I slap his shoulder. I'm panting, my eyes jumping from his to his lips.

"Let's get you fed and working on that van, my love."

He stands up to grab a key from his desk, one I can't reach if I'm bolted to the wall. As promised, he undoes the chain, but not the collar.

"T-shirt, no panties." He points at the Diggy Graves shirt laid out on the end of the bed.

"How's the pain?" he asks as he opens a kitchen cabinet. He grabs a box of pills and turns around, leaning against the beige counter.

"I don't need pain meds," I answer, sitting at the table. "The bruises are ugly, but I feel fine."

He licks his lips, smiling. "You do?"

I nod, avoiding his gaze. Does his have to be so fucking tempting? Fucker.

Turning to the stove, he prepares an omelet in no time. The brothers have lived on their own for so long, they learned to do everything around the house efficiently a while ago.

I don't say anything. I bring my feet flat on the chair, my knees to my chest, and wrap my arms around my shins, resting the side of my face on the top of my knees as I watch him work. He's still shirtless. His shoulders are wide, his back strong. Every little muscle moves when he works the pan. Unlike Ethan, who has multiple tattoos covering his chest and abs, Elliot opted for a huge one on his back. A dark angel cloaked and without a face covers him from shoulders to lower back. Its wings spread across his shoulders and all the way to his elbows.

I remember when he got it, it took four days at the tattoo shop all the Kings go to.

He's got other ones peppered on his arms, mainly the Kings' crown on his right forearm, but the angel is the one you really can't miss.

Running a hand through his hair, he pushes back wild, blond strands. They look like he spent too long at the beach, surfing salty waves and lying in the sand. That kind of mix of bright and sandy blond. My fingertips prickle. I want to feel them too. I want to pull at them.

Apart from that tattoo, everything about Elliot makes him so approachable. So warm. His hair, his words, his smiles. The mask he puts on.

Warm everything, cold heart. Surely, that's valid.

He cuts the omelet in half and splits it between two plates.

"Jade, my love." His enchanting voice resonates without him even turning back to me. He's grabbing cutlery now.

"Mhm?" I hum with closed lips, my eyes slowly blinking.

I feel like I've been watching a film. Elliot feels surreal. How can such a gigantic man cook so gracefully? He's forced to keep his head down to not hit the overhead extractor fan, and yet he's been moving around the kitchen like a chef. Or maybe that's just me being enchanted by anything Elliot Pearson does.

"Bend over the table and lift your t-shirt to your hips."

My head snaps up, my lips parting. He's still not watching me, grabbing some napkins.

"What?"

"You heard me. We have a deal, and I've let you rest for almost a week. Now don't make me wait."

Without controlling my body, I'm up, pushing the chair away.

Why? How embarrassing is it going to be when he walks to me and realizes I've been wet from watching the guy *cook*?

How humiliating that it's just doubled from the order he gave me?

I bend over the table, my cheek burning against the wood imitation plastic wrap covering it.

It's with a tilted vision that I watch him turn around. Two plates in his hands. He puts one next to my face, and one out of view. I think it's by my hip. I hear a chair being drawn and feel him sit down.

Dying to know what he's doing, I lift my head, looking back to see him sitting right where I'm bending over, his plate next to me, and his gaze on what I'm guessing is a great view of my wet pussy.

"Elliot—" My own shriek cuts me off. He slapped my ass with something.

"Lay back down, cheek on the table."

I do so, not before seeing the exact utensil he slapped my ass cheek with. A fucking plastic spatula.

"Asshole," I mumble.

It earns me another slap to the ass. I shift, hissing.

"Grab the edges of the table and stay still. I'd like to enjoy my breakfast without you making my plate shake if you don't mind."

I do as he says, the smell of the omelet right next to my face making my stomach grumble.

"If you're a good girl who keeps still and quiet while I eat, you'll get to eat too. And if you're extra good, I'll even sink my dick inside this dripping pussy."

I feel the plastic of the spatula against the back of my thigh before a light tap lands on my pussy. I have to bite my lower lip to keep from releasing a humiliating noise of pleasure.

"So wet," he chuckles. "This is why we're perfect together, my love. Who else but you is so responsive to being treated this way?"

I squeeze my eyes shut, begging the embarrassment to

leave my body. I fail. I'm only left with one thing to save my pride. Stubbornness.

"Watch what you say, Elliot," I say as loud as I can for someone face down on a kitchen table, who has just been spanked with a spatula. "You and I aren't together. You offer protection, and I give you my body in return. That's not being boyfriend and girlfriend in my book."

The first thing I hear is the chair falling to the floor. Next is the swoosh of someone sweeping everything off the table, and the crashing of his plate on the floor.

The slap of the spatula is hard this time, intent on hurting and leaving a mark. I grunt, tightening my jaw not to scream.

"Watch what *I* say?" he hisses behind me. Another strike makes me realize this isn't a game. He's upset.

Shit. Shit, it hurts.

"How about the little slut selling her body for protection watches what *she* says."

The next strike burns through my skin, and the one after that makes me scream. I can feel sweat rolling down my back.

The next three make me feel like my cheeks have swollen. Tears are brimming in my eyes, and I choke on them when I scream again.

"S-stop," I gasp. "Oh my god, please, Elliot."

"Does it hurt?" he growls behind me.

Another strike makes me cry, "Yes!" My cheeks puff as I breathe out a stuttered "F—fuck." I take in a painful breath. "It hurts."

"Probably another well-learned lesson, then. Isn't it?" When he strikes again, I'm on my toes, attempting to avoid the pain.

"Feet flat. Spread your legs wider." He hits again and my

knuckles are near popping from how hard I'm holding the edges of the table. "Whose collar are you wearing, Jade?"

"Yours." I don't hesitate for one second. I just want the pain to stop.

"Louder." I expect another hit, but it doesn't come. I'm speechless from the surprise. "I said *louder*." *Strike.*

"Yours! It's your collar."

"That's right. Now tell me, if that's my collar around your neck, my protection you're getting, and my fucking kitchen table you're bent over, then what are you?"

I bite my lip, waiting for a strike. It doesn't come.

His voice is calmer, needier when he talks again. "Say it, Jade. What are you?"

"Yours," I rasp. I squeeze my eyes shut when I can't hold the tears anymore.

"Good girl." Instead of a hit, it's a tap against my pussy this time.

It forces me to acknowledge how wet I am, and that surely doesn't help with the tears. Another tap, and I cry out weakly.

"Say it again, my love."

The taps accelerate, getting closer to my clit every time. "Yours," I moan. "I'm yours."

"Mm, that sounds so beautiful on your lips."

I can feel his satisfaction weighing heavy in the air. His need for me wraps the both of us in a bubble of lust and pain.

He keeps tapping rhythmically against my clit, and I shift, the pleasure starting to take over from the burn on my ass cheeks.

I writhe and moan, struggling to stay still.

"Shh, don't move, baby."

I hear him shift, then the zipper of his jeans. It's loud in a room when all that is heard is my short pants and the sound of the plastic against my wetness.

When the tapping stops, I feel his tip at my entrance. He doesn't understand how big he is. How much he stretches me even when he's barely entering me.

"Fuck," I gasp when he pushes in. "Slow down, Elliot." I grunt when he doesn't listen and keeps pushing in. "You're big, b—be careful." The tears have stopped, but my teeth are clattering from being pushed to my limits.

I'm scared.

Elliot Pearson scares me.

Because he has eyes that resemble an angel and reflect the needs of the devil.

Because his hair is the same color as the sun, but what's inside his head is darker than the night.

Because he has warm hands that grab my naked hips as he holds me in place and pushes inside me violently.

Because he grabs the back of my neck when I try to lift from the table, crying out as his length makes me choke on a breath. And he holds me down.

"Too much," I squeak desperately. The pleasure doesn't matter right now. I feel it all, I moan from it, and I squirm under him at how hot this is. But what matters is that he doesn't. Fucking. Fit. And that he refuses to acknowledge it.

I can't take a breath. I can't move one inch, too scared he's going to break me.

"Fuck," he rasps. The hand at my hip slides to my lower back, rubbing gentle circles.

And when he finally realizes the truth, it doesn't scare him like it scares me. It exhilarates him.

"Jade, my love, you're taking me so well."

He pulls back, and slams back in, my hips hitting the table as I cry out.

It shouldn't feel so good. His praise. The thrust of his hips.

"I'm so proud of you," he keeps going.

Stop. Stop making me feel so good with your words. With your *everything*.

"I wish you could see how beautiful you look stretched around me. Fuck." He moans when he bottoms out and makes me whimper.

"Too much...please, stop."

"You're doing well, my love. So well."

He pulls back slightly, allowing me to breathe again. Still, he's deep. He doesn't come back out, instead he thrusts slowly inside me, short movements that make my mouth fall open.

I writhe with need, pushing back against him and forgetting my body is incapable of taking all of him.

"Very good girl. Fuck yourself against me." I accelerate as he stays still, forgetting about the humiliation and focusing on the pleasure. "Beautiful." He gasps, and I go on my toes. "Beautiful slut."

And then he loses it. Uncaring of everything around him, he grabs both my hips and pushes all the way.

"Fuck!" I scream. "Elliot..."

I don't understand what hurts and what makes me feel like I'm in heaven anymore. I just take it. I let him use me and drag out my pleasure from his violence.

When his fingers force their way between the table and my hips, when they press against my clit, I can't hold it.

"Scream it, my love. Say who owns you. I want the whole of the North Shore to know Jade Alva takes my dick like the good slut she is."

"Elliot," I moan. "Elliot...Elliot...*Elliot!*" I know my scream resonates inside the entire house.

He explodes inside me the same way I do around him.

Elliot Pearson scares me. For all the things he does, and all the things he is.

He scares me because his hands are warm, yet his heart is cold, but mainly because he makes my own heart beat to an unhealthy rhythm. The kind I never want to feel around someone like him.

When he pulls out, he lays on top of me. I can't breathe, my ribs killing me, but the post-orgasm high makes me unable to voice anything.

It's his phone ringing that interrupts our silence.

He groans a complaint and casually answers, "Boss."

It's Kay. There's nothing that can take me out of my blissful state like the reminder that Kayla King is just one call away.

When I try to push myself off the table, Elliot flattens me back with a hand between my shoulders. I stay there, boneless under his palm while he talks to her with his bright voice.

The tone is jovial, but because he's not facing her, he doesn't bother with a fake smile and a beaming face. That's the real Elliot right in front of me, speaking fake cheery words. His voice is the act he puts on, his blank expression and empty eyes, the man he really is.

A shiver runs down my spine. I'm playing a dangerous game with a dangerous man. It's unfortunate he's the only one planning on keeping me alive. Unfortunate that I need him to survive in this town.

He hangs up and smiles down at me. Is that real? That smile?

Brushing strands off my sweaty forehead, he leaves a kiss there. Is *that* real?

He traces my damp cheek with his thumb, following the

same trail my tears did. Grazing the scar at the corner of my eye, he presses another kiss there. He drags his nose against my neck, inhaling my scent, whispering how proud of me he is.

And with a flat voice that sounds more like him than anything else he's ever intoned, he murmurs, "I missed you, my love. All my life, I missed you."

Is that...real?

When he straightens up again, I feel like I'm coming back from a trip on ecstasy. What just happened?

My ass cheeks burn, my pussy aches beautifully. My brain is too foggy to process anything.

And Elliot is back to being himself. Or his fake self. Whatever he is in his everyday life.

"I have to meet Kay. Clean up this mess, eat breakfast, and work on the van." He pins me with a stare. "That's it, Jade. Nothing else until I'm back."

I nod, and he lets go of me. He helps me up and kisses my cheek before leaving the kitchen.

I hear the front door close and stay still, staring at the stove for I don't know how long. What the hell just happened? Why does it feel so good and wrong at the same time?

I'm still in my head when I kneel on the floor with a dustpan and brush. I don't hear him walk into the kitchen, only see two black boots enter my line of vision and crush the shards of plates left on the floor.

"Tell me, Mi Cielo, what did he do to you?"

22

JADE

Honest - Bazzi

Ethan used to call me *Mi Cielo* because that's what the main character called his love interest in the series he watched with his mom and dad when he was little. It was some Mexican telenovela he doesn't even remember the name of. All he remembers is that Luis loved Gabriela with a fervor he thought was impossible and could only ever hope for in life. Gabriela was Luis's *cielo*. It meant everything to a boy whose parents didn't love each other anymore. They divorced before he turned five and that was the end of his nights watching Luis and Gabriela. His dad moved back to Mexico, and he never saw him again. His mom stayed on the North Shore and married Joel Pearson, Elliot's dad.

I didn't know Ethan when he was five. I met Elliot and him in elementary school, but when we started dating and he began calling me *Mi Cielo*, I asked what it was. He explained it meant that I was his heaven, his everything, and he also told me where he'd heard it from. It became my favorite term of endearment. Whenever I heard it, butterflies would erupt in my stomach, and my chest would swell with pride to know I was Ethan Torres's *everything*.

That's not how I feel now when I hear him purr the nickname. I sit back on my haunches as I look up at him. He's tall. Not as tall as Elliot, but tall enough to make me feel powerless at his feet.

"I'm not in the mood for your little game right now, Ethan," I mumble, going back to my task.

He stays still, silent, and after only a short moment of him not moving, I look up again. His arms are crossed over his naked chest, and my mouth falls open.

Do neither of the two men living in this house ever wear shirts? It's...unnerving.

Fuck. Ethan's tattoos on his strong chest and rigid abs look absolutely delicious. Is it wrong that I want to lick each and every single one of them?

They're not the only ones, of course. He's got an entire sleeve on his right arm. But the ones on his stomach are peppered on there, each a fucking treat that tempts me a little more.

The owl that looks back and stares at you, no matter where you stand. The music notes that are scattered across his entire stomach. One could almost hear them when they dance on his skin with every breath he takes. The four evergreens at his hip. The ouroboros he got with Caden in high school.

The thorny rose he got after I told him it was my favorite flower.

And his Kings' crown, of course. The one we all have.

I hate it. The day Ethan joined the Kings is the day he assassinated the both of us. He threw it all away to become powerful and feared. I hate Elliot for roping him in. I hate Caden for convincing him it would change his life.

It did.

It changed mine when I followed blindly. If Ethan was there, I wanted to join too.

Fucking stupid girl joining a crew who never took my side.

I go to stand up, but he stops me right away with a hand at the top of my head. He pushes me back down, forcing me to sit on my heels.

"This position is too perfect for you to move." His voice is low, eyes darkening.

"This is not going to be a thing." I try to twist from his hold, which only makes him grip my hair. "Ethan," I grit out. "I won't let you *use me* every time Elliot has, just because you suddenly decided it would be fun to play with me too."

"If you can do it with him, why can't you do it with me?" His mouth curves smugly.

"Because he never broke my fucking heart," I snap. Fuck, I hate that I still let him get that kind of reaction out of me. "He didn't pretend to be in love, didn't promise me forever and then throw me away. You're not getting anything from me. Not ever again."

His smile drops, his gaze narrowing.

"You'd rather belong to him, huh?"

"I'd rather you both leave me the fuck alone, but here we are."

His hand leaves my head so he can hook two fingers under my collar. Pulling me up, I'm forced to kneel and extend toward him.

"Has he walked you on a leash yet?"

My heart drops to my stomach. Something twists inside me, a band tightening around my gut. My eyes widen when I realize I'm getting wet again.

No. Don't let him fuck with your mind.

I shake my head slowly, unsure of what else to do.

"This little collar makes me want to put a tail in your ass and walk you around the house on all fours."

I gulp, forcing myself to believe it's because he's holding something tightly around my neck. Not because it's turning me on like never before.

"How exciting would it be to know I keep his girl as my pet while he's away working for Kay? You'd never tell him because you'd be too humiliated." His eyes flutter closed, and the corner of his lips tips up. "Fuck, Jade." My gaze drops to the hard-on growing in his jeans. It matches my wetness perfectly.

That shouldn't be allowed. My body should know better.

When he drops into a squat, it forces me to go from being up on my knees to my ass resting on the soles of my feet. His dark eyes dig into mine and I want to cry at how much I miss him. The old him. There's a hole in my heart where Ethan's love used to be, and all the sex in the world with all the different men who exist will never fill it.

He releases the collar to cup my jaw softly. I'm on my knees, and he's squatting. Our difference in height is still showing. I blink up at him.

"Ethan..." There are so many words at the tip of my tongue, that I don't know which one to say.

Ethan, I would do anything for you. Don't make me do something insane.

Don't do this to me just because you can.

I still love you. Tell me you love me too.

"Shh." His lips trace my jaw, and he kisses the bit of skin just before my ear. "We'll take it slow, Mi Cielo." Another kiss, soft as a cloud. His other hand leaves my jaw to grab the leather around my neck again. He moves it down and kisses his way to the same spot he bit last week.

And he bites again. He sucks and nibbles until blood rushes there. My head falls to the side, giving him better access. I cry out when his teeth practically draw blood. He puts the collar back in place and whispers, "Get on all fours."

When I hesitate, he pulls at the leather around my neck. "Do it for me. Just this and I'll leave you alone."

Maybe I don't want you to leave me alone.

He lets go, stands up, and takes a step back to give me enough space.

I don't look at him when I flatten my hands on the floor. I look down at the broken plate Elliot left for me to clean.

I ignore that some shards bite into my skin, and my dry throat works over a lump as I swallow.

I hear his harsh exhale, trembling and desperate. I watch his boot disappear from my field of vision, and when he talks again, I can tell he's somewhere else in the kitchen.

"Crawl to me, Mi Cielo."

I shake my head, not even bothering to look up. I can't look him in the eyes. I'll crack. I'll give in and do it.

"You said you'd leave me alone if—"

"Look at me."

I can't resist. I look up, first catching his hand holding his hard cock through his jeans, then his beautiful body, and finally his eyes. Two black orbs calling my name.

"Do you see what you do to me? Do it, Jade. For me."

I hate myself when I take a step. I crawl forward, maybe four or five steps; I don't know, I'm too lost in his gaze.

The humiliation is so intense I want to scream. I want to hurt him and cry and claw at his face.

But then how would I explain the intensity of what I feel

inside? The wetness between my legs. The rumble of a moan in my chest.

I stop when my hands align with the tip of his boots.

"Enough," I beg, looking right at his shoes. "Enough, please."

Walking behind me, he lowers himself and pushes up my t-shirt. I don't say anything when he traces my wet seam. I don't push him away. All I do is tremble under his touch.

The silence is unbearable when he pushes a finger to my entrance slowly, sliding through my wetness. The only sound is my hitched breath when he presses inside me. And when he pulls out, only to tease me with two fingers, I let my head drop.

I slowly accept the fact that I won't push him away and allow my moan to resonate in the room when he fucks me with two fingers. I let the pleasure overtake me, as if I haven't just come twice from his brother fucking me.

"You're still full of his cum," Ethan murmurs behind me, his voice portraying a jealousy I'd never heard from him. "It's dripping out of you."

I'm speechless, too turned on by the exact fact he pointed out. He fucks me relentlessly, and I push back, rocking on my hands and knees. I don't care what I look like, I don't care what he thinks of me. All I care about is having my ex-boyfriend bring me the pleasure I need.

I tense up, panting and so close to exploding.

"Jade." His voice is overflowing with lust. The entire room is under a tension I can't take. "I think I could teach you to come on command. Would you like that?"

I nod, not even caring about what he says as long as he keeps thrusting inside me.

"Then come, you filthy slut."

"Fuck!" I whimper as I reach the peak I've been chasing.

My muscles tense and my stomach contracts under the pleasure, and he keeps going, draining me until I can barely breathe anymore. My arms give up, and I fall onto the floor.

He doesn't give me much respite, helping me up, even though I can barely stand on my own two legs.

Pushing my hair away from my face, he cups the back of my head so I look up at him. "This stays between us. Say it."

But I shake my head. "Why are you doing this to me? I don't want this. I don't want stolen moments with you." A wave of unwanted feelings crashes into me. "You need to let me move on from you."

I know he doesn't miss the despair in my voice. He doesn't say anything, though. Instead, he grabs my wrist and drags me with him to the bathroom.

He's silent as he sits me on the edge of the bath. My back prickles when I stare at the sink, heart accelerating, but I don't say anything.

No one believed me.

He turns around to open the cabinet above the sink, grabs something I can't see, and closes it again. Our gazes lock in the mirror that covers the cabinet door. Still, he doesn't say anything.

"Are you going back to ignoring me for a week now?" Anger is simmering just below my skin, hot and sticky. "Will you only acknowledge me if Elliot fucks me?"

Nothing.

He turns around, holding a cotton ball, which he just sprayed with something. It must be disinfectant because he grabs my hand and twists it palm up. I wince at the sting when he cleans me with the cotton, wiping blood and dust away. He sticks on a band-aid and moves on to the next hand.

On the other hand, he has to pull out a shard before he

can wipe. I hiss, and he throws the tiny bit of porcelain in the sink. Another band-aid. It's done, but he doesn't let go of my hand.

He just frowns as he stares at my palm.

"Surprised that you care if I'm hurt?" I tell him. "Me too."

When his eyes flick to mine, I know I'm right.

"You have to stop this, Ethan."

He shakes his head, a sarcastic puff of air leaving his mouth. I stand up and force him to let go of my hand. Cupping his cheek, I inhale his scent. I could swim in it all day, drown, and take my last breath by his side. Beautiful death.

"You let me go. Your bursts of jealousy because I let Elliot do whatever he wants to me, the hate you throw my way...those aren't proof of love or even interest. It's pure male ego. Don't involve me in that."

His lips part, and I know he understands what I'm saying. Ethan is a highly sensitive person. He's aware of everything. It's all heightened in his beautiful mind. He feels what the normal human feels tenfold. There's a reason he's such an impressive artist. He experiences emotions in extreme ways.

But when I think he's going to say something, agree with me, he grabs my hips painfully, moves us around, and pushes me against the sink. I cry out when my back hits the cold, hard surface, the pain reverberating in my ribs.

His lips crash on mine before I register anything else. He holds me in place, but there's no need. I let him ravage my mouth, my soul. His kiss is unlike Elliot's. It's deeper, monstrously full of feelings. Like him.

I gulp air when he lets me go. That felt...that felt like the kind of kiss he would give me when we were together. I'm dizzy, panting. This isn't right.

"Do you know why I hate you, Jade?"

Being hit by a car was less painful. How can he say he hates me after that kiss?

I barely feel the shake of my head, so I wonder if it's even visible to him.

"Because you think me breaking up with you was a *choice*. It makes me hate you to realize that the girl I loved more than anything doesn't know me. Not at all. Not even a tiny bit."

I fall to the floor when he lets go of my hips. My knees give up from the shock of his revelation. He slams the bathroom door, but I don't even react.

Did he just say he didn't have a choice in our breakup?

That someone *made* him do it?

Am I reading too much into this?

I look at the palms of my hands. At the two band-aids that he plastered on there. They're the kind with yellow smiley faces on them, but there are X's instead of eyes, like the face is dead, and they have a little tongue popping out. The ones I used to buy. They made me laugh because it didn't give much hope for the person who needed them. Ethan thought it was hilarious too, so he kept buying these ones every time I needed fixing. Pretty often, since we live on the North Shore.

Oh...fuck. I don't think I'm reading into this.

My ex-boyfriend was forced to break up with me.

23

JADE

Ghost - Halsey

"Stupid fucking...you're dead. So fucking dead," I grunt, before licking my bleeding finger.

That stupid van is a mess. It's fixable, but it'll snow in hell before I can tune it to the minimum standards of a *racing* vehicle.

Kay is deluded. This entire plan is going to get us arrested at best, killed if we're lucky, victims of police violence at worst. I can't believe I'm back to working for the bitch again.

The hate I felt for her in senior year is coming back tenfold. We were such good friends before *it* all happened.

What kind of leader are you if you're incapable of protecting your crew? If you throw them to the wolves. If you don't defend them when they tell you what's been done to you. Out of all people, I thought Kay would be the one to understand me. Everyone in the Kings knows her dad was abusive. That her mom left because her and Caden are the results of just how much he forced himself on her.

And yet when she heard of what had happened to me...*nothing*.

No one believed me.

"I do wonder at what point in your life you became such a violent, angry little thing."

Elliot's voice startles me. I whip around, narrowing my gaze on him. My hair is in a high ponytail today, but the length is thickly falling onto my neck and between my shoulder blades. Despite the outside freezing temperatures, I'm hot from working on the van, and I can feel sweat dampening my back and my chest.

"I'm not violent and angry. This van is just driving me insane."

Ignoring my lie, he keeps sharing his thoughts as he leans against the doorframe that leads from the garage to the kitchen, crossing his arms.

"I think it was in high school, because you were as sweet as they come through middle school."

"Whatever." I turn back to the open van. I wipe my hands from the black oil and take the notepad I've been using to write down everything that needs to be changed. So pretty much everything.

"Thinking about it," he carries on. I'm not sure if he's talking to me or just sharing his thought process out loud. "You were fine in your first years of high school. Was it when Ethan broke up with you?"

Doing my best to ignore him, I keep my eyes on the notepad. "I need you to take me to a garage."

"But then again, you were still sweet when you joined the Kings. I remember because Kay would make fun of you for it. *That one is going to run back to her mom the first beating she gets.*" He chuckles to himself. "You didn't, though."

I drop the notepad and grab the edge of the van.

"Elliot, shut up," I grit out. "I'm serious."

"Was it when you started sleeping around?"

I don't even remember why I wanted to be like the other Kings girls. What kind of validation did I even get from sleeping with random guys? I wanted to do what the pretty girls did.

My eyes close, my teeth grinding. "I need you to hear me when I tell you to *shut. Up.*"

I grab the adjustable wrench with my left hand. Pretending to work on something, I tighten it around a bolt.

I hear him shift behind me, but soon the buzzing in my ears takes over. "You were fine at my nineteenth birthday. You came even though Ethan was there, and you were still desperately in love. You came for me."

My chest freezes. An immovable block of ice. I can't fucking breathe.

"That was in March," he calculates. "By April, you'd become an insufferable little brat who screamed and attacked anyone she disagreed with. Fuck, Kay came back on her words. Even she wished you'd stayed *nice*. I'm not sure which version I prefer."

"Shut up!" In the blink of an eye, I turn around, attempting to throw the wrench at him.

I don't get to complete my movement. He's right behind me. I didn't hear him move over the anger beating like a drum in my ears. He grasps my wrist before I can hurt him, the tool falling to the floor.

"See what I mean?" He smiles smugly, so satisfied that he made me angry.

"I told you to shut up!" I scream, not controlling the fury. It's exactly that; *uncontrollable*. If I could do anything about it, I wouldn't let rage guide my life.

But I wasn't given a choice in who I would become. Someone took that from me. They *made me* that way.

His head tilts to the side, like a curious golden retriever. "What's that on your palm? Did you hurt yourself?" He's staring at the dead smiley face band-aids Ethan put on me yesterday.

"Mind your own fucking business," I hiss in his face.

"Your anger will be the end of you, Jade," he purrs calmly. He easily turns me around, grabbing both my wrists in one hand and keeping my back to his chest. "Was it at my birthday? What happened?"

"Fuck you! Fuck you, Elliot. Fuck you!" I shriek as I thrash around violently.

The past hits me in the face. A slap that makes me gasp. I swallow a sob and scream instead. "I'll kill you. I swear to God, I'll kill you if you don't let me go."

"Come on, my furious love, let it all out."

I explode into a crazy laugh. That's impossible. I tried everything. I killed and I hurt. I beat people up. I took it out on the world. There is always more. If anything, rage feeds rage. Anger feeds animosity. It's a vicious cycle I will never escape.

So I scream to be heard. I scream to be saved.

I scream and no one ever listens.

With his free hand, Elliot closes the hood of the van. He bends me over, my cheek hitting the metal. "Talk to me, Jade."

"No!"

"Talk. To. Me," he groans, pressing his hips against my ass.

"I tried," I yell, my voice raw. I push back against him. "I tried and none of you wanted to *fucking. Listen.*"

My body is exhausted. There's no point fighting against someone twice my size.

"I will never talk to you," I murmur, struggling to gulp down my tears. "I will never talk about it again."

That gets him off me. He takes a couple of steps back as I straighten up and turn around.

When Elliot came back from Kay's yesterday, he didn't want to pretend to be nice. He was annoyed, broody. He told me to go to bed and made me touch myself until I was exhausted. I orgasmed from my own fingers until I passed out from overstimulation. This morning, I came right to the garage, and this is our first interaction.

This is what we are, him and I. One fucking interaction and it all explodes. In case I was stupid enough to convince myself that he cared, here's the proof that nothing could ever work between us.

He runs a hand through his hair, impatience showing. He can't stand when things don't work his way and they always do. His manipulative behavior should make him a patient man, but it works so well that he never had to wait for anything.

He nods, seemingly accepting defeat. He won't get information out of me, and he knows it.

So I move on for the both of us.

"I need you to take me to Racer and Logan's repair shop."

He snorts, looking away before realizing I'm serious. "NSC Racer? Not in your wildest fucking dreams, my love. If you want to go to a repair shop, you can go to Ashley's."

"Ashley is a bitch. There's a reason I never worked with her. Racer is nice, a gentleman, and he knows what he's talking about. I have questions for him."

There's a flash of annoyance before he puts his mask back in place. "Jade." His smile is poised. "I don't know what makes you more reckless. Admitting you've been working with a man from NSC for a long time. Or admitting you've been working with a man you think is a nice gentleman in front of *me*."

"Please," I scoff. "Everyone already thinks I'm a traitor. What's a little more? Racer might be NSC, but he's been nicer to me than any Kings' member I've ever known."

His jaw works from side to side, the mask slipping. "Are you dying for me to teach you a lesson?"

I tilt my head to the side. "You know what I noticed? I've been holding my end of the deal. You're having lots of fun with me, but I don't see you finding who wants to kill me. I told you it was Ethan, and you don't want to believe me."

"Are you dead?"

I narrow my eyes at him. "Obviously not."

"Then Ethan doesn't want to kill you."

"If you're so sure of yourself, who is it?"

"I believe it's me right now."

That makes me take a step back, only remembering I can't when I feel the van hit my ass.

His smile is back, loving that I'm afraid of him.

"I bought you some clothes yesterday. Go put them on, and I'll take you to Racer's garage. Then, as a thank you, you'll get on your knees and suck my dick in the parking lot. That pretty mouth needs to be kept busy before you get yourself in trouble."

My thighs squeeze together. I'm pretty sure I didn't mean for that to happen. Neither for my clit to tingle the way it does right now.

"In the...parking lot?"

"Yeah, at the back, where no one can see. Don't worry."

"Racer and Logan will be able to see."

But of course, he knew that.

"Oh yeah. Let's hope they'll look away, then."

"I really fucking hate you, you know that?" I twist in the passenger seat of Ethan's truck. Elliot is the one driving since he doesn't have one of his own.

I should have known him buying me clothes meant nothing good. I pull at the fishnets with wide holes, trying to get comfortable. I love the black combat boots, but I'm not sure how I feel about the pleated mini skirt. I'm wearing one of his hoodies. He loves dressing me in his clothes too much to let me wear anything else. Today is a Måneskin merch hoodie.

It does feel good to have taken the time to do my usual makeup. Cat eyes, red lipstick, black pencil on my lower eyelid. I hate to admit I feel more like myself.

"You used to dress like that all the time." He makes it sound like he's doing me a favor to dress me as his doll.

"Yeah, when I was eighteen," I grumble, shifting again as I press the skirt between my thighs. I feel so naked with fishnets.

Slapping my hand away, he lifts the skirt to my hips.

"Elliot! Are you done, you fucking perv?"

He wraps his huge hand around my upper thigh and smiles. "Now I'm done."

I narrow my eyes at him, pretending I hate his gesture when I love the reassurance of his skin against mine.

I'm so fucked it's ridiculous at this point.

"You're so annoying," I huff, turning to the window. He brushes my outer thigh with his thumb, and I have to bite my lower lip not to smile.

"You're trembling," he notices.

"From all that hate I have toward you."

"Sure, my love." He pauses, turning right at an intersection.

"That's not the way to the garage."

"I know."

I look back at him. "Where are we going?"

"I'm trying to do something nice, and if you can't trust me on that, I might change my mind."

I cross my arms over my chest, huffing as I look out of the window again.

"Fucking brat," he says under his breath.

I don't realize where we're going until we're parking.

"The cemetery? Cute date idea." I don't think he likes my condescending tone, judging by his scowl.

"Five minutes. No more. No less. You have work to do. Clear?"

I feel my brow furrow. "What are you talking about?"

I follow him out of the truck, not liking the way he ignored my question. We walk along a few graves, and I stand next to him when he stops in front of a headstone.

For a full second, my heart stops.

"Oh."

I read the name on the grave over and over again.

Manishita Alva

"That's my mom." Those are the only words that leave me.

I stopped going to my dad's grave years ago. It came to a point where the questions would never leave me, and there was no point asking him anymore. He took his own life, and I had to keep on living, knowing there's nothing I did to help him.

But my mom...

It was easier to deny she was gone when I didn't know her resting place. Right now, this all feels too real.

"That's your mom," Elliot repeats, as if to confirm. "It didn't sit right with me that Kay refused to tell you where she was. Just don't tell her I showed you."

I swallow thickly. I can't describe the feeling. I'm sad, devastated, but I'm not crying.

"I don't think it's hit me yet." I can tell that's it by how flat my tone is.

I feel him nod next to me, and he brings his hand to my back, rubbing it in a soothing gesture. "That's okay. Just have a minute with her. I'll be in the truck."

I still don't cry when he leaves me alone. I just sit down in the grass, clearing the weeds around her. There's nothing else but her name on her headstone. Kay didn't know her date of birth, and she surely didn't have anything nice to say about her.

I don't lie to my mom. I tell her that I'm not in a good situation, that it's not about to get better, and that I'm still deep into criminal activities. Saying the whole truth out loud makes it so much worse than I thought, but I stay strong for her.

"You remember Elliot and Ethan, right?" I murmur. "It's getting...complicated, *Ma*. Ethan is still Ethan. I know you weren't a big fan of him, and you thought he was weird. But I think I still love him. It's so stupid because he is not very nice to me." I pull out a bit of grass. That's a way to put it.

"Elliot is being strange. And I know what you're going to say, he was your favorite. But that's just looks, *Ma*. He's the worst." I sigh. "But also, I guess he's not. 'Cause he's the one who brought me here today. And he took care of me when I got hit by that car. Oh yeah, I got hit by a car, by the way, but I'm okay. And Elliot, he also...he said I was beautiful. Like,

227

for real. The same way Ethan used to say it. And he keeps making me feel beautiful, even though I know I'm not."

I rest my head on her headstone, imagining the way I used to lay against her shoulder in bed.

"Hey, I miss you." I poke the stone, a wave of sadness engulfing me when I realize that it's just that...a stone. "I wish you were here to tell me those two stinky boys don't deserve me. Neither of them. I wish...I wish Dad was here to say *no boy in the world* deserves me." I huff, looking at the sky to hold back the tears. My throat is starting to hurt from the thickness in it.

"Maybe I'm just being selfish, and I miss having someone who loves me unconditionally. You're good where you are. You're not suffering anymore." I pause. "Right?"

Swallowing past the tightness in my throat, I nod to myself. "I should go. Got things to do that'll really piss you off. Like robbing a bank and shit." My mouth twists as I stand up. "Sorry, I didn't mean to say shit. I love you, *Ma*. You get some rest."

Elliot doesn't say anything when I get back in the truck. He just observes me, his eyebrows scrunched and a sorry twist of a smile on his face.

"I'm fine," I rasp.

"I know," he lies. "You're a strong woman." That doesn't sound like a lie when it comes from him.

I look at the time, realizing I've been out there for half an hour.

"You said five minutes."

"I know."

We exchange a look full of meaning. I want to ask why he changed his mind, why he brought me here, why he's looking at me like he cares.

"I told her you were the worst."

He chuckles, the sound resonating in his chest making me melt. "As you should. I *am* the worst."

On this lighter note, he drives away.

He huffs as we enter NSC territories. "I can't believe I'm driving your bratty ass to your bestie's garage."

"Oh, Racer's more than my bestie." I smile to myself, hiding it by facing the window. This is fun. "He's also a super cute guy. Scratch that. He's *hot*. And smart too."

His hand lands on my thigh again, fingers digging into my skin. "Watch your mouth."

"Is that jealousy, Elliot Pearson?" I turn to him, trying to appear serious.

"Jealousy?" he snorts. "I've gone past jealousy with you, my love." My heart stops, and his next words kick it back into a dangerous rhythm. "You don't want to know the things I've done to make you mine. The jealousy line was crossed, left behind, forgotten."

Oh God.

Oh God, oh God, oh God.

Stop it, heart.

"But keep talking about other men being cute, and smart, and hot." We stop at a red light, and he turns to me. "And watch me cross the line of insanity."

Goosebumps ripple down my spine when he smiles brightly. His blue eyes dance all over my face, gauging my reaction.

I have no idea what I look like, what I let out. My cheeks feel hot. I doubt my skin shows that. I'm mixed between an Indian mom and a Portuguese dad, so I'm a fairly light brown, and I don't blush often.

But damn, my cheeks *burn*.

And my hands are sweaty, my legs weak.

I exhale heavily, brushing it all off. "You're not serious."

"Not serious?" His deep voice wraps around my heart, squeezing tightly. "Why don't you ask Ethan how serious I am, baby?"

I feel my eyes round. My hand goes to his on my thigh. "What?"

He shakes his head, immediately regretting his words. It's clear as day that he's surprised he admitted it. Whatever *it* was.

"Let's make things clear, Jade. Don't try to make me jealous. Ever. Because I would actually love to see your face when I rip a man's heart out just so there's no risk it can beat for you."

The car slows down. He turns left and comes to a stop. "We're here."

He opens his door and gets out of the truck. I'm too shocked to move, but when I don't follow, he opens my door. "What are you doing? Waiting for someone from NSC to shoot us?"

"What did you mean?" I refuse to get out. "When you said to ask Ethan how serious you are."

Because Ethan said breaking up with me wasn't a choice, he warned me about the things Elliot did to make me his. And now, Elliot...

That makes no sense. Elliot didn't really care about me back then. When Ethan and I were together, he was fucking girl after girl. Hot girls. Kings' girls. Not at all the same as what I looked like back then.

"Did I bring you here to have a talk about our relationship, or to do you a fucking favor?"

I grind my teeth together, breathing in and out through my nose. It's right here, the rage. Bubbling in my chest. Squeezing my stomach. Making me so aware of how heavy my heart is.

"You brought me here so I could fix the van you and your boss are forcing me to drive to a bank robbery. What fucking favor?"

He closes his eyes slowly, reopening them even slower. His patience really is being tested today. He licks his lips, taking a deep breath. "Mention that outside the house one more time, and I'll have to walk you around with more than a collar. What's your favorite color for a gag?"

His words are the reminder I needed. My hands go to my neck, remembering the collar. "Oh my god, take it off. I can't go in there with this stupid thing."

"You wanted to come here, my love. That was your choice, not mine."

Have I become so comfortable with a piece of leather around my neck that I forgot about it when I asked to come here?

What is wrong with me?

"Elliot, take it off." My simmering anger makes him chuckle.

"So feisty." Grabbing my wrist, he pulls me out of the truck.

He drags me along as he strides to the repair shop. We don't need to go through the reception, since the large garage doors are wide open. Cars are spread out in the whole space. We walk onto the polished concrete flooring, but I can't hear any repair noise. Anything at all.

"Hello!" Elliot calls out cheerily. "This is a robbery. Anyone in here?"

The very last person I expected to see here shows up through the back door that leads to their offices and apartment.

"Oh." That's the only sound Barbie makes.

Xi's girlfriend is holding a huge cake. It says

Congratulations Racer! and her bright pink apron burns my retina.

"Jade!" Her enthusiasm at seeing me almost gives me a headache. No one is this sweet.

Her gaze follows mine to the cake. "Racer got a job as a mechanic at Silver Falls Sports Car Club on the South Bank. How amazing is that? I mean, I know you and him must have...differences. But I'm so happy for him."

I don't think she really understands Kings and NSC are not just enemies. A violent, bloody war is a little more than *differences.*

"Jade." I turn to Elliot, who's pinching the bridge of his nose with his thumb and forefinger. "You just elongated my day, you know that? What a fucking headache you are."

"I didn't know," I fight back.

Barbie seems to realize who's with me, and her smile drops. She takes the slightest step back. "Elliot."

"Don't worry, Alex. I'm not here to hurt you. I promise."

My gaze snaps to him. "What did you do to her? What could you possibly do to a soul as innocent as hers?"

I don't even know why I'm suddenly protective of the girl. She texted me a million times in the last week. She created a group chat with Rose White, her, and me, and I guess she's starting to win me over.

But also, who sends that many pictures of their pet bunnies?

Elliot shrugs. "I was looking for you, my love. What I did to find you doesn't really count."

A sweet voice cuts off our interaction. "Racer is just out." Barbie smiles politely, her words as articulate as ever. "In the nicest way possible, you might want to...not be here when he comes back. He's with—" She stops herself, her eyes widening as she looks behind us. "Xi, hi baby." Fuck my life. "Cake is ready," she concludes awkwardly, lifting the sweet treat to show it to her boyfriend.

"You have got to be kidding me," Xi's annoyed voice rises behind us. "What kind of fucking death wish do you two have?"

We don't get to answer.

"No, no...*Logan!*" Barbie's last word is a high-pitched screech. It's drowned out by the sound of a gun firing.

Reflexes make me lower myself as my hands come to protect the back of my head. A car window explodes, probably where the bullet lands. Barbie drops her cake, and it weirdly lands perfectly. The metal mold doesn't break, and nothing happens to her perfect cake.

I can't say the same about us.

Elliot's pained grunt makes me flip around. He's still standing, turned around to face the shooter.

Logan is standing between Xi and Racer. Xi sighs heavily, like he can't be bothered by the drama, but Racer's wide eyes are stuck on Elliot. I follow his gaze to my friend's shoulder. Blood slowly spreads through his gray Sum 41 t-shirt.

"Fuck, fuck, fuck," I mutter.

"Oh my God," Barbie panics. She runs toward us, her hands hovering over Elliot's shoulder. "Are you alright?"

"Alexandra," Xi hisses. He grabs her by the upper arm and drags her to him. "Do you need me to remind you this is the exact same man who threatened your life?"

"I know, but—"

"We don't want trouble," I manage to say calmly. "I just wanted to talk to Racer."

"Yeah?" Logan takes a threatening step, his gun still aimed at Elliot. "You don't need your little boyfriend for that, do you?"

"Not my boyfriend."

"Really, Jade?" Elliot admonishes. It's hard to tell if he's gritting his teeth because of the pain or because of what I said. "Take that shit back."

Right, it was because of what I said. "For the millionth time, we are *not* boyfriend and girlfriend."

His hand comes to press on the wound on his shoulder. "I will make you eat your words. You just wait."

"You think you can just show up here." Logan's furious tone brings us both back to the present.

"Logan, put your gun away," Barbie begs, now forced to stand behind Xi.

"How fucking *dare* you?" Logan presses his gun against Elliot's forehead, making him wince in the slightest. The barrel must still be burning hot.

"I'm guessing you're not over it, then?" he chuckles mockingly.

"I will fucking end you right here. Right now."

Xi doesn't say anything. Even though he's meant to be out of this business. He stands still, holding his girlfriend back.

Racer is quiet too. The most peaceful guy I know doesn't even blink watching that gun against Elliot's forehead.

"Logan, please," Barbie insists. "I know...I know what he did, but violence is never the answer."

"What you did?" I ask Elliot.

"I should have killed you long before now." Logan presses harder against his forehead.

But none of that impresses the man I came with. He's as cool as ever, not minding the situation in the slightest.

"Elliot," I insist. "What did you do?"

"He killed Zara." Xi's voice is as neutral as ever, but his eyes tell me all the pain he's still feeling.

Shit. That was their best friend. She was a known member of NSC, climbing up the ranks.

"See, I think your memory is failing you. *Ethan* is the one who stabbed her," Elliot says coolly.

"And whose fucking order was it?" Xi's grip on Alex tightens from the anger he's trying to control. "I was there, Pearson. I remember correctly."

"What? Wait, wait, wait…Ethan did *what*?" I bring a hand to my temple, attempting to process what I'm hearing. "Why…why would you do that, Elliot?"

"We were looking for you. Xi just needed a bit of convincing to tell us where you were."

My mouth drops open. "You. Fucking. Psychopath." I barely manage to form the words.

"Say bye-bye, Elliot," Logan sneers.

My heart drops heavily when I see his index finger tensing around the trigger.

"Logan!" Barbie barks at him. "That's enough. There will be no more gunshots in front of me." Her eyes dig into Xi's. "This stops now."

"Alex." Logan's fury is quiet, but so real. "You don't know what you're talking about. You can't understand. That was unforgivable."

"I can't understand?" Her voice comes out strong this time, unlike what I've heard from her so far. "What because you three"—she looks pointedly at Logan, Racer, and then Xi—"never did anything unforgivable to me?"

That calms all of them. Racer pinches his lips, shifting from one foot to the other awkwardly as he looks at anything but Alex.

Logan bites his tongue, literally, unable to answer anything.

And Xi lowers his gaze when Alex comes to stand next

to him. "This. Stops. Now," she repeats to her boyfriend. "No more violence."

"Logan, lower your gun." Xi's order shouldn't mean anything. He's not their boss anymore. He's out, as everyone keeps saying.

But sometimes it isn't about who is higher or not in the hierarchy. Sometimes it's just your best friend trying to protect his girlfriend from the violence of our world. And you have to respect that.

Logan shakes his head, defeated, and lowers his gun. "Get out of my shop." His voice is somehow stuck in his throat, grief coating it and making it painful to hear.

I know too well what it feels like to lose someone you love too early. Especially in such a surprising way.

"I'm glad we finally agree on something." I could make Elliot eat his winning grin right now.

He casually walks past all of them, and I have to follow. But when I'm almost out, stepping past Racer, he grabs my arm gently.

"What did you need?" he whispers as the three others go back to their normal activities.

Barbie is picking up her cake, Xi patting Logan's shoulders as they walk through to the back.

"I had some questions about fitting a twin turbo to a van."

"A van?"

My eyes dart to the side. "I was thinking of drag racing it. A new project to keep me busy."

"You got a budget for that project? That shit is going to cost you at least thirty grand."

"And it's not even the only thing I need," I chuckle. "It's a really shitty GMC Vandura."

"Fuck, Jade. Only you come up with that sort of shit."

I shrug. "It's fun, though. Isn't it?"

He nods, smiling at me. "Almost makes me want to lend you the twin-turbo I have. It's an old thing we took from a stolen car. But if someone can bring it to life, it's the girl who put a winning race car together with no money."

His compliment makes me look down. It's been a while since I've heard something sweet about me. Not my body or how good I look while I'm being fucked, but about *me*.

Racer rips a piece of paper from a small carnet he keeps in at the back of his blue mechanic coverall. He writes down his phone number with the pencil he keeps behind his ear.

"Here. A lot of drama could have been avoided if you'd just texted me instead of showing up with your boyfriend."

I grab the piece of paper. "Not my boyfriend."

"You might want to mention that to the man hoping his stare is going to kill me over there. Or maybe next time at least take off the collar. That all looks like a possessive *boyfriend* to me."

I turn to see Elliot staring daggers at us from the driver's seat of the truck. He knows his own limit. It might be complicated to get in a fight with Racer right now when a bullet went through his shoulder.

He probably could. But Racer, Logan, and Xi? Maybe not.

"Thanks, man. And congratulations on the job. I'm envious, but you deserve it," I say. "I should get going."

"Yeah, better." He laughs as I jog back to the car.

"Exchanging numbers with your crush?" Elliot growls as I sit down and close the door.

Fuck, his jealousy couldn't be more palpable if he tried. Maybe if he wrote, *I'm jealous* on his forehead?

"I just got us an engine for free. What did *you* do apart from almost getting us killed?"

"Collected this from the windshield before anyone saw." He hands me a piece of paper folded between his index and middle fingers.

My blood freezes when I read what's inside.

Did you know it takes around fifteen minutes for someone to bleed to death once their throat has been slit? Not long left for you. Tick Tock.

24

JADE

Gasoline - Halsey

My wild eyes keep looking from the paper to Elliot and back. I'm speechless. This is graphic to the point it makes me feel sick.

"They're getting worse…" Am I hyperventilating right now? *Me?*

"Hey, hey," Elliot whispers as he tries to take the paper back. I can't seem to let it go, and he forcefully makes me. "That shit is just empty threats, Jade. Nothing is going to happen to you."

But I can't talk. The blood has drained from my face and my lips are numb. I only realize I'm shaking when he puts a hand on my thigh.

"Jade," he insists. "Look at me."

I can't. I'm going to die. Someone is going to slit my throat, and I will bleed to death in fifteen minutes.

I can't breathe.

How badly does it hurt? Will I feel my blood draining, or will I pass out quickly?

"Jade, breathe." My hand is subconsciously at my throat. I only realize that because he moves it away before grabbing my chin tightly and forcing me to look at him. "Breathe, baby."

When my lungs refuse to stop inhaling in a staccato rhythm, Elliot grabs me by the waist, easily lifting me and dragging me across the center console. I land on his lap, my knees on either side of his thighs.

"Stop..." I whine. "Your shoulder. You're bleeding."

"Logan can't aim for shit. It's just a graze."

"That *graze* is bleeding profusely right now."

He waves a hand in the air, showing he doesn't care.

"Look at me. You're fine." He holds me with a hand wrapped around my jaw. "I will never let anyone hurt you."

He untucks my t-shirt from my skirt and slides his free hand under it, rubbing soothing circles in the middle of my back like he did earlier. "My love, I'll kill them before they get anywhere near you."

"Like—Like you killed Zara." It's terrifying to think Elliot would ever order Ethan to kill someone because he wanted to know where I was.

Every day the blond brother becomes more and more dangerous in my eyes. What level of lethal is he?

He freezes under me. His eyes are void of any emotion when he fixes them on me. "I wanted to find you. I did."

This is insane. My life is spinning out of control.

"You don't know who they are. That person sending me notes. You don't know...what they can do."

"It doesn't matter who they are. They can be a fucking assassin, for all I care. No one touches you."

"Because we have a deal." The words barely make it past the knot in my throat. They taste bitter on my tongue.

He shakes his head, his hand resuming his circles on my

skin. "You're mine, Jade. Deal or not, I promise you they'd have to go through me if they want to touch you. I'll die before I see you hurt."

His hand at my back pushes me forward until my lips land on his.

And here it is. The kiss that holds a million feelings. He doesn't bite my lip this time. Instead, he strokes my tongue in a way that should be illegal.

It's criminal to communicate how much he cares for me in a simple kiss.

It complicates everything to kiss him back and show him I want everything he has to give me.

Elliot and I were never serious. Fucking around was fun in the past...and he's turning this into something beautiful.

How terrifying.

We spend two hours at our guy's house. Our guy being the doctor who works for the Kings. I don't even know his name. He fixes us whenever a band-aid doesn't suffice, and Elliot definitely needs a good stitching and some painkillers. I still wonder how he's not even sweating.

Elliot pays him a hefty amount to keep his mouth shut and not let Kay know what happened today.

"Hiding shit from your boss, huh?" I say quietly as I hoist myself up on a dresser near the back wall, facing the metal table Elliot sits on. I'm not taunting him, just trying to relax the tension in my head.

"Kay doesn't need to know I gave in to your tantrum. Going to an NSC repair shop. Another great idea, my love."

I roll my eyes. "We got a free engine."

"For the price of my shoulder. Great deal."

His sarcasm makes me laugh. "Shut up, you're being stitched." I tilt my head to the side. "Do you even feel pain?"

"Only the pain of you denying I'm your boyfriend. I know you're not the commitment type since you and Ethan didn't end in the best way, but do you know how many women would die to be in your place?"

I shrug, picking at my fishnets. "Don't let those poor, innocent souls die. You and I are as incompatible as they come."

"I don't want *them*, Jade. I want you," he growls.

When I look up, his eyes are on me. Despite currently having a needle going in and out of his wound, I see nothing but the frustration that I won't give in to his ludicrous demand.

"You have my body. You need my heart for me to be your girlfriend." My gaze drops when I add, "You don't have my heart, Elliot."

Why can't I look him in the eye when I say that? Elliot can't have my heart for many reasons. Mainly because no one can, since a part of it still belongs to Ethan.

"How dare you say this to me after that kiss?"

My mouth parts at the boldness of him putting that kiss into words.

Of course. Of course, I feel like a fraud saying that after our earlier kiss. The things I felt were strong enough to drive away any fear of death. Any disturbing thoughts of Elliot admitting he had Zara killed to find me.

Elliot terrifies me for so many reasons. What if the main one is that he wants me badly enough to make me give in?

The silence is broken by such simple words they shouldn't even have the right to be spoken.

"Does Ethan have it?"

My eyes dart to our guy. He's working quietly, ignoring

our conversation. He rarely talks. He takes money, does his job, and pretends he doesn't hear or see anything.

Still, I feel weird talking about our situation in front of him.

"This isn't the right time to talk about this," I mumble, going back to playing with the strings of the fishnets.

"I decide when we talk about what. Answer me."

I can't look him in the eye. "You were so good at pretending you're a nice guy today. Why don't you go back to that and leave me alone."

The clattering of metal against the floor makes me look up. "A nice guy?" he snorts. "You think I'm a *nice guy*, Jade?"

The doctor picks up the surgical tweezers he dropped when Elliot stood up in a sudden movement. He steps back, knowing trouble when he sees it.

"I don't think you're a nice guy," I correct him. "But you *pretend* so well, one sometimes wonders who you really are."

He chuckles coldly, and I gulp the ball forming at the back of my throat. Fear.

"Oh baby, you look so confused. Would you like me to explain who I am?"

"I just—"

"I'm smart enough to not let everyone see my rage like you do. When I want to scream and throw shit around, I smile and take a deep breath, *unlike you*."

"You're an asshole who's so used to getting what he wants, he has no patience when anyone refuses him anything. I don't want to be your girlfriend. You bring me pleasure, and I do the same. What more do you fucking want from me?"

He takes a threatening step toward me, the thread the

doctor was using to stitch him hanging by his wound, the needle still attached and dangling by his upper arm.

"I might be impatient, but I know what I'm doing when it comes to the things I want. And guess, Jade, just take a wild fucking guess at something—or someone—I've been wanting for so long it could drive a meditation guru insane with *impatience*."

My lack of an answer brings him closer to me.

"I don't need to spell it out for you, do I?" His hand is surprisingly soft when he cups my jaw.

"You're the one who always said we were just having fun back then. That it was just sex."

"I was trying to take it slow. I didn't want to scare you away when you'd just broken up with my brother. How's that for patience? But then"—his sarcastic chuckle makes me tremble—"then you saw a better opportunity in Sawyer. *We can't see each other anymore, Elliot. I'm with Sawyer now. It's serious.*"

He lets go of my jaw to run his hand across his face. "Fucking Sawyer?"

"I—"

"*Fucking. Sawyer.*" While his voice stays calm, everything that was on the metal table is swept out of the way with a violent movement from him.

He turns back to me, pointing an accusing finger. "And then you ran away. So I waited. I found you. I brought you back. I made you mine. And now there's something again. Always something. Now," he growls, grabbing the back of my head, wrapping my ponytail around his fist, and pulling so I look up at him. "Now you can't give me your heart?"

When he pulls harder, I whimper. "So my question is legitimate, Jade. Is it because of Ethan? Tell me. What do I have to do for you to belong to me *entirely*?"

"You're scaring me," I admit in a trembling voice.

"Yeah? Don't you think I got scared as shit when I started to realize the effect you had on me? When I realized I wanted to kill my motherfucking boss because you chose him over me?" He snorts. "Fucking Sawyer."

"Everyone needs to leave me the fuck alone with that guy." There it is. The comfort of fury brewing in my veins. Better that than being terrified of Elliot, isn't it?

"Why?" he snarls. "Because you fucked up? Wrong choice of guy to go up the ranks?"

I try to shrug him off, but he pulls my hair harder.

And when I try to slap him, he grabs my wrist. "Because you miss him, baby?"

"Fuck you," I grunt. "Let go!" Who has that much strength after being shot?

"Ah, there she is. My furious little love." I try to pull my arm back, getting off the dresser this time, and when I can't get myself free of him, I attempt to headbutt him. I scream from frustration when I miss. He's too fucking tall.

"Let me go!"

"I could fuck you right here, right now." He whips me around, forcing me to bend over the dresser.

"Stop."

"You'll let him watch, right, baby? Just like the perfect whore you are."

He pulls my skirt up, rips the fishnets, and pushes my panties to the side.

"Elliot," I panic.

"We have a deal, Jade. Now fucking take it. Little slut like you who went through the whole town, you would let anyone—"

"He was blackmailing me!" I shout at the top of my lungs.

He stops.

A beat later, he lets me go, but I stay in the same position. Too ashamed to look him in the eye.

"Are you happy? I fucked him because he was blackmailing me. I did everything he said because he forced me to. I stopped seeing you because he *forbade* me to!" My voice is raw, my heart beating crazily, my lungs straining from the need to breathe.

I try to catch my breath, panting. "He was..." A short breath. "He was blackmailing me, for fuck's sake. Beating up Billie, setting her up, trying to get Caden to stop dating her," I try to catch my breath and calm my racing heart, but I'm unsuccessful. "That was all Sawyer making me do it. Just– please, just...stop."

Even that shameful admission is not enough to convince Elliot. Because he's a bastard like that. "What with?"

And he can ask that question as many times as he wishes. He'll die trying to know what it was.

"I can't tell you that."

I feel him bending over me. "Do you know why no one trusts you, Jade?"

"Let me go."

"Because you're a *liar*."

That word. It stirs something within me. Because the person who broke me knew it. He said no one would believe me.

But it hurts even more when it comes from someone you wish with all your soul would believe you.

"I'm not a liar. Let me go."

"What was it?"

"I'm not a liar," I repeat.

You're lying, Jade. Stop fucking lying. Ethan's mom is the first one who didn't believe me.

Jade, are you sure? I know girls your age are desperate for attention, but...this is a bold statement. Are you lying, Jade? You're doing every real victim a disfavor by doing that. What kind of school counselor says that to a seventeen-year-old? She was the second person to call me a liar.

Oh my god, Jade. Don't make that kind of shit up. Have you seen yourself? Who would do that? Vickie didn't want to hear me. *Seriously, lying doesn't look good on you.* She was the third person to tell me I was lying.

And then it was Kay. She refused to hear the truth.

"I'm not a liar." Why is my voice so weak? What is happening to me?

I'm unsure with what strength I finally turn around.

"I'm not a liar." Why are my cheeks wet?

I feel my knees buckling, but my vision has narrowed. All I can see is Elliot's gray t-shirt.

Sum 41.

My favorite song from them is called *"Pieces."* Elliot is the one who showed it to me.

"I'm not a liar. *I'm not a liar. I'm not a liar.*"

Why would no one believe me? I cried, and I screamed, and I called for help, and they didn't listen.

I'd never done anything to make them doubt my word. I'd never lied to anyone. I'd never started rumors.

Like Elliot said, I was as sweet as they came.

And still...they didn't. Believe. Me.

25

ETHAN

With Me - Sum 41

I can't wait to prove Jade wrong. That no, we did not move on from each other. I know that with deadly certainty when Kay's new recruit, Maria, throws her head back in a fake laugh.

"You're too funny, *papi*."

Kay eyes me, then Maria. Yeah, if there's something we all know, it's that my humor really isn't my greatest asset.

I let Maria flirt with me tonight for one purpose and one only. Just to prove to myself yet one more time that I feel absolutely nothing for other women. I haven't since high school. Since Jade and I started dating. Even before that.

I've not fucked one woman since Jade, and it isn't going to happen tonight. It isn't going to happen *ever*.

"Anyway," Kay yawns. She's been bored to death for the last thirty minutes. "Now you know where to bring them, yeah?"

Maria's new mission is to flirt with the men who owe us

money and bring them here so I can easily torture them in our basement until them or their families find a solution.

"Absolutely." Maria nods. "And do I also get an invite when I'm not bringing anyone with me?" Her suggestion takes this to a level of uncomfortable I'm not willing to deal with.

"No."

She frowns, confused, and sits back. "Okay, *papi*. Next time."

"Maria, I'll start giving you names tomorrow," Kay explains. "I can give you their addresses, but where to find them exactly is a different problem—"

Her phone rings, and she looks down, huffing. She hangs up on whoever.

"Often they know we're coming for them, so they'll be avoiding staying at home and—"

Her phone rings again. "For fuck's sake," she mutters.

"Everything okay?" I ask.

"Got this unknown number that keeps calling me."

I lean forward. "Maybe it's important."

"Or maybe the feds are trying to lock me up," she grunts. "If they want to talk to me, they can serve me or arrest me."

I nod. It wouldn't be the first time the feds looked closely into Kay. She's the head of a gang, after all, but they never end up finding anything. That's what having the Wolves' protection is like. The Bratva has her back because she does good work for them.

"It'll be fine." She shrugs, unaffected, just annoyed that she can't keep going with her conversation. There's not much that can faze the girl.

Her phone rings again. She looks down at the screen,

initially annoyed, but her face relaxes right away, and she picks up, not caring about this situation anymore.

"*Mommy!*" The little voice is loud enough that I can hear it even without the speaker on. "*Nana screamed because Livie she doesn't say thank you. Nana screamed!*"

Exhausted, Kay runs a hand across her face.

"*Mommy! Can you hear, Mommy? Can you hear?*"

"Yes, Lia, I can hear. Give the phone to Nana."

As I'm assuming the phone is being passed from her daughter to her mother, Kay stands up. "I'm off. I'm driving to my mom's tomorrow morning, but I'll see you next Friday?"

"Next Friday?" Maria asks.

"Yeah, it's Ethan's birthday. You should come. I'm sure he'd love you to be here."

I narrow my eyes at my boss, and she snorts, bringing the phone to her ear again. When she closes the front door behind her, Maria turns to me, a salacious smile playing on her lips.

"So, how old are you turning, Ethan?"

It takes all of me not to throw my head back and huff. Couldn't she just leave with Kay? What the hell does she think is going to happen?

"Twenty-one," I mumble. Looking around the room while I think of any excuse to make her leave.

"Fuck," she laughs. "I think my friends are right. I like them young."

Now that doesn't sound creepy as fuck. And people say *I'm* weird.

"How old do you think I am?" She winks at me, clearly hoping for me to say something much lower than her actual age.

She's the type of person who refuses to age. She's

probably between thirty-five and forty, which is fine, really, but I'm not into her. I'm into Jade.

When I take too long to answer, she laughs again. "You don't want to take a wild guess in case you offend me. I get it." She settles more comfortably on the sofa.

"So, twenty-one, and how long have you been part of the Kings?"

"Four years." Are my answers not unenthusiastic enough for her to get the hint?

"That's a long time torturing people for Kay."

People just pry and pry...

"Kay wasn't the leader back then. Her dad was. Then Sawyer. Now her."

"Gotcha. Still, four years of what you do..."

She puts her hand on my chest. The feeling makes me want to scream, to claw at my own skin. I want to break every single one of her fingers.

I don't think she understands the many ways in which I'm already thinking I could cut her body up. Limb by limb, until she has nothing left to touch me with.

People look for something until they find exactly what they want. Something they will love, or a sign to finally. Fucking. Drop it.

"I don't mind," I admit, eventually at ease with the topic. "Torturing, killing, chopping up body parts. I finally found a healthy, useful way to do it."

Her hand is quick to leave my body. Fuck, I thought I was actually going to have to knock her unconscious.

"Before that, *that* was when it was bad. Leaving body trails all over town. Having to kill people to feed my need for blood. They were people who had pissed me off, but did they really deserve to die? I don't know."

I lean forward, smiling at her when her face falls.

"There's nothing like the silence of a heart that stops beating, and how aware you are that yours still is."

She shifts away from me delicately, like she's terrified I'm going to grab her and pull her heart out of her chest. "And you, Maria. What do *you* like to do for fun?"

She opens and closes her mouth a few times before finally saying, "I-I should go."

"Yeah, sure. Whatever you need to do."

But she's already up, bag in hand and by the door.

"So I'll see you for my birthday?" I shout at her retreating back.

"I'm busy next Friday!"

Slam!

That was our front door.

And it reopens right away, but it's not Maria this time. It's Elliot carrying a shaking Jade. A *crying,* shaking Jade. And if there's one thing the beauty never does, it's show her tears to the world. Her legs are wrapped around his waist, and her arms around his neck.

"What the fuck?" I'm up and on them before he can step farther into the house. "What did you do, Elliot?"

"Nothing," he grits out. "Get the fuck out of the way."

"It's the second time you bring her back into this house in a state. I think it's time you admit she doesn't fucking want you."

"Don't make me kick your ass, Ethan." But I keep walking alongside him.

I bring my hand to Jade, caressing her trembling back. "Mi Cielo, what did he do?"

"I didn't do shit."

He's angry. Probably because this is his fault.

Everything is always his fault. I might be the careless killer, but being the mastermind is so much worse.

"Ethan..." Jade's rasp makes my heartbeat accelerate.

"I'm here." I put more pressure on her back, giving her as much reassurance as I can.

Elliot is about to cross the threshold of his bedroom when she cries out, "I want Ethan."

Time stands still for a second.

I can hardly believe it, my brain unable to process her words. It's my heart that understands. It beats wildly for her.

Elliot is frozen on the spot.

"My love," he pleads softly. "I'm sorry...I'm sorry, please, don't go to him." The deep desperation in his voice is only a fraction of how hurt he is. Elliot has gone through everything to make Jade his. He broke every rule, went to hell and back.

But *she* doesn't know that.

She shakes her head, sniffling as she looks up. Her jade eyes cross with mine. They're borderline gray when she cries. The green is drowned in her sorrow.

"I want Ethan," she repeats without looking away, entirely unashamed of her need for me.

26

ETHAN

Scumbag - Goody Grace, blink-182

"I want Ethan."

I nod frantically. "Let her go," I order Elliot.

I grab her waist, and she hooks her arms around my neck. But he won't let go of her hips, his arms wrapped around her and forcing her to keep her legs around him.

"Jade, please." For a fraction of a second, I feel bad for him.

Because no matter how hard he tries, he will never understand what Jade and I share.

No matter the timeline, the galaxy, the fucking dimension, Jade and I are meant to be.

"Let me go," she whimpers, burying her face in the crook of my neck.

His gesture is the most reluctant act I've seen in a long time. His hands go to his blond hair, gripping the roots.

"*Fuck!*" he snaps. He storms into his room and slams the door in my face.

"I'm not a liar," Jade cries against my shoulder.

"I know you're not a liar, Mi Cielo."

I walk us to my room, but when I try to drop her on the bed, she tightens her legs around my waist and shakes her head.

"Okay." I lie down on my back with her on my stomach.

Undoing her ponytail, I let her wild strands fall around her shoulders. I slip my hand through the silk and rub her neck.

"I'm not a liar," she repeats, and I can't help but wonder what the hell Elliot did to break her this way.

"You're not a liar," I assure her for the second time. When she doesn't stop shaking, I add, "You're a fighter. You're an amazing racer. The bravest woman I know. You're not a liar. You're my *pedacito de cielo*."

My little piece of heaven. That's what Jade is.

That seems to calm her. She nods against my neck, and I hold her tighter.

I know what the consequences will be tomorrow morning. But for now, I'll hold her close to me if that's what she wants.

Jade falls into a deep sleep around ten, after hours of her holding on to me like I'm her lifeline. All I did was run my hand through her hair and told her that she wasn't a liar on repeat.

I want to understand what happened. So around midnight, I shift from under her, move her onto the bed, and cover her with the duvet.

She won't wake up now. Once Jade is asleep, absolutely nothing can get her out of it.

I close my bedroom door behind me and take my time going to the kitchen. I don't doubt Elliot is finding it impossible to sleep. He's probably scheming how to get her back. How to fix his mistakes and mind twist her so she forgets what he did, the way he hurt her.

He's standing by the window that looks out onto our small backyard, a cup of coffee in his hand like a 60s housewife.

I can see the wheels turning in his psychopathic mind. Bolts twist into place, screws drive deeper to find the exact thing he can use against her.

Elliot Pearson, master manipulator. The man who destroys everything in his way with the sheer power of his mind, and if it doesn't work, he snaps.

"Just ask already." His voice hits the window in front of him and reverberates back to me.

It's calm, but it won't last long because the situation is out of his control. His jealousy is palpable.

But since the problem that needs to be solved is to my advantage, I go first.

"What did you do?"

He takes a sip of coffee, at fucking midnight, swallowing slowly, his eyes on the backyard when he answers.

"I got jealous."

I take a step forward. "About?"

"Sawyer."

Another slow step. "And?"

"She told me the truth."

Things start to fall into place as I take another step. Now close to his back. "And?"

He sighs, unintentionally blowing on the steaming cup of coffee. "And I called her a liar."

I stop right behind him, staying silent.

I'm a broken man. I was born with a darkness inside me that calls for blood. I kill people, leaving their bodies to be found like a man dying to be put away for his sins. There's a screaming violence inside me.

But I've never wanted to kill my brother.

Until now.

The voice that usually screams in my head is only a whisper right now. So calm and assured.

"She told you the truth about Sawyer blackmailing her and you called her a liar." I'm not asking. I can put two and two together.

Before the truth even hits him, I grab the hair at the back of his head and slam his face against the window.

He grunts, bouncing against the glass. I'm quickly hit by the cup of coffee slamming into the side of my head. Glass breaks against my face, quickly washed away by burning coffee.

I hiss as I take a step back, wiping away the hot liquid. We stand apart, panting, eyes narrowed at each other.

I tilt my head to the side. "What happened to your shoulder?"

"Logan shot me."

"Huh." I shrug and punch him in the face.

He hits me back, and I try to grab the back of his neck, bringing my knee to his nose, but he grabs my leg, pushing it to the side. I have to let go of him to find my balance again.

I take a second to collect myself and so does he, running a hand through his blond hair and flicking back the strands that always fall in his eyes.

Clearly, this is going to lead us nowhere, and our agreement to stop is silent.

"You knew?" he asks.

It takes a lot to surprise Elliot, and it comes as a shock to the man who's always five steps ahead.

"That Sawyer blackmailed her? Of course I knew. Why do you think I did all those things you're happily holding over my head?"

"Oh, get over yourself, Ethan. I fucking own your ass. I have for years. Time to accept it. You helped her run away. It's not the only thing I can tell Kay to get your ass killed."

My jaw becomes so tight I can barely talk. The buzzing in my fingertips doesn't announce anything good.

"You own my ass because I made sacrifices for her. It doesn't make you better than me. It certainly doesn't make you worthy of her."

He runs a hand across his face, shaking his head. "No," he laughs. "No, the first time you ceded to me wasn't a sacrifice *for* her. You sacrificed *her*."

"Because of you!"

"Yeah. Unlike you, I'd do anything for her. And no matter what offer is on the table, I would never let her go. Not like you did."

My chest burns from my speeding heartbeat. I let Jade go because of what he offered me. It was his calculating mind that convinced me and my stupid ass that accepted. I was fucking seventeen. I knew nothing back then.

I shouldn't have let her go. I should have stayed a loser, a reject, bullied and unwanted. It shouldn't have mattered because I had *her*.

I made a deal with the devil, and I've paid the price every day since.

His plan didn't even get him what he wanted so badly. That's what bothers him the most.

"You can own this entire town, threaten, kill, manipulate...the only person you want doesn't *want you back*, Elliot. She'll *never* want you."

The dangerous rage I see in his eyes does scare me a bit. Elliot becomes deadly when he's inconsolable.

He's back in his head right now, calculating what he should do next. I stand silent, my back hurting from how tense I am.

Kill him now. Small, deep cuts all over his body, and he'll bleed until the morning before he dies.

I shake my head. That's not a good idea.

"What was it? What did he blackmail her with?" His voice is calm, but I think it's more dangerous than when he raises his tone.

I shrug. "I don't know."

"You don't know?"

"I never asked her. I never told her I knew. I don't do things for her to notice; I do things to protect her."

He laughs, throwing his head back. "Bravo, Ethan." He claps his hands slowly with such cynicism I want to break his fingers. "Bravo! You're officially her hero. Look at you"—he pouts mockingly—"saving her without her knowing. Sacrificing yourself for her. Suffering in silence."

One step and he's in my face, his voice dropping. "And making her come behind my back when you know I could end your fucking life with one conversation with Kay. *He's the one who helped her escape, Kay. He's the one who—*"

"Enough."

It takes all of me to keep a blank face as he observes me slowly. "You've always loved marking her," he chuckles. "You think I wouldn't notice your pretty bites on her neck? They were placed perfectly under her collar, but I'm not fucking dumb in case you never noticed."

I snort. "Yeah, we know, you're so smart. And yet look at you, you blackmail your own brother for the woman you want. You search the country for her. You make a deal with her...and *still,* you don't have her." A smirk splays on my lips. "That's a bit pathetic, don't you think?" I shrug again. "All I had to do was wait for you to fuck up. Remind me whose bed she's sleeping in tonight?"

There's a pause in space and time for almost a minute. We just eye each other intensely like we're in some fucking Western movie.

We hover our hands over our pistols.

Dust flies around us.

Tumbleweeds roll past.

But Elliot just smiles.

"She'll wake up in my bed tomorrow morning, Ethan. Or the next thing you'll hear from Kay is the sound of her gun firing at your face."

"No. She won't. This is it, Elliot." A certain excitement bubbles in my chest. "I think you're finally going to be my next victim."

"You want to kill me? Cut me into little pieces? Who's going to clean up after you?"

"I don't fucking care! I'd rather go to prison than know you're alive and stealing her from me."

"Go on, Ethan. Fucking kill me. Fucking try..." His voice dies down as a light brightens his eyes. "Unless..."

And here it is.

His new master plan.

27

JADE

you broke me first - Tate McRae

I giggle to myself at the new text from Alex.

> Alex: He literally grabbed it all in one go.
> Look at his cheeks!

The picture of Jean-Paul Sartre—yes, she named her bunny after a French philosopher—eating a whole baby carrot makes my laughter double.

> Jade: I'm surprised you don't feed him pink glitter.

> Alex: Oh, I did when I was a kid. That vet bill was humongous.

> Alex: Sadly, Mr. Shakespeare isn't with us anymore.

> Alex: Not because of the glitter. He died of old age.

"This girl," I murmur to myself.

I don't even know how she got to me with her twenty-four-seven good mood, but her sweetness is becoming my daily dose of sunshine. Especially in a house as gloomy as the brothers'.

> Rose: Aren't you meant to be in class?

I roll my eyes, imagining Alex doing the same. Rose White is weirdly motherly for someone who says she doesn't care about shit.

A hand grabs my ankle, and I scream from surprise my body is pulled from under the van.

Elliot's face appears above me. Without a word, but with a beaming smile on his handsome face, he shows me the brown paper bag he's holding.

"Breakfast, my love."

I ignore the nickname that makes my insides twist with excitement, and keep my face blank.

If he thinks he's getting away with calling me a liar. He can think again. I've been sleeping in Ethan's bed for a week, and I don't plan on changing that any time soon. Elliot has been leaving me alone, but I wonder how thin his patience is getting.

I need Ethan's soothing voice when I fall asleep. The smell of him on his crumpled sheets. I can't deal with Elliot's fake sweetness. I know it's just another mind twist from him.

No one was in the house when I woke up this morning. It was around six, and both brothers were gone, so I forced myself to shower, got changed in some clothes, and got back to working on the van.

I sit up and check the time on the old, plastic clock hung

on the garage wall. It's eleven a.m. I've been at this for hours and barely made a difference.

I eye the bag held by Elliot's strong hands. "I'm not hungry."

He nods, his smile not faltering one bit. "Okay, but I'm assuming you didn't have breakfast, and I can't have you starving yourself. Plus, it was Ethan who got it for you. So, really, you wouldn't be accepting gift from me, but from him."

I did skip breakfast. I pinch my lips, looking down at my stomach. I've been eating well since coming back here. Eating what I want in quantities I want rather than starving myself like usual. I can already see the difference from the small bump rather than the flat stomach I usually have.

"If you keep feeding me like this, I'll go back to being ugly." I look up. "You wouldn't want your toy to be ugly."

There's a flash of anger in his eyes, his smile straining. He takes a step back, like trying to stop himself from doing something stupid. "My love," he says calmly. "I'm in a situation where I want to make it up to you. I'm deeply sorry for the state I put you in, and I want to take care of you, to show you how much I regret calling you a liar when you opened up to me. I truly am sorry, Jade."

He looks away, comes closer, and squats in front of me. The hand not holding the bag cups my cheek before sliding to my loose hair and grabbing the strands tightly.

"But if you ever talk shit about yourself like that again, I'm going to have to punish you. Hurt you until you learn your lesson that no one talks about my woman that way. Not even yourself."

Every time he calls me his, or his woman, or anything to do with being in a relationship with him...it gets less strange. Even while being mad at him and sleeping in

Ethan's bed, it's becoming something I like to hear, and it worries me.

Dropping the bag next to me, he stands up. I keep my eyes on the brown bag rather than him. I need my heart to calm down before I can look into his angelic eyes again.

"I'll give you space to work today. But I want you to be present at Ethan's birthday party tonight."

"Awesome," I snort. "I can't wait."

"I'm not doing this to annoy you. I'm assuming the person after you is from NSC since we found a new note while we were at Logan and Racer's repair shop. But that might be too simple of an assumption. I need to see if anyone tries something tonight."

I put two thumbs up in front of me. "Even better. I'm bait."

He shakes his head, not willing to get into an argument I so desperately need. I want to scream at him and hit him. Anything to let some anger out.

But he plays it smart and turns around. "You know." He stops, his hand on the garage door. "You were always beautiful to me."

"Please," I snort.

He shrugs. "Beauty is a gift given to everyone. Being beautiful is only what society made out of it. I don't care that you finally balanced your weight, that you pluck your eyebrows obsessively and to perfection. I couldn't give a shit about your obsession with skincare or the way you now do your makeup."

My eyes accidentally cross his, and he holds me prisoner. "You were always beautiful to me, Jade. Just because you are...you."

The small smile he offers me is the most honest thing

I've ever seen from him. It's beautiful, kind. It makes my heart stop and my jaw drop.

The moment he's gone, I look into the paper bag. It's a waffle sandwich from my favorite diner in town. I pull it out. Sausage, bacon, double egg, caramelized onions. And a flooding of ketchup.

Ethan remembered my favorite breakfast.

I throw my head back, wincing when I hit the door of the van behind me.

"Ow," I moan. "Fuck you both."

Fuck them for making me feel inexplicable things for two completely different people.

I huff and stand up. I need a plate and a ton of napkins if I want to eat this without ruining the black jeans and Green Day t-shirt I'm wearing.

It's Elliot's, of course.

I walk into the kitchen with the brown bag in my hand and freeze on the spot. My eyes round, looking from Elliot to Ethan, and Ethan to Elliot.

Again.

And again.

And...again.

The shock keeps me speechless, and they stay silent while they think of how to explain themselves.

"Well," Elliot finally says. "I must admit, this is a tricky one to explain."

Ethan stares at me, blinking through the blood covering his face.

It's not just his face, though. It spills down his topless body, his jeans. All the way to his black combat boots. It has dried by now, some of it flaky on his skin, but some thicker parts are still wet.

The swollen veins in his arms beat like his heart can be

felt throughout his whole body. It gives life to the red liquid covering his skin, making it look like a snake slithering its way to his fingertips.

My eyes track the serpent down to a knife he's holding tightly in his right hand. It is just a kitchen knife.

A bloody kitchen knife held by a maniac.

I think Elliot can read my mind before I can even process it myself.

"Jade...*no*."

Life comes back to me in a rush of emotions. I gasp so much oxygen I feel dizzy. Flipping around, I make a run for it through the door I just came from.

"Jade!" I hear Elliot's irritated bark, but I don't stop.

"Oh my god, oh my god," I whimper as I grab the garage door handle and pull it up so quickly, I practically dislocate my shoulder.

I always knew Ethan was deranged, but I never saw the darkness from inside show up so clearly on the outside.

Whoever the person was, he didn't just murder them. He decimated them.

With a kitchen knife. Black hilt, silver blade. Such a simple utensil.

And now I can't help thinking I was right all along. That the person after me is him. That he's going to kill me slowly, painfully, like that person he just drained of blood.

Why did I believe him when he said he wouldn't hurt me? Why did I believe Elliot when he said Ethan wasn't the one wanting me dead? They've been out to get me since the beginning.

I escape whoever's hand is trying to grab me by a millisecond. Running out, I trip over my feet, only catching myself on my car parked right outside.

I don't have the keys, so I run.

"Ethan, come back here, you crazy motherfucker!"

Elliot is pissed. Probably because his brother is running after me down the street, covered in blood.

I'm too small. My legs can't run nearly as fast as Ethan's. I know it's over before I even feel his hand closing on the back of my t-shirt.

"No!" I cry out as he drags me back and slams me against the nearest random parked car. It's freezing. The car still covered with morning frost that burns my cheek.

"Shh," he hisses in my ear. "Don't be scared, baby." As his face presses against the side of mine, I can feel the disgusting thickness of blood, smell the copper scent of it.

I slept next to this man all week. I felt *safe* next to him.

I whimper when I feel the knife at my throat. "Don't be scared," he repeats with a voice I've never heard from him.

It's an empty rasp. Void of any emotion. From a man I've always known as full of feelings, I can't identify this side of him.

"Please, let me go. Let me go, let me—"

"Shh." His other hand comes to caress my hairline. "I won't hurt you. I would never hurt you. I promise."

I'm shaking to the point that my skin presses harder against the knife, despite him making no movement.

"Please," I squeak. The fear makes me feel sick. The smell of blood causes bile to rise up my throat.

"I'm going to bring you home, and we'll talk. No need to run, no need to be scared. I swear, Jade... I would *never* hurt you."

The weight of his body disappears quickly, forcibly. The blade accidentally cuts me just above Elliot's collar.

"Get off her, you fucking psychopath. Do you want us all to go to prison?" He pushes Ethan in front of himself. "Walk, asshole."

Ethan looks at me, life finally coming back to his black eyes. He turns and walks toward the house.

"Hey." Elliot wraps an arm around my shoulders. "It's okay."

"It's him." I say it with such conviction, Elliot's eyebrows rise.

"No, I told you it wasn't him who was threatening you."

"It's him."

He looks like he doesn't want to say it, but he says it anyway. "He wouldn't hurt you, Jade. Believe me, the way he is right now...he's always been like that. It's got nothing to do with you."

Still, the shaking doesn't stop.

"W-wh—" It's hard to formulate any words through my clattering teeth. "What happened?"

He observes the state I'm in, his jaw tightening. "We'll explain everything. At home. Come, my love."

We walk close to Ethan while staying behind. He keeps looking back at us. At me. My eyes won't leave that bloody knife.

Violence is usual on the North Shore. We grow up surrounded by it. We see dead bodies from a young age, friends and family with bloody faces or gun wounds.

We're victims of it ourselves. A good beating every now and then or are you even from here? The scar on my face is proof of our everyday lives.

Violence is our closest ally and biggest enemy.

But a wicked man covered in a stranger's blood?

No, I can't say I've seen that in my life.

I know Ethan is dangerous. People are scared of the things he can do. I *know*, but I never wanted to see it. I never wanted to be confronted with the reality of who he is under the weird behavior and dark tendencies.

I don't think I have a choice now.

I get another dead smiley face band-aid before we settle around the kitchen table. It's on my neck this time. Elliot had to take off the collar to stick the adhesive bandage to my skin.

I'm covered in Ethan's hickeys where the leather should be. We might not have had sex this week, but he still marked me. He'll usually wake me up by sinking his teeth into my skin.

When I sit at the table, Elliot still hasn't put the collar back on, and it feels weird to not have the weight of it around my throat.

What started as an annoyance now feels like a reassurance I need.

Elliot sits down next to me, leaving a chair on the other side of the square table. When Ethan walks in, showered and dressed, he avoids my gaze.

Maybe it's for the best. I've never been so terrified of him.

He sits down across from us.

"How are you feeling?" Elliot asks him.

I don't doubt he couldn't care less if he's feeling *good* or *bad*. All he wants to know is if his brother is still feeling psychopathically murderous or if we're all safe here.

Ethan refuses to reply. He puts his hands on the table, holding them together like a convict in a prison visiting room who's not allowed to have his handcuffs taken off.

His gaze stays on his hands and mine does too. I just want to keep reassuring myself there is no bloody knife there anymore.

"Alright," Elliot finally says. "I guess I'll be the one fixing your shit. As usual."

The lack of response doesn't seem to bother him. He

softly takes hold of the back of my neck, his thumb massaging behind my ear.

"Ethan and I had a...disagreement last week when you decided you wanted to sleep in his bed. Since then, he's been desperately wanting to kill me. Instead of doing that—because I'm his brother and he loves me—last night he went out on a stroll and took out his anger on someone else. What was his name again, Ethan?"

He mumbles something, still looking at his hands.

"Sorry?"

"Mike," he repeats louder.

My eyes automatically flick to the paper bag I dropped on the floor earlier, and my stomach twists. Is that why Ethan was at the diner in the first place?

"Right," Elliot nods. "Anyway, that sleazebag cook from the diner who looked at your tits last time we went. Unfortunately, our little slayer is quick to murder, but not very useful when it comes to cleaning up or covering his tracks. When our boy is done, he just goes home, happy with himself. And guess who has to fix his shit every time?"

"Every time?" My lips are numb, and I don't even feel like I'm the one talking. All I know is I can't take my eyes off my ex-boyfriend. "H-how often does it happen?"

I'm really talking to Ethan, but Elliot is the only one who wants to answer me. "Too fucking often, if you ask me," he snorts.

My ragged breathing worsens. "Why?"

"Why is the sky blue," Elliot says lazily. "Why are oranges...orange?"

"There are scientific explanations for that," I tell him.

"Yeah, but in reality, they don't matter. Knowing why the sky is blue doesn't make it green."

"But they *do* matter," I hiss. "Because if we knew what's

wrong with him, we might be able to help him. To make him stop."

"Don't start getting angry at *me*. I do my best to limit the damages. It's not my fault he has a need to slit people's throats and cut them into pieces. What can I fucking do apart from cleaning up?"

"I don't know!" I throw my hands in the air. "At least—"

"Stop talking about me like I'm broken." I finally recognize Ethan's voice. Not like the deadly tone I heard earlier. "And stop acting like I'm not right here."

I bite my inner cheek, observing him silently. He might be a little scary, but...he's special. Beautiful. He's not that man from earlier.

But then I get it. I look at him so calm, like he doesn't care one bit about what he did.

He doesn't care because death lives inside him. He made it his best friend over the years, living by its side, hoping one day it'll snatch him for being so familiar.

"The body?" I ask him. His eyes go to Elliot right away.

The blond brother waves a hand in the air, like this is nothing. "Taken care of earlier. That's why we were out late this morning. I came home, gave you the breakfast Ethan so kindly bought you before killing the cook, and was about to give him a good scolding before sending him to his shower. You're welcome." He looks pointedly at his brother. "And you're welcome." He smiles at me this time. "Daddy got everyone covered and fed."

I ignore the fact that I didn't even touch my breakfast.

My gaze stays on Ethan. "Why?"

"Elliot told you. I wanted to kill him, so I killed someone else."

"Most people can control their urges to kill," I say plainly. "Why do you give in to them?"

He smirks. "Because the sky is blue, and I wish it was green." Shrugging, he stands up. "Because I'm still in love with my ex-girlfriend, and she's falling for my brother."

My lips part. "I—I'm not—"

"Watch your mouth," Elliot cuts me off. Ethan is already leaving.

I'm speechless and I'm not even sure why.

Is it because he admitted to still being in love with me?

Or is it because he pointed out what I'm trying my best to ignore?

That I'm falling for Elliot.

I snap up, striding after Ethan. "Fuck you!"

"Here she is," he snorts as he turns around. "Getting angry because she can't fucking take the truth."

"I can take the truth," I snap. "But I can't take a hypocrite. So take it back."

"Take it back?"

"You don't love me. You stopped loving me when you broke up with me. Probably before. *Stop. Lying.*"

"I'm not lying, and I still loved you when I broke up with you." How can he be so calm? "You want to choose him? Then you have to at least know half the truth, don't you? Do it while knowing how I feel."

"Liar." I can't take this. They're playing with my head. The both of them are trying to make me crazy.

"I'm not ly—"

"If you still loved me, then where were you!"

My sudden scream keeps everyone silent. I'm doing it again, losing my cool, letting rage take over.

"Where were you when my dad killed himself, Ethan? Where were you, *four. Fucking. Months* after our breakup? Did you forget me that easily? How close I was to him? Where were you when I cried and buried him? Where were you when I was holding my mom in my arms after each round of chemo, when she let herself give up because she missed him so much and *I* was the one who had to stay strong."

My voice breaks. Like every time I scream, my lungs empty. "Because Elliot was there. He held me and he wiped away my tears. He held my hand while my dad's body was lowered into the ground."

I bring a shaking hand to my hair, gripping the roots and resisting the urge to pull every single one out. "You can break up with me, you can destroy my heart, but you can't *abandon* someone you love when they need you the most. So if you still loved me then, and you still love me now, tell me. Tell me where you were."

I'm ready for him to demolish me all over again. When I met Ethan, I wasn't whole. Our jagged pieces didn't even fit together until we polished them, reshaped them, and melted them together.

He smashed the masterpiece we had built and crushed the shards until they turned to dust.

And he dares say he's still in love with me?

No.

I refuse.

I want the truth. I want to hear from his mouth that he was nowhere special. At home, in his bedroom, making music. Throwing my stuff away. With another girl. *Unbothered*.

"Crack me open and stomp on my heart, Ethan. Once and for all, let's end this. Do it. Tell me the truth."

With eyes reflecting a broken soul, his gaze goes to Elliot behind me.

"Do you see what you've done?" he tells him, his voice barely audible.

When his brother doesn't answer, he looks at me again. "Why don't you ask him why I wasn't there for you."

He doesn't stay to hear the truth. Elliot won't bother saying it anyway.

What a great start to his birthday.

28

JADE

Strange Love - Halsey

The party is raging. Of course it is. It's Ethan's birthday.

I'm back in Elliot's room now. My head is spinning from changing brothers' rooms. I should get my own so I can sleep soundly when they're both being assholes.

Staring at my phone screen, I bite my lower lip.

Is it possible to be in love with two people at the same time?

Who the fuck googles that?

I startle when the door opens and delete my research. Locking my phone, I look up at Elliot.

He's biting his lower lip, looking at me like I'm his next meal.

"I really have great taste." His eyes go to my thighs.

I'm wearing a black vinyl miniskirt that he chose, and knee-high socks held by thigh ring garters. They're made of faux leather and have a heart each at the front, the rest of the bands covered by spiked studs.

Instead of wearing one of his t-shirts, I'm wearing a

black bandeau to cover my boobs and a fishnet mesh crop top.

"I bet your rich sugar daddy never dressed you like this."

I shake my head. With everything happening here, I completely forgot about Stan. He probably still doesn't know I'm gone. He's capable of leaving me for a long length of time before contacting me. Especially if he's working. I've only been back for about two weeks.

"This is more"—I look for the right word, unsure if I should admit it—"*me* than what Stan would make me wear."

He nods, clearly not wanting to hear more about the man who paid hefty amounts to keep me at his house.

"I washed this for you. Wear it tonight."

He hands me the vibrating underwear, and I roll my eyes. "Nothing can stop you from being an asshole, huh? Not even when you're meant to be making it up to me."

He chuckles. Grabbing something from his pocket, he shows me a bright green heart-shaped lollipop. It has a little post-it note roughly stuck to it that reads *I'm sorry.*

When I look at him, unimpressed, he waves it in front of my eyes. "Apple. It's your favorite."

I take a deep breath, observing him.

"You talk about Ethan being a psycho for murdering people, but I think you're the most broken one, Elliot."

His hand drops, and he tilts his head to the side. "I don't get it."

"No, you don't. Because you think you can apologize for not believing me by giving me my favorite kind of lollipop. You think you can keep lying to me when I ask you what happened with Ethan in high school." I shake my head in disbelief. "That is not how it works. I'm hurt. Really hurt. You're so...so focused on always getting what you want, on controlling everyone's behaviors and emotions that you never realized you don't know what the emotions you impose on people *feel like*."

For a second, I think I see something unknown crossing his gaze. Empathy, maybe? But it's gone as soon as it came. There's only confusion now, because people like him don't understand basic feelings.

"What did Sawyer have on you?"

I throw my head back. "For fuck's sake, that is not what matters!" I fist my hands, trying my best to control the rage inside me and knowing perfectly well it's impossible. "Sawyer's dead. The things he forced me to do and the secrets we shared are gone with him." I angrily put on the panties. "There. I'm ready. Have the best time torturing me tonight."

Ignoring my last comment, he keeps going on the topic he wants to talk about. "We all thought you were being horrible to Billie because you were jealous of her. Because Caden wanted her and not you."

"Please," I snort. "Was I ever the kind of girl who *competes* with other women? I'm the ugly one. If any other woman wants the same man I do, I'd give up right away knowing I don't stand a chance. I was so insecure about my looks when Ethan broke up with me that I slept with any man who showed the slightest interest. It wasn't because I wanted it, it was because they offered it. I would have never gone for someone who so clearly wanted someone else. So no, I wasn't after Billie because I wanted Caden. He can go fuck himself, for all I care."

The hurt in his eyes makes me retreat slightly. There is so much pain there, and I don't understand it until he talks again. "I hate when you talk about yourself that way. When you call yourself ugly."

It's a simple statement that portrays a truth I've been refusing to accept.

Elliot Pearson thinks I'm beautiful.

Not because he wants to fuck me, and not because I put effort into making myself look pretty.

He thinks I'm beautiful in a way only he can because it's through his eyes.

"I'm sorry," he says again. "I was so blinded by my own infatuation for you, so jealous that your actions were because you wanted another man, that I ignored all of those actions weren't...*you*."

I don't grant him any mercy. "You all saw what you wanted to see."

His eyes drop, the wheels turning in his head.

"What happened that night? At Sawyer's?"

"Sawyer wanted to teach Caden a lesson, and he wanted me to help get Billie to his house so he could rape her." I massage the back of my neck, discomfort crawling under my skin like a million insects digging into me. "You know... nothing kills a person the way sexual assault does. Your body is alive, but your soul is dead. It's like...it's like wearing a head-to-toe costume that doesn't fit. It's too tight, painfully uncomfortable. Everything is unclear, your vision blurry. Moments pass, but you're not sure they actually do. You hear things, but they become muted. People see you a certain way and have no idea what's underneath. You helplessly watch yourself become another person. Someone who isn't you. Something someone else made you. And all you can think about on repeat is one thing and one thing only: I never asked for it. This. Isn't. Fair."

I attempt a breath. It's so painful that I choke on it. My chest is frozen, a block of ice sitting on my lungs.

I spoke about it.

It's been two years and ten months since I spoke about this.

And I choose *Elliot*?

Does my brain truly have something against me? Or are my instincts that broken?

He takes his time analyzing me. He always does that, and people just let him. If maybe someone cut him off while he does that thing of trying to get into your brain, then he wouldn't have so much power over all of us.

"I was there that night. I saw you stop him before he did that to her," he says, his words calculated. "Why did you stop him?"

This is the moment he expects me to say what happened to me. He isn't stupid; he knows I was talking from experience.

But I refuse to let another person tell me I made it up. So the topic is closed.

"I didn't stop him. I beat her up."

"To stop him," he insists.

"Oh my god, yes! Will you drop it now? Why would I want another woman to be raped?"

"And he just...let you stop him."

I throw my head back, cackling like a maniac.

"Have you ever met Sawyer? He took out his sexual frustration on someone else that night. Don't worry."

His nostrils flare. "Jade." His voice is low. It's his anger that's palpable now. "Don't tell me you stopped him assaulting her, only for you to be on the receiving end of it. You sacrificed yourself for Billie?" A beat. "*Billie?*" he hisses. "Who cares about an NSC bitch Caden fell for if you had to be the one to get hurt."

I shake my head. "He didn't rape me. Sawyer and I had sex all the time. It didn't change anything."

"Because he was *blackmailing you*." He steps closer, fisting my shirt. "That is not consent."

My throat closes up, but it's anger that prevails. Always anger. "And what do you do, Elliot? Your protection in exchange for my body. What is that?"

"Don't. We have a history, we…" He stops himself, his face falling. "Jade…tell me this is more than just me giving you protection. Tell me you just used it as an excuse…that you wanted me."

There's no point lying to him. Why? To make him feel bad? I go for the truth instead.

"I wanted you," I admit. "You needing me so much that you wanted to make a deal for it only made me want you more. I'm a slut, remember?"

A smile slowly spreads on his face, so terrifying I steel myself so I don't retreat.

"No, my love. You're not a slut. You're *my* slut."

He reaches into his back pocket, pulling out something he holds tightly. A collar. Different from the one I had on until this morning.

This one is partly leather, partly chain. The delicate metal links that run through it have a heart dangling at the front. He doesn't hesitate to put it on me, and I let him.

I don't even fight it.

Maybe because Ethan is right; I'm falling for a borderline psychopath.

Or maybe because when Elliot calls me *his* slut, my stomach does a backflip despite me forbidding it to.

The front chain is adjustable, and that's when I realize it's a choker. He hooks his index finger in the heart and pulls. The collar tightens and I'm forced to follow his movement.

A surprised gasp parts my lips when he raises his hand and I have to go on my toes until his mouth grazes mine.

"I'm sorry for not believing you," he whispers. "Truly. I was angry and jealous. I should have known right away that it's exactly like Sawyer to do something like that. If you don't want to tell me what he had on you, that's okay. Take your time. When you're ready to open up again, I'll be ready to listen."

My heart tightens, but thankfully, my brain keeps me sane. He still hasn't admitted anything about his involvement in my relationship with Ethan. About him and I getting closer while my ex slowly disappeared into the background.

For heaven's sake, I can't fall for his pretty words when he is practically choking me with a collar he just put on me.

"Tell me you're mine," he whispers, his beautiful gravelly voice pulling at my heartstrings like a puppet master.

I can feel it. My heart...it...

It's betraying me.

"Say it, my love. Who do you belong to?"

I swallow past the gigantic ball in my throat. It physically hurts to do so.

"You."

When I talk, my lips brush his, and the current that sparks from the touch travels all the way down to a place he already controls.

"Mm." He smiles against my lips. "Again. Tell me you're mine."

"I'm yours, Elliot."

"Sawyer wanted you, Stan paid money to keep you, Ethan is still in love with you...but whose are you?"

I'm trembling when I answer again. "*Yours*."

"Good fucking girl." He bites my lower lip in that way I love so much, making it swell and redden between his teeth. "Soon I'll hold your pretty little heart in the palm of my hand. Eventually, you won't be able to breathe unless I allow that heart to beat."

I can hardly breathe *right now*, and it's got nothing to do with the collar.

No, it's because of the monster of a man telling me what my future looks like.

When Elliot speaks of when he'll take control of my heart, his words feel like a prophecy rather than a threat.

He takes a step back, his eyes shining with a need for me I've never seen before. Not in anyone else. Ethan wanted me, needed me, but he had me willingly. He was never like this...so unhinged from trying to keep me to himself.

The heat from the party contrasts harshly with the freezing temperatures outside. I don't like winter. It's too cold. In the studio apartment where I lived with my parents, we couldn't afford the heating. My mom would cook something in the oven, and when she was done and had turned it off, she'd leave it open to warm up the place while it cooled down. I guess it's a good thing we lived in such a small place.

I'm surrounded by people like me. People who got hit with the realities of life at a young age. Right in the face.

People I used to call my friends.

Uncomfortable, out of place, pariah...these words can't even begin to describe how I feel tonight.

I can hear their whispers, despite the loud music. I read the questions in their eyes.

Is Elliot fucking her again?

That traitor? Surely, he can't be touching her.

Vickie and her friends have been eyeing me from the other side of the room for what feels like hours. They can't do anything because I've been forced to sit on Elliot's lap all night. The other guys he usually hangs out with don't mind. They get a great view of my skirt and legs. Probably what's underneath the skirt too. Out of four men sitting with Elliot and I on the sofas and chairs around the coffee table, two I had sex with during the period between Ethan and Elliot, and one I had sex with while I was already seeing Elliot. I don't think he knows. It was meant to be just fun, so we weren't exclusive. Or at least I thought we weren't.

I'm starting to understand there was never any fun between Elliot and me. Just him and his elaborate plan to keep me to himself.

Because he couldn't have just *asked* like a normal person. Or even suggested it. No, he waited until Ethan and I were over. He advised me to join the Kings to keep me close. He insisted we do most of the work together, seduced me, pretended it was a fling...and when I ran away, he had someone killed to find me, came back for me, dragged me back here and offered me protection in exchange for...*me*.

I shift on his lap. Putting it like that makes it sound so wrong. It truly highlights that fucked-up part of me that's falling for him. The part that feels ecstatic a man went through all of this to have me.

Elliot is so much worse than everyone thinks. It's those sweet eyes and that bright smile. We all fucking fall for it as if he never proved to us that he is capable of scheming sins that would make the devil shiver.

Every two minutes or so, my eyes scan for Ethan between the sweaty bodies.

I'm still in love with my ex-girlfriend.

I want to talk about what he said. To understand why he broke up with me. Mainly...I want to hear it again.

I'm still in love with my ex-girlfriend.

A shiver runs through me despite the suffocating heat of the party.

People near us are banging their heads to *"FIGHT MODE"* by Beauty School Dropout. No traces of Ethan, though. I eye the beer bottle in front of me, convinced that I should keep a clear mind tonight.

I look out again, desperate to find the black eyes of the man who admitted he's still in love with me, and when I find him, my heart freezes into a block of stone. That beer sounds a lot more like an option when my eyes cross with vivid green ones.

Caden is speaking with Ethan, his arm draped around my ex's shoulders, but his eyes are on me. His mouth is right in his ear so he can hear him over the music.

Fucking. Dick.

I can't believe Ethan is letting Caden *touch him.* I'm the only one he allows to do that.

Elliot is so surprised by how quickly I stand up that he's forced to let me go. He doesn't have time to ask anything as I mutter, "Bathroom."

His hand comes under my skirt, skimming my ass before he nods and goes back to his conversation.

I push past Kings' members, disregarding the insults some throw my way. Ethan and Caden are against the wall near the kitchen, and I can't ignore the infuriatingly cute smile Caden King has put on my ex's lips.

Those are so rare, Caden doesn't deserve them.

"I can't believe you *dare* approach me, Jade," he says casually. "Do you know how quickly I could kill you right now?"

"You told Elliot you wouldn't."

He cocks his head to the side, blinking at me. "I'm unsure what your point is."

"You told *Billie* you wouldn't."

When he doesn't say anything, I know I've got him.

"I thought you lived in NYC now," I snap so hard my teeth clunk together. "For someone who hates this town, we see you here way too often."

He smiles down at me, but talks to Ethan. "I told you it would work."

"What would work?" I snarl, my hands already forming into fists so tightly my nails cut crescents into my skin.

"That you'd come over the second I put my hands on him. You're a jealous, volatile little thing." Caden's eyes light with mischief.

I look at his arm still around Ethan and everything becomes clear to me.

There's something known to many Kings' members, but is rarely talked about. And that's the few brief months Caden and Ethan dated when the latest joined the Kings. If we can call Caden using Ethan as his favorite fuck toy *dating*.

What it really was, was Ethan getting attention from someone else other than me for the first time in his life. He always knew he was bisexual, and it's no secret from Caden either, but finally a human other than me showed Ethan he was attracted to him, and he was done for.

The frustration of seeing my ex walk around with Caden's love bites was more heartbreaking than I ever cared to admit.

I look at Caden's hand hanging over Ethan's shoulder and the brightest fucking lightbulb lights up over my head.

I narrow my eyes at him. "It was you."

"Me?" Caden chuckles.

It's becoming so clear that he's the one who forced Ethan to break up with me. Or why would he have jumped on him the second we were separated.

"You made him break up with me."

Caden laughs, throwing his head back. "What the fuck."

"Jade," Ethan says low, separating from his friend. "It wasn'—"

"Bastard!" I scream, hitting Caden with a hook.

It just...left my body. My eyes widen when his face slams to the side.

There's a party raging behind me, so I don't think anyone really notices what's going on in our little corner.

Caden massages his jaw as he stands to his full height, looking down at me.

I don't feel fear, only anger. Which, really, has always been what gets me in trouble.

"You fucking..."

I can't control myself when I jump him. We both stumble to the side as he tries to avoid me, and through the kitchen door. No one's in here since Elliot said it was a no-go. It leads to the garage, and he doesn't want anyone finding the van.

Caden is too strong for me to take him to the floor, but he's forced to take multiple steps back to keep his balance.

He pushes me back, clearly not intending to hurt me, and I land in Ethan's arms. He wraps them around my waist, my arms stuck to my body. "Stop it," he hisses in my ear. "It wasn't him."

"How could it not?" I rage, thrashing in his grip. "He was all too happy to fuck you the second he could."

"And it was amazing, too," Caden taunts me, leaning back against the kitchen table. He crosses his arms and tilts his head to the side. "He's just so irresistible when he moans, isn't he—"

"Shut up!"

"Jade, that's enough." Ethan's grip tightens to the point I'm struggling to take a full breath. "If you don't calm down, Caden will happily witness me putting you on your knees and shutting you up with my cock."

"Charming as ever," I grunt.

But it has the desired effect. I calm down in his hold until he feels it's safe to release me. Still, he keeps a hand wrapped at the back of my neck.

"And you," Ethan insists. "Will you leave her the fuck alone? I told you not to get her angry."

"Name one thing that doesn't anger her," Caden mocks.

"I will—" My threat dies in my throat when Ethan drags me back to him, my shoulders hitting his muscly chest.

"So possessive of me, Mi Cielo," Ethan whispers in my ear. "If that's how you feel after seeing Caden touch me *once*, imagine how I feel seeing Elliot fuck with you every day."

I twist in his hold, refusing to listen.

"I wasn't going to fuck your man, Jade," Caden jumps back in. "I found the love of my life. When that happens, you can't feel anything for anyone else, believe me. Why don't you ask Ethan what it feels like?"

Ethan freezes behind me.

"What?" Caden laughs. "You never told her that apart from me you haven't dated or fucked anyone since you two broke up?"

Ethan huffs, his warm breath tickling my neck. "I can honestly say you were the biggest fucking mistake I ever made, Cade."

Caden's smile is as smug as they come. "I don't think you

mean that." He pushes off the table and murmurs, "You're welcome," to Ethan as he leaves the kitchen.

The music becomes loud again as he opens the door, and it goes back to a dull bass as soon as it closes.

Silence stretches for a long minute. Our breaths synchronize, our hearts beating at the same pace. I can feel his between my shoulder blades, dictating the rhythm of mine.

I should move away. His grip is loosening, and I'm free to leave. He's quiet as his hand falls back to his side, allowing me to go back to Elliot.

No matter what is unsaid, no matter how he feels about me, Ethan knows his brother calls the shots, and that if I know what's good for me, for him, for everyone's sanity, then I should step away and go back to the living room.

It's a shame I don't want to.

His next breath is slow, deep.

"You're unbearable."

Those are the only words he exhales harshly as he flips me around and his lips capture mine.

I whimper when he grabs my waist, and he presses harder. Lips against lips, hard, unrelenting pressure. He lifts me and sits me on the kitchen table. I spread my legs to allow him to stay close to me.

And finally.

Finally, his tongue breaches past and strokes mine. I moan into his mouth, kissing him back with all the love I've ever felt for him. It's deeply emotional, and I want to cry out how much I still feel for him. Always have.

I don't need to. He can read my mind. I'm an open book to the man who never stopped learning about me, teaching me how to exist, to be myself. I don't need to express one word to someone who never stopped loving me.

Ravaging my mouth, he bites my tongue, then licks the wound. He moans when I bite back, starving for him.

I fucking hate Caden for being the only other person who knows what I know; Ethan is irresistible when he moans.

His forehead rests down on mine as we catch our breaths.

"Mi Cielo," he pants, his lips grazing mine. His hands leave my waist to press on either side of my head. "I'm sorry."

I want to cry. The emotions in his voice are breaking me. So much longing and regret. So much unrestricted love.

I can't breathe, a sob stuck in my throat.

"I'm sorry I pushed you away." His hold tightens, my neck straining from the way he's forcing me to look up at him. The angle is uncomfortable, unnatural, but I don't want to move. "I'm sorry I let you go. I'm sorry we found you."

He kisses my hairline with a strength that would have made me fall back if he wasn't holding me so tightly.

"I make selfish mistake after selfish mistake when it comes to you, Jade. I can't think straight... I shouldn't have helped him look for you. I'm sorry you're back here, in my arms. I'm sorry because I'll never let you go again. I helped you run away, only to drag you back...and I wouldn't change that for anything."

Gulping a breath, memories of the morning I ran away crash into me.

My phone lights up with a message from Stanislav. We only met a week ago, and he's already obsessed enough to give me anything I want.

But anything I want always comes with a price when it's offered by powerful men. Whether they're the kings of the world, or big fishes in a small pond, men always find a way to shackle you the moment you reach out to grab what they're presenting on a silver platter.

> Stanislav: I didn't think I'd hear back from you after you told me to, and I quote, use a cactus as a dildo and go fuck my own ass.

I guess my initial response to his offer was not what this man is used to. But I wasn't desperate back then, and I didn't need him. Things have changed, tables have turned, and I need to leave this town...yesterday.

Word travels fast in our town. Last night, Caden King killed Sawyer after keeping him in the brothers' basement for weeks. I should have run away the moment they caught him. But I was stupid, thought myself invincible.

Sawyer is dead, and I'm next on the list.

A knock on my door startles me. My heart drops so low it turns my feet heavy and stops me from pacing around the studio my mom and I live in. She's sleeping right now, exhausted from the round of hard chemo yesterday. That's the only reason I didn't leave the second I learned Sawyer was dead. I wanted to make sure she got home safely, that she had someone by her side until at least the morning.

"Jade!" I recognize all too well the voice shouting behind the door.

My thumbs fly across my phone screen.

> Jade: I was playing hard to get...

I see the dots at the bottom of the conversation, but my head snaps up when Elliot Pearson slams his fist on my door again.

"Sawyer's dead."

Yes. I know that.

"Now, now," Elliot's voice is a satisfied drawl. The tone of someone who is about to get his long-awaited prize. "Spare your mom the distress of seeing us grab you from your home. Come out like a good girl."

And to think I let the bastard choke me the last time he fucked me.

My phone pings.

> Stanislav: Do you accept the rules? It's a simple exchange, but I'm a very demanding man.

I don't even hesitate.

> Jade: I accept. If the money stays the same, I accept anything as long as you come get me today.

I had better plans in life than to become an escort for a rich man. Especially one who wants to keep me in his vacation home so he can visit me whenever he wants. Especially a man who seems to have tastes that could kill me.

When I was little, I wanted to be a stunt woman. Drive cars for a living. What a dream. Look at me now.

> Stanislav: Are you that excited to come to me, little puppet?

My throat tightens. The distinctive disgust of using my body as a means to an end never gets easier.

> Jade: I am. Just promise me the money is what you told me last week. $2000 every month.

I look at my mom, her sleeping form unmoving. That money will cover her chemo and whatever she needs. All of it is for her. Kay used to pay for it. All I had to do in exchange was to be at her beck and call for any jobs she wanted me to do. Being part of the gang who runs our town doesn't mean we're all earning beautiful money. There's a hierarchy, and I had to fight my way to be even remotely close to the top.

"Jade!" *The knocking intensifies. Elliot is losing the little patience he has.* "I know you're in here. Stop being a little bitch. Sawyer told us everything."

It takes all of me not to stop a whimper of fear. Elliot is going to kill me.

> Stanislav: The money is the same. Plus, I'll be taking care of you full time. You can have anything you want, as long as it's within my rules. And I promise the dildo I'll be using for your ass won't be a cactus.

I sit on the bed I share with my mom and put the phone next to me on the mattress. I don't often sleep here anyway. It won't change much for her. And she's always so tired...

I swallow roughly, forcing the tears away. And then again to bring me strength.

"Ma," *I murmur. She barely stirs when I slide my hand in her hair.* "Meh tenu pyar karteh hu." *I love you.*

My mother is probably the only person I love.

"I love you, Ma," *I repeat as I get up and grab the bag I packed. It's a small overnight bag, but Stanislav will have everything I could possibly need anyway.*

The knocking is hard.

I go to the kitchen window and look out. The blocks of public housing I live in only have three floors, and I'm on the second.

I've jumped it before, and I can do it again. I just need to watch my knees.

I throw my bag first. Then I tie my thick, dark brown curls in a ponytail and look at my mom one last time.

"I'll be back," I promise in a whisper.

The landing isn't gracious. I roll onto my shoulder, but at least I don't break anything. A few bruises at worst. Grabbing my bag, I sprint to the back of the blocks. I run to the gate, a steel gate that's the only way out. I pull at it and freeze when it stays stuck.

I look down at the lock.

Shit.

Shit, it's locked. Of course, it's locked. It's always locked and only the residents have a key so they can take out the trash from the back.

The key is in my apartment. Hooked on the side of the cabinet, right next to our trash can.

The rush of the situation is making me stupid and careless. That mistake could cost me my life.

I follow the brick wall on either side of the gate, unsure what I'm hoping for.

No such luck.

I don't care. I'm not going to die today. I throw my backpack high over the gate. I have to try twice to pass it over. It's high and so are the walls. Way too fucking high to climb.

And still, I don't care. I try to climb it, not realizing it's a hopeless situation. I'm too small. I'd have to be a trained soldier to climb this shit.

It's impossible to get in without a key. Mainly, it's impossible to get out.

I throw my head back, looking at the gray sky above me. "Fuck."

A sense of resignation washes over me. Elliot is after me

because Sawyer spilled my secret. Maybe he wanted to save himself. Elliot is going to kill me for what I did. Ethan will encourage him to do so.

I'm stuck here...a lamb waiting to be slaughtered.

Struggling to breathe, I take several steps back, craning my neck, looking up at the top of the gate as I lean against the brick wall of the building. I let myself drop to the ground, bringing my knees to my chest, my head falling onto them.

I'm going to die.

It's too soon that I hear the building's back door open, and someone approaches, feet crunching the gravel I'm sitting on. I don't look up. I don't want to see Elliot's beautiful eyes tainted with a need for murder.

He's on me after a few steps. I sense him right there. Observing me.

I don't need to look up to feel him squat.

He softly puts a hand at the top of my head. My heart is beating in my ears, an insufferable ringing. I've had this hiding mechanism my entire life.

When debt collectors came to our apartment to speak to my dad, I'd hide in the corner near the bed, my head on my knees and my eyes closed.

When my mom announced her cancer, I hid in that same spot, refusing to hear her.

When Ethan broke up with me, I sat on the floor of my kitchen, knees to my chest, blocking out the world.

The second I learned Sawyer was dead, I sat right next to my mom. My ass cheeks got numb from spending the night on the floor, my head down, not wanting to accept the truth.

I can't look up right now. Just put a bullet in my head and let me die a coward.

"Jade."

My heart stops. This isn't Elliot.

It's Ethan.

That's what makes me look up and gaze into the black eyes.

My own fill with tears. "Don't bring me to him, please." Throat closing, my voice becomes barely a squeak. "I know you hate me. But he'll kill me."

And then he says the few words that will change my life forever. "I'm not bringing you to him. I'm helping you leave."

I can't speak. I can't utter a single word. My eyes wildly look around as he helps me up. Surely, this is Elliot's plan, fucking with people's minds again.

"He's still at your front door," Ethan explains. "I said I'd check to make sure you don't escape from the back. Now come before he starts wondering what I'm up to."

He grabs my hand and drags me toward the gate again.

"I'll give you a leg up."

When I stay frozen on the spot, he grabs my wrists and slams my hands against the gate. He holds me there until he feels the strength coming back to my body. "Come on, Jade. You're stronger than that."

Grabbing my waist, he starts lifting me up. It's the gesture that brings me back. I press my combat boots into the gate with all the need for survival that surges inside me.

"There you go," he says softly. I pull myself up as he grabs my thighs and pushes me higher. One strong shove from him, and I throw an arm to grab the top of the gate. I feel him grip my ankle and put me on something solid. I glance down to see my foot on his shoulder, and I don't hesitate to push as I throw my other leg over.

I almost lose my grip when I get to the other side.

"Focus," he snaps.

Holding myself harder, I slide down, hanging by my hands, and finally let go.

"Atta girl. I need you to be more reactive if you want to make it out of this town alive."

I can hear him fine, but I can only see him through the gap between the gate and the wall now.

"Wh-why are you helping me? After what I did...you should hate me. What about Elliot?"

"Stop thinking, Jade. It's time to act now."

I nod dumbly, my brain foggy from what just happened.

He shakes his head, coming closer to the gate. We're standing on either side of it, but I feel the need to reach out for him.

We spent the last year and a half silently hating each other. Me because he broke up with me. Him because I kept sleeping with his brother.

"You got your car keys?"

I nod again with a new fervor. "I do."

"Then pick up your shit and go."

It feels wrong to leave just like that. He just saved my life. What am I meant to do now?

I want to touch him. Hug him, kiss him. It's intense, something I can't control. I take half a step forward. "Ethan—"

"Hide and hide well," he growls low. "Because if we find you... I'll never let you go."

His black eyes stop me on the spot. I don't need anything else to conclude the short moment we just shared.

I spin around and sprint to my car. Freedom already tastes bitter.

Undeserved.

Ethan's thumb tracing my lips brings me back to reality.

Elliot was looking for me because he thought I had stolen money from Kay. But why did Ethan help me leave?

"That's what you said that day," I murmur. "That if you found me, you'd never let me go."

He nods, the guilt in his eyes larger than life itself. "How can I?" he whispers. "If there's something I know deep down, it's that you're mine. Aren't you, baby?"

He spreads my thighs wider with both hands. Then he wraps them around my waist, squeezing until I can't breathe.

Kissing my jaw, he traces it until he travels down to my neck. "When did you stop loving me, Jade?"

He brings a hand to my panties, pushing them to the side. When his thumb grazes my clit, I swallow back a moan.

My heart is ready to explode. It kicks against my chest, and for a second, I'm sure it's going to jump out and claim him.

"I never did," I admit quietly, tilting my head to the side to give him better access.

"I know."

Without warning, he presses two fingers inside me. They slip in through the wetness and curl instantly, driving a whimper from my chest. Our kiss, our proximity, that's all I need to stir my unending desire for Ethan.

We become a madness of feelings. A rush of skin against skin. He doesn't even take my underwear off. He only undoes his jeans and barely lowers his boxers.

There's a burning need inside us.

Do you know what it's like to feel like you've missed someone your entire life?

Because the Ethan from high school, my strange boyfriend, isn't the man he's become. He's worse now. Stronger, sharper. He's a serial killer, his mind darker than it's ever been. He's the man who helped me escape and dragged me back. The man who suffers while his brother parades me around as his.

I never knew *this* Ethan. And I missed him.

I moan when the tip of his hard dick nudges against my entrance.

"You still love me," he repeats. "You never stopped loving me."

"I never stopped loving you."

He kisses me, licks my open mouth, bites down my neck and all the way to my shoulders. I hiss, but I let him mark me. He loves marking me. That's the only thing that hasn't changed.

"Say it again." It's a plea, not an order. Something that fuels him.

"I never stopped loving you, Ethan. Not when you pushed me away, not when I joined the Kings."

As he presses slowly inside me, I tremble against him. "I never stopped loving you when I met up with Elliot or Sawyer. When I ran away...aah..."

He presses harder, deeper.

"I know," he growls. "I *know*." They sound more like *I knew it*, than *I know*. They sound like *I've won*.

He pushes all the way, making me cry out. When he grabs my hips, I wrap my arms around his neck. He moves inside me with pure, unyielding need. He does it for me and for him. Our bodies stay tight against each other. The only thing separating us is every time his hips pull back to pound against me.

He fucks me into the kitchen table, so hard that at every thrust, it moves back a little. It grates against the floor, and he follows.

"You're going to love me forever." Now *that* sounds like an order. "I swear to God, Jade, don't you dare stop." A threat even.

"I won't...I won't," I pant.

As Ethan fucks me for the first time in more than three years...it feels almost indescribable.

Almost.

Because deep down, I know exactly what it feels like.

Coming home.

I come once from his thumb on my clit. Twice when he explodes inside me.

We're two panting messes, our foreheads against the other.

"I love you," he whispers like a secret. "I never stopped loving you, Jade."

"I love you too." My smile feels real, unlike anything I've experienced since being back.

He smiles back. Something so delicious and contagious. "You're mine, Mi Cielo."

"I'm yours." I nod against him.

We both startle when slow clapping erupts between us.

One single person condescendingly applauding us.

"If that's not the cutest fucking thing I've ever heard."

Ethan pulls out of me, quickly putting my panties in place and zipping up his jeans. I stand up when Elliot takes a step toward us, putting myself between the two brothers.

"Oh, it gets better," he laughs. "She wants to protect him."

"Elliot." I lick my lips, hesitant.

What am I meant to say? How am I meant to explain this?

Suddenly, the party is just out there once again. It never left. I'm the one who went to another dimension, who let Ethan bring me to a place where no one can touch us.

Elliot cocks his head when Ethan's fingers come to my waist, holding me tightly against him.

"Don't hurt him," I finally say.

Ethan is strong. Ethan is a *serial killer*.

But it's not about strength when it comes to his brother. Elliot can get in his head. He can put him in the same state he was in high school. Weak, easy to break.

"Him?" Elliot's smile is carnal. "Oh, my love, why would I hurt him?"

Elliot is closer now. Close enough that I feel the need to retreat farther against Ethan. Behind me, his grip on my waist becomes borderline painful all the while I feel him relax.

I hear the smile in my ex's voice when he talks behind me. "I told you I could get her to say it."

I freeze.

What?

"Ah, you were right, brother." Elliot tips an imaginary hat toward him. He's so close that I have to tilt my head up to look at him. The back of my head presses against Ethan's chest, and Elliot cups my cheek, keeping me in position.

"You told two different men you were theirs tonight." The gentle way in which he caresses my cheek is the opposite of how I feel.

But I can't move. I can't talk. I'm frozen between the two men who clearly played me.

"What are we going to do with you now?"

29

JADE

Pretty Little Addict - Haiden

I try to turn back to Ethan, to look into his eyes. I need to see the truth, the blackness of his mind.

But he doesn't let me.

First, he grabs my wrists, pinning them to the small of my back. He only needs one hand to keep me like this. With his other, he fists my hair, keeping me in the exact position he wants.

So I can't look at him. I'm forced to look at Elliot instead. At his playful blue eyes that promise nothing but trouble.

"You tricked me," I rasp.

"No, no, my love. That's not true. We tried to let you choose."

"What?" I twist in Ethan's hold, but it only makes him tighten his grip. "You didn't!" I rage, feeling the heat of anger pounding in my ears. "You both made me say—"

"We didn't *make* you say anything. We wanted to give you a choice. We shot our shots and wanted to see your reaction. Turns out"—he shakes his head, almost impressed

303

by my reaction—"you can't choose. You can't because Ethan was right. You fell for the both of us."

I go to speak, lips parting to shout like I know so well, but he slams his hand over my mouth.

"No. You don't get to be angry, Jade. For once in your fucking life, you're going to shut up and listen. Or I swear, baby, I will shut you up myself."

When he pulls his hand away, it takes all of me to stay quiet. I fidget, feeling the need to hit back. He gives me time to fight, but I must be getting wiser, because I stay quiet.

He smirks, so proud of himself that I chose to listen.

"You wanted the truth? Here's the truth; we've both wanted you for longer than you could ever imagine. Ethan got you first. Fine. You fell for him. Fine. But it would not be knowing me if you ever thought I'd give up after that."

His gaze flicks above me, looking into his brother's eyes. "I can make the two of you do whatever the fuck I want. If nothing can stop me, why would I stop myself?"

"You came to get me all the way from New York, just to prove you can do anything you want?" I hiss.

He throws his head back as he explodes into a terrifying laugh.

His eyes catch mine when he straightens his head again.

"You think that's all I did, baby? How much more naïve can you get?" Coming even closer, he kisses the top of my head. "That's why I love you, you know? Because for someone so feisty, so ready to always fight back, I could still control you like a little puppet on a string. It makes me special to be able to do that."

My nostrils flare when I try to take in a calming breath.

"It started long before that. You want to know everything. Here it is. The man you love so much let you go for a place among the Kings."

I feel Ethan's entire body steeling behind mine, and my chest tightens in response.

"What?"

"That's not the entire story, Elliot," Ethan mumbles, but shame coats his consonants, making them sound dull rather than biting.

Elliot's shrugs. "The details are boring. But if you insist. Kay's dad didn't want him because he was too weak. Kay saw the way he was bullied at school and didn't want any weak link in her dad's crew either."

He smirks at his brother. "But his big brother helped him. As usual, huh? I told them Ethan was capable of more than they knew. He was already an amateur serial killer back then. Funny how everyone who disrespected you disappeared, don't you think?" He shrugs. "I knew he had it in him. I told Ethan I'd convince them. That he'd get into the Kings' crew. He'd finally get the respect he deserved. A place among the gods."

That's not true. That's not true because the direction he's heading right now...

"All he had to do was break up with you."

No.

Ethan wouldn't break up with me just to be part of the Kings.

But he *is* part of the Kings, isn't he? And he did break up with me.

"Oh, baby, don't look so sad. He really, *really* didn't want to. I had to get in his head to convince him. It took me months. I told him it was the only way he could protect you. How could he keep you safe by being a bullied loser? I told him eventually I'd get tired of you, and he could have you back. I must admit, that was quite a big lie. Ah, here's something I said that was true; that it was the only pacific way in which I'd try to get you from him. That he might as well get something in exchange. Because what if I had to get hostile? Who knew who I'd hurt? Maybe you. *That* really got to him."

"Stop," I rasp, tears brimming in my eyes. "Ethan." I try to get some mobility back, but there's nothing to do. "Tell me he's lying."

The silence kills me. I feel like I'm going to be sick.

"Tell me he's lying!" I hit my head back against his chest, thrashing in his grip. "Fuck...*Fuck!*" I panic. "This is complete madness..."

Elliot nods, looking too proud. "It really is. But in his defense, I ordered him to stay away from you. That's why he wasn't there for you, my love. That's why he stayed away when your dad died, when you needed him. Because I *made him.* He hated you for dating me because he never wanted to break up with you in the first place. He only did it because he owed me for getting him a place in the Kings' crew."

I thought Ethan had broken my heart. I thought I would never hurt more than when he told me to stay away from him. That he was done with me.

But *nothing* has ever hurt like what Elliot is currently admitting. He kept the only person I loved away from me. He took his place in my head, in my heart. He fucked me, held me in his arms, pretending to be a savior when he was a villain the whole time.

He manipulated Ethan into staying away. He played me.

And Ethan let him.

For years, I've been wondering which of the brothers is worse.

The one who broke my heart or the one who constantly lies to me?

The serial killer or the master manipulator?

Ethan or Elliot?

There's no answer.

They're both out to get me. My heart. My soul. My sanity.

"No, no." Elliot shakes his head. "Don't cry, my love."

Both of his thumbs on my cheeks make me realize I'm doing what I hate, showing vulnerability.

I'm crying warm tears of betrayal. As hot as my blood feels. Boiling from rage. But in a room full of heartless men, they freeze from the coldness of their presence.

"Ethan and I have been arguing over you for years. *Years,* Jade. And we finally came to an understanding. Why would you cry when life just became easier? No more fighting over you. No more breaking this family apart. No more threats and blackmail."

His bright smile scares me to the bone. He is so, *so* broken.

"Now we get to share you. You said it yourself earlier, didn't you? You're mine."

He pauses, and Ethan nestles against my cheek. "And you're mine," he whispers.

I take a ragged breath, my entire body shaking. "This... this isn't fair. You *played* me."

"Fair?" Ethan chuckles in my ear. "When does Elliot ever play fair, Mi Cielo?"

I squeeze my eyes tightly shut. "The only thing he likes playing is *God*. We're all just pawns on his big chess board."

I try to shake my head, but I can't. Their hands are everywhere. On my cheeks, in my hair, wrapped around my wrists.

"Let me go," I panic. "Let go..." My chest heaves, the tears running, but they don't relent.

"No, my love. We're not letting you go. Never again." The certainty with which Elliot pronounces these words makes my heart drop to my stomach.

"I hate you," I croak. "Both of you."

"Mm." Elliot lets go of my face to grab something in his back pocket. "It's going to be the best hate sex of your life, baby."

I cry out when my underwear starts vibrating. "Fuck! Don't you dare...don't you—aah."

Ethan's hand leaves my hair, and he wraps it around my throat, leaving me just enough air to breathe. Just conscious enough to feel the pleasure without being able to fight back.

My eyes squeeze shut, and I inhale sharply through my nose. The setting is still on low, and it feels too good. I can't hate them when it feels this good.

I start chasing the pleasure, shifting my hips and thrusting, trying to press myself harder against the vibrating toy in my panties.

The moans rumble deep in my throat, and I'm incapable of keeping them down. I attempt to hide my face away, pressing against Ethan and twisting to the side against his strong chest. But I can't move with the way he holds my throat.

My body starts shaking, and I press my legs together. I feel my hands closing into fists behind my back. There's something there pressing against me. Ethan's hardening dick.

Shame engulfs me the second I know I won't be able to control myself.

"Go on, baby," Ethan whispers against my neck. "Keep your eyes on Elliot as you come."

I refuse, and Elliot ups the vibrations a level.

"Aah...s-stop."

I squeeze my thighs tightly, but it doesn't change anything.

"Let go," Ethan rasps. "Do it for me. Come for my brother, and then you'll come for me."

My eyes snap open. I want to beg Elliot to stop again, but it's a moan that escapes my throat instead.

"Let it go," Ethan repeats softly. He releases my throat to rub my nipple, gently playing with the hardened peak.

I throw my head back as I explode without warning. My knees give up, but he holds me as I tremble against him.

"That was one," Elliot says. His voice is heavy with lust, a low tone that promises nothing but more insanity. "Should we see how long you last until you pass out?"

I shake my head manically. My hips keep shifting since the toy is still vibrating, but I'm trying to avoid it now. "N-no. It's too much. A-already too much...stop..."

"I think we'll do that," he insists. "Do you know what would be fun, baby? If I take it up a speed every time you come." He smiles at me, and I shake my head *no* again.

"I c-can't," I gasp as the vibration goes up. My complaint turns into a moan again.

"I think she likes it," Ethan laughs.

"What a good little slut you are," Elliot praises me. Always praising me.

Ethan? He prefers humiliation. That's what he told me he wanted to do to me when we were younger. That's what I wasn't ready for.

And now?

Now nothing makes sense anymore. And I might be ready to lose myself in the madness of it all.

"Fuck!" I scream. Elliot just slapped my cheek. It wasn't hard, but it's the gesture that angers me.

"Focus on us," he growls low. "I can see you trying to escape mentally."

I whimper a wordless complaint, and he smiles back at me. "Spread her legs open, brother."

Ethan doesn't need to be told twice. But before he does so, he slides his hand inside my underwear and grabs the bullet vibrator. Once he's got a hold of it, Elliot rids me of the soaked material.

From behind, Ethan presses the vibrator against my clit again, making me hiss. The pleasure turns a little more into pain with every minute that passes. My pussy is tightening around nothing every time I explode into a powerful orgasm. But my clit is overstimulated, burning all the way to my toes, and every vibration sends a whole new sensation through my body. That hesitation of what I'm truly feeling. Does it feel good? Is it horrible? Does it feel so horrible it's good? What is it?

Ethan brings both his forearms under my upper thighs, one hand holding the vibrator, the other keeping my pussy lips spread. He sits back against the table, pulling until my knees come to my chest.

I'm wide open for Elliot, and his eyes light up. "Fuck," he rasps. "The way that toy vibrates against you. The way your thighs strain...You're a goddess, Jade."

Undoing his jeans, he pulls out his cock in a rush that translates his need for me.

He strokes himself as Ethan gives me a short break from the vibrator. I'm still shaking.

"Open your mouth, my love," Elliot says softly.

I hesitate, my eyes looking around wildly. He grabs the heart hanging in the hollow of my throat and pulls, making the choker tighten.

"Don't make me wait." The drop in his tone is enough

for me to open my mouth. "Good. Stick your tongue out. Mm...just like that."

He releases the collar to press his thumb against my tongue, still stroking himself. "That's good, baby. I'm so proud of you for doing that."

God, I hate his praise right now. The man turns himself on by doing that while he fucking tortures me.

"Wider, Ethan."

I cry out when the man behind me spreads my legs wider.

"Oh shit," Elliot hisses. He runs a hand against his mouth, his smile widening. His eyelids turn heavy. "Ethan, I wish you could see what a very, *very* wet slut she is. Such a good girl you are, Jade."

Ethan groans, pressing his hard-on against my ass. My skirt has ridden up to my waist, and all I have left are the ring garters holding those high-knee socks in place.

I shake my head, moaning when Ethan presses the vibrator against my clit again. My thighs are trembling, my muscles aching.

Extending his arm, Elliot grazes one of my nipples with the knuckle of his index finger. Then he moves to the other, enhancing the feeling of ecstasy spreading through my body as I come yet again. The buds are so hard they could cut glass. Scratch that, I could fucking shape a diamond right now.

When he pinches a nipple, I scream against his thumb.

"Very good, baby."

The pleasure is quickly becoming overwhelming. That's three. Three fucking orgasms. I can't take one more. I'm sweating so much, I can feel my hairline dampening by the minute. There's a single drop of sweat rolling from my temple to my cheek.

"God, you look so beautiful." He presses against my entrance, slowly pushing inside me.

I can't breathe at how good this feels.

"Fuck," Ethan rasps. "You're wetting my jeans."

Why is this so hot?

They manipulated you.

They're playing you right now, Jade!

I whimper when Elliot bottoms out.

"Too big..." But instead of listening, he pushes three fingers inside my mouth, flattening them against my tongue.

He hits my cervix, making me scream around his fingers.

"You're doing so good," he growls. "Look at this beautiful cunt taking all of me."

When he pulls back, the tip of his curved dick hits my G-spot. He rubs against it repeatedly, as Ethan plays with my clit again, using the vibrator.

"Shit," I moan with a mouthful.

My pants accelerate, and I come again in a dizzying rush with Elliot inside me.

"That's right. Feel it all for me. You're beautiful. So. Fucking. Beautiful." He punctuates his words with punishing thrusts, contradicting his praises.

I feel him explode inside of me. From the way he accelerates and from his grunts of pleasure.

The moment he pulls out, Ethan throws the vibrator away. He lets go of my legs, grabs my hips, and switches the two of us around. Within a split second, I'm lying on my back on the kitchen table.

"Let your head fall back on the other side," he orders, undoing his jeans again.

I can't even think anymore. I do as he says while he lines himself with my entrance again.

"You're such a dirty fucking slut," he growls. "Letting us both fuck you like a little toy."

I cry out when he enters me violently, and I feel Elliot settling by my head.

"You're going to come again while we both fuck your pretty holes, aren't you?" Ethan insists as he thrusts inside me.

When I don't answer, he pinches my clit. "Answer me."

"Yes!"

"Clean me, my love," Elliot orders softly. "Clean your wetness off me."

My mouth drops open, and he pushes all the way down my throat, the angle opening me widely.

When he pulls back, I lick his dick, just like he said. He tastes of me and his cum, maybe his brother's too. Something that could easily become addictive.

Ethan shifts, and I feel it deep inside me. "I want you to admit you're a dirty slut who's going to come with a dick in her mouth and one in her pussy."

So that's what it is? Ethan and his need to degrade me. That's what it looks like?

"Jade."

I shriek when he slaps my clit.

God, this is intense. So different from Elliot's praise.

Elliot presses his dick in my mouth, and I have to try to formulate words around him.

"I'm going to come," I choke.

Fuck, it's true. I'm going to come.

"Keep going." Ethan slaps my clit again.

"With a...with a dick in my mouth." The words are

barely understandable, but what counts is that I'm humiliating myself for him.

"Mm, what else?"

"One in my pussy."

I choke on Elliot when Ethan fucks me harder.

"That's right." Another slap on my oversensitive clit. "Come, then, pretty slut. Come for us."

I don't need more than that. One more slap, and another release overtakes me.

I've lost count.

Encouraging the other with each of their thrusts, I let them use me for their pleasure...but I think I let them use me for my own pleasure the most.

Elliot is the first to hold me once they've both pulled out. He sits me up on the table and holds me to his chest, caressing my hair. "I'm so proud of you, my love."

I shake my head, but my mind is too foggy to speak.

I do manage to spit out something before I pass out.

"I hate the both of you."

I even manage to catch his response.

"That doesn't matter. You're ours now."

30

JADE

hell is a teenage girl - Nessa Barrett

I groan when I twist in bed. I know I'm not in Ethan's because it doesn't smell like him. And I know I'm alone because no one is touching me. Elliot can't keep his hands off me when he sleeps next to me.

My pussy aches in such a good way I hate myself for it.

I lie on my back, staring at the ceiling as I recall everything Elliot admitted yesterday.

Ethan broke up with me because his brother told him to. He chose the Kings over me. He tells me he's still in love with me after sacrificing me for his own good.

And Elliot tells me he cares when he's done nothing but manipulate me and the people around us to have me.

I can hardly take a breath without wanting to dissolve into tears. It looks like the sun is barely rising. I must not have slept more than a few hours.

I don't know what to do with myself, but I know I don't want to go into the living room. There are probably still people sleeping on the floor and furniture from last night's party.

But worst of all, Ethan and Elliot are in there, kicking everyone out. I can hear it from here.

I don't want to see them right now. I need time to process. I've spent the last weeks seeing them all day, every day. I need a minute without the pressure they both put on me.

Getting up with a sigh, I start looking for Elliot's cigarettes. He never smokes, but he used to keep a pack for me in here. Seeing how obsessed he is, I'm sure he still has one.

Looking under the bed, I see a duffle bag where he probably keeps money and weapons, but something else catches my eyes.

A box.

That's where I find my cigarettes. But that's not it. It has my favorite apple lollipops, and apple bubble gum too. I sit on the floor and empty the box.

Hair pins. A photograph of me and him. A note I had slid in his locker once.

Thank you for kicking Sean's ass. I know Ethan won't say it, so I wanted to thank you myself.

There's a small heart drawn in blue ink below the words, and I rub my thumb against it.

Sean used to be one of Ethan's bullies, and Elliot kicked his ass once for slamming his brother's head against the lockers.

A week later, Sean spat on my lunch in the cafeteria. Ethan didn't say anything, just stared at him. The next day, he disappeared. His body was never found.

Funny how everyone who disrespected you disappeared, don't you think?

So, one brother killed people for me.

And the other calculated the way he would get me for himself to a T.

How...reassuring.

I huff to myself, hating the way I feel my heart beating faster, my chest growing warm.

You hate them.

I look at more of the objects on the floor and my heart stops completely. There's a family picture of my mom, my dad, and me.

I know for certain that it was in my apartment the day I ran away. I kissed it and left it to my mom because I was too scared Stan wouldn't let me keep it.

Elliot kept it.

Because he knew it meant something to you.

No, no, please, my heart, shut up.

He kept it because he's unhealthily obsessed. He planned on finding me and forcing me to make a deal with him. His protection against my soul.

I must never forget that.

He's no better than Sawyer.

No better than Stan.

The thoughts feel like a lie.

Because Sawyer and Stan didn't find me pretty when everyone thought I was hideous.

Sawyer and Stan didn't put elaborate plans in place to have me. They just jumped on the first occasion of a girl in distress. It could have been anyone.

Elliot did it because it's *me*.

I swallow thickly and look at the rest. A pair of white cotton panties I must have left in his room at some point.

Thankfully, they're clean. My album of *Chuck* by Sum 41. I know it's my own and not his because it's missing the little leaflet with the lyrics. I would always take them out to read them as I listened and ended up losing them more often than not.

A lock of hair.

He definitely went into my apartment after my mom's death and helped himself. This is the lock of hair that she kept when she cut my hair for the first time. It's tied in a soft pink ribbon.

"Elliot," I sigh. "You are so fucking creepy."

I don't bother to put the shit away. It's all mine, after all.

Picking up the pack of cigarettes from the floor, I go to his window. I need some fresh air, maybe a walk. Then I can think about what happened last night.

He put me in a Bad Omens hoodie to sleep. Another one of his most listened to bands. I put on a pair of his boxers, not really bothering with anything else since his hoodie reaches mid-thigh, and my combat boots.

I eye my knuckle duster on his dresser, then chuckle to myself. Surely, I can catch a minute of peace without getting myself into a fight.

Opening the window, I jump out. The house is only a single story, so I don't need to worry about hurting myself.

Holy shit, it's cold. I should have grabbed a coat and a scarf. Maybe some pants. I'm going to freeze to death in this.

Elliot's window opens into their backyard, and I make my way to the other side of it. For lack of a gate, they have two metal trash cans to delimitate the entrance to their property. I move one to the side and step onto the back alley. It's not very long, and it leads straight back onto the road.

But I don't get to make it that far.

Because Vickie and her friends are leaning against the walls of the alley, blocking the path.

It's not like they were waiting for me. They're just out here smoking a joint. Vickie's house isn't very far. She's often in the back alley. Looking at them right now, they've probably just left the brothers' house and stopped here to chill some more before all heading back to their own house to sleep off the alcohol and drugs.

So much for a calm walk for me. Kay's bestie is with her forever on-and-off boyfriend who's always cheating on her, and her younger sister who's about my age. Pretending I didn't see the three of them, I turn back around.

No need for a fight when my body is already battered from Elliot and Ethan.

"Hey!" Vickie whistles with her lips to call me, and I suddenly wish I had taken that knuckle duster with me. "Don't act like you didn't see us, Jade."

I freeze on the spot. They're already making their way to me. One wall of the alley is the back of the brothers' garage. The other is the same but for the houses from the street over.

It's narrow. Too narrow for two people to stand shoulder to shoulder. There's absolutely no way for me to make it past them.

They're right behind me.

I should run back inside.

That's my first thought when Vickie speaks again. "Trying to escape?"

Instead, I turn around. Because I'm dumb and stubborn. Because my pride means more than my safety, apparently.

"Escape where?" Vickie's sister, Lea, laughs.

We used to be friends.

Practically best friends. Then she took Vickie's side when I told them what happened to me. Her sister convinced her that I was lying, and my friend decided she didn't want to believe me anymore. Or that I was worthy of friendship.

"She's a stray," Lea insists. "Where is she gonna go?"

I clench my jaw, unsure of how to reply.

"Fuck," Vickie bursts into a laugh. "Which one of them got you good like that?"

She points at my neck and cheek. Ethan marked me. I'm covered in visible love bites.

I press a hand against my neck and narrow my eyes at her. "Why, jealous?"

"You know she's the queen of sluts." Lea is quick to defend her sister. "She's probably fucking both."

I keep my mouth shut, but my stomach twists.

I let both Elliot and Ethan fuck me last night.

"Lucky bastards," Andrew scoffs.

There's a short silence before Vickie registers what her boyfriend just said.

"What?"

"No, I mean...You know what I mean."

"She's a fucking slut, Andy. What the fuck?"

"How about you stop calling me a slut before I knock your teeth out," I spit. "One quick hook, huh?"

That was stupid.

That was so fucking *stupid*.

Anger makes me too reckless.

Lea is the first one on me.

"Bitch, shut up!"

I avoid her punch, but I'm pressed against the wall now, and it's easier for them to surround me.

"Always stealing other's boyfriends." Something I never did, but I don't think it matters.

Vickie punches me in the stomach. I can't avoid that one, but I throw one back in her face before Lea smacks me.

I feel dizzy, but thankfully don't get knocked out by a palm to the cheek.

"Grab her," Vickie hisses.

"Fuck off!"

Both Lea and Andrew take my arms and pin them to the wall.

Vickie lets her anger out on me. I grunt from the hits to the stomach, and my vision narrows when she punches me right in the temple, then my lips.

"Not so fucking cute now, is she?" She spits in my face.

"Fucking cunt," I groan, blood dripping from my lips.

I feel sick from her saliva on my cheek, and I want to puke on her shoes. But nothing fucking comes.

"Go on, Andy. If you find her so fucking hot, get your fix. A slut is a slut. You'll probably catch something, but hey."

Vickie slaps me in the face when my eyes close for a little too long. "Stay up, bitch. Andrew wants a taste."

"She'll probably enjoy it too."

Lea's words make Vickie smirk. "Yeah. She'll enjoy herself, and then pretend that she was assaulted. Boohoo."

"Shut up." More blood spills from my mouth. Fuck, I feel dizzy, and the alley is tilting.

"Remember, Jade?" Vickie insists. "Remember when you made all that bullshit up about Elliot's dad?"

"Oh yeah, that was some big fat lie," Lea snorts.

"I. Didn't. Lie," I grit out.

I didn't. I remember it. Everyone wants me to forget, to ignore it, to convince me it didn't happen. But I remember the sound of the bathroom lock behind me, and his face appearing in the mirror.

I remember my stupid self being too polite and smiling back at him. I was confused.

Are you okay, Joel?

He didn't reply, and I felt the discomfort right away.

I'll be done in a second.

I was washing my hands.

That's it. All I did that day was go to the bathroom to wash my hands before lunch. It was Elliot's birthday. He turned nineteen the day his dad broke me forever.

I didn't expect it. I didn't see it coming. He'd never talked to me much.

I was as surprised as all the people I told. All the people I sought for help.

People remember Elliot's dad for being violent. To the world and to his son. He was unpredictable, and Elliot still bears the scars.

Why is it so surprising that he could have hurt me too? Because it wasn't in the same way? Because it's easier to blame me?

I don't think I'm really present when Vickie hits me again.

"Imagine being such a sucker for attention that you make up lies like that. Some girls really go through it, Jade. You're fucked in the head."

But he did it.

I remember his hand grabbing my breast from behind me. The confusion. I could see his face through the mirror. The water was still running.

I remember the fear of asking what he was doing. I just...froze. I should have asked. I should have screamed.

Maybe, then, *maybe* someone would have come running. Elliot or Ethan.

It wasn't even violent.

That's the worst of it all. He was disgustingly soft when he pressed my cheek against the mirror.

He was silent.

I was silent.

Why was I so silent?

Something chokes me. A sob.

No. No. No.

"Oh my god," Lea cackles. "She's crying."

I shake my head, but I'm a prisoner to my thoughts. So. Fucking. Silent.

Did I let it happen? Is that why I'm being punished? Because I let him do it?

He didn't rip off my clothes. He didn't call me names and hiss for me to keep my mouth shut.

He just slipped his hand under my skirt, pulled down my underwear.

"Why are you crying, bitch? You're the traitor who stole from us and dares show up here again. You should be keeping your head down and your eyes to the floor." That's Andrew.

"You're so fucking pathetic," Vickie mocks.

But their words don't reach me anymore.

And when they let my arms go to beat me up some more, I don't really feel it either. I'm curled into a ball on the ground, but the pain doesn't register.

Because nothing will ever hurt more than Joel Pearson pushing his fingers inside me.

Tears fall today when they didn't that day.

I was just watching my breath fog against the bathroom window, my hands gripping the sink. Silent. Motionless.

He only stopped because his wife called for him somewhere in the house.

He brushed some curls away from my sweaty face. He flattened them against my head.

You're okay, he murmured.

That's the only moment I whimpered. Because I was *not* okay.

So he said it again. *You're okay.*

This stays between us, huh? It's better for you, Jade. You're not pretty. I don't want people to hurt you when they don't believe you.

He made sure my underwear was back on and my skirt wasn't out of place. He even patted my back in what would normally be a reassuring gesture.

Then he left, and I didn't say anything. I sat at lunch with him and his son. With his wife and her son. I ate lasagna that I threw up the moment I got home. And that was it. Just like that, I was broken forever.

Nothing hurts when you're dead; you only feel the phantom pain of what killed you.

So Andy's, and Vickie's, and Lea's hits don't really do anything. They get bored of it pretty quickly.

"Sort yourself out, you pathetic bitch," Vickie spits my way before they stroll out of the alley without a care in the world.

I pick myself up like I always do. Sitting back against the wall of the alley, I grab the crumpled pack of cigarettes they stamped on, and I take my time to smoke before I come back to reality.

It only starts to hurt when I walk back inside the house through the back door. My mouth tastes like blood, and I can feel that my lips are swollen. I hold my side when I walk in. My ribs had barely healed from being hit with a car that I'm already back to not being able to breathe properly.

I fucking hate this town.

Elliot is alone in the living room, sitting on the sofa texting someone. He looks over his shoulder when I close the door and his face falls.

The panic in his gaze makes me wonder what I look like. He's up in a split second.

"Ethan!" he calls for him as he approaches.

"I'm fine," I rasp.

I try to look away, but he grabs my jaw delicately.

"Who?"

"Elliot, I'm fine," I insist, taking a step back. He cups the side of my face that isn't currently pounding from pain.

"I said *who*?"

"I—"

For the first time in my entire life, I hear what Elliot's voice sounds like when he screams from fury.

"*Who did this to you?*"

My ears ring in the silent aftermath. I'm pretty sure the walls are still shaking.

I'm the screamer. I'm the angry one out of us three. The gunpowder that lights up at the flick of a flame.

Not today.

He's angry.

Fuming.

Murderous.

"Vickie." But he knows she's not brave enough to attack me on her own.

"And Andy?"

I nod. "And Lea."

Ethan jogs into the room. "What? What's—" He freezes on the spot. "Jade...what happened?"

"You go to Andy's house," Elliot orders without answering. "I'll get Vickie and her sister."

"Wait...wait!"

They don't.

They're just...gone.

31

ELLIOT

A$$A$$IN - Beauty School Dropout

"Why don't you try again, huh?" I push my gun into Vickie's mouth, making sure it goes all the way to her throat. "But try to add a little bit of truth to your response this time."

She retches around it, and I press farther. Spit drips from her mouth, and still...I push farther. Her body contracts, then extends, and I pull out. She rolls to the side, vomiting on herself and the plastic sheet she's lying on.

It does nothing except annoy me.

"I don't know," she cries. "Please, Elliot..." I broke one of her front teeth when I pushed the barrel into her mouth earlier, and she struggles to talk now.

Not liking her answer, I press the gun against her busted lips again.

"Stop! Stop!"

"The car, Vickie. Who was driving it?"

I'm going to have to start shooting if she keeps giving me the same answer.

"I don't know what y-you're talking a-about." Snot runs

down her nose, and she twists her face. She's particularly ugly like that.

"Elliot." Jade's rasp is the only thing that can take me out of my trance. "She says she doesn't know."

I turn toward her. She's sitting on Ethan's chair, splitting her attention between me torturing Vickie and watching the road to see if Ethan is coming back yet.

She brought her knees to her chest, hugging them tightly. Only those who know her can understand this as the only sign of vulnerability she shows.

"Jade, please," Vickie cries. "Please, tell him we didn't try to kill you."

Her gaze lazily goes to her, then to me. "They didn't try to kill me." The lack of emotion in her voice breaks my heart.

"See!" Vickie's voice is more than desperate right now. "Elliot...the knife, please..."

I look at her leg. I put a knife in there earlier.

"Oh yeah, I forgot about that. Better if it stays there. I don't want you to bleed to death."

Pulling my gun away, I walk to Jade. Vickie won't go anywhere with her wrists and ankles tied up. She'll stay on the floor where I left her.

I caress Jade's hair as she looks out of the window. "He'll be back, my love. Don't worry."

Ethan isn't here. He's busy with Andy right now. I'm not sure if she's worried about his safety, or worried about what he's doing to Andy. I've got the sisters at home. Lea is in the basement since Vickie was the first one I wanted to interrogate.

"It's not them, Elliot." Jade's voice is only a whisper. "If they were the ones behind the threats, they would have simply killed me."

I turn back to Vickie. "We didn't hit her with a car. I-I— At least I didn't. We didn't send her death threats, Elliot. Please, *please,* you have to believe me."

"Well, you still cornered her in the back alley to beat the shit out of her. Didn't you?"

She cries again when I mention what they did.

"Spare me the fucking tears, Vickie."

"I'm sorry!"

I squat next to her face. "You know, Ethan is probably dismembering your little boyfriend one limb at a time right now. Knowing him, he's doing it with a butter knife to make it more painful. When he gets to the tendons..." I hiss. "Man, I wouldn't want to be him. You're lucky you're with me." I snatch the knife in her thigh and wipe it on her jeans as she thrashes around like a lizard that just got decapitated.

"Elliot." Jade's head falls onto her knees. She takes a deep breath before looking up again. "I can't hear her cries anymore. Please, I'm exhausted."

I straighten up, nodding at her. "Okay, my love. We'll get you to bed."

I think Jade believes she's sparing Vickie by saying that. I don't doubt she wants to sleep. Her face is swollen, her eyes bloodshot red. She just wants this to end and for Vickie to leave.

"She learned her lesson, let her go. Lea too."

Vickie cries with relief this time. "Thank you. Thank you, Jade. I'm sorry. So sorry."

"You must be tired too, Vickie," I say.

She nods, eyes full of tears.

I smile at her. "Yeah, you get some rest."

Her body jerks one last time when my bullet hits her between the eyes.

"Elliot!" Jade is up, her head clearly spinning, since she has to put a flat hand on the window to balance herself. "You fucking killed her."

"That I did, yes. Why do you think I put a plastic sheet on the floor?"

"For the torturing... The—" She waves a hand toward Vickie's now dead body. "The whatever you were doing there."

"Ah, right." I grab the cloth I'd put on the sofa and wipe my gun before putting it at the back of my jeans. I squat next to Vickie, observing her dead body. This feels very good. "No, it's because I was going to kill her the whole time."

Jade watches with an open mouth as I casually roll the plastic and wrap it around her body.

"I know we have a deal, but I don't need you to fucking kill people for me!"

My shoulders are the first to tighten, muscles freezing. Then comes my jaw. I should have told her to keep quiet. Not to piss me off more than I already am.

"This has nothing to do with our deal. This has to do with the fact that anyone who hurts you gets a bullet to the head. Period."

I slowly stand up, taking my time to breathe.

"She just beat me up. It's the North Shore, Elliot. That's how we live."

Be patient. She's in pain.

I swallow thickly as I turn around and try to force a smile, but there's nothing to do.

"*Just* beat you up. Just..." Two strides, and I'm on her, my hands on her hips because I know those aren't bruised, or only from Ethan yesterday, and push her against the window.

330

"Just beat you up?" I repeat, hissing in her face. "Jade, do you have *any idea* what it's like for me to see you in pain?"

She huffs, attempting to push me back. "You're possessive, we get it—"

"I'm possessive, yes, but that has nothing to do with it. This is me, hurting, because I know you're unwell. Because I see you wince when you breathe, and your left eye has so many busted vessels, it looks like you're crying blood."

"It's not the first time I've gotten beaten up," she fights back weakly. Her hands grip my wrists to ease the tension on her body. "I'll get better."

"That doesn't matter. What matters is how I feel right now, seeing the woman I've loved for as long as I can remember *in. Fucking. Pain.*"

I inhale sharply, realizing what I've just done.

I've always hated seeing Jade in pain. Every time she'd get in petty fights with NSC girls, I'd be the one fixing her. Every time she was in danger, I was right behind her, making sure nothing happened to her.

I've seen her bruised and bleeding. I've wiped the blood away from the scar she has on her temple. I watched it heal and scolded her for putting herself in trouble again.

I've seethed countless times when she would get furious and slap a man twice her size in the face. Always protecting her, always suffering in silence when she got herself hurt.

We live in a town that breaks every single one of us on the daily. I've got more scars on my body than I can count, but the scar that has always hurt the most is the one she left on my heart without even knowing.

How long can one keep sane when loving someone who has no idea about it?

My gaze roams over her face. If her lips weren't already

split and swollen, I would have captured her mouth already. It takes everything in me not to.

Just like it took everything in me to let her date Ethan when we were in high school. I wanted to give her a chance to choose who would make her happy.

But the longer they dated, the more I knew *I* was the one who would make her happier.

I feel the way my jaw twitches uncontrollably. My molars are grinding.

"Don't say you love me," Jade whispers. "Please."

I let my head drop against the top of hers, my fingers gripping her hips tighter. I have to hunch over to be able to keep my hands on her. Because her head doesn't even reach my shoulders and her hips reach the top of my thighs. That's how fucking ridiculous our height difference is.

"My love," I chuckle. "You don't understand." I breathe in her smell of cigarettes and apples.

I want her to know. I'm done manipulating her into being mine. I *need* her to know.

"Do you know when I memorized apple lollipops were your favorite?"

She hesitates, and I feel her head shake *no* under my chin. My eyes are on the road behind the window as I go down memory lane.

"On the last day of second grade, I was with Ethan's mom at the convenience store. She was buying cigarettes. There was a long line, and you were at the front with your dad. We were all the way at the back. You asked your dad if you could have an apple lollipop. He told you he would buy it if he had any money left after buying the little he'd gotten for dinner. He counted his change to pay for the groceries. He paid for them and then, to my surprise, pulled out a roll of cash and bought I don't know how many scratch offs. It felt like a hundred in my eyes."

I'd known Jade for less than a year. She was a grade below me. She was shy at school, like Ethan. They were the same year, so they just sat together all the time in silence.

"I just couldn't understand why he bought all those and not your lollipop. He told you he'd get it as soon as he won more money. You waited so patiently as your dad stepped to the side to play, and the line moved forward. I remember you shifting on your feet, quiet, with your wide green eyes stuck on that fucking candy. I was the impatient one, waiting and waiting for you to get your treat as the line got shorter and I got closer to you."

God knows I would have thrown the tantrum of my fucking life in her place. Getting what I want is the only way I function.

"He bought some more, cutting in front of people, cursing every time he lost. And you were just there, being so good. I just didn't understand how you could be so sweet and still. The A/C was blowing on your high pigtails. Your hair was *so* curly back then. And your only movements were to get them out of your face."

That day is the most vivid memory I have of my childhood years.

"He lost again. Just as I got to the front of the line, he grabbed you by the wrist and dragged you away. Your little legs struggled to keep up with him, but you still did. You didn't understand why he was so angry. Your naïve mind thought he was annoyed he couldn't buy you the candy. And with your high-pitched voice, you said, 'Don't be sad, Daddy. We can get the lollipop another time.'"

She's quick to defend her dad. She loved him like nothing else in this world. She misses him every day, I know it. I know it because it was my shoulder she cried on when he killed himself.

"So, my dad spent a lot of money on scratch offs. It's basically a scheme made to rob poor people by dangling a dream over their head. I don't...I don't even remember what you're talking about, Elliot. It wasn't a big deal."

"But I remember," I grit out. "Because *that's* when I fell in love with you. The pureness of your heart clung to me. It left a mark I've been trying to get rid of since. And I failed. Your wholesomeness gripped me that day, and it never let me go, Jade. From that moment on, everything you did was like a call to worship."

I close my eyes, appreciating the fact that I'm currently holding the woman I love in my hands.

"I begged Ethan's mom to buy an apple lollipop that day. I—"

"Brought it to school. You gave it to me. I remember that because Ethan said you never did nice things for him. He wanted to know why you did something nice for *me*."

"Yeah. And you said they were your favorite. That smile on your face...fuck me, that smile, Jade. The most beautiful thing known to man." I huff, knowing that her reaction was the reason I started doing so much shit to get her.

Not right away, of course. I was too young. But it was the catalyst. Because I knew when I acted a certain way, Jade *reacted*. And as I grew older, and started testing all her reactions to my actions, it got worse. I became more ruthless as a man. My actions toward her were good, but I was becoming bad.

And then she started dating Ethan. That's when everything I did that involved her turned black and poisoned. Manipulative, and with only one goal in mind; to make her mine.

"I've loved you forever, Jade. I know I did the wrong things to get you. I know I hurt those around me. You and Ethan. I did unforgivable things to you and innocent people, but it didn't matter to me. It still doesn't. I would do it all over again if it means it gets you right here, in my arms. So *no,* you don't get to tell me whether I love you or not, or if I'm allowed to say it. I'm in love with you. Don't ever fucking test me on it again."

I shift to drop a kiss on her forehead, but she's the one who looks up, puts her hands on either side of my face, and presses her swollen lips against mine.

She whimpers, probably from the pain, but when I try to pull away, she holds me close. Her tongue licks the seam of my mouth, and I open for her, letting her take everything she needs.

Jade Alva can take anything she desires from me. My heart? Stolen. My sanity? She obliterated it a long time ago. Take my body, my soul, the very base of my existence.

Fuck, she doesn't even have to ask, I'll hand it all to her. On a silver platter encrusted with diamonds and anything else she wishes.

She pulls away and softly falls back, flat on her feet. I'm frozen in place, waiting for her to say it back.

That she loves me.

That despite what I did, she understands *why.* That loving her made me crazy and unhinged and I didn't have a say in it.

I count the seconds. One. Two. Three.

I drop my chin on the top of her head again. Maybe if I don't look in her eyes expectantly, she won't feel the pressure, and it'll just come out.

Tick. Tock. Six.

By ten, I understand it's not coming. And I do my best to not hold it against her.

I must give her time.

I try my hardest to hold down the rage, the disappointment, the heartbreak.

It's hard when I see Ethan approaching the house through the window.

I swallow through my tight throat. I've been jealous of my brother many times in my life. Envious of the times he could touch the woman I love obsessively. For the moments she shared with him and not with me.

But nothing has ever quite felt like this. Knowing that she is in love with him, that she said it to him again yesterday, that he got to hear those words over and over again coming from her mouth.

I never did.

I'm still waiting.

And who knows how much longer I'll wait.

The life expectancy on the North Shore is low. I'm turning twenty-two at the end of the month, and I can't help thinking; will I die before I hear those words from Jade?

"Ethan's back," I murmur, watching my brother coming to our porch covered in blood.

The fact that he's never gotten caught doing what he does is a straight up miracle.

Jade comes alive again, twisting in my hold and forcing me to let go of her. She runs to the door, ignoring her bruised ribs and struggling to breathe. She's opening it before he can even do it himself, and she hugs him despite the blood dripping from his clothing.

"Oh my god," she whimpers. "I was so worried for you."

My eyes drop to Vickie's dead body, and I walk to our

kitchen, through the door that leads to the basement, and slowly down the stairs.

I'm met with Lea's cries.

"Please...Elliot. I'm sorry I hurt her." She puts her hands in front of herself. She's probably terrified because she heard the gunshot upstairs. "I'll make it right by her. I'll do anything. Please, I'm sorry."

"Yeah," I huff. "And I'm sorry I'm in a shit mood." My fingers wrap around the handle of my gun.

I kill her swiftly. No pain, no torture like I did her sister. She pays for the consequences of her crime toward Jade like I'm still paying for mine.

32

ETHAN

Trick of Cheat - Diggy Graves

"This little piggy went to the market," I murmur as I drop the butcher hatchet on Andy's big toe.

He screams against the rag I shoved into his mouth before wrapping duct tape all around his head.

"This little piggy stayed home." I leave it intact. "This little piggy had roast beef." I slam the hatchet again, accidentally chopping the one I had just tried to avoid too. A frustrated huff escapes me. "You're shaking a lot, Andy. It's very hard to aim. I'll admit, using a hatchet doesn't help."

I lift my arm again. "This little piggy had none." I skip it. "This little piggy...Shit, what is it? Hold on."

I leave the hatchet on his wooden table and grab my phone in the pocket of my jeans.

I take my time to google 'the little piggy song lyrics' while he thrashes on his table, crying and desperately attempting to get away. He won't. I've tied him to his kitchen table legs, arms and legs spread.

"Calm down, will you? I'm trying to focus." He's already missing all his fingers and his other toes, but I wasn't doing it *depending on the song. Now I can't finish if the lyrics don't match what I'm doing.*

"Oh, that's right." I throw my phone on the floor and turn back to him. "This little piggy cried wee wee wee." I raise the hatchet high above my head. "All. The. Way. Home." I slam it on his ankle with enough strength to cut off his entire foot in one go.

His screams feed my anger.

The moment I saw Jade's face beaten up, I knew someone was going to die painfully, but I was just missing who. Elliot found that out right away.

Now I need to let myself be.

And Andy needs to die slowly and painfully.

The moment Jade slams into my body, I wrap my arms around her.

"Oh my god. I was so worried for you."

My eyebrows lift all the way to my hairline. "For me?"

She looks up, goes on her toes, and presses a kiss against my lips. Nodding, she flattens herself again. "What if you got caught? What if...Andy hurt you. Ethan, you can't just go around slaughtering people."

"He hurt you." My sentence doesn't leave anything up for discussion. So I'm not too sure why she keeps going.

"I don't care. What are you going to do? Kill every single person who hurts me? That's fucking ridiculous."

"Yeah, that's already done, my love." Elliot comes out of the kitchen as he says that. "Hurt you, disrespected you, breathed a bit too hard your way. All gone. He's a serial killer with very specific victims. But you're right, it *is* ridiculous."

I wonder why she's not scared when I smile wickedly at

her, but I love her for it. I grab her tighter, leaning down to bury my face against her neck.

The closer she is, the closer I need her to be. I hear her whimper, but I squeeze my arms anyway, needing her warmth and the smell of green apples.

I do it until I'm pulled away violently by the neck of my shirt.

"Ease up, Ted Bundy. She's in a lot of pain."

I'm in a lot of pain when I don't touch her, but I don't say that.

"Where is it?"

I keep smiling at Jade, ignoring my brother because her hand is touching mine, holding my big hand with her small fingers.

A slap at the back of my head takes me out of my happy moment. "Hey, how about you tell me where I have to clean up, or the next time you hold her hand will be through prison bars."

"I don't think they let you hold hands through prison bars," I retort, my eyes still on Jade. It makes her smile, and she has to bite her bottom lip to stop it.

Another slap at the back of the head forces me to turn to Elliot. "Where?"

"At his house," I groan. "Where do you think?"

Elliot is a psycho. A manipulator. Borderline narcissist. We argue and fight, and we hate each other sometimes. All the time when it comes to Jade.

And yet, through all of this, he is still my big brother. We might not share the same parents, but we've never needed that to feel like family. And like a big brother, he fixes my messes even when he doesn't want to. Even when he hates me. Even when he'd rather stay with the woman we both love and have been fighting over for as long as we can remember.

"There's a dead body right here," Jade says, her nose scrunching up in the cutest way. "And one in the basement, I'm assuming. Can't we take care of those?"

"You two take care of nothing. You touch nothing. I'll be back for those. Ethan's bloody slaughter is more important because anyone can find Andy at any moment."

He points a finger at me as he grabs his jacket. "Shower. No fucking, no touching the bodies, no leaving the house. You call no one, and you answer if I call."

"No fucking because you can't stand for me to touch her when you're not here, huh?" I smirk.

"No fucking because she's in pain, Ethan. Your brand of fucking will make her worse."

I lift my hands in front of my chest, palms out in a sign of innocence. Funny, since they're covered in blood. "I'll be good."

He smiles brightly at the both of us. "You two kids stay put while Daddy fixes everything."

The moment he's out, Jade and I turn to each other.

Putting a strand of curly hair behind her ear, she looks at her feet. "It's really weird when he calls himself Daddy."

"So fucking weird," I agree.

She looks up, and we stare at each other for a few seconds. I'd say we last about four before we both throw ourselves at the other. My hands are on her waist as she pushes her lips against mine.

Jade is ravenous. I think it's the killing.

She hisses as I pick her up, but her lips stay glued to mine. Wrapping her legs around my waist, I walk her to my bedroom.

"This isn't right," she moans between two strokes of her

tongue. "You and Elliot killing for me shouldn't turn me on. It's so fucking wrong…"

I push her against the wall of my bedroom. "We're on the North Shore. There's no right and wrong here, baby. Just wrong."

Her head drops back against the wall as I kiss her, biting until I can see new marks on her again.

"God," I growl against her soft skin. "I love marking you. I love that you let me do it. That you know who you belong to."

She moans when I bite harder. I grab the collar of the Thirty Seconds to Mars t-shirt she took from Elliot and rip it off her.

Gasping, her eyes round as she looks at me. I pin her harder with my hips, smiling down at her perfect tits.

When I start playing with her tight buds, she moans into my ear, and I could die right here, a very happy man. "We really shouldn't," she pants. "Elliot said—"

I wrap a hand around her neck, cocking an eyebrow. "Don't even finish that sentence. If you think I give a shit what Elliot says, I can easily prove to you otherwise."

She nods, her mouth opening in need of air, so I let her go.

"You're hurting," I murmur against her skin.

"I don't care. Really"—she pushes her core against my lower stomach—"don't"—and again—"care."

I smile against her skin. It's carnal.

"I won't hurt you more. I won't make it worse." I press her harder into the wall. "But when you're better, I'll fuck you the way I want to."

Nodding, her hands slide in my black strands. She pulls until I look up, and captures my lips. "Okay," she agrees against my mouth.

I hook my index finger in the heart dangling from the choker Elliot put on her. It tightens around her throat. "I'll hook a leash to this. I'll walk you around the house on all fours and plug your gorgeous ass so I can watch a pretty tail swing between your legs when you crawl past me."

"Fuck," she pants, grinding the heat between her legs against my abs.

I wrap her hair around my fist, pulling until we're looking into each other's eyes, tugging at each other's heartstrings.

"You remember, Mi Cielo. Right? The things I wanted to do to you."

She nods, a barely perceptible movement because of how tight my grip is.

"Tell me. Tell me the things you refused me back then." Pinning her harder with my hips, I slip my free hand beneath the boxers she's wearing. A guttural groan resonates loudly, and it takes me a second to realize it's coming from me. "Tell me the things you didn't want to do then and that make you wet for me now."

So wet.

My fingers slip through her slickness, finding her entrance. I press the pad of two fingers against it, making her gasp.

"Go on, baby."

"You said..." She closes her eyes, swallowing thickly. "You said you wanted me at your feet, worshiping you."

"Open your eyes."

They snap open, following the order. "What else?" I smile, expectant. Every single word that falls off her lips makes me harder, more desperate for her. I push my fingers a little farther in, teasing her.

"That you would be my master, and I'd be nothing. That

344

my place was on my knees at your feet...ah...please, Ethan...more."

"Keep going and I'll give you what you crave. A good little bitch begs her master for pleasure."

"Oh god," she moans. "Please..."

"What else did I want?"

"You wanted me to degrade myself for you."

She's so unbelievably wet. I've never felt her like this, and it takes all of me to not slam into her right this second.

"Yes," I insist. "You didn't want that, baby."

"I'm sorry!" She bucks her hips against my fingers, attempting to push them deeper.

"Don't be sorry," I murmur. "You weren't ready. Do you want it now?"

"Yes. Yes, please."

Her eyelids drop as I smirk. "How badly?"

"Please, Ethan."

"What is it you want, Jade?" My voice is sterner as I give my order. "Say it."

"I want it." She licks her lips. "The degradation. Please, I want it now. I want to get on my knees for you."

"You want to kneel at my feet, baby? To worship your master?"

I press all the way in as she screams, "Yes!"

"Beg me for it," I growl as I bite her neck again.

"Please...please, let me worship you."

"Who am I, Jade?"

She struggles to let it out, so I curl my fingers inside her, making her cry out. "You're my master," she gasps.

"And what are you?" I rub against her G-spot firmly, pressing my fingers in and out of her.

I feel her legs tighten around my waist, her moans turning high-pitched.

"Did you not hear my question, toy?"

"I-I—"

"You're *nothing*," I growl. "You're a fuck toy, a little cum whore, a slutty little pet who deserves nothing but to be under my boot."

"Yes. Yes, Master." She detonates around my fingers, convulsing as her wetness running down my hand.

"Dirty little slut loves to be degraded, doesn't she?"

"Yes," she pants, catching her breath. "More..."

Her eyes flutter open, a need for me I've never seen before in her life shining brightly in her gaze. The green is practically black, oozing desire. The opaqueness of her usual jade mixes with her dilated pupils. The strength in it makes me step back. I let go of her hair to hold her waist, keeping her close to me. I can hardly breathe.

"Fuck," I grunt. I carefully lay her down on the bed, holding myself on top of her. "You drive me crazy. I knew it. I knew you'd be the perfect toy. I just had to be patient."

I undo my jeans, the action reminding me I'm covered in Andy's blood. It's not easy to forget. The smell, the feeling of it heavy on my clothes.

But when Jade is around, nothing matters. My brain can only focus on one thing and one thing only: her.

"I want more," she moans as I lower my boxers and press my pierced tip at her entrance.

"I'll give you anything you need, Mi Cielo," I rasp.

She shakes her head. "I want to degrade myself for you. Make me..." She thrusts her hips, rubbing herself against the hard ridge of my dick. "Make me worship you, Master."

I lick my lips at the sight of her like this. She looks possessed by lust, insatiable. I grip both her wrists in one hand, pinning them above her head.

"You'd do anything for me, wouldn't you, Jade?" She

nods frantically. "You love me so much, you'd debase yourself for me in the most primal way."

"Y-yes."

"Settle down." My tone lowers, taking over her mind. "You'll get what I give you, when I give it to you."

She whimpers, and I push inside her slowly. "Not today, toy. You're tired, in pain—"

"I can take it," she grits back, but it turns into a muffled sound when I push hard inside her.

"When I talk, you shut the fuck up. Say 'yes, Master.'"

"Yes, Master."

"Your body is not in a state to take what I have to give. So you lay down like a pretty toy, and let me fuck you softly."

She nods, gasping when I bottom out inside her.

"Atta girl." With a hand on her wrists and the other coming between us, I fuck her with slow, purposeful thrusts, rolling my hips and controlling her breath with my movement. I press my thumb against her clit, splaying my fingers on her mound, and continue moving inside her at a rhythm that drives her crazy.

"Please..."

I ignore her plea, staying on my trajectory. She comes apart beautifully, writhing under me.

"I love you," she moans. "I love you..."

I come inside her, feeling her tightening around my cock. "I love you too," I grunt. "Fuck, baby, I missed you."

Having Jade to myself right now is worth the chaos Elliot will cause when he realizes we didn't listen to one word he ordered.

And chaos he will cause.

33

JADE

MAKEUP - Chris Grey

"Bad girl."

I gasp when I feel a finger pushing inside me. It quickly turns into a moan, and my eyes flutter open.

"I said no fucking," Elliot growls in my ear.

I'm finding it hard to locate my own body in the space around me. It's dark outside, and I can't see anything in the room. Ethan and I showered after another round and went another two times before we fell asleep. The sun was already gone.

I feel a pull at my hair. I'm on my front, and someone is keeping me pressed against the mattress. Someone else shifts beside me, an arm leaving my waist. That must be Ethan. He was holding me so close in our sleep, I could barely breathe. I felt his arms brushing against the bruises even in my dream. But I didn't want to move away from him. I love his skin against mine.

"You're back," Ethan's groggy voice rings to my right as he sits up, leaning his back against the wall.

I can see him, my left cheek flat on the mattress. But I can't see Elliot holding my head, and I'm assuming, he's standing next to the bed on my left.

"I'm back." His grip tightens, making me groan, but Ethan doesn't seem bothered. He looks at me, caresses my cheek, and turns to his brother.

"His cum is still hot in your pussy," Elliot growls. "How many times?"

"Oh God," I moan when his one finger becomes two. He pushes inside me, not giving me a chance to reply.

Ethan opens his mouth, but Elliot presses my head harder against the mattress. "I'm talking to you, my love."

"F-four."

"And how many times did you come?"

I struggle to breathe when his rhythm accelerates. "Fuck," I pant. "Three."

He tuts Ethan, chuckling low. "Not your best form."

"She's the one who said it was too much," Ethan mumbles, his black eyes on me, so clearly belonging to the night.

"So what?" Elliot snorts. "You let her dictate how many times she comes? That's not very good girl behavior, my love, is it?"

"No, but—"

"You're going to give her the last orgasm you owe her, Ethan. And then you'll hold her down while she gives me as many as she gave you."

"What?" The shock wakes me up further. I try to push up from the mattress, but he makes sure to hold me there firmly. "That's too many."

"Is it?" Elliot laughs. "I guess you should have listened to me when I said no fucking. We have to make sure we keep everything balanced, or who knows what jealousy will drive us to do. You gave him four orgasms, so you give me four. Spread your legs and lift your hips, my love. Ethan is going to lick his own cum from your pussy so I can replace it with mine."

Said pussy pulses from his words. Elliot's grip on the back of my neck doesn't relent, so I know it's Ethan's hands that grab my hips and pull me up, that spread my ass cheeks and expose my wet pussy. And I know for certain it's his tongue that comes to lick my entrance.

I inhale sharply, exhaling on a moan. He laps my wetness and his cum. And like an addict who finally gets a taste of what he craves, the moment I press back against his mouth, he pushes his tongue inside, ravaging me. With his fingers splayed on my cheeks and his thumbs spreading my lips, he pulls me up until he can lick my clit, but the access is difficult, and he changes his mind. He lets me go, and I hear him move, then the next thing I know, he's lying on his back between my legs. His hands are back on my ass, and he pulls.

I try to resist, but he leaves me no choice. He uses all his strength to force me to crash onto his mouth.

"Fuck," I whimper. "Yes...Ethan..."

A frustrated growl rumbles in Elliot's chest, and he twists my head until my mouth is pressing against the mattress. "I'm still not used to hearing you moaning his name. It'll take time."

His fingers curl tighter around my hair. The mix of his possession and Ethan's tongue teasing me forces a shiver through my whole body.

Until I realize I can't breathe. Probably the same way Ethan can't breathe, suffocated by my weight and my pussy against his face.

Panic seizes me, and I struggle in Elliot's hold. Ethan

feels it too, and he grips my ass harder, the pads of his fingers undoubtedly leaving bruises on my skin.

"Settle down," Elliot says calmly. "You're fine." And he pushes me farther into the sheets.

I attempt to scream, using my hands to push against the mattress, but my strength is nothing against his.

For a second, I think this is it. I wanted them both, then their jealousy over me got the best of them, and instead of letting me destroy their family, they decided to take me out of the equation.

Because what a ridiculous concept it would be to actually have both of them.

Right?

Ethan and I share the kind of love that can never leave one's body.

You can convince your brain that you're over someone, but the heart is a muscle, and muscle memory never leaves.

I love Ethan the same way he plays his instruments. So fiercely that my heart can never forget it. He can stop playing for months, if he picks up his guitar, closes his eyes, and lies down in bed, his hands will play any music without the slightest effort.

That's how I love him. Effortlessly. The muscle that is my heart does it with graceful ease, and I have no control over it.

Ethan laps at my clit in a repetitive rhythm. I'm the strings he's so used to stroking, and nothing can take him out of his tempo. His hands go from my ass to my hips, and he lifts me up slightly, holding me at the exact distance he wants.

I attempt to grind back against him, wanting to get more than what he's willing to give. He chuckles against my pussy, and I moan against the mattress.

I'm feeling lightheaded, my body in desperate need of air. Elliot moves beside me, squatting, I think.

"My love." I tremble from the lustful rasp in my ear. "You'll breathe when you come." His lips press against the soft skin just under my earlobe. "Take your time."

I thought I couldn't get any more aroused. I was wrong.

Ethan's teasing becomes unbearable, and tears of frustration burn in my eyes.

"Please…" I whimper, the sound swallowed by the mattress.

"Ethan," Elliot chuckles against my ear. "You're being mean."

But he doesn't stop. A stroke of my clit. A long beat. A teasing lap at my entrance. A beat.

I scream against the cotton sheet under me. I'm drooling over it, the material damp and making the situation even more humiliating. I can't breathe…I need to come. Heaven is so close and unattainable.

"She's going to pass out," Elliot continues. It's not a warning, not a threat, nothing that gives any order whatsoever. It's simple information for his brother to do whatever he wants with.

Exactly like they're doing with me; whatever they want.

"I'm working on making her come on command," Ethan says. His breath on my needy clit makes me tremble.

I feel myself go, a fear of never waking up seizing my entire body. It's at this exact moment that Ethan lets me come.

"Come, Jade," he orders simply.

He slams me back down on his face, keeps his mouth on my clit and loses himself against me.

I can't scream, the sensation too intense, the madness overwhelming. I tense and shake and tighten around nothing. Everything inside me shatters from immeasurable pleasure, and Elliot finally pulls at my hair, bringing my head up. Ethan rolls me onto my back like a rag doll and lets me go.

"Here you go, my good girl. You earned your right to breathe."

A sob bursts out of my chest, stopping the air I'm trying to gulp in.

"Shh." Elliot caresses my sweaty forehead. "You're doing so good, baby."

I shake my head. "Enough," I cough. "Enough..."

I feel Ethan stand up, and he grabs both my hands softly. "Come, sit up, Mi Cielo."

I let him help me. He settles behind me, his back against the wall, and spreads his legs so I can rest my back against his chest. His hands grab my waist, sliding down to my hips, then my thighs...

"No," I whimper when he wraps his fingers around my thighs and spreads my legs open. "Please, please, no more."

He nuzzles his nose against my neck. "Remember what you said? That you'd do anything for me? I want you to let Elliot use you. Be a good little toy for me."

"Elliot," I panic. "You said it yourself; I'm hurt and tired and—"

"And you still had enough energy to get fucked by my brother while I was cleaning his mess. Wider, Ethan."

Ethan spreads my legs wider, uncomfortably so. I'm drenched from being teased and from coming so hard.

"Jade," Elliot chuckles as he kneels between my spread thighs. "Your cunt is a greedy little slut."

As he pushes two fingers inside me, I cry out, my back lifting off Ethan. He pulls them out, lubed with my wetness.

354

"Fuck," he rasps. He repeats the movement with his thumb, exploring my pussy with his thick finger.

I grunt, twisting and pushing against him.

He pulls his thumb out, dragging it lower. "No!" I rush out, but Ethan holds me tighter. A rageful growl escapes me. "Elliot."

Smiling to himself, he looks into my eyes and presses his thumb against my asshole. I bite my lower lip to stop the proof of the pleasure that zaps through my body.

"You've been fucked in the ass before, baby. I know it because I did it," he says.

I don't say anything, embarrassed at how much I love it.

But I'm exhausted, too spent. They've overused me.

"Good little toys just take it," Ethan whispers in my ear. "Are you a good toy, Jade?"

I moan when Elliot presses on the tight entrance again. "I am..."

Maybe it's Ethan's voice that does it. Maybe it's Elliot's strong topless body between my legs, or the way the black-haired brother slides his hands behind my knees, pulling until my spread legs are on either side of my chest.

"Oh God..." His thumb pushes past the tight muscle, well lubricated by my own wetness that spread down to my ass.

"What a good fucking girl," Elliot growls. "Fuck, look at what a perfect slut you are. I'm going to make you come with my finger in your ass, baby. We have to start training you to take both of us."

I freeze. To...what?

"Fuck," Elliot rasps. "She just got wetter. The little whore can't wait for us to DP her."

I shake my head, attempting denial. "That...that's not true."

355

Elliot freezes, hard eyes looking up at me. "Do you want to lie to us? Really?"

"I—"

"Open the little liar's mouth, Ethan."

He doesn't need to be told twice. Ethan lets go of one of my legs to grab my jaw. I wince from the force he uses to open my mouth. He hooks two fingers against my lower teeth, marking himself with my incisors and keeping my mouth wide open.

Still with his thumb playing with my ass, making me pant, Elliot uses his other hand to push two fingers inside my pussy, then three, making me scream with a wide-open mouth. He pulls out, only to press his three fingers on my tongue.

As he keeps playing with my ass, moans rumble at the back of my throat.

"Lick my fingers, Jade. Taste your fucking lies." His order spurs me on. I push against his thumb in my ass and lick his fingers covered in my arousal.

"Isn't it so delicious to be a slut for us?"

I squeeze my eyes shut, but he doesn't even let me escape. "Look at me." When I snap my eyes open, he's smiling. "Don't ever lie to us again about the pleasure we bring you. You're our whore, baby. Better start acting like it."

He pushes his fingers deep inside my mouth, hitting the back of my throat and making me gag so hard I'm practically retching.

There's a string of my saliva at the tips of his fingers when he pulls out, making the humiliation a million times worse. "What a dirty toy," Ethan chuckles in my ear.

Elliot wipes his fingers on my cheek. "Covered in her spit and come. Pretty slut."

He fucks my pussy with his fingers while pushing in and

out of my ass with his thumb. "Beg me to make you come, Jade."

"Please!" I cry out. "Please, make me come."

I move to his rhythm, Ethan holding both my legs again.

"Do you know why you have to beg?" he grits out. "Because no one, *no one* will make you come like we do. We own this pussy, own your body." He smirks. "We own your fucking soul."

Ethan's grip tightens. "You're nothing," he adds. "You exist through us, and us only. Say it."

When I try to talk, it's a moan that rolls past my lips. "F-fuck..."

Elliot's hands freeze.

"No!" I shriek with need. "Elliot..."

"My brother gave you an order. Execute."

"I...I only exist..." He starts fucking both my holes again, and my body lights up like an addict getting their hit. "I only exist through you."

"That's right. Whose slut are you?"

"Yours...both of you. Oh my God, I'm going to come...I-I—"

My scream is so fucking loud, I wonder if the whole North Shore hears it.

Elliot is smiling like the cat who got the cream, and when he licks the fingers that were in my pussy, I think he did.

He hums and digs his gaze into mine. "Only three to go."

A whimper is my only response. I'm not fighting him anymore. I know there's no point.

The next orgasm comes with two fingers in my ass. He uses his mouth for the third.

And he fucks me dead for the last.

I feel when they shower me, but I'm not really here.

They're both in here with me, naked, and the only thing I wonder in my numb mind is if they'd ever shared a girl before.

I must ask them because Elliot answers my question. Unless he really is a mind reader? Surely, that's impossible. Fuck, I feel high.

"Just you, baby," Elliot answers. "Ethan has never fucked another girl but you."

My traitorous heart flutters, spreading warmth in my body that's hotter than the water falling on us.

I force my heavy eyes open. Ethan is standing in front of me, so it's Elliot at my back. I lick my lips. Seeing Ethan's naked body almost kills me. All those tattoos on his ripped muscles. His skin isn't pale like Elliot's. It's a few shades lighter than mine, but it's clear that not both his parents are Caucasian. He's skinnier than his brother, his muscles tight, his body narrower.

Ethan has never been with another girl. I know it's true. Not because Caden said it and not because Elliot says it. The truth is in Ethan's eyes, in the looks he gives me. In the way his calloused hands roam over my body as he washes me.

"If you loved me that much," I mumble so quietly, it must be hard to hear under the splash of the shower jet, "then why did you choose to let me go for the Kings?"

He freezes, his gaze dropping in shame.

"That's not fair to ask," Elliot says softly behind me.

"It is," I fight back weakly. "I loved him, and he chose them over me."

"He chose what he thought would protect you," Elliot continues, his hands grabbing my boobs from behind. He brings me closer to him, but my eyes stay on Ethan's face. "I made him—"

"You don't need to defend me," Ethan says through gritted teeth. He fists his hands hanging by his sides, his gaze down. When he looks up, there's only regret dulling his already black eyes.

"I let you down," he tells me. "I did it because I didn't want to be the loser who couldn't take care of his girlfriend anymore. Who couldn't defend her. Do you know how it felt every time someone made fun of you, or hurt you, or *touched you*, and I just stood there and watched because there was nothing I could do about it? I was a coward."

He runs a wet hand against his face, brushing away drops that are splashing in his eyes.

"You were fine before you met me. You had never been bullied or mocked. Then you associated yourself with me because you were a good friend. Because you were in love. And then they got to you too. They hurt you and teased you and humiliated you. You didn't deserve that. You didn't deserve a boyfriend who let it happen because he was scared of being beaten up by NSC dudes who thought they were the kings of the school."

"I didn't care." My voice is barely a squeak.

"Fuck, Jade. Billie Scott made you crawl around the cafeteria if you wanted your lunch, and you did it because you knew you couldn't afford to buy anything else. What did *I* do? I stood there, and I watched."

I'm exhausted, and the emotions are pouring out of me without a filter. "I didn't care about any of it as long as you were by my side."

"*I cared*," he hisses. "How many times could I just *watch* you take on the humiliation that came with being my girlfriend? Elliot might have been the catalyst, but I made my choice. I wanted to be stronger, to be violent, to be feared. I *wanted it*, Jade. To protect you from them. That came with being part of the Kings, and to be part of the Kings, I had to let you go."

"You said breaking up with me wasn't your choice."

"Because I still blamed Elliot for it. But I'm done hiding behind his actions. Yeah, he's a fucking manipulator—"

"Hey," Elliot jumps in.

Ethan gives him a pointed look before both his hands grab my shoulders so I focus on him. "But it was my decision, and I fucking regret it, believe me. So no, I haven't slept with anyone else—"

"But Caden," I cut him off.

He presses his lips together, clearly pissed that we keep cutting him off.

"But Caden," he agrees. "Once."

"Oh. It looked like you guys were dating for a little bit."

"We had sex once," he repeats. "And—"

"He just wasn't that good, was he?" I tease.

"Will you just let me fucking talk?" he seethes. "I'm trying to apologize here."

I cock an eyebrow at him. "I believe apologies of that grandeur should be made on your knees."

His mouth drops open just as Elliot's burst of laughter escapes him. His hands are still on my tits, both of them fitting in his palms perfectly.

"Do you want to die, Mi Cielo?"

I shrug. "Do you want me to accept your apology? I'm not in a rush, are you?"

He looks away, a puff of air leaving his lungs. "Unbelievable."

But as he says that, he drops to one knee in the bath, and then the other.

His hands wrap around my thighs, his head by my stomach. "I'm sorry, Jade. My actions made it seem like I wasn't in love with you anymore, or that I was capable of forgetting about you. I'm sorry that's what they portrayed, and I'm sorry I broke up with you so Elliot would get me into the Kings' crew. Since I met you, I have not spent a day not loving you. Please, forgive me."

Looking up at me makes his black eyes look bigger and looking down at him makes my heart jump crazily in my chest. I'm awake now. Awake and ready to let the past go.

"I forgive you, Ethan," I say as I slide my hand in his hair. "I love you too."

He smiles, pressing his cheek against my stomach. "I'm never letting you go again. I promise you."

I nod, but our moment is cut short by Elliot's bitter laugh and his grip on my body tightening. "She got you on your fucking knees, brother. It's a good look on you." His voice is strained, like there's something he's dying to fight about, but he's keeping to himself.

My back stiffens, remembering that half of my heartbreaks come from Elliot and all the plans he put in place to have me.

"You think this is funny?" I twist my head back to see him. "You're the one who led him down that road. You planned my entire life without me having a say in it because you were obsessed and didn't have the courage to let me know."

He narrows his gaze at me. "If you expect an apology, don't hold your breath."

My nails scrape against Ethan's scalp, and he nuzzles closer to me.

"Let go of me, Elliot." There's a surge of power inside me, and it's too big for me to control.

Elliot lets go of me, and I shift to see him properly. "You manipulated him into breaking up with me. You manipulated me into giving you what you wanted in the guise of protection against people you rallied against me yourself. You know you do the things you do because you can't stand even the slightest chance of me rejecting you. Own it. Get on your knees and apologize for breaking me apart so you could build me back together the way you wanted it."

"All I hear is that my plans worked, and you fell for me. You may call me a genius."

"Is it worth me falling for you if a part of me forever loathes you for what you did? It doesn't have to be that way."

He opens his mouth, but nothing comes out. He waits, and waits, staring at me, waiting for me to break. I won't.

"I did what I did because I'm in love with you," he says in his sweetly manipulative tone. "I can't apologize for that."

"You can apologize for your actions. For humiliating me at that party. In front of our entire crew."

He licks his lips, smiles, and to my surprise...drops to his knees. But it doesn't feel the same as Ethan. It's not because he's taller and his head reaches my boobs despite kneeling at my feet. It's because of his eyes shining with mischief, and the tip of his smile taunting me.

Elliot might be kneeling for me, but he is in complete control, and he knows it. He is doing it because he wants to, because it'll get him something he wants, not because I told him to.

"I am sorry for loving you so hard I couldn't stay away. I'm sorry that I would do anything wrong or right to have you." His smirk falls, a flash of honestly crossing his gaze. "I'm sorry my love is selfish and destructive, but it's real. You can hardly blame a man for his obsession when his obsession is you."

My mouth parts when his hand wraps around my right upper thigh, his fingers so close to my core. On my left, Ethan is still holding my leg with two hands.

I thread my fingers in both of their hair. "I forgive you," I murmur. "If you forgive me for loving you both."

The silence stretches for an eternity. The love is light, but it's stuck in a heavy web of tension.

Elliot's eyes keep going from mine to my pussy. "I only ever imagined a reality where I would have you to myself no matter what, Jade. It's going to take a while to adapt, but if that's the only way, then I'll do it."

Ethan's grip heightens.

"She was mine," he says softly, an undertone of anger lowering his voice. "She was mine from the beginning and you knew it. She was *my* friend. My age in *my* class. She sat next to *me*, and she would come to our house to hang out with *me*. She liked the music I showed her and held my hand. She became *my* girlfriend, Elliot. *Mine.*" A gasp escapes me when he holds me even harder. "We loved each other. You had everything you wanted. The physique, the brains, the acceptable social behavior. You had the girls, the friends, the Kings. I had *nothing*. Nothing but her." He looks up at me, his voice now a rasp. "And you stole her from me."

"Ethan..." *I'm sorry* is on the tip of my tongue, but I can't say it. I can't because all the events that led us here happened because...well, because I wasn't his.

If I was, Elliot would have never been able to steal me away from him.

"I'll do it." My heart drops to my stomach when he says that. "Not because I forgive him, and not because I love him. I'll do it because I would do *anything* to get you back. No one can control their heart, or I would have stopped loving you a long time ago."

I look at both of them, one after the other. "You guys had already agreed to it, didn't you? Or you wouldn't have done what you did in the kitchen last night."

They both nod. "We talked about it after I got shot," Elliot explains. "When you told me about Sawyer and I didn't believe you. When you asked for *him,* even though you were meant to be with me."

"I wanted to kill him for hurting you," Ethan admits. "Then he proposed a new plan, and I wanted to give it a try. You want us both, Jade. We can't change that."

"So no matter how much we will make you scream that you're ours..." Elliot smiles up at me, the knowledge that it will happen *many* times etched on his face. "We're yours too, my love. At your feet, ready to be owned by you forever."

I take a shaking breath.

"You've got our hearts, Jade. Fucking take care of them," Ethan concludes, just as Elliot brings his hand higher.

He spreads my pussy lips, his eyes shining with a new fervor, and before I can react, his tongue is licking my clit. Ethan grabs my leg, hoisting it over his shoulder, and I almost faint when he presses his face against me too.

For a few seconds, I'm pulling at both their hair, keeping them tightly against my pussy. Both their tongues are on me, one on my clit, one at my entrance.

I almost lose my balance, letting go of Ethan to slam my hand against the shower wall.

I wonder what it feels like for them. I know they're not attracted to each other, yet I feel their tongues connecting to bring me more pleasure than imaginable.

People can say what they want about me.

That I'm a traitor. That I stole from the Kings. I'm a heartless bitch, angry and out of control.

They can say anything, but they don't know me the way these two men do.

And despite that...they love me.

It doesn't take me long to explode against their tongues, my knees buckling. But I hold myself up. I keep my head high.

Ethan Torres and Elliot Pearson are kneeling before me and no one else, ready to love me for who I am.

That kind of power is dizzying. Overwhelming. *Addictive.*

34

ELLIOT

Use Me - Emerald Royce

Jade gasps when the covers are pulled off us, and the cold of the house shocks me awake.

"What the fuck?" I groan, immediately standing up and grabbing a pillow when I realize I'm naked.

Ethan jumps out of bed, a gun already in his hand.

The curtains are pulled open, and Kay turns back to face us again.

"What. The. Actual. Fuck." Considering she's usually someone who manages to keep her calm, the hiss that just escaped her like a pressure cooker about to explode tells me she is not happy about finding us all in the same bed, hugging naked, with Jade between my brother and me.

Ethan lets out a sigh, lowering his weapon. "How did you get in?" He's standing on the left side of his bed, wearing nothing but boxers.

"I own this town, Ethan. I get inside any fucking house I want."

"You better not have broken a window," I huff, holding the pillow to my crotch.

Jade sits right in the middle of the bed, covering herself with the first shirt she found.

"Put some fucking clothes on. I'll be in the living room."

We eye each other the second she leaves Ethan's bedroom.

I grab the clothes I'd discarded on the floor yesterday. "I talk, you two shut up. Daddy will handle this shit."

"Stop calling yourself Daddy," Ethan huffs. "It's weird."

I turn to Jade, waiting for her opinion. "It's weird," she confirms.

"Daddy doesn't care." I smile at both of them, and a laugh bursts out of Jade.

Kay paces in the living room, biting the nail of her thumb, by the time the three of us show up. I sit on the sofa with Jade on my left, and unsurprisingly, Ethan decides to sit on Jade's left rather than his usual seat. The guy would rather die than leave me to sit alone with her.

Kay's jaw works from side to side as she observes us. "Seriously?" She pinches the bridge of her nose with her thumb and forefinger. "The two of them?"

I have to adjust myself in my boxers when Jade bites her lower lip, probably to stop herself from retorting with anything that could make the situation worse.

"How can we help?" My voice still sounds sleepy, and I scratch my eyes. We're not exactly used to waking up early, and judging by the sunrise out the window, it must barely be eight a.m.

"Oh." Her voice trembles with anger. "There is plenty you should already be doing to help. And that you're not."

Right. I guess she's pissed about me not showing up yesterday.

I run a hand through my unruly blond hair, graze my front teeth with my tongue, and smile brightly at Kay. "I'll find another way."

"No." Kay's nostrils flare up as she inhales. "Elliot, you *fucked me over*. I swear to God, if you don't fix this, I will cut off your balls and watch you choke on them."

"I didn't fuck you over," I answer lazily, lying back on the sofa. "I put the plan on hold while I look for another one."

Some of the things Kay and I had planned for the robbery don't work for me anymore, and I need a bit of time to come up with something new. My brain has been focused on Jade non-stop, on my brother and I deciding to share her. It's a big step for us, and I haven't been giving work the attention Kay's used to.

"The plan *you* helped me put together in the first place."

My hand comes to rest on Jade's naked leg, since all she put on was her underwear and Ethan's shirt, and my fingers tickle the soft skin of her inner thigh. It grounds me to touch her. Everything is fine as long as she's within reach. "It's all gonna work out."

Kay's eyes narrow on my hand. "Right," she scoffs. "Of course."

She moves like a panther. In a split second, she's got a hold of Jade's hair, dragging her off the sofa and to the floor. Three steps back, and she's pressing a gun against her head.

My stomach drops. Ethan and I are up right away. My brother steps forward, but Kay clucks her tongue. "I don't think so."

Jade closes her eyes, taking a deep breath. The pull at her hair looks unbearable, or at least that's how it feels to me, and my eyes can't look away from the barrel of the gun against her temple. But she stays calm, quiet.

"You had one job, Elliot."

She pulls harder, getting a whimper out of Jade. I can see on her face that she hates that. That she thinks it shows weakness. I know grown men who would have already pissed themselves being held at gunpoint.

"You had to go on a fucking date with a *fucking* banker. We all have a role in this robbery, and you've been failing at yours miserably. So what do I do, huh? When my right-hand man becomes fucking useless."

I hope she doesn't recognize my signs of panic. My index finger tapping repeatedly against the side of my thigh, my jaw tightening, bulging just below my ears.

"I expected this one"—her gaze goes to Ethan—"to fall back for her like a desperate puppy, but I thought you were smarter than that. That you knew business comes before everything."

"Business *does* come before everything," I say calmly.

"Ah, great," she mocks me. "Then tell me you didn't stand up that banker because you were scared Jade was going to find out and think you're seeing someone behind her back. You didn't show up to the fucking date, Elliot!"

Confusion etches on Jade's face. Her eyes wildly roam around the room, settling on me and begging for information. "What date?"

"Is my van ready, Jade?" Kay presses the gun harder against her head.

She swallows thickly. "No."

"Then shut the fuck up."

I look at the woman I love, steeling myself for her reaction. I want to answer her question.

"Part of the plan for the robbery was for me to seduce

the bank manager who will be present on the day. She's the one with the keys to the safe."

A crease forms between her eyebrows. She's upset, just keeping it to herself.

"On the day, I'm meant to convince her to have sex in the safe. Doing something forbidden as a sexy game."

Her chin trembles. She's probably biting her tongue to reel back her jealousy right now. It's so clear on her face.

"I started seducing her," I admit. "I went to the bar where she hangs out every Thursday with her girlfriends and I hit on her. I asked her on a date. But I didn't show up." My eyes dart to Kay and back to Jade. "I couldn't do it... because I finally have you, and I don't want to fuck it up."

"It's just a *fucking plan!*" Kay snaps. "No one is asking you to marry her."

"Plan or not, I'll only do it if Jade is okay with it. Now will you put your gun away so we can talk?" I huff. "That shit is so unnecessary." It takes a patience I'd never thought I'd have to gather to not jump Kay right now.

And I'm not even doing it because she's my boss or because I respect her. I'm not even doing it because I love her like a sister.

I'm staying calm because I don't want her to hurt Jade. Plain and simple.

"Is it? Or do you only act when you risk losing her?"

"Put the gun away, Kayla." My cold voice makes the February freezing temperatures feel warm.

"Your girl has been relaying information to NSC, did you know that?"

"What?" Jade's panicked gaze goes to me. "I didn't. Elliot, I promise I don't know what she's talking about."

I see it now. I don't know how I never noticed it before. I'm not sure when it started, but since I made the mistake of doubting that Sawyer blackmailed her, I noticed the way she panics when accused of something, or when she has to justify herself.

Jade's biggest fear is not being believed. And God knows how long we've all spent calling her a liar.

Kay clocks the hammer, making Jade gasp. "Lie one more time and your two lovers will be cleaning your brains off the floor."

"I didn—" She stops herself, too scared, but her pleading eyes don't leave me.

One more threat...just *one. More.*

"Kayla." My tone has less life in it than death. The threat makes my boss look right into my eyes, checking how serious I am. "Put the gun away."

Ethan shakes his head at me, warning me not to do anything stupid. A mix of the fear we all have of Kay and the fact that he's worried about Jade too. Ethan would rather let this go so he can sort things out later. My brother has always been one who can stay leveled and take things silently. He didn't have a choice when he was too weak to defend himself, so he learned to endure. But it doesn't mean he isn't dangerous. If I'm an earthquake, he's the deadly aftershock that comes when no one expects it. You think you got him, and that same night, he comes to slit your throat.

I've always been an observant man. Gauging human reactions saved me from my dad's volatile moods more than once. Later in life, it helped me manipulate the people around me. I'm not about to stop myself now. I see the small shift of Kay's feet, the slightest movement of the gun. Kayla King doesn't react well to threats, but she's hesitating, and I cling onto that.

"You don't only have a problem with me, or you

wouldn't be this angry. Put the gun away and let's talk. I'm here to listen. To help you. It's not just my job, Kay. We're family."

And just like that, I got her.

She pushes Jade violently, the movement making her slam against the floor. But the gun is off her, and Kay puts it at the back of her jeans.

"Alright," she chuckles. "You want to talk?"

Ethan helps Jade up and sits her on his lap.

"What's happening?" I ask seriously as I sit back down.

"Emma Scott is threatening me. That's what's happening. And I'm pretty sure it's because of this traitor. And this fucking bank robbery isn't happening any time soon with the pace at which you work."

"Emma is the head of NSC. Her very existence is a threat to you." My deadpan tone doesn't seem to help the situation.

"Emma isn't a threat if she has nothing on me." Her eyes narrow on Jade. "But *someone* told her that Jade was with Stan, and that Stan is a Bratva Wolf. A pretty important one. And now she's threatening us to tell them that we're the ones who have Jade if I don't accept to set up a fight in the Death Cage."

My back stiffens, and my head snaps to the side. Ethan is frozen on the spot, his hands on Jade's hips.

She looks at me, doing her best to hide her panic and failing miserably. "I thought you knew," she whispers.

Oh. The little...

"I didn't snitch to Emma!" Darkness envelops her pupils, that rage inside her showing. "I didn't do shit. I don't know how she knows—"

"Stan is a Wolf?" I don't think she likes the undertones

of violence pouring out of my mouth, the warning that she's about to pay for hiding that from us.

"Whoa. Hold on." For the second time today, Kay pinches the bridge of her nose.

I'm sure that's how she reacts when her kids do something stupid. She talks slowly, like she can't believe what she's hearing.

"You two fuckers found Jade. Convinced me to let you go get her. Went all the way to New York. Brought her back to the North Shore against her will...and at *no* point did you check who the fucker was who paid her to be a stay-at-home whore?"

Jade's angry eyes go to Kay. "Fuck you," she hisses.

"If you knew, why didn't you tell us?" Ethan jumps in. "Of course, we didn't fucking know."

"Because I thought two of my most important men had enough brain cells to rub together between them," she snaps. "I only learned about it once you came back. I thought you'd done your fucking homework. I have other shit to worry about than looking after you two. You're meant to be useful, not bring more trouble to me. Now your girlfriend is using the only thing she has on us to threaten us."

"I'm not!" Jade stands up, not scared of anything now that she's angry.

This is how she's going to die one day. I'll be looking away for one minute and she'll be getting herself into trouble by shouting at the wrong person.

Exactly like she's doing right now.

"Jade." Ethan tries to grab her at the same time as he warns her, but she jerks away from his hold.

"No," she fights back. "Don't even try to tell me to calm down because I didn't do shit!"

There's a stretched silence before Ethan says. "Okay."

"Okay?" Kay hisses.

I nod, supporting my brother. "She says she didn't go to Emma." I shrug. "So she didn't."

Jade's gaze hops from me to Ethan, back and forth with wide, surprised eyes. "You...believe me?"

I nod, and Ethan does too. "If you say you didn't do it, then we believe you," he says softly.

"Oh my God." Kay throws her head back, silently praying for God to give her patience. "You two are so pussy-whipped, I can't even trust you anymore."

"I'm telling the truth," Jade says firmly, seeming to calm down now that we have her back. "I didn't talk to Emma or anyone else. NSC has been seeing me around, so someone from her crew might have told her."

"No one knows you were with Stan, or who Stan is." Kay settles down on Ethan's corner chair, biting her nail again.

"How did you know who he is?" I ask.

"Ivan told me. You guys mentioned him when you came back from New York, and I told him. He said Stanislav is big player in the Wolves. Close to Viktor Volkov. Ivan isn't going to fucking tell Emma, is he?"

"I'm more worried he's the one who's going to tell the Wolves at this point."

She shakes her head. "He wouldn't. He barely talks to them anymore, and he would never do anything to hurt me."

She believes us, and she's thinking hard to try to solve this.

"I told you there were cameras at that house," Jade says to Ethan and me. "He must have seen them."

"I cut those off before we entered the house," I explain. "Xi," I suggest. "He knew where Jade was."

Kay shakes her head, looking out of the window. "He's out."

"No one is ever really out," I snort.

"His girl would cut his balls off."

As I answer her, I grab Jade's hand, pulling her back to the sofa. She sits on my lap this time. "That's a lot of ball cutting you've mentioned today. Not sure I'm liking it."

"Someone's after Jade." Ethan's voice is quiet, like he's still thinking.

Kay rolls her eyes. "Everybody is after Jade. She deserves it too."

"Bitch," my girl murmurs under her breath.

"He means someone is directly threatening her," I elaborate, taking in the scent of apples.

Ethan is already up, grabbing the notes from a little box on the living room shelves. He gives them to Kay. She reads them one by one, and her brows lift to her hairline.

"Shit. Someone is after her, okay," she mumbles.

"They're clearly trying to set her up now. They knew if Emma threatened you, you'd think Jade had snitched." Kay listens to me, staying quiet.

"Any idea who?" she finally asks.

I shrug. "We're slowly narrowing the possibilities."

She looks at me, unimpressed. "And I'm assuming narrowing the possibilities includes killing three people from my crew."

I smile. "I don't know what you're talking about."

"Vickie was my friend, you know." And yet, no expression shows on her face because she's a cold bitch like that.

"Have you found her body?"

"I don't need to find her body, Elliot. I know when three

people disappear so *cleanly,* you've got something to do with it."

I run a hand through my hair and drop my chin on Jade's shoulder, holding her closer to me. "I guess we'll never know, huh?" My left hand comes to play with the heart from the choker.

To my surprise, Jade lets her head fall to the side and on mine. My heart skips a beat, my arm tightening around her.

Oh, boy. I thought having her would finally calm the effect she has on me, but I think her willingly giving herself to me is worse. I'm so in love it scares me.

For a second, Kay lets herself go. Head dropping into her hand, she takes a deep breath. Her vulnerability permeates the air, and I feel bad for her. Ethan and I do whatever we want, our responsibilities rarely affecting others.

Kay has the weight of the Kings on her shoulders. The fate of entire families rests on her. Will people eat? Pay their rent? Be able to live another day? That's what goes on in her mind every day. Money, lives, survival.

She's been doing so well leading this crew since her father and Sawyer died, but she has no one to turn to.

It recharges me to rest my head on Jade right now. It shows me I'm not on my own. Kay has no one to do that. Ivan is as useless as they come, and she feels nothing for him, only using him because he's a Wolf.

When Kay wants to give up, she only has herself to keep her going.

Ethan moves closer to Jade and me. His hand rests on her thigh and she wraps her small fingers around it.

"Kay," I say softly. "We'll sort this out. We're here for you."

She looks up, her face stern, but her words trembling. "Elliot," she sighs. "If Stan learns we're the ones who have Jade, he'll no doubt tell Viktor Volkov. We're talking about the head of the Bratva Wolves here. He's ruthless. Nothing matters to him but business. We'll lose their protection, their money."

Her gaze drops to her hands. "We'll lose *everything*." She looks up, her green eyes full of doubt. "Remember what happened when NSC lost the support of the Cosa Nostra? We jumped in, we fought them in the Death Cage, and won the town back. Look at our fucking situation. If she tells them, we're fucked, and if I give in to her threats, what's to say we'll win the fight?" She throws her head back. "I don't want to lose the North Shore to NSC. I am not going back to a town controlled by the Scotts."

The petty gangs of the North Shore are unbeatable when they're supported by big criminal organizations. When things start falling apart, we send two fighters to the Death Cage. Whoever comes out alive, their crew takes over the town. It's bloody, deadly. It keeps a semblance of order in a town ruled by violence.

NSC used to be backed by the Bianco family from the Cosa Nostra. But then Bianco went to prison, and we jumped on the occasion, kicking NSC while they were down.

We won the last decisive Death Cage fight and took over.

It'll be four years in May. Four years that the Kings rule the North Shore. But NSC is backed by another Cosa Nostra family now. Emma Scott got herself a deal with the Lucianos. Now she's threatening Kay because she knows if we lose the Bratva protection, the imbalance will be such that we'll be forced to agree to a fight in the Death Cage.

We'll always send our best fighter...but so will they. And then only fate can decide our future.

"We're not going to lose the North Shore," I tell her.

"The only way to have enough money to survive without the Wolves is that fucking robbery," she grits out. "I can't force you to go with the plan, Elliot. You're in or you're out. We're talking about ten million in the biggest bank of Silver Falls. If I don't have someone I can trust, if you fuck up with that manager, we're done for. Once we're all in prison, the North Shore will go to NSC all the same."

Guilt pulls at my chest. I feel Jade's breathing stuttering before she can get it under control again.

I run my hand through my hair, hating myself for what I'm about to say, yet knowing there's no other way I could do this. "It's up to Jade."

She freezes, her back straightening. "W-what?"

Kay's gaze goes to Jade. I can see the way she wants to scream at me, but if she wants me on her team, then she needs to give Jade the respect she deserves. No more threatening the woman I love.

For the first time since Jade has been back on the North Shore, the power is in her hands. It's up to her to see what she'll do with it.

"He'll do it," she rasps. I can feel it takes all of her to agree.

She's jealous, possessive, so fucking angry inside...but she says yes anyway.

"Are you sure?" I check.

She nods stiffly, then gets up, walking to Kayla. "I'm only doing it because you used to pay for my mom's treatment, and you paid for her funeral. There must be some sense of family inside you despite what you did to me. I don't like you. I don't respect you. I *hate* you for not protecting me when you should have."

Kay's eyebrows furrow in confusion.

"But why should everyone be punished because you can't hold it together?" Jade sneers. "If Elliot wants to support the plan, it's fine with me. I can kill that banker bitch when we're done."

She doesn't wait for Kay's reaction, storming back to the hallway. I hear a door slam and already know she *isn't* okay with me doing it, but willing to sacrifice that for the Kings.

"What does she mean she hates you for not protecting her?" Ethan asks. There's a certain loathing in his voice. Something that truly makes him tick.

Kay shakes her head, looking confused. "I...don't know."

Ethan leans forward, his elbows on his knees and his fisted hands falling between his spread legs. "You don't know, or you don't want to tell us?"

"What did you do, Kay?" I insist.

"I don't know," she snaps back, getting up. "Maybe I forgot. Maybe it was something meaningless to me. I don't fucking *know*."

Ethan and I eye each other, silently agreeing that we need to find out.

Once Kay's left, I unsurprisingly find Jade sitting on my bed, her knees to her chest, her arms wrapped around her shins, and her head down.

"My love," I say softly as I sit on the side of the bed. I caress the top of her head, but she doesn't look up. "Talk to me."

She shakes her head, and my fist closes around her hair, pulling back. "Jade," I sing-song. "In this family, we talk when there's an issue. If I force Ethan to do it, I can do it to you too."

Her sad eyes twist my heart. "You won't fall for her, right?"

A smile spreads on my lips. She still hasn't said she loves me, but it's so fucking damn obvious.

When I don't reply, she panics. "I know you share me...I know it kills you. But I can't do it. I can't, Elliot. Sharing you isn't an option for me. Not you. Not Ethan. I guess I'm selfish, what can I say? I'm selfish, and I want you to myself. Both of you. I can live with being a selfish bitch, but not with sharing you. So tell me you're not going to fall for her...please."

Unshed tears sparkle in her eyes. "I thought it would kill me to share you with Ethan," I admit. "But it doesn't. What I want in life is *you*. You're my ultimate goal, my love. So, no. I won't fall for her. I won't fuck her unless I'm forced to on the day of the robbery. I'm going to pretend so she takes me to the safe. I'll get it opened for Ethan and Kay, then I'll move to another room with her, but I'll occupy her with something else. And I won't fuck her before the day either."

I let go of her hair, hooking a finger in the heart of her collar.

"You might have to kiss her if you date her."

"Or maybe I'll make her wait. It'll make her want me even more."

"Don't be yourself with her," she murmurs. "Only I get the real you. Me and Ethan."

I nod. "Only you two." I pull at her collar, forcing her closer to me by her neck. "Kiss me, baby. Show me how much you don't want to share me."

Her lips crash onto mine, her hunger for me insatiable. I pull away between strokes of her tongue, murmuring that I love her against her lips.

I say it again, and again.

"I'm in love with you, Jade. You. No one else."

And still, her response doesn't come.

It's okay. I'll be patient. I can do it. I've waited all my life for her. I can wait a little longer to hear her whisper that she loves me.

In the meantime...I guess we're robbing a bank.

35

JADE

Love is Madness - Thirty Seconds to Mars, Halsey

The next few weeks pass in the blink of an eye. Kay has to go see her daughters in West Virginia again, so it's just the brothers and me working on the robbery. The van is the most important thing, and Ethan and Elliot have been helping. They follow everything I tell them to a T, and it's been nice to be the one to give the orders for once. Except at night. Or lunch. Or any other time of the day we're outside the garage.

It takes a lot of energy to date two men who are demanding, like to be in control, both dominating. They don't fight for power anymore, as they quickly realized there was enough energy in me for both to get whatever out of me. And I'm weak. I'm not a weak woman, but fuck, I'm weak and desperate to please those two like it's a fucking save-the-world kind of mission. Only our world, but that works too.

I wouldn't say we've found the perfect balance yet, and I don't know if they'll ever not have those bursts of possessive actions they sometimes do, but we're working on it. Falling in love with two men is not easy. There's a reason it doesn't really happen. It's hard, it hurts sometimes, and I can't help the slight pulls of guilt when I spend time with one more than the other. But it's working and things can only get better.

Every now and then, when one is jealous, they'll take it out on me. Not in a bad way, more in a deliciously wrong way. I like it.

They still haven't held some promises they made. The kind they taunt me with and hold over my head. Like the two of them inside me at the same time.

Ethan has started becoming more demanding, showing me the ways he likes to use me, and I can't stop thinking about it. This morning, he made me kneel on the floor of the kitchen in nothing but my choker and a small skirt while he was having breakfast. He hand-fed me and made me thank him afterward. My eyes couldn't leave the bulge in his jeans the whole time. He teased me with it, but ultimately didn't give me what I craved.

I slam the hood of the van closed, my thighs squeezing. Ethan's degradation is somehow always perfectly balanced with Elliot's praise. I'll never get a *good girl* from Ethan, but Elliot was right there this morning, caressing my hair and telling me how proud he was for listening to his brother. And he fucked me to reward me. He focused on my pleasure, on how much I deserved gratification.

It's a strange balance, yet so perfect.

I walk around the van, taking in the details. I know what it looks like from the inside out, having built in every single add-on to make it faster. There wasn't much I could do about corners, but this thing is going to do exactly what I need in a straight line, which is the main concern anyway. Enough speed will get anyone off our ass.

"Shit," I murmur to myself. "You're done, you little beast." I tap the hood and go to the kitchen.

Every time I cross this doorway, I remember discovering Ethan covered in blood. This time, it's only Elliot cooking some noodles for lunch.

I walk past him, going directly for the sink to wash my hands, but his long fingers wrap around my upper arm.

"My love," he drawls, dropping the wooden spoon he's holding into the pan. "Don't ever walk past me without giving me a kiss."

I giggle like a teenage girl on a date with her crush and push onto my toes to kiss his cheek. He hasn't shaved in a few days, a blond stubble covering the lower half of his face.

"Scratchy," I tease as I walk to the sink. He comes behind me, hugging my waist and dropping his head on top of mine.

"Wanna shave me?"

"You'd trust her with a blade near your face?" Ethan walks in, holding a bottle of water and twisting the cap back on. "A desperate need to die, maybe?"

With a snort, I grab a tea towel to dry my hands. I turn around in Elliot's arms, my back now resting on the counter. "I have good news."

A hand sneaks to my side, grabbing my jaw and pulling my head until Ethan can drop a kiss on my lips.

"I'm listening."

"The van is done." I smile brightly at both, feeling giddy. "I want to take it for a ride. A race, more specifically."

They pause, eyeing each other and doing that thing where they communicate silently.

"Hello. I'm right here. Care to share your thoughts?"

Ethan nods subtly, and Elliot takes a step back, running his hand through his hair. "Well, the last time Ethan went to one of your races, someone died. It was ugly as fuck too."

"He said some really rude things to her. What was I meant to do?" The way he says this sounds like a child justifying giving the dog candy because it looked like it wanted some.

"Not kill him?" I suggest, right at the same time as Elliot says, "Clean up your own mess?"

Right, it seems we have different ways of dealing with things.

"I have to test that van in a straight line, and there's nothing like a drag race for that."

"We'll have to bet some money so we don't have to give it away if we lose," Elliot says.

I look up, narrowing my eyes at him as I cross my arms over my chest. "I do not *lose* races, Elliot. That word isn't even in my fucking vocabulary so take it back before I cut your fucking tongue."

Ethan whistles. "Damn, our girl is feeling feisty today."

Elliot chuckles, grazing my cheek with his knuckles. "Yeah. I think the effects of her humbling session with you this morning didn't last into the afternoon."

My heart drops to my stomach, my thighs tightening out of my control. I drop my arms to my sides as my feet shift, but I can't step back since the counter is behind me.

Elliot laughs when he notices my reaction. "Still feeling like snapping at me?"

"I just..." I wet my lips, unsure how to justify my sudden spurt of violence. "I just don't lose races, and it annoys me that you think I would."

"Fair." He nods. "There are ways to communicate that

without threatening to cut off my tongue, though. Aren't there? Like keeping your cool and saying how you feel."

"Right." I take a deep breath. "Sorry?"

"Sorry," he snorts. "Yeah, you'll fucking be sorry, my love. So do you want to eat your second meal of the day at Ethan's feet, or should I take you over my knee? Ethan, what's your favorite food to feed her?"

He shrugs casually. "Don't have any."

My eyes dart to Ethan, smirking at me like a demon about to make a worshiper sin. "I just wanted to race..."

"And you will," Elliot agrees. "Just choose your punishment first. Although being fed noodles while kneeling on the floor is messy."

"You'd have to beg me really hard for me to agree to that." Ethan moves closer, both of them cornering me tightly against the sink. "I don't really want to hand feed you right now, so you'd have to beg with all you have."

"And I know you love being spanked," Elliot comes back harder. "So I'd have to add a little something. Like teasing your pretty cunt until you're desperate and then leaving you hanging."

I struggle to take my next breath. "You guys aren't being fair," I whisper, unable to push a clear sound through the lust and fear invading me.

This is all too exciting and yet terrifying at the same time.

Elliot tuts. "Punishments aren't meant to be fair, my love. So, choose."

"I can't choose. It—it's ridiculous."

"Consider choosing your penance part of it."

They both stare at me with fire in their eyes. It burns so bright, I can feel the heat spreading on my skin.

"Tick tock, Mi Cielo. You wouldn't want to have to do both."

"You have about three seconds left," Elliot taunts. "Three."

"Wait—"

"Two."

"I'm thinking," I panic.

"One..."

My heart stops, the words spilling out as a desperate gasp. "The spanking!"

They smile at me, but it's Elliot who wraps his hand around my jaw. "Great choice. Now beg for it."

"Come on." I squirm under his touch. "You said—"

"Take your punishment like a good girl and beg for it, Jade." The threat in his voice doesn't help with the wetness dampening my underwear.

"Please," I murmur. "Spank me."

"I can't quite hear you."

I narrow my eyes at him, but it has little effect when I give him what he wants anyway. "Please, put me over your knee and spank me," I say louder.

"That would be my pleasure, baby. Pull out a chair for me."

Ethan sits across the table as I pull a chair for Elliot. He takes his time turning off the stove. Then he undoes his belt and turns to me.

"Put your hands behind your back." He slowly slides it out of the hoops of his jeans, each inch forcing my eyes to grow wider.

Putting my hands behind my back, I turn away from him. He takes his time looping the leather around my wrists, making sure I can't get out of it easily.

I squeeze my eyes shut when he kneels before me and

undoes my jeans all the way to my ankles, then my underwear to my knees. That way, he knows I'll struggle to move my legs.

"Oh, baby." His condescending tone does nothing to help. "So wet for me already."

"She loves her punishments way too much," Ethan says. His tone tells me he loves them too. "She's becoming a sucker for them."

"Better make sure she never forgets this one, then." He's speaking to his brother, but his eyes are on my pussy.

He stands up, sitting on the chair, and maneuvers me until I'm over his lap, my face hanging on the side and my toes barely touching the floor.

"Mm," he hums, massaging my cheeks. In the process, he grazes my entrance with the tips of his fingers. "What a wet little slut. She'll be dripping in no time, and then crying shortly after when I don't give her what she craves."

My stuttered breath is loud when I inhale, but I don't say anything.

"What should we do, brother? Five for snapping at me, five for taking so long to choose her punishment?"

I bite my lower lip not to whimper. Elliot's spanking is not a walk in the park. His palms cover most of my flesh, and he always makes sure to use enough strength to mark me.

"Sounds about right," Ethan agrees. I turn my head to the side, looking under the table just as he spreads his legs and palms his dick through his jeans. They're ripped black jeans today, and he's wearing a red plaid shirt tied around his hips.

"You'll count, my love. And don't forget to thank the both of us after each one."

The blood is already rushing to my head, and I know this is going to feel surreal. It always does.

I gasp on the first one. I didn't expect it so quickly. My eyes stay on Ethan's crotch under the table.

"One," I say in a fairly casual tone. "Thank you, Elliot. Thank you, Ethan."

The bulge under my stomach is instantaneous. Elliot is already turned on hearing his name from my lips.

The next one feels the same, even better since I'm prepared. "Two. Thank you, Elliot, and thank you, Ethan."

It's the third one that makes me cry out. It's harsher, because he clearly wasn't getting what he wanted out of me. Thanking them is harder this time.

The fourth and fifth bring tears to my eyes, and my ears start ringing when I see Ethan unzip his jeans and take out his cock. I lick my lips, feeling spit gather from being upside down.

It's not from seeing my boyfriend's beautiful pierced cock. I promise. Kind of.

From the seventh, I lose myself. The pain doesn't register anymore, as I feel lightheaded, and reality starts to leave my mind.

My cheeks are burning, my pussy wet.

It feels good. Too good not to try to meet his hand on the eighth one.

"That's it." Elliot's voice resonates in my head, but I can only respond with a moan. Spit is falling from my parted lips, and as I pant, it drips to the floor, making everything worse and yet better.

These men turn me into anything they want, and in exchange, they accept anything I already am. There is no match more perfect than ours. Nothing more powerful in this world than the unconditional love they give me in exchange for my sanity, my body, and my heart.

He slaps my pussy on the ninth one, making me groan with pleasure.

"I can't hear you thanking us."

My eyes are stuck on Ethan's hand fisting his cock. I want it in my mouth. I want him to face fuck me while Elliot fucks my pussy and makes me come.

"Nine," I moan. "Thank you, Elliot. Thank you, Ethan."

"Should I slap your little clit for the last one, my love?" There's a laugh coming from somewhere, but I'm not sure who it is. "You're dripping." He drags his finger down my inner thigh. "Feel that? That's me tracing your wetness." He pinches where it stops, and I squeeze my eyes shut at how low it is down my thigh.

"Please," I pant. "Slap my clit. I need to come."

"I'm sure you do." Tapping all the way from my ass to my slit, he spreads my pussy lips open with his other hand.

I scream when he slaps my clit. I use the occasion to grind against his hand, desperate for more.

But he pulls it away, tutting me. "Absolutely fucking not. If you think you're coming from this punishment, think again. You are going to feel your wetness all day long, sit on your sore ass, and beg us to make you come until we decide you've waited long enough. Is that fucking clear?"

"Yes," I whimper.

"And why is that?"

"Because I got angry...I—I snapped at you instead of communicating how I felt calmly."

"At least you're capable of learning. Now beg for me to make you come."

"Please," I squeak. "I learned my lesson. Please, Elliot, let me come."

He laughs, tapping my ass softly. "There will be a lot more of that today before you get what you want, baby."

"Ethan," I plead. "Please... I need it." When he ignores me, accelerating his thrusts into his palm, I try with all I have. "Master." I writhe on Elliot's lap, more desperate than ever.

None of this feels real. My head is heavy from the blood rush, my ass stinging. My own voice resonates around my head like a bouncing ball that got loose. I'm fucking flying, high as a kite. And all I need is to come.

"I'll do anything," I whine. "Please, Master. I'll do anything for you to make me come."

"Fuck," Ethan grunts. I got to him. Fuck, fuck. He's going to make me come, I know it. And then they can argue over their failed punishment. "Bring her here. Right now."

Elliot doesn't hesitate. He carefully lifts me off his lap and makes me kneel in front of his brother.

Ethan gets up, holding himself on the table not to lose balance.

"Open your mouth, toy."

God, I shouldn't love it so much when he treats me like a fucking inanimate object. And yet here I am, opening my mouth wide for him. Showing him my tongue and silently begging for him to fill my mouth with his cum.

"Fuck," he moans as ribbons of his warm cum cover my face. A lot of it lands on my tongue as he aims for it. "Stay like this," he rasps when he's finished.

He takes his time pulling his jeans back up, taking his phone out of his pocket.

The telltale sound of video recording doesn't even bring me back down from my high. It doesn't taper my need to come in the slightest.

"Tell your master what you want," he says.

With a tongue covered in his cum, I ask for him to make me come. I beg, writhing on my knees.

"Please, Master. Let me come."

He tuts me when I lower my wet cunt on my heel.

"No, no," he taunts. "Sit up."

I reluctantly follow his order.

"Swallow my cum, baby."

I do it. And since there's more on my face, he drags his fingers across it and into my mouth. I lick him, taking more of him than I should, pushing his fingers down my throat. He keeps going until he's satisfied and turns off the camera.

"What should I do with you now?" He smiles, knowing exactly what I need the most.

"Touch me," I whisper, my desperation at its height. "Just touch me and make me come, please."

He steps back, sitting down on the chair again. "Sorry, toy. This is a punishment, remember?"

"No," I whimper. "No, no, no." I turn back to Elliot. "Please."

The blond brother undoes his belt from my wrists. He puts it back on, not even looking at me anymore. "Go wash your face. You need to eat."

"But—"

"Don't you dare wash your pussy, Jade. And no underwear. I want you to feel your wetness all fucking day."

"Please."

"My love." He smiles, but it means nothing good. "I'm being kind enough to stop here. Don't test my patience. You know I have very, *very* little of it."

My head drops, eyes stuck to the floor.

"Go on," he urges me as he helps me up. "Go wash your face."

.   .   .

This is the worst lunch of my life. The embarrassment of knowing I'm leaving a wet spot on the wooden chair keeps my cheeks burning the whole time. I can barely eat, the need to come still too hot inside me. The brothers keep their eyes on me the whole time. While they talk and debate what day we should race.

It's Elliot's birthday tomorrow, and he said he didn't want a party. That he's done with that shit and just wants to watch me race with our new baby. I agree silently, and the moment he sees me shift on the chair, he slaps my thigh.

I hiss, turning to him. "I didn't—"

"Don't even fucking try to lie. You're such a little slut you can't help but attempt to grind your pussy on a chair? Behave yourself."

"She's like a badly behaved little pet," Ethan taunts, his dark eyes on me. "Can't control her urges."

My eyes narrow. The pet allusions multiply every day, and the lust in his gaze when he talks about them is making me hot. Hotter than I would have thought. I would have never imagined in a million years getting bothered by someone talking about making me their pet, but when it comes out of Ethan's mouth. Fuck. Love makes you stupid, truly.

"I want to take you somewhere this afternoon," Ethan says. "There's a shop on the South Bank. I want to get you some stuff from there."

Elliot's phone vibrates on the table, and I catch the name on the text before he can put it away.

Natasha.

The banker.

"Are you for fucking real?" I snap. "I'm right here!"

Elliot takes his time putting his phone in his pocket,

then turns to me. "Let's try that again. It would be a shame to punish you again so soon."

I tighten my jaw, trying to control myself and not absolutely lose my shit. Lesson well learned; I decide to talk calmly.

"I hate her," I seethe. Nope, not calm.

Ethan snorts. "That's her holding herself back, you know?"

"I know." But Elliot doesn't seem to find it funny. "Jade." He licks his lips, clearly thinking of what to say next so I don't blow up the place. "She wanted to see me today, and I said I couldn't. That's because I want to spend the day with you. I want to go to that shop Ethan's been talking about for days. You're going to try some stuff on for us there."

"I'm not trying shit for you two. Have you kissed her yet?"

His eyes flutter closed as he clearly tries to keep his cool. "No. I haven't."

"But you told her how pretty she is, I'm sure. *Natasha*. I bet she has great tits."

Ethan laughs this time, loving that I'm fucking miserable.

"Enough, Jade." Elliot's patience is getting very thin.

But no. Not enough. The jealousy inside me gnarls at my rational side, and I snap. Again.

"If she touches you, I swear she's fucking dead. I'll go to that little bar, where she hangs out with her friends every Thursday, and I'll put a fucking bullet between her eyes." I press my thumb between Elliot's eyebrows. "Right there."

Ethan throws his head back, enjoying the show way too much.

But Elliot is up in a split second, wrapping his huge hand around my jaw and forcing my head up.

"Do you think this is easy for me?" he hisses. "You agreed, Jade. You agreed to the plan and now I have to follow through with it or none of us is getting any fucking money. Our power over this town is hanging on by a thread. You said yes. You knew it would hurt. But if you think it hurts you more than it does me, oh, baby, you're so fucking wrong. If you have feelings to communicate, you share them with a soft tone and controlled words. Or you're going to get the punishment of your fucking life. I've been holding back Ethan on the things he wants to do to you. I've been taking things one at a time. That's all for you. I don't have to do that. How about I stick my cock in your ass without prep and we see how you behave. You want that, baby?"

I shake my head, or as much as I can. "N-no."

"Good. Your job was to fix up the van. Mine is to get that bitch to open the safe for us. Trust me when I say I will delay any fucking touching as much as I can, but if it comes down to it, I need you to promise you won't kill her."

"You two killed out of jealousy for me."

"No. I killed people who hurt you."

Ethan stays silent until Elliot gives him a pointed look. He shrugs. "I'm a jealous person," the dark-haired brother says lazily. "So what?"

Elliot rolls his eyes and looks back at me. "Promise you won't kill her."

And here comes my brat side they both have come to live with. "I promise I won't kill her," I mimic his words in a way higher voice. He waits, knowing something else is coming. "Before she opens that safe."

"Fucking hell." He lets me go, wiping his hand over his mouth, probably to hide the smile that's spreading on his lips. "You're incorrigible. Go put some clothes on, we're taking you shopping."

. . .

I grab the sides of the two front seats, bringing myself forward in the middle to talk to the guys. "Can we go thrift shopping too? There's an amazing shop on the South Bank. All the rich people donate their stuff there, and we can get them for super cheap."

"Our little queen of finding gems," Ethan says.

"What shop is that?" Elliot asks, looking up from his phone. I know he's texting Kay, but I get weird now when he's messaging. "I'll put it in the GPS."

"No need," Ethan says casually as he drives across the bridge separating the North Shore from the South Bank. "I know where it is. Used to take her all the time."

Elliot stiffens, looking at his brother in a way that makes me wonder if he's about to grab the wheel and throw us into the river.

"Don't say that," he says in a low voice.

"What? That I took her to a thrift shop?" Ethan doesn't seem to get it. Or maybe he does and he's riling Elliot up on purpose.

"Mentioning your past together. That shit is over now."

"Yeah." Ethan shrugs. "But you can't erase it. I'm just saying I know where her favorite shop is."

"And I know what she looks like with a cock in her ass. Now shut the fuck up."

My stomach twists at Elliot mentioning some of the things we did before I ran away from the North Shore.

"It's not a competition, Elliot. Chill." Ethan doesn't lose his cool, but again, that's Ethan. He can take and take and take. Then when you look away, he...apparently, he cuts people's limbs off and drains them of their blood.

"Then shut—"

"Hey." I slam a hand on Elliot's shoulder. "Hey, enough. You guys are taking all the fun out of the shopping trip."

Ethan parks in front of the huge warehouse, and I look outside with bright eyes.

My mom and I used to spend hours treasure hunting. She made a game out of it when I was a kid. For as long as she could avoid saying we were buying me clothes here because we had no choice, we were treasure hunting like the adventurers she read to me about. But even when I finally understood, I'd insist on coming back to find treasures.

And I always did.

Elliot grabs my hand a little too forcefully when I jump out of the car.

"You seriously need to control your jealousy over him —" I'm cut off by Ethan grabbing my other hand just as tightly.

"For real?" I huff as they start walking toward the entrance and I'm forced to follow. "Can I get one of them back?"

Their simultaneous *no* is one of those things they do that makes butterflies flap their wings in my stomach.

"I feel like a child being dragged somewhere by their parents," I giggle as we walk past the door and into the warehouse holding thousands of donated items. It smells of dust in here, and I kind of love it. Just because it's familiar and reminds me of my mom and I being here.

"Do you often think of us as your two daddies?" Elliot laughs.

"I bet she does. Especially when she's sucking our cocks."

"Ugh, shut up."

A woman not far looks at us with wide eyes. Her gaze

drops to both my hands being held by two different men and she shakes her head.

I attempt to pull out of their holds, but there's not much I can do when I'm gripped by two men twice my size.

"Ma'am." Ethan nods his head, but Elliot isn't done making my life a living nightmare.

"She looks confused. Jade, help her out. Tell her we both fuck you."

The woman gasps, and my own eyes round. "Elliot!" I hiss.

Why am I even trying to keep face in front of a random woman? She's the one judging us, after all.

"What? We do." He laughs and finally lets go of my hand. "Alright, my love. Get anything you want."

Ethan lets me go too, and I'm off like a kid running to their presents on Christmas morning. The warehouse is huge, with mountains of clothes piling up and aisles of shelves from floor to ceiling.

Ethan walks behind me, giving me space but keeping an eye on me. When I stop by a rack holding what looks like fifty black hoodies with different patterns I know the three of us would love, I jump with excitement. I grab one for me. It's black with a white smiley face that has two crosses instead of eyes. I chuckle to myself, knowing it matches the band-aids we have at home.

I pause.

Home?

Is that what I think of the brothers' house now? That messy place where my clothes are scattered between two rooms, where I have no space in the bathroom whatsoever for my cosmetics and everything I use for my skincare routine. Where I get on my knees for two men I love, where

I watch my favorite movies and listen to punk rock and metal bands all day long.

Yeah.

That's home.

Smiling to myself, I grab another hoodie. One black one for Ethan that has a giant white death ripper. In blood red at the top it says, *painted with the blood of my victims.*

I want to laugh at how accurate this is.

I take one last one off the rack for Elliot. A simple black hoodie of the band Slipknot. Their name written in huge white letters.

"I love them too."

I turn around to find a young man, about my age, with bright blond hair and a killer smile.

Shit, that really is a *killer* smile. I find myself grinning back, just because it's that contagious.

He points at his current t-shirt, and I laugh when I see it's a Slipknot logo. "Is there another one of those hoodies in there?"

"There are about a million, so I'm sure you'll find something."

He starts going through them, moving one hanger at a time.

"What's your favorite song from them?"

"Um..." Why is it when someone asks you what your favorite *something* is, it never comes?

"Mine's '*Surfacing.*'"

"Oh yeah," I exclaim. "So good."

He releases a hanger, his hand reaching toward me. "This is cool." It's heading toward my neck, and my eyes widen. Is he about to grab my necklace? Well, not necklace. It's a fucking collar.

The tips of his fingers graze the heart at my neck, when a strong hand grabs his wrist.

"What the—"

"Shh, shh," Elliot cuts him off. "That's a cute little smile you have. Do you know what would be a shame? Me destroying it with the barrel of my gun when I put it in your mouth to blow your brains off."

The guy's face falls, his mouth opening and closing like a fish out of water. Behind Elliot, Ethan is watching the scene with a tight jaw, his arms crossed over his chest.

Oh, this isn't good.

"And '*If Rain is What You Want*' is the best Slipknot song by far. So take your shit tastes and your hands away from my girl before I decide I'm bored with teaching you a lesson and go straight for the kill."

"Elliot," I hiss. "You're fucking insane—"

"I'm busy right now, Jade. I would never hurt you, but I will punish your cute little ass for entertaining him, believe me."

He releases the guy's wrist, and he races toward the exit like his life depends on it. Well, I guess it does.

"You're a maniac, you know that?"

"It's called love, Jade. Look it up."

I roll my eyes, shoving my findings against his chest. "Here. It's for you."

"Sweet. Hey, Ethan, what's your favorite Slipknot song?"

His good mood is back on, but not his brother's. Ethan is staring toward where that man ran, and I don't like it one bit.

"Don't have one."

He steps away, going to another aisle.

"You put him in a mood," Elliot says.

"*You* put *me* in a mood."

He clucks his tongue. "When are you not in a mood?"

I turn my back to him, walking away. "I'm going to shop *on my own,* Elliot."

"I'll see you at the register when you need Daddy to pay for your shopping, my love!"

I flip him off without even turning back.

I quickly lose my two crazy men. As I pile things on my arms, I look behind every single item for a better one hidden behind.

I stop by a gigantic metal-wired basket that could fit three of me in there. It's full of toys and stuffed animals. My mouth falls open when I see a necklace attached to a cat toy made of Legos. It's part of the cat's collar. I drop all my items to the floor, stick the front of my boots through the bottom of the basket, giving myself an extra few inches. I grab the edge of the basket, hoist myself a little higher, and bend at the waist over the metal to grab my perfect finding.

With the cat in my hands, I undo the collar. It has a heart dangling from it, made of two flat pieces of Lego. Each piece is a rectangle with one side curved. Pressed together diagonally, they form the heart. They're attached to the collar by the rounded edges, one hole in each piece.

I feel my eyes sparkle, my heart beating faster. This is so perfect. I let the cat go, keeping the heart in my hands. I undo the two pieces and slot them back together. I'm going to take out the main chain and put a separate one through each hole. That way, they can both wear half of it. And to make it even more perfect, it's a jade color. I couldn't have asked for anything better.

In my haste to add it to my pile of things, it slips from my hands and back into the basket. The small heart finds its way deep in there.

"Come on," I grunt.

I bend over at the waist again, digging through the stuffed bears and other toys. The moment I close my fist around the little collar, my foot slips, and I fall forward into the giant basket.

A short shriek escapes me, my body joining the stuffed toys just as someone grabs my hips. I startle, but don't push away the help as the two hands drag me back up and onto stable ground.

I chuckle awkwardly as I turn around. "Thank you so—" My voice dies in my throat when I realize the proximity in which he stayed.

He's close enough to hold a gun against my stomach without anyone seeing. My head whips from side to side, but no one else is in this aisle.

Looking up, I open my mouth to talk, but he brings a gloved finger to his lips, tapping twice. As my eyes drop to the side of his neck, a tattoo grabs my attention.

My heart drops, and that's when I know.

I still count the number of moons on his tattoo. Seven. The entire cycle of the moon on his neck.

The Bratva Wolves tattoo.

There is no doubt. No doubt my life is over.

Because there is only one motto the discreet Bratva Wolves follow; A wolf's face is the last thing you see.

Their organization works in total anonymity. They're invisible, and if they decide to show you who they are, it's because your minutes are now counted.

Panic grips my chest, its frozen claws shortening my breaths. I want to beg and plead, but that would be stupid now that he told me to stay quiet.

I can safely say this is the most scared I've ever been since the disappearance of Elliot's dad.

Stan might have been rough, but he desired me too much to ever truly hurt me.

Kay wants me dead, but she wants to use me for money more.

Elliot and Ethan love me too much to ever break their favorite toy.

And since Elliot killed Vickie, the threats have stopped.

No. This is it. Someone who truly wants to do me harm and has no reason to keep me alive.

He grabs my arm with a lack of violence I didn't expect. He's calm, knows I'm not about to fight back. He comfortably brings me in front of him, his gun now in the middle of my back, and he presses gently.

I walk, praying with all I have that we don't bump into Ethan and Elliot. The last thing I want right now is for them to see him too and sign their death warrants. If one of us has to go, I'd rather it be me.

"In there," he says with a calm voice when we come to a door with a sign that says *staff only*.

I can see he's already unlocked it. That's probably the way he came in. I push it open, walking into a back room. There's an exit on the other side, and judging by the small rectangular window above it, it leads outside.

I gulp. There's a way out. If he lowers his guard for even a second, I could run. He turns me around with a hand on my shoulder, keeping his gun trained on my stomach. A bullet there doesn't have to be lethal. That's a good thing, right?

"Hello, Jade."

My hands are shaking at my sides. I don't know what to do, where to go. I silently observe him. Dark skin, the beautiful Pacific Islander type, and the shape of his almond eyes tell me he's from islands in Southeast Asia. He's tall compared to me, but nothing next to men like Ethan and Elliot. No one compares to Elliot's height.

His deep brown hair is cut short, but long enough to fall just above his ears and onto his forehead.

"You don't know me," he says in a smooth voice. "My name's Aaron. I work with Stan."

I can't help the snort that leaves me. "With or *for*?"

Oh God, I truly have a death wish. Elliot was right, even facing death in the eyes, I can't stop snapping at the man who holds my life in his hands.

A small smile tips the corner of his lips. "With, but that's of no importance either way."

A noise rattles behind the door that leads to the warehouse. Someone is tapping the code. Aaron's eyes go to the door, and in a split second, the gun is tucked at the back of his jeans.

An elderly woman enters, probably a volunteer helping with the place. She squints her eyes behind huge round glasses.

"Hello, Yvette," Aaron says politely. She frowns, and so do I. How the fuck does he know her name? "Just training the new girl. We'll be on the shop floor in a minute."

My jaw drops open, and Yvette nods. "We need more good kids like you two."

She drops two items in a box labeled *defective* and leaves again.

I don't wait one more second. Not leaving time for Aaron to pull his gun back out, I run for the door leading outside. My arms twist the handle keeping it locked, ready to push with all my weight. Before I can, a body slams into mine, dragging me back, and turning me around.

I whimper when my back hits the door, and Aaron slams his hand on my mouth.

"That wasn't smart." He points his gun at my neck. "Pretty stupid, actually."

I shake my head, attempting to get away from his grip.

A muffled *please* attempts to leave my lips, pressed back down by his palm.

"I'm not here to kill you. So calm down. I have questions. You're going to answer them, and I'll be on my way. With or without you, but that's your choice to make."

My eyes widen from the shock.

He's lying.

But then why am I still alive?

"I'm going to remove my hand, and you're going to sit down in that corner." He points at a secluded corner between two shelves. "If you keep still, I'll put the gun away. Nod if you understand."

I nod, starting to suffocate from his weight on me.

"Good." He lets go of me, taking a step back, and points at the corner with the gun. My eyes stay on him as I move to where he told me and sit down.

It's a smart move. Without having to threaten me directly with a weapon, I'm still in a weak position. I'm cornered, and if I want to run, he'll catch me before I get to stand up. He's much stronger than me, and it's hard to overpower someone when you're on the floor and they're towering over you.

He knows what he's doing. Of course he does, he's a Wolf.

"Stan has been worried about you. He's been looking everywhere for you."

"So he's back from his trip, then."

"He is. And he isn't happy."

"Was it Emma Scott? Who told him?"

Aaron laughs softly. "Emma Scott only gets the information people bigger than her provide."

I look up, confused. "So who told her? And who told Stan?"

"That's none of your business. What you need to know is that he isn't happy that the small, insignificant gang that works for us took the toy he paid a lot of money for."

I narrow my eyes at him. The Kings are small and insignificant to the Bratva, but our lives matter just the same.

"I'm not a toy," I hiss back.

He smirks. "You know exactly what you were to him. You agreed to his terms. And then you left while he was away."

"I got taken."

"Which brings me to my visit. Being taken means it was against your will. I can bring you back to Stan, but I need your consent for that. He doesn't want a kidnapping. He wants the deal you had."

My chest lightens for a second, my heart accelerating. "You mean he'd let me stay?"

"Of course. You can stay, you can come. That's up to you." His pause is heavy with meaning. "Although, I have to say both options come with conditions I think you should be made aware of before you make a decision."

And just like that, the lightness in my chest is crushed down by two heavy weights.

"I'm listening," I rasp.

"If you don't want to come back, Stan will talk to Viktor Volkov" —aka the head of the Wolves—"and tell him to drop the deal with the Kings. Your crew will be on their own out there."

My heart drops.

"You're telling me the entire fate of the Kings' Crew rests on this fucking decision?" I seethe.

He shrugs. "I didn't say it was going to be an easy one to make."

"You're blackmailing me into coming with you!" I fight. "That's not a *decision*."

"Watch your tone with me." With that voice, I almost expect him to add *young lady*.

I take a deep breath, my anger calming down under the threat. "So I have to come, that's what you're telling me."

"If you care about the Kings and their fate on the North Shore, I guess you should come."

A sense of dread overcomes me, and yet I can't get myself to decide. The Kings betrayed me many times in the past, but not everyone who is part of this crew is bad. Some people aren't greedy; they're just trying to survive in our broken town.

"I'm not finished."

I glance back up.

"If you decide to come, Stan assumes it's because you really have been taken against your will. Then the people who did it must pay. I work quickly, Jade. I have no time to waste. Agree to come back with me, and Elliot Pearson and Ethan Torres will be left behind in the parking lot with a bullet in each of their heads."

"What?" I gasp. I'm up in a split second.

"Sit down."

"You fucking sit down," I seethe. "You're not touching them."

"Stan had very specific orders. Come, and he eliminates the threats. Stay, and the deal with the Kings is over."

"Fuck the Kings! I'm not sacrificing Elliot and Ethan for them."

His smile is as condescending as they come. "Taken against your will, huh?"

"Fuck you. Fuck you and Stan. I'm not going back to him. Burn the North Shore to the ground if you must and tell the entire Bratva Wolves to go fuck themselves. I don't care as long as they stay alive."

"If you think losing the Wolves' protection means they stay alive, that's a pretty ridiculous thought. They're important players. They'll be killed the second NSC takes over."

"At least they have a chance." Something that strangely resembles a growl leaves my lips.

"So that's it? Is that what I should tell Stan? There's no going back from this."

"No, that's not it."

He cocks an eyebrow, and I can't help the smirk that spreads on my lips. "Make sure to tell Stan they make me come in ways he never could."

Aaron pinches his lips, clearly holding back a smile. "For your sake, I won't. Goodbye, Jade."

The second I'm back on the shop floor, I sprint to the front of the store. Ethan and Elliot are standing by the doors, pacing. Elliot is on the phone, and I realize mine is vibrating in my pocket. I hate the looks on their faces. The worry, the anxiety.

Tears wet my eyes. They're alive and well. They're going to kill me for what I've just done, but I don't care.

As long as they're alive, I can take anything.

I run to them, the noise of my boots hitting the floor grabbing Elliot's attention first. Without giving him time to react, I jump into his arms, wrapping mine tightly around his waist. I press my cheek to his chest.

"You're okay," I murmur.

One of his hands lands in my hair, caressing the curls. "Where the hell have you been?"

"Jade." Ethan's panicked voice reaches me, and I pull back in the slightest, keeping my left arm around Elliot as I wrap the right around his brother.

"I was so worried."

"You were?" Ethan chuckles. "We've been looking everywhere for you. We thought something happened."

I look up at both of them, and they notice the tears brimming in my eyes. They're going to fall, I know they will, because I can't stop them when I imagine anything happening to them.

"Something did happen," Elliot grits.

"I'm so sorry." My voice is small, reduced by my throat narrowing. "Kayla...she's going to lose her shit."

Elliot steps away, softly untangling himself from my hold. He looks around suspiciously. "Let's go to the truck."

I'm shaking when Ethan wraps his arm around my shoulders. They guide me back to the truck, Elliot sitting next to me in the back, and Ethan in the driver's seat.

"What happened, my love? Talk to us."

Something hurts in my palm, and I realize I'm still holding the Lego heart tightly. My fingers are stiff when I relax my fist. "I forgot to pay for this."

The three of us watch my trembling hand.

Stealing is not something we have a problem with on the North Shore. It's the least terrible thing we do. But not from thrift stores. Not when the money goes to charity.

Ethan opens his door. "I'll be back in a minute."

And he is. He runs to the store and is back quickly.

"Feel better?" he asks. "I threw a twenty on the counter. That shit is surely not worth twenty dollars."

"Now talk," Elliot adds.

"I'm sorry," I rasp again. "The Wolves..."

"The Wolves?" Both of Elliot's hands come to grab my shoulders. "Did you just confront a Wolf?"

I nod awkwardly, not sure what to do.

"Words, Jade," Elliot insists. "Is that a yes?"

"Y-yes. I'm sorry," I repeat. "I'm so sorry."

"You're alive," Ethan observes almost clinically. That's his way of being surprised.

"Stan knows. He knows it was you two."

"Was it Stan?"

I shake my head. "No. He sent someone. His name was Aaron."

The brothers eye each other, but they don't seem to know him. The only Wolf we know is Ivan. He's our only link to the Bratva. The only one we're allowed to see and that's because he's a soldier no one really cares about.

"What did he want?" Ethan asks softly. He's easier to speak to than Elliot right now. The blond brother is too intense.

"He...he wanted...oh God." The reality of what I've just done hits me right in the guts. A punch to the stomach. Kayla is going to kill me. For good this time. "I'm so sorry," I cry. "He said if I'd really been taken against my will from Stan's house, then I could go back, but then...then he'd kill you."

Elliot's jaw tightens, but his grip on me relaxes. "You don't have to go back, my love."

"I don't want to!" I cry out. "I hate him. I fucking...shit." I gasp a breath. "I don't want him, and I want you to die even less. I couldn't...if something happens to you two."

Panic seizes me violently, and out of nowhere, my breath disappears.

"Mi Cielo." Ethan is half in the back seat now. He grabs my face, forcing me to look into his eyes. "Breathe. Nothing is happening to us. We're right here."

"But..." I choke. "If I stay..."

"Take your time," Ethan says. "Just breathe."

"The Wolves. Oh fuck...the Wolves...our deal with them." I squeeze my eyes shut, unable to look at them. "It's over."

The silence stretches for so long, I'm obliged to reopen my eyes. Both of them are looking at me similarly. Brows furrowed, jaws tight, but a shared look of understanding in their eyes. It's mixed with a resignation I only understand because I felt it less than half an hour ago in that room with Aaron.

"You chose to stay," Ethan says quietly.

I nod, incapable of talking through the tears.

"And our deal with the Wolves...it's gone," Elliot clarifies.

And I nod again.

"I am *so* sorry."

Elliot's hand comes to my left cheek, and Ethan's stays on my right. "Sorry for what?" the older brother whispers. "For choosing us? For saving our lives?"

"The deal—"

"Fuck the deal," he snorts. "We've got a bank robbery that's going to get us all the money we need. And even if we didn't, it doesn't matter. Nothing matters as long as we have you by our side. Do you understand, baby? Nothing. Fucking. Matters."

Ethan smiles softly at me. "You chose us."

"I didn't want anything to happen to you. I love you."

"Sounds overprotective as fuck," Ethan chuckles.

"You're one to talk." I look at Elliot. "And you."

"Our girl can't stand us getting hurt." Elliot's smile brings me life.

"Our girl survived a confrontation with a Wolf," Ethan adds, impressed.

"Only because he let me live. I didn't have anything to do with it."

"I bet you still got angry at him. Even a Wolf can't get you to keep that pretty mouth quiet, huh?"

I smile at Elliot, running a hand through his blond hair. "I might have told him to go fuck himself. And his entire organization."

"Fucking hell." Ethan runs a hand through his black hair, the sun glinting on it and giving it a purple hue. "Yeah, our deal is done alright."

"We'll handle Kay," Elliot says softly. "You made the right decision, okay? You don't worry about anything."

I nod, but my heart sinks anyway.

The pressure of the robbery has just gone up a notch. Or ten.

If we fuck this up...there's no saving us from NSC.

36

JADE

Circus Psycho - Diggy Graves

"Wake up, pretty girl."

As I roll onto my back, reality comes back. I yawn, stretching my stiff limbs and slowly opening my heavy eyelids.

Ethan is standing by the side of the bed, a cup of coffee in his hands.

"Is that for me?" I ask, my voice groggy.

When I couldn't sleep last night, too scared of Kay's reaction and the future of the Kings' crew, the brothers worked all my energy out of me.

And yet, they still didn't let me come.

Ethan takes a sip from the mug and smiles at me as he swallows.

"Asshole," I chuckle.

"Get it all out now. I've got a surprise for you today and you won't get to be so bad later."

I sit up, rubbing my eyes and stretching some more. "A surprise? Not one I'll like if I don't get to be bad."

"You can be as bratty as you want if you can bear the consequences." He takes another sip, his black eyes on me.

His hair is wet, water pearling at the tips that reach his mid-forehead and his ears.

"You showered without me? How rude."

"Mi Cielo, I will shower ten times a day if I get to have you naked with me under the water."

I lick my lips, smiling. "Deal."

"I guess you'll need a few showers with the number of times I'm going to come inside your pretty pussy. And on your tits. And your face. And the rest of your body."

"Sounds like you're going to exhaust yourself with all that coming." I drag my body to the side of the bed, letting my feet rest flat on the floor. "Is Elliot here?"

Ethan shakes his head. My heart drops. "A date? What time is it?" It's annoying that Elliot doesn't keep a clock in his room.

"Nah. Kay's back and he went to talk to her. You know, about losing our deal with the Wolves."

"Don't," I groan. "My anxiety has been through the roof since yesterday. I can't imagine Kay's reaction."

"Don't worry," he says softly. "She listens to him."

I finally get up, throwing my arms around Ethan's neck and going on my toes to drop a kiss on his jaw. I trace my lips upward until I'm stretching to my limit and kissing just below his ear, and when I pull away, something catches my eyes.

Blood. In the shell of his ear.

"Your ear is bleeding, babe," I say with concern. "Are you okay?"

He steps away, almost making me fall, and grabs the towel he's just thrown on the bed. Wiping the inside of his ear, he mutters that he's okay.

My eyes narrow into slits as I observe him. "Ethan."

He throws the towel away again, cocking an eyebrow at me. "Yeah?"

"This isn't your blood." I know that with certainty, but I still add, "Is it?"

His silence keeps me going. "You killed."

"Don't worry about that."

"You killed someone and showered before I woke up so I wouldn't notice. Except you missed a fucking spot."

"Jade," he growls. "Drop it."

"Who? Does Elliot know?"

"Yes, Elliot knows. He cleaned up during the night."

"Ethan! Who was it?"

A sudden look of guilt crosses his eyes, but he shrugs. "Does it matter?"

"It matters to me."

"Why? He's dead. It was painful too. People need to think twice before they flirt with you."

My ass falls back on the bed, my mouth dropping. "Oh my God. It's the guy from the thrift store, isn't it?"

"I said I was a jealous man. Why are you so surprised?"

I throw my hands in the air. "Because there's jealous and..." I point at him with both hands. "That!"

He shrugs, crossing his arms again. "I'm not saying sorry."

"Yeah, well, it's too fucking late for sorrys anyway!" I grab my roots, trying to ground myself. Taking a deep breath, I do my best to *talk* through how I feel rather than scream through it. "He didn't do anything wrong."

"He flirted with you." His deadpan voice is going to be the end of me. He's talking about this the same way one would let you know they're off to the grocery store. "He tried to touch you."

I'm speechless. I have zero words to answer him right now.

"Are we done with this conversation?" he asks calmly. His hand comes to caress my cheek before it cups my jaw, and he forces me to look up at him. "Can we be done? I have an exciting day ahead of us."

"You're a complete sociopath."

"I don't think I am."

"No, you are. I'm telling you, you are."

"We can agree to disagree. Now let's feed you breakfast. You're going to need the strength."

On his lap. That's what he didn't mention when he said *let's feed you breakfast.* That it would be on his lap, with his fingers grazing my pussy through the boxers I'm wearing. I don't even know if they're his or Elliot's. It doesn't matter because all I can think about is the way he traces the material around my clit, yet never quite touches it. It doesn't help that he took off his shirt, and I feel his heat searing into my back. My legs are over his thighs, and he spreads a little wider, keeping me open for him.

"Elliot said I could play with you today. The way I've been wanting to."

I gulp the spoon of cereal I have in my mouth. "So you do listen to him?"

He chuckles, nuzzling against the side of my neck. "Only when it comes to playing with you safely. If I had it my way, it would have scared you away. But he thinks you're ready now."

I take in a trembling breath. "Ready for what?"

"For me. Are you finished?"

It's hard to eat. My body is coiled, my pussy thrumming.

They've been edging me for a day and it's getting hard to think clearly. I drop the spoon in the bowl in front of me.

My eyes stay fixated on the cereal swirling in the milk. "What's your favorite breakfast food?"

"Don't have any," he mumbles.

"You always say that. Did you notice you don't have a favorite anything?"

I feel him shrug. "You."

"What do you mean me? I can't be your favorite everything."

"But you are. You're my favorite taste. You're my favorite quote, book, movie, season, holiday. You're my favorite everything, Jade. Every experience in life is dull unless you're there. Then, well, then it becomes my favorite."

"That's a little crazy."

"Call me crazy then."

He wraps a hand around my jaw, pulling sideways until he can see my face. Dabbing a napkin across my mouth, he says, "You're beautiful, you know? So fucking beautiful."

He puts the napkin on the table, smirking. "Now." His fingers graze the boxers again, and my eyes flutter closed. "There's no need to change the subject again. If you're scared, we don't have to do anything."

But his voice is taunting me, because he knows I'm not scared. Not of him or the things he wants to do.

"Maybe we can start with things we know...that we've already done? Maybe if you let me come—"

"The next time you come will be because you listened to me like a good little slut."

The words only make me attempt to squeeze my thighs together. Something I can't do with his legs spreading mine.

"Tell me if you're scared."

I huff out a long breath, attempting to calm my racing heart. "I'm scared," I admit.

His lips leave a soft kiss on my jaw. Then another. "Of?" He speaks against the corner of my mouth.

"Of liking it."

I feel the way his lips spread into a satisfied smile against my skin. "You should be, Mi Cielo. Because you're going to love it."

He cups my pussy firmly, making me gasp. "You're going to love following your master's orders, aren't you?"

My breathing is already shortening, my heart palpitating at the idea of all the things he wants to do to me. "Y-yes."

"Yes, what?"

I swallow thickly. His teeth graze my jaw, and then they come to rest on my neck. He bites, making me cry out. "Yes, Master."

"That's a good slut. Now get on all fours."

He releases me, helping me stand up.

"Undress first."

That comes with an ease I didn't realize I had around him. I'm so comfortable, the t-shirt and boxers drop to the floor before I even notice I'm moving.

And I stand there.

I shift on my feet as he relaxes against the kitchen chair, legs spread and a look of indescribable hunger in his eyes.

He waits patiently for me to be ready. Saying nothing, he doesn't make any move. He just looks at me.

It feels like forever when I finally kneel, but I needed the time to gather my thoughts. To know I'm doing this because I want to.

Not because he has a secret of mine he's dangling over

my head like Sawyer did. Not because he's paying for my mom's treatment like Stan.

Ethan and I are on the same level. It's my choice to surrender the power for the sake of this game.

I press my palms to the floor, looking at my splayed fingers before looking up at him.

He points at the space between his legs, nothing but a snap of his fingers indicating what he wants. I crawl forward, closing the short distance between us, and settle back on my heels in front of him.

His hand caresses my cheek, my hair. Grabbing a thick, curly strand, he pushes it behind my shoulder.

"Here's what's going to happen." He readjusts in the chair, the hard-on looking painful. We haven't even started yet, but the idea of what he wants to do is clearly getting him going.

"You're going to be mine, and mine only until Elliot comes back. I get to do what I want with you, and you know how much I've been dying to have my little pet just for myself."

I do know. I know because he says it all the time. Because he always promises he's going to leash me and walk me around the house on all fours.

I just...didn't realize it would actually happen.

"I-I know."

He smiles softly, but there's a lust behind it he can barely keep control of. "First rule, baby, is that pets don't talk."

I gulp. It's loud, surprising the both of us. I didn't expect that right away.

"Right," I murmur sardonically. "Of course."

He cocks an eyebrow at me. "And if my pet does, I might have to keep her gagged for the whole day."

This time, I don't respond. The message is clear enough.

"That's what I thought." He stands up and points a finger at me. "Stay."

I don't move when he leaves the room.

Oh my god. What am I doing listening to this man?

He walks back in before I can come to my senses. There's a chain in his hand, and I know exactly where it goes.

"This power exchange is more than sex," he explains. "That's why I need you to give it to me willingly. I'm going to spend the day using you, Jade. To calm my nerves, to help me creatively, to heal with the only person I know can heal me."

I look up at him silently. The pause in his sentence is testing me, and I stay just the way I am until he smiles happily. "I need to quiet the thoughts in my head for at least a few hours, and only you have that kind of power to help. I might be your master today, but you have the real control, baby. Nod if you understand."

I do.

And weirdly, there's nothing more arousing than knowing Ethan Torres, the man I've loved my entire fucking life, *needs* me. Not because of my body and the things I can do, but because we know each other's hearts and souls so well, I'm the only person in which he can find respite.

"If you want this to stop at any time, I want you to talk. You're not allowed to talk unless it's to tell me you want to stop. Nod if you understand."

And I nod again.

"I'm going to push you to your limits. I'm going to test you and it might come across as cruel sometimes. But I need you to know I love you and none of what's going to happen changes that. If anything, I'm doing it with *you* because you're the only person I love and feel safe doing it with. Nod if you understand."

I blink up at him, dying to tell him I love him too, but I simply nod.

"Knowing all of that, now is your chance to stop it all before it starts. There's no fun in me forcing you to do something you don't want. This isn't a punishment. I might punish you if you behave badly, but that's not what it is. You're going in because you want to. Now..." There's a look of despair on his face, knowing he's about to give me a chance to walk out. "Talk if you don't want to do this." His face hardens, and he adds, "Or nod if you're in."

I wish I could say I hesitate, think over it a million times, and take my time to make my decision. But I think I had my entire life to think whether I could take on Ethan and every single little corner of his mind that holds the weirdest yet most delightful things. He's a peculiar man, and I've known that for as long as I've known him.

Instead of pushing me away, it's always attracted me to him.

So I nod without hesitation.

His shoulders relax, and my breathing relaxes with them.

"That's a good pet." He smiles and squats in front of me. "Now let's put this leash on your collar so you can follow after your master."

He hooks the end of the leash to the heart dangling from the collar, and the truth hits me right away. If he pulls, I'll choke. That's the whole concept of this thing. So I have to follow him before the chain extends.

It comes quicker than I thought. Without a word, he's walking, one hand holding the other end of the leash, and I'm crawling after him.

It's a blessing that he's in front of me because I'd be too embarrassed at him seeing the wetness glistening at my slit.

He walks directly to his room and to his desk. Pulling the chair away, he guides me under the desk before sitting down. As he wraps the slack of the chain around his palm, he spreads his legs so I can settle there.

"You're going to stay here while I do some work. You have no idea how much I've been needing you like this, baby. Just so I can focus."

He slides his hand in my hair, the cold links touching the side of my face. "So fucking beautiful."

Then he lets go and starts working. First, it's the guitar, then I heard him write, probably on music sheets, for what seems like hours. Then comes the keyboard. I can't even hear the music. It's all plugged into his laptop and all I pick up on is the clicking of the mouse and tapping of the keyboard as he puts it all together.

"This song is for my mom."

My breath hitches. He knows I can't respond, and he keeps on explaining. "I miss her, Jade. Every day I miss our relationship and the kind of love only she could provide. I can't accept that she just...left. We were so close. It makes no sense to me."

For lack of being able to say anything, I nuzzle against his inner thigh and drop a kiss there before pulling away.

I'm glad I can't talk because he wouldn't like what I have to say. Ethan is allowed to miss his mom. They had a beautiful relationship, but I don't feel the same way about her anymore, and he doesn't need to know that.

He spends hours like this. Or at least that's what it feels like to me. My vision is simply his legs and his crotch. Every now and then, his hand will come to caress my cheek or my hair, but nothing else.

Being naked at his feet and yet not being the object of his attention is the worst torture I've ever endured. I don't just want him to talk to me and acknowledge me. I want him to tell me I'm what he desires right now.

I am naked at your feet!

I want to scream at him so badly. How can he just focus on music when I'm right here, desperate for his attention.

I shift on my knees, eager for him to notice me moving, and yet not sure I'm allowed. He ignores me anyway, and I hear him using the keyboard again, the dull sound of the keys being pressed.

Still resting my ass on my heels, I press my palms between my spread thighs and lean forward, trying to look up at his face, but he's too tight against the desk, and all I see is the underneath of it, and his beautiful...so fucking beautiful stomach.

Even sitting down, his ripped figure shows his abs, each tattoo moving to the rhythm of his breath.

I shift again. I'm wet.

I can't believe I'm wet from just being forgotten and admiring the god-like creature in front of me. This is fucking embarrassing.

Before I realize what I'm doing, I nudge his inner thigh with my head, just above his knees.

He ignores me, clearly too focused on his task.

But I can't do this. I can't have him so close, feeling his heat, and not having him touch me. So I do it again, more forcefully this time.

"Settle down," I hear above me. "I'm working on something for you now. And I'm not finished."

My heart accelerates. For me? This doesn't help at all.

I try. I try really hard to settle down for at least a minute. But I can't. My skin is buzzing, my clit needing to be touched, and I know all too well I'm not the one allowed to pleasure myself.

It has to be one of them.

Right now, it *has* to be Ethan, or I might combust.

I nuzzle against his inner thigh again, going bolder this time. I put both my palms on the chair, between his legs, and pull myself as high as I can without hitting my head. Pressing my face against his crotch, I feel the way he starts growing hard under his gray sweatpants. And I do it again.

Fuck, I need him right now.

His hand comes under the desk, grabbing my hair as he pulls the chair back.

"What do you think you're doing?" he hisses. He acts angry, but there's a fire in his eyes that matches the one in my body.

I can't talk, so I just eye his face and then his crotch.

"My pretty kitten wants to please me?"

Kitten.

Of fuck. This is actually happening.

I attempt to get closer to his crotch again, but he holds me back. With his other hand, he lowers his sweatpants, pulling out his half-hard dick.

"You can have it in your mouth, but you're not allowed to suck. Cock-warming only, Kitten."

I lick my lips and nod. I don't care. Anything to feel him against me, inside me. Just for him to know I'm here and desperate for him.

He guides my head toward him, and I open my mouth wide. I take him all in, swirling my tongue against his piercing.

"*No*," he scolds me, his grip tightening. "What did I just say? You just stay there, mouth open, and wait for me to give you the authorization to pleasure me. Am I clear?"

He looks down, and I nod, my eyes on him.

"Good. Now let me work. I'm almost finished."

If I thought it was horrible before, I have no words to describe what goes through me as I keep his dick in my mouth, not allowed to move.

Saliva pools at the corners of my mouth, making me wish I'd not tried to get his attention at all.

I wait for what feels like forever, my mind wandering, my eyelids closing heavily.

I startle when he grabs my hair again, pulling the chair until I can finally see his face.

"Is it really so hard for you to behave yourself that I had to gag you with my dick?"

I blink up at him, feeling in a haze of a million emotions. Mainly, I'm desperately horny.

He pushes inside me, his dick hardening to the point that I choke. "You want to suck, Kitten?"

I nod as eagerly as I can. "Take my cock deep, then. Show me you're sorry for trying to distract me."

As he thrusts his hips, I gag around him. He pulls at the leash, my collar tightens, and I choke, my throat closing around him. I lick and suck, bobbing my head up and down as I try to pleasure him.

Because I know what comes after pleasing him. And it's worth giving the best blow job of my life.

He hisses above me, thrusting harder inside my mouth. I moan around him, writhing from the need to be touched.

"Fuck, Jade..." He thrusts deep into my throat, coming so far inside me all I can do is swallow.

He lets his head fall back as I pull away and catch my breath. But his hand is still in my hair, and the other one is holding the leash. "We're going to have the best day, you and me, Kitten."

. . .

And fuck if he meant that. For the third time today, Ethan makes me crawl from the living room to his bedroom.

He fucked me on all fours after he worked, my body under the desk and his dick ramming so hard into me I could barely breathe.

But he didn't let me come.

And when he made me climb him while he was watching TV, holding the leash to decide at which pace he wanted me to ride him, he didn't let me come either.

Back in the bedroom, he fucked my pussy while his fingers were in my ass. Bent over the bed, he called me the perfect pet. But he *still* didn't allow me to come.

We've just had lunch, me at his feet as he fed me, and he's walking me to the room again.

I'm more than desperate. The need to come has become an anxious pulse inside me. It's different when they tease me in the morning and then we go about with our day.

He's been edging me all day long, bringing me to the brink of orgasm and back so many times I think I'm losing my mind.

So when he helps me on the bed and lays me down on my back, I open my mouth to beg. He's quick to press his thumb against my lips. "Remember, Kitten. If you talk, we stop. I need you to stay in character."

I whimper when he grazes my drenched pussy with his knee. I just want to scream and beg him. To wrap my legs around him and not release him until he's made me come.

Maybe I could run to the bathroom. Lock myself in there and—

I gasp when his mouth presses against my pussy. I didn't even realize he moved to kneel on the floor.

"You've been good so far today. Such a good little pet. Look at how wet you are from crawling around for me. From being at my feet and doing exactly what you're told."

My entire body electrifies. I should not be loving his words so much, but mixed with his tongue lapping at my clit...

I scream, pushing against his mouth. Shit. I'm going to come. I can't speak to tell him, but he feels it and murmurs against me.

"Don't you dare come. I swear you'll regret it."

But how the hell am I meant to resist this? His mouth is calling my body, ordering it to bend.

I feel myself falling over the precipice, just as he pulls away, dragging a desperate scream from me.

"No!"

I freeze.

Standing up, Ethan looks down on me with fire in his eyes. Not the lust kind. The destroying fire that will burn my soul.

"Do you want to stop?"

I shake my head frantically. No, God no, I'll die if we stop.

So to prove I mean it, I bring my hands to my face, pretending their paws, and wipe my forehead with the back of one.

He bites his lower lip, failing to suppress a smile. It turns into a chuckle that turns into a cute laugh. He's not bursting into laughter, just a beautiful, discreet laugh that shakes his chest and shows me his perfect teeth.

I think I'm dying and coming back down to earth when his dimple shows on his left cheek.

Fuck. That thing is so rare, always too shy.

He runs his hand through his hair, pushing the deep

black strands back so they stop falling in his eyes. His relaxed demeanor reassures me, and I finally understand something.

Ethan can't enjoy this if I'm not fully enjoying it too. And me talking scared him. He wants me at his mercy, but because I choose to be.

I flip around, going on all fours and coming to the end of the bed, nuzzling my head against his stomach.

He thinks he needs me?

He has no idea what it's like to need someone. No one does if they haven't experienced the way I need him.

Pressing his hands on either side of my face, he pulls me up until his lips devour mine. I moan into his mouth, the need to come returning tenfold after the fear he'd stop everything.

"Turn around, Kitten. Show me this wet pussy."

I don't hesitate even a millisecond. I turn around on all fours, lowering my chest to the mattress.

"Mm, baby. You're dripping."

I push myself closer to him, jerking when he slaps my ass. "Stay."

The moment I feel him come back, he parts my ass cheeks, and thick liquid drips between them.

Lube.

He's lubing my ass.

"Bad kitten couldn't follow the rules. Now I have to put you back in your place."

I feel him press something at the entrance of my pussy. It's thick and round. I moan when he pushes inside me, pushing back against it.

"You're going to love your tail, Kitten."

My heart drops, my body freezing. Did he just say...

When he talked about it before, I thought he was joking.

"You're making it so wet."

He pulls it out of me, speaking softly. "Spread your ass cheeks for me."

My face is burning as I bring my hands back and part my cheeks for him. The moment he presses the plug against my asshole, I recoil.

"Don't be scared. It's a very small one. We'll take it one step at a time, and I promise I'll make it feel good."

Slowly and firmly, he inserts the plug, playing with the way he makes me feel. He pushes in, retracts, does it again a little farther. All until I'm writhing under his touch.

And when I'm the one who starts pushing back, he murmurs, "Take a deep breath and release slowly."

I do. As I release, he pushes the plug all the way in.

The mix of sensations is overwhelming. I feel full, but so turned on by it that I squeeze around the plug. I feel the furry tail against my ass cheeks and at the backs of my thighs, deepening the embarrassment of doing this for him.

"Oh, Kitten," he sighs. "You are so perfect." He caresses my lower back. "Come back down now, on all fours."

The sensation of being on the floor with that thing inside me is indescribable. I feel it so distinctly when Ethan grabs the leash and starts to make me crawl beside him.

"Fuck," he rasps. "Come, baby. Go wait at the door for Elliot. He'll love it."

So I do. He takes me all the way to the doorway, makes me kneel on my heels so the tail doesn't hurt, and I wait for Elliot.

It must take him hours to come back, but when he does, he freezes in the doorway.

"Oh, shit." He squats, messing the top of my head. "Hi, little kitten. Did Ethan put you here for me?"

I nod. I've never been so desperate in my life. I don't wait for him to take action. I crawl between his legs and nudge him with my head.

"Fucking hell, Ethan." He talks to his brother now standing behind me. "What have you done with our fiery girlfriend?"

"Shh, she's in character. Don't break it."

Elliot grabs the leash in front of me, takes me to the sofa, and makes me turn around. He unzips his pants. "Let's test what this kitty's tongue can do."

His hand goes to my hair, and unlike Ethan's patience earlier, he pushes his already hard dick in my mouth. I choke on it, pulling back. But then Ethan grabs the leash and pulls me in their direction again.

"Be good," he threatens.

Elliot does this thing where he forgets how thick and long his dick is and tries to push to the back of my throat, making me gag.

"She's not trying nearly hard enough," he chuckles.

He pulls back slightly, and Ethan brings his fingers to my mouth, tracing the outline of my lips. He pushes his index finger in, then stretches the corner of my mouth. "Say 'ah,'" he taunts me.

I whimper when he presses his pierced tip against my lips, pushing next to Elliot's.

Elliot has to pull back some more for Ethan to be able to fit. Both their tips are pressing on my tongue, keeping me quiet.

Elliot pulls out and presses my head against Ethan's dick until my nose grazes his crotch. He pulls me back by my hair, giving me a second to breathe before he does the same on himself.

"Good little kitty," he grunts.

Pulling me away again, Ethan drags me onto the sofa,

my knees on there, bent over the back. He settles behind me and taps the tail, making me moan at the sensation of fullness in my ass.

"She's ready to play," Ethan murmurs. "This is your training, pretty kitten. You're going to keep the tail in your ass while I fuck you. And then we'll remove it so you can take both of us at the same time."

I practically mewl my agreement. I need them so badly.

Elliot stands behind the sofa, by my mouth, and pushes in slowly while Ethan stays in front of the furniture by my pussy.

I moan around him when Ethan starts pressing against my entrance. I feel full from the tail already, but his dick inside me brings me to another level. I don't care that he has to be careful not to break me. I want more.

I push back against him, making him groan. "Slowly." He slaps my ass. "I don't want to hurt you."

I let him take control, slowly pushing in and pulling out, rolling his hips and making me moan. He grabs the tail, doing the same with it. Every time the thicker part goes through the ring of muscle, I whimper loudly around Elliot's cock.

The pleasure is too much. I'm going to combust if he doesn't let me come.

He finally pulls the tail out, discarding it to the side before pushing two fingers in. "Let's spread you open a little wider, baby."

A third finger pushes inside, making me feel tighter. He adds some lube, pushes in again, and I cry out.

"Do you want us both, my love?" Elliot rumbles. "Do you want him in your ass while I take your pussy? You're going to feel so tight."

I nod desperately, still swirling my tongue against his dick.

Before I know, they both pull out of me. Ethan sits on the sofa, lying back and bringing his ass to the edge. Grabbing my hips, he flips me around so I'm facing the other way.

"Slowly," he murmurs in my ear. "Just trust me."

His lubed cock presses against the entrance of my ass. It's much thicker than his fingers, but it's also more pleasurable. I like the sting of pain, the feeling of *too much*.

He pushes in little by little, making me take deep breaths and slow releases.

And when he's finally sitting fully inside, Elliot comes in front of me. "You're going to feel so good, baby. Spread your legs wide."

I do as he orders. He puts a hand on the back of the sofa, just above Ethan's shoulder, and holds his face near mine. Dropping a peck on my mouth, he slowly enters me.

I whimper against his lips, and he captures them, entangling his tongue with mine.

I'm sweating, trembling, so tense from the need to orgasm that I can't see straight anymore.

"Shh," he whispers against my lips. "You're doing so well. Look at how good you're taking us, baby."

He goes deeper, tearing a moan from my throat.

"Ah, Elliot...too much."

I fear Ethan's reaction at my calling out Elliot, but nothing happens. Instead, he presses two fingers against my clit and starts circling, bringing me more pleasure than I can handle.

My body is on fire, my heartbeat near explosion, and before I know it, Elliot hisses, "You did it. You're taking every fucking inch of us, my love."

And then they start moving. It's messy at first. The pleasure is there, but we're all looking for our rhythm. Until they start moving in tandem, and Elliot keeps hold of my gaze as Ethan kisses my neck. He keeps playing with my clit, running his fingers over and over again at the same pace they fuck me.

It's not fast. It's not crazy.

It's perfect.

"I need to come. Please," I beg. "Please, you can't do this and not..." I pant, unable to finish my sentence.

"You are so gorgeous like this," Ethan murmurs. "Completely ours."

"Now come for us," Elliot orders.

I shatter so hard I see stars. Every single nerve ending in my body snaps on demand, my belly twists and tingles, my toes curling behind Elliot.

I feel Ethan grunt behind me, emptying in my ass as I tighten around him. Elliot keeps fucking me, accelerating as I cry out my release. He's the last one to explode.

We just sit there after. I can't move because I'm stuck between them. Ethan wraps his fingers around my hips softly, like I'm suddenly breakable. He lifts me off him as Elliot pulls out and away.

I fall back on Ethan's lap as he kisses my neck, my jaw, and whispers in my ear, "You're ours, Jade. Completely ours. We're never letting you go."

37

JADE

Angels Don't Cry - Ellise

The engine rumbles under me, vibrating through my body and highlighting the delicious ache inside me. I want more. More of the two men I've fallen for, more of them inside me, more love, more games, play, cuddles.

I'm greedy for everything and even more than that.

"A fucking van," I mutter to myself. "You're drag racing a fucking van. If that isn't the most stupid thing you've ever done."

I press the gas pedal, holding the clutch right below the releasing point. I focus on the road ahead of me, ignoring the loud exhaust from the car next to me.

It's fine. We're good. I know what I'm doing. I'm a fucking good mechanic, amazing even. I don't have to worry about anything.

I pop an apple-flavored piece of gum in my mouth as Faith raises one flag above her head. The guy next to me must nod, but I don't look.

I press the button of the CD player. What an old fucking

thing this van is. Going straight to the second track, I listen to the beginning of the song and nod when Faith raises her flag.

I turn to Ethan and Elliot right there at the front of the crowd. I do the OK sign and offer them half a heart with my left hand. They both do one back and my chest lightens.

I am so in love it's dangerous.

Lose my mind, lose my focus, lose *myself* type of dangerous.

Facing forward again, the rags go down, and I release the clutch.

"*Na Na Na*" by My Chemical Romance starts screaming in the van, and I'm off.

We start off good. Both of us, but he quickly accelerates and so does my heart. I have enough bags at the back to replicate the weight of the money bags we would have, and I'm too heavy. Fucking stupid heaviness. I watch the speedometer, counting the seconds in my head as I accelerate with all I have, pushing the van to its limit.

The first eighth of the mile is enough for the guy in his tuned-up car to speed past me, but I keep my eye on the needle. I push, and I push, and I fucking push.

But I lose.

By a few seconds too.

Still, I keep a smile on my face.

This is going to work.

I drive back to the starting line, watching as Faith gives my money to my opponent—or rather Elliot's money. He shakes my hand, but I pull away quickly, not caring as I run back to my boyfriends.

Weird. That feels weird to say.

Elliot gives me a pointed look, and I know he didn't

forget our conversation from yesterday, but Faith is quicker than him.

"I think that's the first time I've seen you lose," she says. She doesn't *think* she *knows*, but she's testing the waters right now.

"Yep." I nod, not really caring.

"Feels weird. Are you okay?"

I smile at Elliot. "Yep."

He narrows his eyes at me. "*Yep*?"

"It's fine," I assure him, putting a hand on his chest. "I promise it's fine."

"I believe I have two thousand dollars missing from my pocket telling me it *isn't* fine."

"Right, I'll just leave you guys to it," my friend says. She gives me a side-eye, silently hoping I'm going to survive this.

"Alright," Ethan chuckles. "I'm sure you just made a very nice discovery for you to tell him it's fine. Tell us all about it."

"You know me so well." I wink at him. I turn back to the blond brother, balancing on my heels before going flat again. I like teasing him.

"Jade," he growls. "Talk. Now."

"I went zero to sixty in seven seconds."

"I'm pretty sure that isn't very good for a drag race," Ethan wonders aloud.

"Oh, it's terrible. It's okay for a van, but it's fucking terrible for this race. I put my reputation on the line for this shit."

"And yet things are fine? Get to the fucking point." Elliot's lack of patience shows, and it makes me want to taunt him some more.

"What I mean is..." I let my words hang and giggle when

he takes a step toward me, his hands gripping my waist harshly.

"Your ass is going to be so sore," he threatens low.

"What she means is she can do it. That three-minute drive in fifty-nine seconds." Kay appears from behind the guys, looking at me with her piercing eyes. "What she *means* is she fucking did it. She made that van perfect for our little adventure. Good thing, now that I lost my deal with the Wolves."

I try to take a step back, but Elliot holds me. Kay settles next to him, and he stays close to make sure this doesn't escalate.

"Is it done, then?" Ethan asks. "Official?"

Kay nods, her eyes staying on me. "Yeah. Ivan got a not so nice call from Mikhail, Viktor Volkov's right hand." She takes a deep breath, like she can't believe it. "I think it's worse than my worst breakup." She chuckles sadly.

"You and Ivan broke up?" I ask.

She snorts. "No. He told Mikhail he wanted to stay here, by my side. They didn't even care. I'm talking about my breakup with the Wolves. Only years of work that have become completely worthless."

I wouldn't say she looks vulnerable right now, but it's the least held up together I've ever seen her.

"Kay," I start. "I'm...so fucking sorry."

I'm not even saying this because I'm worried about what she'll do to me. I'm saying it because her entire life has always been about the Kings' Crew. She was born into it, daughter of the leader, but by being a girl, she had to fight her way to the top. She's strong—maybe stronger than I'll ever be—and her empire is crumbling to the ground.

She shakes her head. "You have nothing to be sorry about. The fuckers had you between a rock and a hard place and they knew it. They've been trying to find any excuse to drop us. This was just the perfect timing. I wouldn't have stood for them threatening Elliot and Ethan either." She smirks. "And I heard you gave Aaron Williams quite a piece of your mind."

I laugh softly, confirming what's been said. "He angered me."

"Yes, a rare event." Elliot pokes my cheek, making me giggle.

"Damn. You really are scared of nothing." Kay turns to the brothers. "Your girl survived seeing a Wolf *and* insulting him. I hope you gave her the orgasm of her life after that."

"Oh, we did." Elliot smirks. My cheeks flush remembering taking them both at the same time.

"We have pictures if you want."

"Ethan!" I bark. "When did you take pictures?"

"When you were purring like a good k—"

"Okay that's about enough," Kay intervenes.

The brothers burst into laughter despite my scowling at them. "Assholes," I growl.

"Come, let's get you a beer or something," Elliot laughs.

They start walking away, but Kay holds me back, a hand on my shoulder.

"Jade."

I turn around, unsure what to expect. Her features soften from the ruthless woman she usually is. Her hand on my shoulder is reassuring.

"I'm proud of you," she says. "Really. Thank you for working so hard on the van."

I take in her words, but it's difficult to be nice back. That's not the kind of relationship Kay and I have anymore. She fucked it all up by not believing me. By ignoring what happened to me.

I can feel anger bubbling inside me, ready to burst out like a volcanic eruption. But instead, I express myself calmly. It's kind of annoying to see Elliot's *lessons* in talking about my emotions have worked.

"This doesn't change anything between us."

Her brows furrow, her own anger appearing. "I'm extending a hand here. You still fucking stole from me and ran away."

"Please," I snort. "You know I never took that money. Whoever did it is still in your ranks and that's a you problem. Once we're done with this job, I'm never dealing with you again."

"Don't fucking lie to me, Jade," she hisses, coming closer. "I could insist on you giving me that money back. Where are you hiding it?"

I step forward too, tilting my head up. Facing her head-on. "It's always been easier for you to call me a liar and ignore the people poisoning the Kings from the inside."

Her face twists with confusion, her head tilting to the side. "What are you talking about?"

Because I'm not here to play dumb, I give it to her once and for all. "I. Am. Not. Lying. But someone in your crew is."

It takes all of me not to scream that I'm not a liar. That they're the ones who let me down, and I was just a teenager who didn't know what to do.

But I swallow it back. Breathe. Screaming and breaking things never got me anywhere. What does help is spending time with Elliot and Ethan. It's laughing with them, listening to music together, the sex, the limits we push through, discovering each other.

I smile to myself. "I'll never forgive you for what you did," I explain with a calmness I didn't know I had inside me. "Or *didn't* do."

I ignore the pretense of her confusion, and, not waiting for an answer, I turn around and jog to catch up with my two men.

I hear her shouting she has no idea what I'm talking about, but I'm above that. Above her. I'm flying high with Ethan and Elliot as I take them into my arms.

"Alright." I tap Elliot's back. "Let's win your money back."

"Maybe there's been enough damage for one day," he chuckles.

"Do you even know me? There's never enough damage. Did you drive my car?"

"I did, Mi Cielo." Ethan throws the keys at me, and I catch them with a smile on my face.

"Now watch what a real car can do on these roads."

"Na, Na, Na" by My Chemical Romance has never felt so freeing. I only did a drag race with the van, but I'm doing a proper race with my baby.

When I press the gas pedal, my hate for the Kings and the North Shore stays back while I speed across the asphalt. My opponent eats the smoke I let out as I drift the corner, leaving skid marks behind. As my body hits against the side of the car, I scream with joy.

I accelerate back to the finish line, cheers exploding as I hop out of the car. Using the side as a step, I pull myself up and tap on the roof. "Show me the money, fuckers!" I shout at the crowd, getting myself some more cheers.

I throw up two middle fingers at everyone, sticking my tongue out, before jumping back down. Thrumming with adrenaline, I wipe my sweaty hands against my ripped blue jeans. I wore them with large fishnets and a chain going from the back to the front. It's Ethan's chain, and I fucking love wearing it on my clothes. Especially knowing he likes to hook it to my collar when we play together.

"Jade!" A tornado of pink hits me right in the chest, wrapping her arms around me. "You were such a queen out there." She pulls away, keeping her hands on my shoulders. "You're so badass," she giggles.

It makes me laugh. If only she knew how *not* badass I am.

"And you're delusional."

"I couldn't believe it was you when you came out of that van. Someone like you doesn't lose." Her eyes light up with pride. "And then you raced with your car and...whoa." She giggles, shaking me. "That was *crazy!*"

Her contagious smile gets to me. "Thanks. Are you here alone?"

She shakes her head. "Rose is somewhere around. Probably arguing with someone over something. I better go find her. I'll catch you later. Enjoy the win!" With a wink at me, she's on her way.

The people crowd me, tapping my shoulders and grabbing me until Elliot and Ethan push through. With bright smiles on their faces, they both grip my waist, pulling me up and settling me on a shoulder each. I'm on Elliot's right and Ethan's left. I have to grip both their necks. The height difference between them is minimal when you see them next to the other, but when you've got a leg on both, Elliot seems like a giant.

I can't stop giggling. Even as they put me down and Faith brings us the money. "That's the girl I know," she cackles.

I wink at her, grabbing the bills. I take a twenty out.

"Racer's tax." I laugh at Elliot's face as I give him his money back.

"You really are pushing me tonight."

The three of us can't stop laughing. Everything feels so fucking light. Almost like it shouldn't be.

We're criminals. We'll be robbing a bank in just over a month. Surely, this kind of happiness shouldn't even exist. Nothing in my life has ever felt like this. So happy I don't care about anything and anyone else in the world.

"Happy birthday," I tell Elliot, lifting onto my toes to give him a kiss.

Grabbing the back of my head, he presses me harder against his lips, and devours me like there's no tomorrow. He bites my lower lip the exact way he loves, making it swell between his teeth.

As I go flat on my feet, I slip the twenty in the front pocket of my DiggyGraves hoodie. Well, Elliot's.

Feeling something inside, I pull out a piece of paper.

My heart drops before I even open it.

If I shoot you through the head, you'll be gone instantly.
If I shoot you through the heart, you've got a few minutes.
And if I put a bullet through your lungs, you could suffer for hours.
Soon, dead girl

My knees buckle, the weight of the words crushing into me.

"Fuck," I whisper. Ethan is the one who catches me just as Elliot rips the paper out of my hands.

He looks around, circling us as he crushes it in his fist.

"H-how?"

It's been long enough without notes that I started to believe it might have been Vickie and her friends. And that by killing them, we'd gotten rid of the threats.

I convinced myself I was safe.

My entire body shakes, but Ethan keeps me close to him. "We're here. You risk nothing when we're here, baby. I promise we won't let anything happen to you."

Elliot and Ethan might be killers, but they can't stop a bullet. No one can.

"Let's get you home," Elliot finally says.

They eye each other, silently communicating. "What? What is it?" I don't like the way my voice shakes. I *hate* being vulnerable.

"Must have been when people crowded you earlier. They slipped it in your pocket," Ethan explains.

It takes all of me not to burst into tears. The fear of knowing they were close enough to touch me. That they could have killed me right there and then.

"Fuck." My chest freezes. A weight sitting on it. So heavy that I can't take my next breath.

Elliot is on me right away. "No, no, no. Stay with us. Everything is fine."

"Everything is fine?" I scream. "*Nothing* is fine." My eyes widen when the truth hits me. "Oh my god," I gasp. "It's Kay."

"What?" Elliot pushes hair out of my face. "What did she say to you earlier?"

"What she said doesn't matter. She used the moment to slip the note in my pocket."

Kay knows what is going around town. People's whereabouts. What my car looks like. She could have been present every time I was somewhere.

The bitch fucking hit me with her car.

"It's not Kay," Ethan jumps in. "Let's get you home. Somewhere safe where we can talk."

"It's Kay," I fight back, jerking out of their holds and turning to face them. "It's her. I'm telling you it's her."

"Jade," Ethan says calmly. "You're panicking, and I get why, but it doesn't make sense. She needs you."

"Does she? Or did she stop threatening me while I was working on the van, and now that I'm done, she's ready to end me. She doesn't fucking need me anymore."

"Jade." This time, his tone is nearer scolding than reassurance. "Listen to yourself. You are not making sense."

"Why are you defending her?"

"Calm down." His cool voice riles me up.

"When has anyone ever calmed down when being told to calm down!"

Fuck. Fuck. I'm screaming again. No one is listening to me.

I inhale a shaky breath, but it doesn't work. I'm not calming down. I'm working myself up even more by the simple acknowledgement that I can't control my emotions. My heart is speeding, my blood beating in my ears.

I can't notice anyone or anything else. My vision is narrowed on Ethan and my mind is blaring a deafening alarm. *He isn't listening.*

"I'm not defending her."

"You're defending her," I scream, my voice raw.

Stupid. I pull at my roots, attempting to ground myself. But nothing works. I'm stupid, stupid, *stupid*.

I fucking hate myself when I can't think straight.

"I need you to listen. By focusing on the wrong person, we're letting the real threat get away. I'd be putting you in more danger by agreeing to your ludicrous accusations. This isn't Kay's style. She would kill you and be done with it.

This is stalker shit. They're taunting you, scaring you on purpose. They're *playing* with you, Jade."

My head falls back as I let out a sarcastic cackle. "Of course." I look back at him. "Of course, you'd know because that's what *you* do," I accuse. "This is serial killer territory. You're in your comfort zone."

"My love, that's enough."

I ignore Elliot. "Do you play with your victims too, Ethan?" I put two hands on his chest. "I bet you're the kind to terrify them before killing them. You cut the lights, drag your knife against the wall. Maybe stalk them for a few days. You put it on me. On your jealousy. Because they talked to me? Touched me? Insulted me? But it's all you. It's you and your fucked-up mind."

The pain in his eyes should break my heart, but I'm angry. I'm hurt and I want to hurt back. Because apparently, I take a step in the right direction and ten steps back to toxicity.

I'm such a fucking loser.

"I think I'm starting to see what they feel like. Someone is coming for them, and the killer is smart enough to drive them crazy. Smart enough that when they seek help, no one fucking believes them."

I step back. "I'll drive myself home."

"Jade, don't," Elliot calls back as I walk away. I flip him off and make sure to go through the crowd. That way they can't find me.

"Jade!" I hear him shout just as I surround myself with people.

And maybe one of them is going to end me.

I'm just coming through to the other side, when the unmistakable sound of a police siren rings out.

Time freezes for a split second, everyone going quiet before someone screams. "Cops!"

All hell breaks loose. It takes me a few seconds of being pushed around as the crowd disperses before I snap back into reality.

"Fuck," I hiss, sprinting in the direction of my car. I look around for Ethan and Elliot, but they're nowhere to be found. People are bumping into my shoulders, trying to go past me.

My phone rings as I run.

Elliot. He talks the second I pick up.

"*Get in your car. We'll take the van. Meet at home.*" The orders are direct. Spoken smoothly. He's not one to panic.

His heart isn't beating crazy like mine. His fingers aren't numb like mine.

His head is clear...unlike mine.

"*Jade. Is that clear?*"

"Y-yes."

There's a short beat before emotions take hold of his syllables. "Be safe. I love you."

I'm pretty sure I'm about to say it back. I don't know. I hesitate too long. Someone knocks me and my phone drops. Next thing I know, it's crushed under someone's shoe as they run past me.

"Fuck." I look around, finding my car in the mess of shouting and hazy movements. I keep on my trajectory as the sirens get closer. The blue lights are right here. There's no time to waste.

I jump in my car, speeding away and making sure I'm not running over anyone. It's one thing to get caught illegally street racing. It's something else to kill someone with said car. Especially when we put everything in place to not hurt anyone. There's a reason we do it in a deserted place.

Smoke trails behind me as I race across the abandoned area.

I'm out before most people, and I think that's actually a bad thing, makes me look guilty as fuck. I know it because there's a blue light speeding after me. My heart is beating three times the rhythm of the sirens.

I drift onto a different street and accelerate again in a straight line. I lose them quickly. Almost too easily. I slow down, catching my breath as I make my way to the truss bridge. No need to hurry anymore. My heart finally calms down, and I wipe my hands against my jeans.

"Holy shit." A sigh of relief leaves me.

I'm about to get on the bridge when a black car coming from the bridge lights up, a siren ringing and blue light blinding me.

I brake hard, skidding across the asphalt. It's an unmarked car.

I veer right, pressing the gas pedal again, trying to convince myself they're not here for me.

How foolish.

I don't give up, though. Speeding again, I follow the Silver Snake River until I find a street where I can take a right. We're closer to the woods now, only some buildings still within sight. I'm about to take a left onto a dirt road, with no choice since there's a building right in front of me. Another police car comes from exactly where I want to turn. I'm forced to slam on my brakes, so I don't crash into them.

"Fuck!"

The other police car blocks me in from behind. I'm

stuck in the corner of that road. Trees, the building, the two police cars. I've got nowhere to go.

My heart drops to my stomach. It's me alone with four cops. I turn the engine off, already expecting them to burst out of their cars, guns pointed at me, so I keep my hands in front of me.

But they stay inside, and only one comes out.

He puts a placating hand in front of him as he walks to my window. It's like he wants to tell me it's all going to be fine.

He knocks on my window, indicating to lower it.

"Evening. Can I see your license, please?"

"I…" *never took my driving test.* "Don't have it with me."

I've never needed to take a test to know how to drive. My dad taught me. It was too fucking expensive, and with time, I just left it. I'd never been arrested for driving before.

He shines a light in my car, checking what's in here.

"Your vehicle has been seen at an illegal street race. I'm going to have to ask you to step out, please."

He's polite, looks like the kind of guy with a wife and a family. Just doing his job, just trying to keep his town safe. I know I'm being lucky right now. They chased after me, they know I was up to no good. But I chance it anyway…

I swallow thickly. "I think you're mistaken. It wasn't me."

"It wasn't you," he repeats. "Is that why we had to chase you to get you to stop? Your car matches the details we've been sent."

"Black?" Suddenly, I'm glad my car isn't pink anymore.

He looks at me, his mouth twisting. Almost like he feels bad for me. "The license plate frame saying *if you see this, I'm winning* also helped. Look, I convinced my colleagues to not jump out of their cars, all guns blazing, because I saw you were a young woman on your own, but you have to give me something to work with here. This doesn't have to be difficult. Step out of the vehicle, please."

I look around. All the other cops are in their cars. It's just him. He's not threatening, neither in his words nor in his physique. A twig compared to Ethan and Elliot. Taking a deep breath, I open the door and come out.

And that's when his behavior changes. His entire stature switches from *I'm a good guy* to *you're fucked* in a few seconds.

My stomach twists, my instincts telling me to jump back in my car right now as I close the door behind me.

And it's too late. He grabs my upper arm violently, flipping me around and slamming my body against the car.

"What the fu—"

"Ma'am, you're under arrest for engaging in illegal street racing, reckless driving, and endangerment of public safety—"

"Wait! Wait, what the fuck..."

"—You have the right to remain silent. Anything you say can—"

"You're hurting me," I squeak as he cuffs me so tightly my blood instantly stops flowing to my hands.

"—and will be used against you in a court of law."

"Fucking asshole," I rage, twisting in his hold.

He slams me harder against the side of my car, his hand coming to the back of my neck.

He talks low when his other hand presses against my wrist, right where my Kings' crown is tattooed. "Kings' crew, huh?"

I open my mouth to talk, but he cuts me off again, making sure he speaks loudly enough for his colleagues to hear he's following procedure.

"Ma'am, I have reason to believe you may be armed or

possess something dangerous. I'm going to perform a frisk for weapons. You have the right to refuse, but if you do, I may have to take further action."

I try to scream. "I ref—" He grabs my hair, slamming my head against the car.

His official tone drops as he hisses in my ear. "Now is the right time for you to shut the fuck up."

"I don't have anything on me!"

"Better check thoroughly," he chuckles, his hot breath irritating my cheek.

"Fuck off," I growl, fighting his hold. "Fuck—" I choke on my words when his hand goes under my hoodie and to the back of my bra.

My hands instinctively try to fight him, instantly being stopped by the tight handcuffs.

His fingers slide under the band of my bra, coming to my side, the tips creeping toward my breast.

"D-don't," I whisper in panic. I can't find my voice anymore. "P—" I swallow thickly, unable to talk.

Like that day.

He closes his entire hand around my mound, making me cry out. "Please," I whimper.

A hundred thoughts run through my mind. Maybe if I'd stayed with the brothers. If I hadn't been such a bitch to Ethan. Maybe if I hadn't decided to test the van tonight...

"All you low-life North Shore criminals are the same." He pulls away from my boob, sliding down to my jeans.

Panic seizes me. He doesn't even take the time to unbutton them, roughly pushing through.

"You ridicule us when we can't catch you on your turf. Taunt us with your petty crimes. Act tough because you're on your side of town."

He grabs my underwear, pulling them up and forcing me on my toes as I hiss in pain.

I watch my breath fogging my window.

Exactly like that day.

"But when we catch you, you cry and beg us to leave you alone, like you're some sort of fucking victim."

He releases my panties, kicking my legs apart with his boot.

"Not feeling so strong now, are we?"

"Hall." The foreign voice barely takes me out of the nightmare. I don't think I can process anything anymore. His hand is unmoving, but it's still right *there,* ready to break me like Elliot's dad had.

"Hall, that's enough."

That's his colleague. I only realize my eyes were scrunched closed when I open them again. He's stopping him. It's over.

It's over.

"Get back in the car, newbie."

No.

"What you're doing...that's not right."

Please, don't get back in the car. Please, don't get back in the car.

"I said get your ass. Back. In. The. Car."

I can't see him, but I heard the fear in his voice and the will to help. Only one out of three witnesses wants to help. I want to scream at him to do it. To rip Hall off my body. To uncuff me and let me go home.

But my chest is too tight to speak.

My voice is non-existent.

There's only a void inside me right now. And there's nothing I can do with that.

I hear a huff. A mumble that it's fucked up. And then the car door closing.

"Now...where were we?"

"Step the fuck away from her!" There's a flash of something, blinding me.

The voice is female this time, and I know it from somewhere, but my brain is too messy to understand what's going on.

His hand retreats, his other one still holding my hair.

"Hey!" he shouts. "Nothing to see here, walk away."

"I'm filming you," the female voice says. "I've got you on camera, you idiot. Now step away from her."

I squint my eyes, trying to see past the flash that I now understand is someone's phone.

My heart is beating in my ears, hope slithering through my veins.

He can't do anything now. He can't.

"I'm going to arrest your fucking ass if you don't stop filming and walk away."

There's a little laugh. Too cute to be threatening. "Do you have any idea who I am? It's incredibly stupid to threaten the daughter of an ex-senator."

He's off me in a split second. "What? What's your name?"

"Me? Alexandra Delacroix. What's *your* name, Officer?" *Barbie.*

He steps away from the light. The panic in his voice makes me wonder if that's what I sounded like a minute ago.

"T-This woman is under arrest for illegal street racing. I'm just doing my j—"

"What. Is. Your. Name?"

She comes closer, pointing her phone at his badge.

"Officer *Hall*. Well, you've got a whole lot of problems coming your way, Officer Hall. I'd start packing your stuff the second you get back to the station."

"I'm just...She's under arrest."

"Not anymore, she's not. Uncuff her."

And just like that. With zero violence or insult from Alex whatsoever, the cuffs are gone.

All it took was one friend with an important name, and I'm...free.

Her arm wraps around my shoulder. "Come, Jade. Let's go."

She directs me away from the cop and to a Porsche sitting on the side of the road.

I'm speechless, unable to find anything to say to her.

She helps me sit inside, driving away instantly.

"Jade, are you okay?"

I stare ahead at the road, despite feeling her eyes on me.

"Do you need me to take you to a hospital?"

I shake my head.

"I can take you to the police station. We can go to Stoneview so we won't have to deal with any of his colleagues."

Again, I shake my head, but no words come out.

"Um," she hesitates. "I'm so sorry about what happened. I mean—his hand...it looked bad. He won't get away with it."

I don't respond, my head falling to the side and hitting the window. I think I'm in shock.

I can't...

Exactly three years ago, day for day, Joel Pearson was doing the exact same thing to me as we celebrated his son's birthday.

Oh, the fucking irony.

456

"Do you want to go home?" Alex asks. "Give me your address and I'll drive you there."

But I shake my head.

"Is there anything you need?"

She doesn't get a word out of me the whole drive. I'm too numb, too shocked to believe anything that happened tonight.

When she parks in front of her own house with the pink door and helps me out of the car, I let her.

When she puts me to bed in a guest room, I let her. When she sits down on the floor next to me and holds my hand...

I let her.

38

JADE

I Need You - Chri$tian Gate$

Could the walls in this house be any thinner?

Alex arguing with her boyfriend is what wakes me up. I jump out of bed, on edge. I'm still clothed, bar my shoes, but I want to burn what I'm wearing. It's tight, sweaty. I feel disgusting.

My entire body feels like there's a layer of dirt covering it. My mouth is dry, my tongue sticky, and there's something inside me that burns. It prickles under my skin, making me want to dig my nails and draw blood.

I try to take a deep breath, but there's nothing to do about the tightness in my chest.

And for having been through this before, I know one thing for sure: it'll never go away.

So I make the same decision I did back then. I crush the despair in my mind, narrowing it to one feeling that will make me feel strong rather than used and dirty.

Anger.

I press my ear against the door, almost jumping back

when I hear Alex shouting. Shit, I thought that girl didn't even know how to.

"No. I swear to God, Xi..."

"Don't even finish that sentence." His voice is stern, leaving no room for discussion. And yet she continues.

"Why would you do this? I didn't tell you so you'd call two guys she most certainly does not want to see right now."

"Alexandra, look at me. I am *not* keeping a Kings' girl in this house."

"She was *attacked*!"

"I don't give shit. And what the fuck were you doing at an illegal race anyway?" His voice booms in the house, much deeper and louder than hers. "You said you were revising with Peach."

"You know you'd never let me go there. You're overprotective."

"Over...*overprotective*? Damn fucking right I am. Now listen to me. My crew and hers are at war. I'm not bringing any of that shit to the house. To *you*."

"*Your* crew? Are you part of NSC again, now?"

"You know what I mean."

There's some moving around, and I follow along the wall, not wanting to miss anything.

"She's my friend, Xi."

"She's not your friend. You have no idea the kind of things this girl has done."

"Ah. Yes. And you, you never did anything wrong. A *saint*."

A chair moves, and there are steps walking toward the room. "Come back here," he calls after her. "Alexandra!"

The steps pause. "What?" Her clipped voice is followed by pause.

"Cupcake, please. I lost my best friend because of that

girl. You don't get to bring her here and rub it in my face. She's leaving. End of the discussion."

There's a sharp inhale. A pause. And the steps come toward me again.

I pull away from the wall, looking for my shoes around the room.

There's a knock on the door, and when I don't answer, it opens slowly.

"Jade?" Alex's high-pitched voice contaminates the room with her worry. "I brought you some tea."

She steps all the way in as I grab my left shoe.

"Are you leaving?" She puts the cup down on the bedside table. "Wait. At least have a hot drink."

"I have to go home."

Where the hell is that? I can't go to Ethan and Elliot right now.

"Just...just wait." She approaches me slowly, clearly concerned she's going to scare me off. "If it's because you heard Xi..."

I go on my knees, checking under the bed and finally grabbing my right shoe.

"I—It's my fault, but I want to make sure you're okay before you leave. Please, at least—"

I stand back up, stopping her with a simple look. "You told him."

"I'm so sorry, I—"

"Why would you do that?" I put my second combat boot on, doing the laces. "Why?"

Panic seizes my chest, fear making my hands tremble.

"I'm sorry. I panicked. I was trying to tell him why I brought you here and—"

"He told Elliot and Ethan, didn't he? It's bad. It—" I lose my voice again. "Fuck," I squeak.

"None of this is your fault," she explains calmly.

"They're not going to believe me," I panic. "No one will."

She pauses, her eyes rounding. "Of course they will. Why wouldn't they? I believe you. Xi might not be happy about you being here, but he didn't doubt what happened for one second."

"I have to leave before the brothers get here."

She grabs my wrist, softly bringing me back. "You shouldn't be on your own right now. Ethan and Elliot will take care of you."

"They won't believe me! Are you not fucking listening?"

I pull out of her hold, turning toward the door, only to come face to face with Xi, arms crossed in the doorway.

"Watch your tone when you talk to her."

I blink up at him, not sure what to do now that he's blocking the way. A loud banging on the door brings all of our attention away from this conversation.

"Sounds like your boyfriends are ready to destroy my front door."

He finally moves out of the way, and I follow. There's no escaping them. No escaping the things they'll say.

Is it true?

Are you lying?

Don't lie, Jade.

"My love." Elliot is the first in, grabbing me by the waist and picking me up as if I'm a kid who had gotten lost in a mall and he just found me. I mechanically wrap my legs around his waist. "Fuck, I was so worried."

I feel a hand caressing my back. "He's a dead man walking, Mi Cielo. I can promise you his days on earth are counted."

"Fuck the days, he's got mere hours left. What was his name?"

He keeps my head to his shoulder, and I nuzzle against his neck. His warmth is making me feel alive again.

"Tell us everything," Ethan says as he pulls my hair away from my face. "Every fucking thing, and we'll make him pay."

A sob constricts my throat, my words painful to push out. "You...I...I'm confused," I admit.

"What's confusing, my love? Tell us."

Ethan's hand is on my cheek, his thumb wiping a falling tear. "You don't have to get into details now. Or ever. We'll be ready when you are. Don't make yourself worse."

"We don't need to know everything to end his fucking life, trust me," Elliot adds.

My arms tighten around his neck.

"Just know we're here," Ethan concludes. "We're here now, and I'm sorry we weren't last night. That we didn't stop him."

I gulp on air, trying to breathe through the ball in my throat. A whimper escapes me.

"It's not a lie," I choke. "He really did attack me."

"Of course it's not a lie," Elliot reassures me in a gentle voice. "We know that."

"Baby, we know you're not lying," Ethan insists.

That's the exact moment my whole world implodes.

Where's the anger I forged inside me for years? It was burning hot, ready to destroy everything in my way.

And now it's just...gone?

I think that's all I needed.

Not screaming and not revenge. Not to kill, and not to hate the entire world.

I just needed someone to believe me.

39

ETHAN

Devil In Me - Halsey

"This is the most exciting thing I've ever done."

Elliot takes a sip of his milkshake. My finger taps on my steering wheel. Waiting. *Patiently waiting.*

My phone beeps, but I don't take my eyes off the house we're watching.

"Don't worry it's just me in the group chat. Jade asked where we were."

Elliot taps some more on his phone and me on my wheel.

"For real, though, I'm so excited."

"Or so you said," I answer flatly.

It's not excitement that runs through my body. It's a need for the kill.

Normally, it's something I have to feed about every six months. It's not too bad. Manageable. When I start having nightmares about high school again, about the bullying, that's when I know it's time to act before I just kill someone for something as stupid as stealing my parking spot.

But since Jade has been back, things aren't the same.

And since she was assaulted by that cop...the growing need inside me is turning insatiable.

Three weeks.

Elliot made me wait three. Fucking. Weeks to let me get my hands on him.

First, we had to convince Alex Delacroix to not take this to the cops. To not get her expensive lawyers on it. If we made some noise about it, it would lead right back to us when we took matters into our own hands.

Then Elliot was on my fucking back. The least patient man on earth just wouldn't leave me the fuck alone.

His colleagues saw the whole thing. It's too obvious, Ethan.

If I'm being patient, you can too, Ethan.

We'll get him when it doesn't link back to Jade, Ethan.

And there was Jade forbidding us to do anything about it.

Forbidding us like she has a right to.

He touched her.

He touched her against her will. He made her feel like we wouldn't believe her.

He made her doubt herself, doubt *us*.

If Xi's girlfriend hadn't showed up at the scene, who knows what could have happened.

The fact that Elliot is coming with me means everything. A line has been crossed. One we can't accept.

That man signed his death warrant when he assaulted her. But we go by our own law on the North Shore.

On the other side of that bridge, I'm the judge, the jury, the executioner. I'm the entire fucking court. That cop is about to leave his house like he does every night. We've been observing him. He leaves his perfect family for the convenience store, buys a pack of cigarettes, takes one out, smokes it, then throws the whole pack away to pretend to himself that he's quitting, and repeats the same thing the next night. Except this time, he won't be coming back home.

The second I see him exit, I start the car.

"Obvious much?" Elliot says in a low tone. "Take your time, brother."

"Elliot," I sigh. "I know you're used to us always following your lead, but this is my territory. I know what I'm doing."

I can feel him looking at me, but I keep my eyes on Hall.

"If you leave right after him, it'll give us away before we even get close enough."

"Maybe I want him to know. To realize he's being followed. To start getting scared of what's going to happen to him."

I hear Elliot inhale, ready to talk. He stops himself. "Fucking hell. You really are one of those psycho killers, aren't you?"

"You have no idea."

I press the gas pedal and follow Hall down his street.

"I knew you were intense from the state of your victims, but I don't think I expected the chasing."

"And yet here we are."

I follow him over a few blocks, making sure to indicate as soon as he does, to replicate his exact driving.

I can tell when he gets it. When he starts going around in circles to test if we're following. And I do. I keep making sure to go exactly where he does. He follows the Silver Snake River and turns into the forest.

Big.

Mistake.

Once he gets on the long road that crosses the woods, his fate is sealed. The trees here are so big they reach over to the other side of the road. It looks like a tunnel made of creepy branches and shadows. The moonlight barely gets through, dangerously isolating the place.

The only lights are the ones from our cars illuminating the ominous road.

"The guy must be scared to death right now," Elliot chuckles.

I smirk. "That's the plan, isn't it?"

My brother turns to me again, and this time I glance at him. "I've never heard that in your voice."

"What?"

"That kind of excitement. It's creepy as fuck, Ethan."

I laugh. "I'm weird. You said it yourself."

"It's a good kind of weird."

Right on time, the front of his car starts smoking. Elliot cocks his head, confused.

"Did you do that?"

"I learned a few things from working on the van with our girl."

Elliot huffs. "It still feels strange to call her *our* girl."

"I know."

"But she is our girl, isn't she?" He pauses, clearly thinking. "I worked so hard to have her to myself. You never had to put in the effort. She was in love with you all along."

"She's never going to choose, brother. The longer it lasts, the worse it gets. She thought she could get out of this situation, but she waited, and she keeps getting deeper and deeper in her feelings. And now look; she's in love with both of us."

"Yeah, right," he snorts.

Hall starts slowing down, putting his hazard lights on.

"What's that about?" I ask, curious of his reaction. It's not like Elliot to doubt someone's devotion to him. He's seen it all from women over the years. They have always wanted him badly enough to do anything to get him.

"Whatever she feels for me isn't love. And to be honest, brother, I don't know if it'll ever be."

"Are you insane?" I press the brake harder when Hall's car suddenly stops working. He's got just enough momentum to pull over to the side of the road.

"Do you know how many times I've heard her tell you she loves you since she's been back?

"You counted?"

"Four. That I know of."

"What the fuck is wrong with you?" I huff.

"I'm obsessed. That's what's wrong. Do you know how many times she told me?"

"I'm going to assume zero," I say deadpan. I pull over right behind Hall's car.

"The only time she used the word love toward me was to say she loved the both of us."

I play with my helix piercing. "So she did say she loved you—"

"Stop pissing me off, Ethan. We're doing some important work, and I don't want to ruin it just because you make me lose my shit."

"I was trying to help. Okay, so she didn't tell you she's in love with you. She is, though."

"I want to choke that smug voice out of you right now."

I smile at him when he turns to me. "You just hate when I have something you don't, so I'm telling you; she is in love with you."

Hall finally gets out of his car, eyeing us suspiciously. He makes a show of showing his gun attached to his belt as he walks to the front of his vehicle.

"Are you just going to stay in your truck and watch him fix his?"

I shake my head. "You stay here and let me do what I'm good at, alright?"

I get out, putting a cap on just for show. Just because it says I want to hide my face and it'll make the cop even more uncomfortable.

"You alright there, pal?" I call out.

He looks up from the open hood of his car.

"Who are you?"

I raise my palms in front of me, coming closer to him. "I was right behind you and saw your car smoking. I just thought you might need some help."

He eyes me suspiciously, his hands going under his jacket and showing me his gun again.

"I'm a cop," he uses as a threat. Something to warn me off. "Don't do anything funny, bud."

"Whoa, okay," I chuckle, stopping a few steps from him. "I was just checking on you. Your car's broken down." A beat. "At night." My pause is longer this time, letting the fear sink into him. "All on your own."

His face falls, but he shakes his head. "I'm fine. Go back to your car."

Flashing him a reassuring smile, I nod. "Alright. Let me know if you need anything. I'm a mechanic, so I've got a few things in the back."

He hesitates, and to push him, I take a step back and turn around, slowly walking to my truck.

The second I wrap my hand around my handle, he calls out, "Yeah, I might need a hand with this."

My gaze crosses with Elliot's, his smile chilling.

I turn around, my eyebrows raised.

"I have to admit"—he massages the back of his neck— "I'm not much of a mechanic."

"Hey, man, you protect our town." I smile brightly. "To each their own."

I make sure my gaze doesn't leave his as I go back to him. Everything I'm doing is reassuring, but the way in which I'm doing it is making his instincts ring alarm bells in his head. Too bad for him, he needs me.

I lean over his hood, checking the smoking. "Ah, it's your transmission fluid, pal. I can fix that in no time."

I have no idea what the fuck I'm saying.

"Let me grab what I need from the truck."

"Thanks." He's still not fully relaxed, eyeing me like I'm hiding something.

I am going to torture and kill him, to be fair.

I grab a heavy-duty wrench from the back of my truck and make sure to hit the end against my palm as I come back. His confusion shows. His instincts are screaming I'm dangerous, and yet I'm just a nice citizen trying to help.

"Alright, let's have a look." I bend over, loosening bolts, tapping random shit and pretending I'm fixing the fucker's car.

"You know"—his chesty laugh rumbles as he finally relaxes—"for a second there, I thought you were some sort of psycho following me."

I laugh. "No way?"

"Yeah. I could swear you'd been following me for ages. I almost called my colleagues for backup." He whistles. "Thank God I didn't."

I straighten up. "Ah, that. No, no, you were right. I *was* following you."

His brow furrows, unable to process.

"And I am some sort of psycho."

He barely has time to understand what I'm saying before I swing the wrench, hitting the side of his head.

His body goes down with a thump, and I feel a smile creeping onto my face.

This is going to be fun.

It takes both Elliot and I to put him in the back of the truck.

"Tree thirteen?" my brother suggests.

"Can't I have a bit of fun with him before?"

"You can have fun at tree thirteen, Ethan. It'll save a lot of cleaning afterward."

I fake a pout that makes him burst into a laugh. "Drive, asshole."

Tree thirteen is a place in the woods of the North Shore that both NSC and the Kings have turned into an unofficial graveyard. It's the only place that we share because if cops were ever to find the bodies there, it would be so hard to lead it to one person that they'd have to arrest the entire North Shore.

Impossible.

We're all protecting ourselves by adding to the place.

I cross the bridge back to the North Shore, drive into the woods on our side of the river and until the road turns into gravel, then into a dirt road, and I keep going until it completely disappears.

"I haven't been here in so long," I admit.

"Really? Maybe I should take you with me next time I clean up your mess."

I take a deep breath, not knowing how to bring this up with him, and yet trying anyway. "Elliot, I...want him to suffer. I need to get it out of me. Don't try to stop me once I've started."

He observes me for a few silent seconds. I can

practically hear the sound of an imaginary clock counting down until it's finally time to make the fucker pay. "Go ahead, brother. Be yourself."

It's bloody.

So fucking bloody.

Elliot sits on the hood of my truck as I let the rage take over.

But my kind of rage has never been loud or out of control.

It's precise, painful, meant to make the culprit die slowly.

All I decided to use is that wrench, but I don't need to beat him with it. I can crush every single one of his bones. I started with his fingers, every single knuckle. Then it's the hand. Now his wrists.

His screams are muffled by the rag I shoved in his mouth, but his tears are free to fall. He tries to ask why. He tries to understand.

But I don't need him to.

I know, and so does Elliot. That fucker doesn't even deserve an answer as to why he's being tortured.

"Isn't it horrible?" I ask. "That you know you're going to die, but it's going to take a long time. It's coming, just not yet."

His pleas are unclear through the gag, but I think I get it.

"Your power is the law. Your gun. The respect or the fear people have of you. And you abused it. My power is that I kill people as a hobby. That I'm bigger and stronger than you. But mainly that I don't fear committing crimes. You abused your power, Hall. Now I'm going to abuse mine."

Instead of hitting him, or compressing another body part between the claws of the wrench, I turn it around, and push the other end onto his closed eye. More...and more...

until his screams of pain send birds flying and I see him cry blood.

"Is it hurting?"

The yes is easy to understand.

"Oh no." I pout, cocking my head to the side. "Where, buddy?"

Elliot bursts into laughter behind me. "You're fucked in the head, brother." He says that, but he's sipping on a caramel milkshake, watching a man being tortured.

"Are you two for *fucking* real?"

Jade's voice startles us both. All we hear for a moment are the pleas and whimpers from Hall.

I'm too shocked to speak, so Elliot takes over. "My love," he says sweetly, as if we haven't just been caught torturing a man who assaulted her in the middle of the woods.

"Don't *my love* me, Elliot. What do you think you're doing?"

He smiles as I stand up, the wrench dripping red on the forest floor. The smell of pinewoods is mixing with the coppery scent of blood. I like it. It's soothing.

"Enjoying a milkshake?"

She narrows her feline-like jade eyes at him, and the eyeliner she draws on her eyelids enhances the effect.

"What?" He raises his palm. "I'm not doing anything."

She cocks an eyebrow, unimpressed, as her eyes flick to me. "Are you going to say you're not doing anything either?"

"How did you know we were here?"

"Because I'm not a fucking idiot," she snaps back at me. "You've not left me alone more than two seconds at a time in the last three weeks and, suddenly, you tell me you're both out tonight? With no serious explanation?"

"And you knew we'd be at tree thirteen?"

"I checked that fucker's house before. Lights were on,

474

his wife and kids were having dinner. Clearly, you weren't there. There aren't many places on the North Shore where you can take someone to kill them."

Hall cries out. Probably something about having family and deserving to live, but we all ignore him.

"Where did you park?" Elliot asks.

We got Jade's car back the day after Hall put his hands on her, but she hasn't been wanting to drive since.

"At the edge of the woods."

"You walked the whole way here?" Elliot jumps off the hood of the truck, his tall form towering over the tiny thing Jade is. "What if something happened to you?"

She throws her hand up, frustrated. "The two most dangerous things in this forest are right here, torturing a man."

"A man," Elliot scoffs. "That guy ain't no fucking man. He abused his position to—"

"I know what he did. I was there."

"Then you understand why we're doing what we're doing too." Elliot takes a sip of his milkshake, shrugging.

Jade pinches her lips. My brother's casual demeanor isn't doing it for her, so I decide to take charge. "Mi Cielo, come here."

She hesitates, and I extend my hand, digging my black eyes into her greens. "Trust me."

She slowly takes the few steps separating us, her eyes going back and forth between Hall and me. Her face twists when she sees the state he's in from up close. I grab her hand, pulling her in front of me, her back to my chest, and forcing her to fist the bloody wrench with both hands.

My palms cover hers, and I talk softly in her ear. "We know there's something raging in you. Something you've been wanting to let out. I don't know what it is, Jade, but you've been punishing yourself for the things you can't control. Every time I watch you get angry, I also see the regret in your eyes. I *feel* it. I don't want to ever see that hate in your eyes that's directed at yourself."

I kiss the skin below her ear. "You are the bravest woman I know. You survived through your dad's death, your mom's illness. You survived on your own in a broken town. You fought Sawyer and you fought Stan. You kept your head high when we brought you back. You are a queen, Jade. You're my heaven and hell, my most beautiful salvation. I want you to feel the way you make me feel. The freedom and the deliverance."

She shakes her head, sniffling. "I'm scared."

"The only thing you're scared of is letting yourself be vulnerable. But we're here. We've got you. It's okay to admit that this man hurt you. It's okay to acknowledge what he did. He put you in a vulnerable position."

"Stop, please."

"He assaulted you when there was nothing you could do to defend yourself."

Her knees buckle, but I keep her tightly against me.

"So let it out. I'll hold you. I'll be there. Don't do it for me or for Elliot. Don't do it to put on a strong face." I bring her hands above her head, some blood from the wrench dripping down and onto her wrists. "Let the pain take a hold of you and do it for yourself."

She doesn't move, so I keep digging. I guide her through it.

"Tell me something that hurts inside." She doesn't understand the question. She doesn't process hurt the same way everyone else does, so I change my tactic. "Tell me something that makes you angry."

"This cop."

"Why?"

"You know why."

"*Why?*"

For a few seconds, I think she's going to tell me to fuck off and leave. Jade doesn't admit defeat, hurt, grief. She'd rather live through the agony, translate it into fury, and let the world know how angry she is.

"Because he assaulted me."

"Yeah, he's fucking vermin and doesn't deserve to live. Now give me something else."

"Vickie."

She's sticking to her list of people she hates, but I want something more. "She deserved to die too. Give me something else. Not a name, Jade. Something *else* that makes you angry."

Her arms are starting to tremble above her. "I let Sawyer blackmail me."

"The very definition of it means you can't *let* someone do it. It's not your fault. Keep going."

"I sold my body to escape this town. It makes me angry."

"What else."

Getting in the rhythm of it now, she barely needs me to nudge her. "My dad. I love him, but I don't understand why he didn't ask me for help. It makes me sad."

She's finally changing the emotion from angry to sad. "More, baby. Give it all to me."

"I'm sad that I was born here, and I never managed to get out for good. I'm sad that I joined the Kings to feel powerful instead of finding it within me. I'm sad because I'm ugly and my body never listens to me. I'm sad that I used to make myself sick to fit in with the pretty girls. I'm fucking exhausted because I want a job and money, and a chance at life. I think of all the times my mom wished she could have gotten me the pet I would beg for, but we couldn't, and I hate myself that I was making her feel guilty. I'm sad because I want a bunny like Alex!"

A scream like I've never heard before tears through her chest, cries into the night...and she slams the wrench down on Hall's face.

Blood spurts from him onto the both of us. She went straight for his face, not bothering with his body.

She screams again when he whimpers and cries. She hits him, shrieking at him to shut up. And she hits over and over again until we're both sprayed with his blood, and he doesn't make a sound anymore.

The hits are only thumps once his skull is broken into pieces, but she keeps going. She continues until there's no strength left in her, no tears left to cry.

She's just panting, covered in blood and hotter than I've ever seen her.

Elliot is standing next to us now, the milkshake gone. His eyes are shining with pride. They probably match mine.

We both watch her as she spits on him.

"He deserved it," she rasps. "All of it."

"He did, my love," Elliot backs her up.

Unable to stop myself, I slide a hand in her hair and pull until she twists and faces me, and I capture her lips in a savage kiss.

She smells coppery, but her tongue tastes of the acidity of green apples. Her hair feels wet and clumpy with all the blood stuck in her strands, but it only makes me fist it harder.

I only pull away for a split second, my lips grazing hers, barely able to resist the temptation. "You're so brave," I whisper. "So fucking brave."

"I love you," she murmurs. Her hands come to fist my shirt and she looks up at me. "I love you, Ethan."

"I love you too, baby."

"A pet bunny, huh?" Elliot cuts in, making us all burst into laughter.

40

ELLIOT

I'm Not Okay (I promise) - My Chemical Romance

"Settle down, will you?" I grab Jade by the waist and pull her back to the edge of the bed.

She's sitting cross-legged, her back to the edge, and I'm standing behind her, brushing her hair after her shower.

"It hurts," she whines.

"I used the entire fucking bottle of conditioner. How can it hurt?"

I think I'm developing a showering kink. Is that a thing? I'm incapable of letting Jade shower on her own anymore. It's become something we do just the two of us, where Ethan doesn't care to join us, and I fucking love it.

I love lathering her in soap, rubbing, massaging every inch of her skin. I love washing her wild hair, making sure to cover every strand in conditioner. I like tickling her while we let it sit.

And I love...oh I fucking love making her come with the shower jet.

She's still flushed from it right now, squirming on the spot.

"Ow!" She slaps my hand before tightening the towel around her.

"That's about enough, young lady."

"You're a year older than me," she throws back, deadpan.

"Which makes you younger. You know it's a fucking mess in the morning when you don't brush it after your shower. I'm not spending tomorrow morning listening to you scream at your hairbrush and throw it across the room."

She juts her chin higher. "You don't have long hair. You don't know the frustration it is when it doesn't do what you tell it to."

"Jade...you called the hairbrush and its entire family a cunt. Hairbrushes don't have families, baby."

"It's very frustrating," she insists.

"Hence why if we brush it now, tomorrow will be easier. Come on now." I grab thick strands, brushing more of the tips, but the second I get to the roots, she slaps my hand away again.

"It hurts!"

I roll my eyes, grab both her wrists, and pin them to the small of her back. With my other hand, I undo the towel and let it fall to her waist. I slap each breast once with the back of the brush, making her gasp.

"What the..."

"How was that? Which one hurts more?"

She squirms, and a smile spreads on my lips. "Oh...you liked it. Look up at me."

"I didn't like it," she lies as she meets my gaze, but her eyes say something else.

"My love," I chuckle. "What am I meant to do with a little slut like you?"

"Stop touching my hair, for one."

"Deal. I'll touch your pretty pussy instead. Spread your legs."

"How about fuck off?"

I slap her tits again, one after the other. And then another time for the sake of it. "Now spread."

"You're infuriating." She says that, but her thighs slide across the sheets.

"I think your pussy disagrees. Wider."

"I hate you." She spreads wider.

"Not even a little bit."

The moment her legs are where I want them, I slap her clit with the back of the brush.

"Elliot!"

"Yes, baby?" I do it again, making her jump on the spot.

"That's..."

"Amazing?"

She refuses to answer, so I keep going until she's writhing and moaning. I slap her little clit until her head falls back against me and her breasts move up and down to the rhythm of her panting.

"Look at you," I purr in her ear. "So fucking beautiful. Such a good little whore desperate to come for me. That's what you want, baby, isn't it? You want to make me proud and come hard."

"Y-yes."

"Of course you do. Come on." Instead of pausing between each slap, I accelerate, my rhythm not giving her time to recover. "Come like the perfect slut you are."

"Elliot," she moans. "Fuck...ah..."

I keep going relentlessly, small taps that wouldn't hurt, only bringing her pleasure.

"Jade," I growl. "Be a good girl and come for me."

That's all she needs to come undone. Her limbs tremble, and her legs come to her chest, folding over. I keep hold of her wrists, relishing the sounds she makes as she reaches her peak.

When I finally throw the brush away, she looks up at me, and I quirk an eyebrow. "What do you say?"

"Thank you," she sighs.

"I'm going to make you squirt tonight."

She blinks up at me. "W-what?"

"Don't act like you don't know what that is." I brush hairs away from her forehead.

"I know what it is, but I don't think I..."

"Are you going to tell me Stan never made you squirt with all the toys he had?"

She bites her lower lip, shaking her head. "I don't think so?"

The question in her statement makes me smile. She's so fucking cute like this. Still damp from the shower, wet for me, and high on her latest orgasm. Her wrists are in my hand, utterly at my mercy.

The image of perfection.

"If you don't think so, it didn't happen." I turn my head toward my bedroom door. "Ethan!" I call out.

He's here in a few seconds. His gaze is on Jade, who's still sitting on the bed uncomfortably.

"We're going to make our girl squirt tonight."

A smirk spreads on his lips. "Oh yeah?" He steps toward the bed, shamelessly tapping Jade's pussy. She startles in my grip. "So wet already. Eager to come all over yourself?"

"It feels...it's weird to talk about it," she admits, round eyes going from me to my brother.

"Why's that? Is it embarrassing to acknowledge you're a little slut who is desperate for us to make her wet herself?"

She blushes, but it only encourages him further. "Come here." I let her go so Ethan can grab her hand and guide her to the other side of the bed.

He helps her stand up, discarding the towel entirely. "Put your hands behind your head."

Jade licks her lips, looking at the both of us. "This doesn't...hurt, right?"

I join her, taking one hand and lifting it behind her head. "Only in the best way."

She does the other on her own.

"Your hands don't move, clear?" Ethan says sternly.

"Yes."

He cocks an eyebrow at her.

"Yes, Master," she corrects herself.

Because I know there will be no praise coming from him, I put a reassuring hand between her shoulder blades. "Good girl. Keep doing what you're told." Her beautiful green eyes looking up at me with devotion get me hard.

Ethan doesn't give her a break. "Spread your legs. Nice and wide. That's it. Your hands won't move. Your legs won't move. You'll stay standing up. I don't care if it's too much, and I don't care if your muscles are begging you to give up. You will stay exactly like this. Is that clear?"

She's already trembling, the excitement clear on her face. "Yes, Master."

I can't help but lick my lips when I look her up and down. She is so perfect like this. She's going to degrade herself for my brother, and I will be praising her for all the good work she puts in. Her reward will be my dick in her beautiful pussy.

Ethan looks at me, satisfied with how he just set her up. He and I don't need to talk to communicate. I settle behind our girl, and he stays at the front, going on his knees.

"Are you wet because Elliot gave you an orgasm?"

"Yes, Master." The simple fact of saying those words makes her shiver.

"You're getting wetter just thinking about it. What a little slut."

His fingers disappear between her pussy lips, and the next second, her back curves. She presses against me, and I wrap an arm around her waist, splaying my fingers on her lower stomach.

"You love it when you've got two fingers pressing against your G-spot." Ethan's statement is accompanied by a loud, agreeing moan from her.

"You're going to show us how you take more, huh? You're going to take mine and Elliot's fingers in this beautiful cunt."

I know he keeps rubbing her because her legs are already shaking, short moans bursting out of her to the rhythm of his fingers.

Keeping an arm around her waist, I slip my hand behind her to find her entrance. Ethan stops pressing inside, scissoring his fingers instead.

"Fuck..." Jade gasps. "That feels...that feels strange."

"I'm just making sure you're open enough to take the both of us, baby," Ethan rasps. "You stay exactly how you are."

Her arms are shaking, struggling to stay up and behind her head.

I push one finger in at first, making her whimper. "You're doing great, my love."

She melts into me, her head falling back against my chest, but Ethan tuts her. "Stay upright if you don't want me to slap this clit raw."

She straightens up, and the moment she's settled again, I add a second finger.

"Fuck," she squeaks. "Wait—wait."

"Shh." I kiss the top of her head. "Be good, baby."

We move slowly, finding our rhythm. Him at the front, with two fingers pressing against her G-spot, and me at her back, slowly coming in and out and adding more pressure to his touch.

Her legs shake as her screams get higher. The sound of her wetness resonates in the room.

"That's it," I whisper. "Relax."

"I can't...I can't..." she pants, her breaths shortening by the second.

I press on her mound. I'm gentle, but I keep my hold firm.

"Let go," Ethan orders. "You're holding back."

"I'm scared," she moans. One of her arms falls to her side, and she hurries to put it back up. "Please...please, it's too much."

"I do whatever the fuck I want with you, now let go and come on yourself."

"Oh God," she whimpers.

We press harder inside her in perfect harmony, at the same time I push on her lower stomach.

"Wet yourself like the dirty little slut you are," Ethan growls.

She finally lets go, her orgasm gushing down her thighs and covering our hands.

"Fuck," she moans. "No..."

We keep at it, taking everything she has to offer. My dick is painfully hard in my boxers, and I keep thrusting into her lower back.

"Look at you," Ethan chuckles. "Covering yourself in your own cum. You're so fucking pathetic."

She cries out when we both remove our hands.

He grabs her hair, pulling her away from me, and I fall back onto the bed, desperate to fist my aching cock.

"Fuck," I groan when I finally free myself.

Ethan pushes Jade to her knees. "Where's our thank you for giving you the orgasm of your life?"

"Thank you," she pants.

He chuckles, looking down at her as her hand comes between her legs. "You want more, huh?"

"Yes. Yes, please," she begs.

"Lay on your back. Put your head where you soiled the floor."

She doesn't hesitate one second, and I thrust into my fist, her submission getting the best of me.

"You're being such a good girl, Jade. Keep going."

She whimpers at my words, her hand furtively rubbing her clit. She's fucking insatiable.

With her head right next to where she wet the floor, Ethan clucks his tongue. "That's not what I asked for, toy."

Her eyes widen as the tip of his boot advances toward her face. He presses it against her cheek, forcing her head to the side until the other side of her face is pressed against the wet spot.

She whimpers, her eyes squeezing shut.

"That's what you get when you don't listen. Are you sorry?"

"Yes. I'm sorry, Master."

"If you disobey again, I'll rub your entire face in it, do you understand? I will flip you around and make you lick your own cum off the floor." His boot presses harder. "Do. You. Understand?"

"Yes," she moans. "Yes, Master."

I'm panting, choking my cock as my eyes go from her wincing face to her fingers furiously rubbing her clit. She's not trying to be discreet about it anymore. Her legs are wide open, her hips bucking.

"You just love being degraded, don't you? You're going to come from just that, aren't you?"

"Y-yes...yes...yes..."

"But not before we both give you permission."

"Please!"

"Fuck, Ethan," I growl. "She's killing me."

He smirks up at me. "We'll wait for Elliot to be ready. He'll take as long as he needs."

I stand up, still rubbing myself as I stand over her. She opens her eyes to plead, "Please, Elliot."

"Stay still," I grunt.

She keeps touching herself as I explode and lean over to come all over her face. Some of it goes on Ethan's boot, most on the side of her face that isn't pressed against the floor.

"Fuck," she gasps. "Please...I need to come. I'm *begging you.*"

"Rub your little clit and humiliate yourself, baby," Ethan rasps. "Come from being covered in Elliot's cum. Come from being under my boot."

She screams, her eyes rolling to the back of her head as she makes herself orgasm.

"You're unbelievable," I whisper to her. "So fucking perfect."

Ethan lets her go, standing right next to her head as I

help her sit up. He looks at my cum on his boot and cocks an eyebrow at Jade.

"Show me you're thankful for your orgasm."

She eyes him, then the boot, before a small gasp escapes her. Squirming on the spot.

"Toy." There's a rumble in his chest. A *need* for her to do it. "Lick it clean. *Now*."

I can't catch a fucking break. My dick hardens again when she goes on all fours, her slick pussy right in my vision. And when she lowers her head and licks my brother's boot, I let mine fall back.

"Fuck...Jade."

I can't fucking wait anymore. I grab her by the waist, pulling her away from Ethan, and sit down on the bed before impaling her on me, her back to my chest.

Her mouth falls open, inhaling sharply. Unlike my brother, I don't want to see her do anything for me. I just want to watch her come undone from what I inflict on her. I want her to let me take control and let me do anything as I want.

Keeping a tight grip on her hips, I thrust up, making her gasp. "I got you, baby," I growl in her ear. "Be good and stay still."

There's no mercy in the way I fuck her, just pure lust. She lets her head fall back on my shoulder, and it allows me to see Ethan getting rid of all his clothes.

I lean back as he approaches, laying on the bed with my feet on the floor. And of course, I take Jade with me. She lies with her back on my front as I keep fucking her, and I only slow down when Ethan grabs her legs, wrapping them around his waist.

"Wh-what are you doing?" she pants.

"I'm going to fuck your pussy."

490

She shakes her head. "Elliot…he's too big for that."

His smirk could be taken as a threat in itself. "We've loosened you good, baby. You're all wet and relaxed now."

"Don't worry," I murmur in her ear. "We'll take it slow. If it's too much, we'll stop."

Ethan nods as he pushes his fingers at her entrance. I feel him on the underneath of my cock. He loosens her some more, making her moan loudly.

"You can't get enough of us, huh?" I chuckle, kissing the side of her head. "Let us both in, baby. Do it for us."

Ethan's fingers retreat, and his pierced tip startles me. "Fuck," I laugh. "That shit feels weird."

"I'm sure you'll be fine, brother. Just be a good toy like our girl."

I thrust up violently, making him wince since he was barely starting to push in. "I've killed people who said less than that to me. Watch it."

He laughs at my threat, but he doesn't insist.

"Focus on her," I growl.

And he does. While I grab a nipple between my thumb and forefinger, he licks the other, then nibbles at it until Jade is so gone, he can push inside her and make her feel even better.

We all stop moving as Ethan bottoms out. "You did it, toy." He smiles down at her. "You're taking both of us."

She's sweating, the back of her head pressing against my chest, and as Ethan and I slowly start moving again, she bucks her hips to our rhythm.

"Fuck. Fuck, it's tight," Ethan grunts, losing his calm. "Fuck, baby, you're so good to us."

I'm just as surprised as him to hear him praise her, but after what she offers us, what she lets us do with her body, I think my brother is ready to worship her altar too.

"I'm gonna come," Jade whines. "This is too much. I need to come."

Ethan rubs her clit slowly, sending new sensations through her body. "Do it, Mi Cielo."

"Come for us," I conclude.

And when she does, it's the end of both of us. Ethan's head falls on her chest as he grunts, accelerating to a point that I can't catch up with him anymore, and I explode as he does, both forcing our girl to take everything we have to give.

Ethan loses his strength, falling on the both of us.

"Heavy motherfucker," I wheeze. "Get up."

But Jade giggles, wrapping a hand at the back of his head and stroking his black hair at the same time as she reaches above herself to touch my cheek.

"That was the craziest thing I've ever done," she pants.

"For now," Ethan mumbles into her tits.

I can't help but laugh. "You two are gonna be the end of me." I smile even though neither of them can see me.

Suddenly, I don't care about the weight of them crushing me. I can feel Jade's hand on my cheek, her skin against mine.

I don't need to breathe if I can keep her this close.

I shower her again. Then I wrap her in a blanket, make her some popcorn, and put on an intense action movie since they're her favorite. Once I sit down next to her, she nestles against me, taking popcorn from my lap.

"You know that's not her doing her stunts, right?" she says, watching with interest.

"Looks so much like her, though."

"Damn, look at that drifting."

"You could do that easily." I caress her hair, watching the TV. "Is that something you still want to do? Stunt driving?"

She looks up at me. "You remember?"

"Of course I remember," I snort.

She falls back on my shoulder, hesitant. "I don't know. I guess, anything with cars will do."

"Like robbing banks?"

She laughs. "Yeah, like that."

Both our phones beep. It's Ethan in the group chat.

> Ethan: Mi Cielo, bring me an energy bar, please. Your screams are going to keep me writing music all night.

> Ethan: I want you crawling to me. Holding it between your teeth.

I roll my eyes. The guy has no fucking limit. Jade groans, starting to shift as if to get up, but I wrap an arm around her waist as I text back.

> Elliot: After care, asshole. Ever heard of it?

> Ethan: Am I talking to you?

> Ethan: Baby, come rest at my feet.

Her hips shift, and I know his words turn her on.

"You don't have to, my love. And if you play with him, I want you to come back to me afterward so I can take care of you some more."

> Ethan: I've got a pretty tail for my kitten.

Jade looks up at me again, eyes shining. "I want to, but

493

I'm exhausted, and I think I should get some sleep for tomorrow."

> Elliot: She says fuck off.

"Elliot," she huffs. "Was that really necessary?"
"What?"
She types on her phone.

> Jade: I didn't say fuck off. I'm just tired and I think I need some sleep. Tomorrow?

"When we're rich," I whisper to her, "he can throw money at your naked body then. And we'll buy you all the pet bunnies on the planet."

She laughs so hard she snorts, making me tighten my grip on her just to have her closer to me.

"How are you feeling about tomorrow?" I ask, playing with the ends of her hair. I finally managed to keep her still long enough to brush it and put in some hair mousse for her curls. Then I braided it for the night.

"I'm a bit anxious," she admits.

"It's the biggest fucking job we've ever done. It's no joke, for sure."

"That's not what scares me. I trust Ethan and Kay to move the money fast enough. I trust the van I built, and I have full confidence in my abilities as a driver. I even trust you to get the safe open and," she hesitates, grabbing a popcorn and crushing it between her thumb and forefinger, "I know you got that girl around your finger. *That's* what makes me anxious."

When I don't say anything, she sighs. "Have you kissed her yet? Fucked her?"

494

"The other day you said you didn't want to know about any of this."

"Well, now I do. I want to know what you've done with her."

I let my head fall back against the sofa, and I look at the ceiling instead of the movie still playing in front of us. People are shooting each other now. There's a car chase, and the sound of guns and screeching tires is starting to get on my nerves. It feels like a bad omen for tomorrow.

"I haven't fucked her. And I haven't kissed her."

She seems to stop breathing for a second. "So, you're really playing the teasing card."

"Yeah. I promise her shit I'm never going to give her. I compliment her like I mean it, but all I can think about is you and how you're waiting at home for me. I think about you in my bed, between Ethan and me. And I think about how good it feels when I fuck you. My body is with her, but my mind constantly screams *Jade, Jade, Jade.* All my life that's all my brain has been screaming."

I take a deep breath, bracing for another disappointment. "I think about how much you mean to me. That I'm in love with you."

She stills completely.

Come on, Jade. Give it to me.

Three simple words.

That's all I need.

"It makes me feel better that you don't give her any part of you," she murmurs against my chest.

And I'm fucking done.

I thought I could take it one more time, but I can't.

I push her off me violently as I stand up, the popcorn falling onto the floor.

"What the fuck," I hiss as I snap around. "What

the...*Why*?"

She sits up in a panic. "What? What did I say?"

"It's what you *don't* say, Jade. Why can't you fucking do it?"

She seems to understand what I mean, slowly getting up. "Elliot." The apology in her voice kills me. It extinguishes the little fire I had in me.

I run a hand through my hair, feeling my throat constricting. "You tell Ethan you love him all the time."

"I know, but—"

"Why not me?" I rasp. "Please, Jade. I would do anything for you. I *did* everything in my power to have you. I have nothing else to give. Do you understand that? You have all of me. I—I'm fucking sharing you with my brother, for fuck's sake. What else am I meant to do?"

She takes a step back, but I grab her hand. "No. You don't get to avoid the conversation this time. You're going to face the fact that I've been desperately in love with you for as long as I can remember, and you're going to tell me how you feel. Even if you don't feel the same. Even if it's to tell me you'll never be able to love me the way you do Ethan."

"What's going on?" My brother's voice resonates softly in the room.

My eyes flick to him. Topless, with his headset around his neck and the cord hanging by his side.

"You're not running away from this, Jade," I say to her.

"Please, Elliot. I can't...I can't do this."

When she tries to take another step back, I grab her other hand. It doesn't really stop her attempt, and I'm too tired to fight.

I drop to my knees, both her hands in mine. "If this is the night you decide to choose, then so be it. But I'm not going to hurt myself over and over again asking for your love. I can't do it anymore." I gulp, my gaze dropping. "It hurts too much."

"I can't do this," she panics some more. "Please, it's not that simple."

"He's right, Mi Cielo. You're unfair, and he's allowed to know how you feel."

"I can't." A sniffle makes me look up. She's crying, but it doesn't stop me.

"Do you want Ethan? Is that it? If that's truly what you want, then I'll let you two be, Jade. I'd rather that than knowing my whole life that I'll always come after him. That there's a brother you love and another you tolerate."

"It's not...Please...I can't," she sobs.

"I want the truth."

"Elliot, I..."

Time stops as she looks me in the eye, so much guilt transpiring. It thickens the jade color around her pupils, it makes her hands shake in mine.

I expect her to break my heart. I brace for it.

But I certainly don't expect her to say what she says next.

"I killed your dad, Elliot." She chokes on the end of the sentence, then gasps a breath. "I'm sorry. I'm so sorry. I love you. I'm in love with you, but how can I say it to you when I live with the guilt of what I've done?"

I fall on my ass, my mouth dropping open.

"What are you talking about?" Ethan comes nearer, attempting to put a hand on her shoulder, but she shrugs him off, stepping out of my hold and away.

"I'm sorry," she repeats. "I'm sorry. He—" Her eyes are wild, going from my brother to me. "He hurt me." She points to the hallway. "He assaulted me...and I...oh my God, I'm so sorry. I tried to tell someone."

I can't say anything as she keeps walking away, putting her palms in front of herself as if to keep us at bay. I just watch her...shock keeping me frozen.

"Your mom," she says to Ethan. "She didn't believe me. And Vickie...Lea...at school...no one believed me." She's wheezing, struggling to breathe, but I think Ethan and I are both too gone to react.

"Please." Her struggle to breathe puts a weight on my chest. "Please, I didn't mean to. He did it once, and when... when he tried again." She stops pointing at the hallway, now looking at the sofa with round eyes, as if rewatching the scene unfold.

"I had come to ask for a ride to school. My dad had been called to work early. And you guys were already gone. Joel dragged me inside and he—he tried again. He said no one was here to save me...he wanted to go further...I just." She shakes her head, wiping her forearm against her red nose. "I grabbed his gun to scare him off. We fought for it, and it just went off. I didn't...I don't know, maybe I did it on purpose. I just wanted him to leave me alone."

Her back hits the wall. She slides down, bringing her knees to her chest as she grabs her roots. "I just wanted him to leave me alone."

She looks up at Ethan as he approaches her slowly, putting a hand in front of himself like someone advancing toward a wild beast.

"Your mom opened the front door just as it happened," she tells him. "And when she saw what he tried to do, my ripped clothes, she said she'd take care of the body. She left with it in her car, told me to tidy the house." She shakes her head. "She never came back."

She gives up on trying to explain herself. Her head

drops to her knees, and she wraps her arms around her legs.

The silence stretches forever. Her against the wall that separates the living room from the kitchen. Me on the floor by the sofa. Ethan, in between us, standing and lost as to what to do.

The movie keeps playing in the background. We're silent until the end credits.

Ethan's gaze crosses mine, his face twisted by the sadness. I must look the same.

Jade killed my dad.

My abusive, piece-of-shit dad tried to rape my friend.

More than once, apparently.

And no one believed her, so she took matters into her own hands.

As if life finally breathes back into me, I stand up, taking deep breaths and wiping my hair away from my sweaty forehead.

I walk to her, squat in front of her trembling form, and put a hand on the back of her head. She startles, whimpering.

I stay that way until her back stops shaking from the sobs.

"The first time," I rasp. "When was it?"

She doesn't lift her head, talking into her knees. "Your nineteenth birthday. When I was in senior year."

"Fuck," Ethan huffs, wiping a hand against his face. "We were here. We were right *fucking here*."

"And then?" I say softly to Jade, caressing her hair.

"He said no one would believe me. And he was right. No one did."

I press my fist against my mouth, trying my best not to scream. I want to cry for her, with her. I wish she'd told me.

I don't blame her for not doing it, and I understand. He was my dad. But had I known, I could have killed him myself.

"And when did it happen? The second time." My voice wavers.

"Two months later. In May. The day your dad and Ethan's mom disappeared. It was because of me."

I eye Ethan. His thumb is caressing his lips, his elbow resting on his arm across his chest. He nods at me, and I know that he's thinking of telling her the exact same thing I want to.

So I do.

"Thank you, Jade."

Her head snaps up. Her eyes are red from the crying, her face puffy.

"W-what?"

"Thank you for doing what we all wanted to, but never had the courage."

"I...killed your dad."

A sarcastic chortle escapes me. I think the shock is fading away. Finally. "You mean the man who locked me in the basement and hit me with the buckle end of his belt?"

Her eyes drop to the scars on my chest.

"The man who knocked Ethan unconscious when he tried to put himself between my dad and his mom?"

Her brow furrows, more tears filling her eyes.

"That's the man we're talking about, Jade. He didn't deserve to live. Especially not if he touched you against your will. I never cared that he disappeared. I was happy about it."

I wipe a tear with my thumb. "You did nothing wrong."

She nods slowly before looking at Ethan as he drops to his haunches on the other side of her.

"Your mom called Sawyer that day," she explains. "She

wanted his help, so she told him what happened." Her gaze drops. "That's what he was blackmailing me with. By December, I knew your mom wasn't coming back. With her gone, there was no other witness. Sawyer said if I didn't do as he asked...he could tell whatever version of the story he wanted."

Looking up again, she wipes her own tears. "I didn't know what to do. I let him scare me." She shakes her head. "I'm not strong. It's just pretend. I'm weak. I let others decide my fate every time. *That's* why I ran away. Because I thought when you caught Sawyer, he told you. I had no idea about any money. I thought you were coming to my house because you knew what I'd done to your dad. I'm such a coward."

"Hey, hey." I grab her face between my palms. "You still being here after what happened, standing strong and keeping on living, that's what makes you resilient. What happened to you doesn't define you. What others imposed on you isn't who you are. You decide who you are, my love. That's all up to you."

"I wouldn't be surprised if Sawyer got rid of my mom," Ethan admits. "It worked better for his narrative." He takes a shaky breath. "I never believed in the whole 'she left and never came back.' It's just not like her." He puts a hand on Jade's knee. "I'm sorry she didn't believe you at first. We do."

Jade pinches her lips, her nose twitching. "You guys are gonna make me cry again."

Her gaze hops from Ethan to me. "I love you, Elliot."

My heart stops. "Say it again," I murmur.

"I love you. I love you. I love you. I will never choose. I can't. And you're not second, because I'm just as in love with you as I am with him. There's more than enough space in my heart for the both of you."

. . .

We wait for her in bed that night. She keeps looking for something in the living room, and when she finally joins us, settling on her back between the two of us, she shows us two necklaces.

Each is a piece of Lego. A rectangle with a curved end.

"They clip together like that, look." She puts them together, and the pieces form a heart. Undoing them, she gives them to us. "Now you know you both have an equal piece of my heart."

We both grab our respective necklace, eyeing each other.

"Yeah, I'm not wearing that," Ethan chuckles.

"That thing is ugly, Jade. What the fuck."

We all burst out laughing.

"You guys are so fucking mean," she laughs.

I give mine to Ethan and he puts both pieces on his bedside table. "We know we have a piece of your heart. No need to dress us in it. Especially when it's that ugly."

"Goodnight." I yawn, grabbing Jade by the waist and pulling her against me, her back to my chest.

On the other side, Ethan faces her, a hand on her hip and his forehead practically touching hers.

In the silent room, Jade's voice is distinct.

"If anything happens tomorrow...I love you."

My heart skips a beat, and I know Ethan feels it too, because his hand on her hip tightens.

"I love you. Both of you," he answers.

I take a deep breath. Tomorrow is going to be okay.

Everything is going to go smoothly, just as we planned.

"I love you, guys."

41

JADE

Roses - Awaken I am

Ethan parks his truck at the back of the abandoned warehouse we'd found months ago. Right off the freeway between Silver Falls and Stoneview, closer to the billionaire town than Silver Falls.

We're meant to meet Kay here, all leave our cars, and get in the van. Then after the robbery, we'll leave the van here, split back into two cars, and meet back at the brothers' house.

Kay is already here, arms crossed, leaning against her sleek black Mercedes A Class. A baby she bought for herself when she made a deal with the Wolves.

"I always forget you have a nice car," Elliot says as we jump out. "Self-made women in our town make a lot of money, don't they?"

She cocks an eyebrow at my boyfriend.

"Emma drives a Range Rover now. Did you know?"

"What? A fucking Rover?"

"SE too. That shit costs a hundred k, at least."

Kay's mouth twists, clearly unhappy. "She can't have bought that herself. Someone got it for her. And I'd bet my life it's the same person who's been giving her info on us."

"The Lucianos?" Elliot suggests.

I scratch my throat. "Can we focus on what we have to do and talk about Emma Scott's car once we're finished robbing a goddamn bank."

Ethan chuckles beside me, holding my hand and squeezing hard. "It's 8:30."

Kay grazes the pad of her thumb against her bottom lip, still lost in thought. "We'll go over the plan in the van. Let's go."

She talks again once we're on the highway back to Silver Falls.

"Right, let's go over the plan one last time. The cameras will be cut off until 9:30, but the bank opens at 9. Elliot, you're walking in at 9 sharp. Natasha is the manager on shift. That's when all your work from the last few months needs to pay off. You convince her to get you to the safe. Make sure to open the fire exit in the basement too. You remember from the pictures Carla showed us. The back door is not too far from the safe, so after that, you'll need to move somewhere else with Natasha. Ethan and I will be waiting there at 9:15. Not one minute early, not one late. Clear?"

The two guys are sitting at the back, and I glance in the mirror. Elliot is already looking at me. He winks. "Crystal clear, boss."

I smile at him, despite the uneasiness in my stomach.

"Who's Carla?" I ask.

"She used to be part of the Kings. Watched my kids a

lot. Then she got a job in a bank, and I let her go. She owed me one, that's why she's helping. She's the one who told us about the work being done and the cameras being cut off."

I nod, my eyes back on the road.

"Ethan," Kay carries on. "You and I will have exactly thirteen minutes to move the money. First, we'll pack all the money in the bags. I'll bring the first two outside by the security door and stand guard while you bring the rest. You keep doing the back-and-forth. You'll have eighteen bags left to carry. Thirteen minutes. Got it?"

He lets his head fall against the headrest and smiles at me through the mirror. "Got it."

"Jade, I want you to leave your exact spot at 9:28. There is absolutely no way in hell we're letting a van wait in front of the bank, or we'll have the cops on us right away. Fifty-nine seconds, which then leaves us a minute to put all the bags in the van and be gone. Does anyone have any questions?"

"Isn't someone going to see you putting the bags in the van?" I ask, my hands tightening around the steering wheel.

My stomach is twisted, my head pounding. This is the most dangerous job any of us has ever done because it's not on the North Shore. We have no control over the South Bank. People there are not NSC or Kings, and they'll call the cops at the first unusual thing they notice.

I don't want to deal with cops ever again.

"The door leads to a back alley. The van is the exact size to fit in there, but it does have cameras, hence why we need to be gone before 9:30."

She searches through a plastic bag at her feet and comes out with four masks. She keeps the simple balaclava for herself, then shows us the others. One of them is a mask like the movie Scream. One is the kind with green crosses instead of eyes and a big green smile.

"That's mine," Elliot grabs the green one and passes the ghost mask to Ethan.

How fitting for a serial killer.

Kay tilts her head to the side when looking at a black leather mask with ears. A kitten mask.

"What the fuck?"

"That's for Jade." Ethan smiles, and our eyes cross in the mirror again.

A wave of arousal shoots through my body. He's dressing me as his little kitten.

"Why do we even need masks if no one is meant to see us?" I ask.

"This is just in case. I want everyone to have an alarm set at 9:30 on your phones. If we're still in the bank when it rings, you put your masks on. No second thoughts, no questions asked."

She grabs something else from the bag. Three guns. I'm assuming she's already got hers on her. "If at 9:30, we're not out of there, we're doing this the North Shore way. Everyone face down on the floor, and we leave the bank by the front door. Jade, if we're not out at 9:29, I want you to drive to the front doors with the mask on and wait for us there. We'll be running out with the bags. That means cops. That means showing us your nice racing skills. Got it?"

I nod. "Got it."

She puts a reassuring hand on my thigh. "But that won't happen. Don't worry."

I feel weird having her touching me. She's been nice to me lately, and I don't like it. Because I know it's all an act.

"What's the plan to wash the money?" Elliot asks coolly,

but I know this has been a well-thought-out question. Timed perfectly.

He's been talking to Ethan and me about it for weeks and wanted to make sure he does it at the right moment. Now is it. Kay can't afford to lose any of us before the robbery or her plan goes to waste. She has to answer him if she wants everything to go smoothly.

She eyes Elliot in the rearview mirror before looking out of the window.

"There's a house for sale in Stoneview. I'm going to buy it with all of our money. Then I'll sell it and we'll split the profit. It's the only place where they don't give a shit where your money comes from."

"Will ten million be enough to buy a house in Stoneview?" Elliot doesn't sound happy. That town isn't called *billionaire* town for no reason.

"I am not stupid, Elliot. I know what I'm doing. It's being sold at an auction next month. It was seized by the government after the guy owning it went to prison. Makes it a little cheaper for us. I'll get it, don't worry. I'll wait about six months and sell it again. That's everyone with clean bills in their hands." She eyes me. "You too."

"What?" My mouth feels numb. "I'm keeping my share?"

She eyes me for a while. "Yeah, your boyfriends convinced me. You get your share, minus fifty grand."

"Oh my god." I roll my eyes. "I did not steal that money. How many times do I have to tell you?"

"You can say it as many times as you want. Sawyer said it was at your place. He saw it, and said it was in the bag the Wolves use to transfer money to us. I know you took it when you and Sawyer set up Billie."

"When Sawyer *made me* set Billie up. I didn't want to." I

keep my mouth tight, my teeth gritted. Now isn't the time to have an argument.

Kayla is about to talk again, when she's cut off. "I'm the one who stole the money."

I brake so hard, we all choke on our seatbelts. I'm right at the entrance of Silver Falls, just off the highway, and someone honks as they pass the van. I pull over to the side, my ears ringing.

"What?" I seethe as I turn around.

Ethan's eyes are trained on his thighs, his hands tight around his mask.

"I stole the money," he repeats.

"Look at me, Ethan. *Fucking look at me!*"

He does, regret flooding his eyes. I shake my head, barely able to talk. "Why?"

I can't find any emotion to display the betrayal I currently feel. It's too much to even put into words.

"Why did you do that? Why did you..." I swallow thickly, barely able to talk. "Why did you let me take the fall?"

"I took it to help you. I knew Sawyer was blackmailing you with something. I understood it the moment you started acting weird. Beating up Billie for no reason? Dating Sawyer? That's not you. Setting her up? You would never do that."

He looks away and out the window. "You were in danger, and I wanted you out of this shitty town. So the night you and him set Billie up, when you all went to bed and I helped Billie get home...I took the money from Volkov and half of Elliot's scams. I put the bag at your house and under your mom's bed."

He hits the back of his head against the headrest. "I didn't realize Sawyer would look for it at your place. He found it and probably left it there thinking you were

508

keeping it for him. We caught him that same day, then we tortured him over a few weeks, and he threw you under the bus, wanted to make you look like the traitor so we would let him live. That's what Elliot and I were coming to collect that day. That's why I helped you escape. I wanted to give it to you, but I had no way of going back in to get it without Elliot knowing. So I just helped you out and...you were gone."

"You did *what*?" Kay hisses, turning around. "You helped her leave?" She turns to Elliot. "Did you know that? And where the *fuck* is my money?"

"I didn't know until we found the money at Jade's. Ethan told me everything then."

"You knew?" I gasp.

He eyes me but keeps answering Kay, solving one problem at a time.

"And chill, will you? Your money is at my house. I'll give it back. I didn't tell you because I didn't want you to hurt my brother."

"Please," Ethan snorts. "He didn't tell Kay because he wanted to hold it over my head." He looks at me, his black eyes sucking the soul out of my body. "So I'd be a good boy and help him look for you, even though I knew you were safer away from here. So I wouldn't talk to you when we brought you back and he could keep going with his life-long plan of making you his without me getting in the way." He turns to Elliot. "Protecting me? It's called *blackmail*, asshole."

I run my hands through my hair, grabbing my roots and pulling.

"You two are fucking insane," Kay hisses.

"You watched her beat me up!" I shout. "You didn't say anything!"

And then the truth comes out, breaking my heart.

"It was easier to keep you docile if you were scared," Ethan admits in a tone that barely portrays regret. His eyes come back to me. "And as much as I hate myself for it, I wanted you close as much as Elliot did."

"*Motherfuckers.*"

They both look at me, not saying anything. They know I'm right. They betrayed me. They have nothing to defend themselves with.

They manipulated me the whole time. They crushed my sanity and stole my heart. And now I'm exactly what they want: nothing without them.

"I hate you both," I rasp.

Kay shakes her head, clearly disappointed in them. She checks her phone and looks at me with pity in her eyes before it's replaced by her usual darkness.

"I don't have time to deal with this shit. We have to get back on the road," she tells me. "We're wasting precious time."

"You're not laundering my money," I tell her. "The moment we're done here, I'm leaving." I look at the two men I love. "For good this time."

42

ELLIOT

Cute Girl - Diggy Graves

I walk into the bank, dressed in a suit that doesn't even belong to me, and dragging my fissured heart with me.

Ethan and I are not good people. We could have lived and died keeping that fucking secret with us. But no, he had to bring his emotions into this, to let the guilt take over, and now Jade is back to square one, hating us.

Fucking asshole.

Maybe we're both assholes. Maybe we should have told Kay we were the ones with the money the whole time.

Of course, it was painful watching her suffer from our lie. Of course, we fucking hated ourselves for it. Especially Ethan.

Me? It gave me something to blackmail him with, and it kept Jade scared, worried for her life, in need of protection. The entire thing worked perfectly for me.

Again, I am not a good man. I've done enough terrible things to keep Jade to myself that one more didn't really tip the balance for me. I don't think the *conscience/selfishness* scales in my head are working the best, to be honest.

Now I have to do this fucking robbery knowing my girlfriend hates me. She probably doesn't even consider herself our girlfriend anymore.

She wants the money and to leave.

I'm scared.

Scared of the things I will do to keep her this time. We won't let her go anywhere. Ethan and I both know that.

But I don't want Jade as a captive. I want her happy. I like the way we play, the way we all take care of each other. We're family, and she should be finding comfort in us. Not betrayal.

"Good morning, sir. How can I help you?" The banker at the counter smiles brightly at me, observing me from head to toe.

I bet I look delicious in a suit. The blond hair, the blue eyes, the sharp jaw. My six-foot-seven figure takes up the whole view in front of her.

If only she knew what kind of monster I really am.

"I'm here to see Natasha Saint." What a poor name for her. The girl is as desperate for kink as they come. That's what I've been playing with in the last few weeks. The promise to make all her dark dreams come true if she's patient.

"Of course. May I take your name, sir?"

"No." I grin, letting the silence stretch before she finally realizes there's no point insisting and goes to the back.

I look around as I wait, checking everywhere for the cameras. Not that I should need to know where they are. Everything is going to go perfectly fine. I trust every single person working this job. They're my family.

"Matt, hey!"

I look up as Natasha rounds the counter, giving me a quick hug. Of course, I didn't give her my real name. If this goes south, she can tell the police that Matt Anderson played and used her to access the safe.

"This is a nice surprise." She blinks up at me, adjusting her blouse and pencil skirt. "Let's go to my office."

I check the time as we walk behind the counter and toward a hallway that leads to her office. It's 9:03. She opens the dark wooden door and lets me in.

This bank is nice. Luxurious. She's got a huge glass desk, a coffee area with an espresso machine, and some velvet seats. She must sign some real nice contracts with rich people in here.

"Coffee? I was just going to make myself one. My first meeting isn't until ten, so you timed this perfectly."

That I did.

"Coffee sounds nice. How are you, beautiful?"

My throat feels tight saying this word only. Natasha isn't an ugly woman, by any means. She's about average height, with long light brown hair, generous boobs, a tight waist. She fits her role as a banker perfectly. She's smart.

But she's naïve.

She's sexually frustrated because she's scared about what she loves in bed. She never had the courage to tell any of her boyfriends what she really wants and ends up leaving them because they're too vanilla for her tastes.

We talked about it. I bet we could have been good friends in another life.

One where I'm not using her to rob the bank she works at, or where I don't have a real girlfriend who is possessive enough to want to kill any woman who talks to me.

One where I don't dangle her sexual fantasies like a carrot in front of her eyes so she does exactly what I want.

She gives me a cup of coffee, then sits down on one of the velvet chairs. "Please, sit. To what do I owe the pleasure of your visit? Missed me?" She winks playfully and takes a sip of her coffee.

"I'm going to give you what you crave today."

Her lips part, eyes rounding. "What...what do you mean?"

"I've made you wait long enough. You've been such a patient girl. Now you get your reward."

"I do?"

"If you listen and behave, then yes."

The excitement in her eyes makes me feel uncomfortable. We can safely say I had the most fucked-up part to play in this robbery.

Her voice is a seductive purr when she talks again. "I'll listen." She puts her mug on the coffee table and shifts her hips with need. "I'll behave."

"Sir," I say, unimpressed. And she probably thinks it's a role I'm playing, but the truth is, I *am* unimpressed. Because all I fucking want is Jade in her place right now, submitting to me like she does so well.

"I'll behave, sir." Her eyes are bright with need.

"First thing you should know, my submissive doesn't get to sit down before I do. And she certainly doesn't sit on a chair."

She's up in a split second. "I'm sorry, sir." I sit down, in her place, and point at the floor between my knees. "Down."

She drops to her knees in front of me and holds her hands behind her back.

This girl knows what she wants. She's done her research, and it shows.

"Very good." I splay my arms at the back of the seat and check my watch. 9:08. "You passed your first test of obedience." I lean forward. "Now I bet you'd like a little reward for that, wouldn't you? Maybe my fingers in that wet pussy of yours."

She shifts on her knees, caught off guard. It's so obvious she's wet right now, I don't need to fucking check.

"Why don't you beg, huh?"

"Please, sir. Please, can you touch my pussy?"

This does absolutely nothing to me. Her voice irritates me, her hips bucking forward make me want to retreat, and it takes all of me not to scream at her to shut the fuck up and go home.

"Good," I rasp. She might think it's because of lust, but it's because I can't stand this fucking situation. I want to die right now.

"Here's what we're going to do, Natasha. You're going to take me to the vault, and I'm going to make you crawl all around it, until I'm satisfied with your performance and bend you over the cash in there. You'll take my dick like a good little girl, won't you?"

She seems to break out of it. "The vault? I can't do that."

"What was that?"

"I can't—can't do that, *sir*. If anything happens, I could lose my job. Or go to prison."

I smirk, taking hold of her chin. "I'm doing this for you, sweet girl. I'm trying to protect your reputation in this bank. What will happen when you scream my name so fucking loud that cute little receptionist hears you? Safer down there, don't you think?"

Fuck. Fuck. Fuck. I need to get her down like *now*.

"It's okay." I slap my knees as I stand up. "You're not ready for what I have in mind for you. Submission takes a lot of time, and I get it. But my sub doesn't question me. Or she gets nothing."

I round her kneeling form, heading for the door. "Maybe another time, Natasha."

"No!"

I freeze, my back to her.

"I'll do it, sir. Please, don't leave."

Slowly turning around, I watch as she crawls to me. "Will you?"

"Yes, sir. I'll do anything, but please...please fuck me."

I wonder how devilish my smile looks when I look down at her again. "Well, then let's not waste any more time. Get up."

She's up and by the door before I can turn around again. I check the time. 09:10.

"Linda," Natasha says as we pass another banker with round glasses and a cardigan in the hallway to the back. "I'm taking Mr. Stanford to his safe. Log it in, please, will you?"

Linda and Natasha stop, but I don't. She can fucking catch up.

"I think you're the one meant to do that, Miss Saint. Only the manager—"

"Can't you see Mr. Stanford is in a rush, Linda? We adapt to V.I.P. clients, now off you go."

Natasha hurries after me, catching up.

"Mr. Stanford?" I query.

"Oh," she giggles. "He's a V.I.P. client of ours. He's got a *lot* of money in that safe."

"Does he now?"

"Yeah. He's a tall blond, not too dissimilar from you, sir."

She taps a code on a *staff only* elevator and we get in.

"Down," I tell her after she pushes a golden key in and presses the only button in here.

She drops to her knees, and I put my hand at the top of her head. "You'll crawl to the safe."

"Yes, sir."

The second we arrive in the basement, she crawls across the white tiles. We take a right, and pass the emergency exit I saw in the pictures, and soon after, the round, thick concrete door of the vault.

"Oh, shit." It escapes me as I look at the gigantic door.

"May I stand up, sir."

Time check. 09:13 and 51 one second.

"Hurry."

She's on her two feet already, grabbing a key attached to her belt by a retractable wire. She puts it in, turns, then another key, turns again.

This is the longest thing I've ever had to endure.

"Hurry, beautiful. Patience is not my best asset."

"Yes, sir," she murmurs.

Something clicks, and she turns the wheel of the giant door. Steel-reinforced concrete. That shit is heavy.

"On your knees," I say as I grab the door myself. "To the side."

I use all my strength to open it quickly.

There are bars behind it. The money is in a fucking cage, and it takes all of me not to snap.

"Go on."

She opens the door, and we finally walk in.

It's a tiny room. The left side is a wall of safety deposit boxes. And the right...I bite my lip not to gasp. The entire right wall is stacks on stacks of cash.

"Sir?"

I shake my head. "Bend over the table, Natasha."

She hurries to the small steel table in the middle of the room, and I settle behind her. I push her pencil skirt up to her waist and my mouth twists when I see how wet her panties are.

She would be the perfect submissive to any dominant. I know so many men who would be weak at the knees for her.

But I take a step back.

Shit. Shit, I can't do this.

I look at my watch. We're ten seconds away from 9:15.

Grabbing her hips, I flip her around and lift her up. She wraps her legs around my waist, her arms around my neck.

And she goes for my mouth.

I turn my head to the side, incapable of offering her my lips.

"Don't touch me unless I allow you to." I slap her ass. "Bad girl."

I take a few steps back and out of the safe.

"Where are you going?" she panics. "I need to lock the—"

I slam my hand on her mouth. "Bad girls who can't keep quiet get gagged. Would you like that? Maybe with your soaking panties?"

She shakes her head as I walk back the way we came. I look behind her, take a deep breath...

And I slam her back against the emergency exit. Her ass pushes on the bar and unlocks the door. We're almost outside.

My eyes dart around, and I catch Kay and Ethan right there, leaning against the wall with twenty black duffel bags at their feet.

Natasha notices my eyes looking behind her shoulder and she moves her head to turn. Kay's eyes widen, as they're too close to hide.

I seize Natasha's jaw with my hand, forcing her to face me before it's too late. "Eyes on me. Always. Especially when I'm about to make you see stars. Say 'yes, sir.'"

"Yes, sir," she pants.

I step backward into the building, going around the corner and to where the elevator is. I walk us both in, press the button to close the doors, and slam my hand on the emergency button.

Pressing Natasha's back against the mirror, she looks up at me through her lashes.

"I want to kiss you, sir." She bucks her hips against my stomach. "Please..."

My heart is beating a hundred miles an hour. I don't want her lips on mine. I don't even want her body touching mine.

Instead, I press the side of her head against the mirror and start unbuttoning her blouse. I do it slowly, biding my time. One...slow...button...at...a...time.

I slide my hand behind her back, undoing her bra.

"More...please."

Slowly, I unzip her pencil skirt at the back. If this was Jade, I would have pushed up the pleated skirts she likes to wear, ripped a new hole in her fishnets, and tugged her panties to the side. I would have impaled her in one go as her black combat boots dug into my ass.

I don't even know what more I can use to distract Natasha.

After forever, I discreetly check my watch. It's 9:22. They've had seven minutes in the safe.

"I want to kiss you." She puts two flat hands on my cheeks. "Please, let me kiss you."

My mistake is looking in her eyes. That's how she sees the truth in mine.

"Matt." Her eyes dart around my face. She tries to kiss me, but I turn my head to the side. "What's wrong?"

I take a deep breath, trying to find my focus, reminding myself why this is the plan and why it's the only way.

I exhale.

"I can't do this."

"What? Can't do what?"

I release her legs, forcing her to stand up again.

"I'm sorry, Natasha," I murmur, putting a strand of light brown hair behind her ear at the same time as I reach for the back of my jeans. "I'm going to hurt you now."

She knows this time it isn't our little game, but she doesn't have time to react. I slam the handle of my gun against her temple, and she crumbles to the ground.

"Ah, fuck," I huff, running a hand across my face.

I grab my phone and call Jade right away. "Put your mask on and bring the van to the back alley. *Now*."

I reach inside my suit, grabbing my own mask and putting it on.

I open the elevator again, running to the safe.

Kay is already outside, and I count fourteen bags at her feet, meaning Ethan is in the vault.

"What the fuck are you doing here?" she hisses. "We're not done."

"Put your mask on."

"No...Elliot. What did you do?"

I don't answer, running to my brother.

He looks at me, and he doesn't need to ask. He knows.

"Grab those two bags," he orders as he puts on his Scream mask. "I'll be right behind you."

He knows I couldn't do it. He probably already knew before I showed up.

How could any of us ever betray Jade? Even if it's planned.

No one could ever replace her.

43

JADE

WE MADE PLANS & GOD LAUGHED - Beauty School
Dropout

"Drive!" Kay shouts at me as Ethan throws the last bag in
the van and jumps in.

The tires screech as I speed down the alley and turn
right, slowing down to not look suspicious once we don't
have the cameras on us anymore.

"What happened?" My heart is beating so quickly I can
barely take a breath. The mask narrows my vision and I
shake my head. "Can I take this thing off?"

"No!" three voices shout back at me.

I guess that's a no, then.

"I'm going to kill you, Elliot," Kay hisses in the
passenger seat. "I'm going to cut your balls off and feed
them to you. I swear to fucking God...you fucking *asshole!*"

"I'm sorry, okay?" He kicks Kay's seat. "I told you this
was too hard. I *told you* we should look at another plan."

"We didn't have time!"

"We had three months," he fights back. "We had all the time in the world."

It's exactly 9:30 when I take a right onto the main street, right where the entrance to the bank is.

I catch a woman running out of the building, wearing a blouse and a pencil skirt, the side of her head bleeding. She stops on the steps that lead to the bank, on the phone. She looks at our van and our eyes cross.

Time slows down, I catch the panic in her eyes. She can't see my face, but I feel like she can see my soul.

"They're right here! Escaping in a white van. It's a blank plate!"

"Elliot." I hesitate to ask because I now think I know exactly what happened.

"She called the cops, Elliot." Kay's not screaming or panicked anymore. She's running the pad of her thumb against the material of her balaclava, exactly where her lower lip is.

"I hope you're ready to show us how well you can race, Jade. Because all our lives depend on you right now."

"I'm sorry, Jade." Elliot puts a hand on my shoulder from the back as I stop at a red light. "I'm sorry we lied to you about stealing the money. Please, forgive me. Forgive us."

I turn my head, looking at his hand on me.

"What happened?"

"I couldn't do it," he whispers. A secret everybody knows, but he now admits to me. "I couldn't kiss her. I just... I couldn't do it. I fucked up, and I'm sorry."

I don't know if he says he fucked up because he knew I hadn't stolen the fifty grand all along, or because he didn't keep Natasha distracted.

"I'm selfish, Elliot," I admit.

The sound of sirens resonates down the main street.

"Jade," Kay calls out. "Now would be a really good time to go."

"The light is red," I tell her before talking to Elliot again. "I'm selfish, and I'm glad that she didn't get to touch you like I do."

"Jade," Kay insists. "I can see them in our rearview mirror. I don't fucking care about the lights, there are two cop cars coming our way."

"I know." I take a deep breath, my hands tightening on the steering wheel. "But forgiving you for the lie?" I tell Elliot. "I don't think I can. Either of you."

"I don't fucking care about your love life right now. Get us out of here." Kay's eyes stay on the side mirror, and mine on the rearview.

"They're almost here...they're slowing down."

"I know," I insist.

One car slams on their brakes, stopping right behind us as the second keeps going to our side.

"Jade," Ethan says slowly. "I know you're mad..."

"Police! Turn off the vehicle and show your hands!"

Elliot's hand tightens on my shoulder, and Kay holds her gun on her lap. We're all wearing our masks. They can't recognize us.

"Jade!" Kay screams at me.

The light goes green just as a cop gets out of the car.

And we're gone.

Our tires screech as we let out a cloud of smoke behind us. They're too slow to get back in their cars, probably already calling for backup.

"Oh my God," Kay gasps, grabbing the handle above the door as we all get crushed against our seats. "For a second there, I thought you weren't gonna move."

"I know what I'm doing," I say, staying focused on the road. I drift around a corner, sending everyone to the side and praying the van doesn't flip over.

I feel two tires leaving the road and steer the wheel all the way back.

"Shit!" Ethan shouts.

We slam back on four wheels, and I speed along the road that leads to the highway.

Sirens scream behind us. Now three cars are after us.

"I'm going through the North Shore."

"That's not the plan," Kay fights back.

"They're South Bank cops. They won't know the roads like we do. I know them by heart; I've raced them my entire life."

I press down on the gas pedal, knowing I can lose them. One gets close enough, and Kay brings her gun to the window.

Someone fires, but it's not us. A bullet hits the side mirror, making me scream. Kay fires back, aiming straight for the tires. I watch the car zigzag behind us before crashing into a tree.

"Everyone okay?" she asks.

I nod, speeding across the truss bridge and onto our side of town.

Kay grabs her phone, texting at the speed of light. "I'm sending some guys to slow them down," she mumbles, focused on her task.

By the time we're on the other side of the woods, three cars speed in the opposite direction as us, braking as they see the cops and boxing one in.

Two down.

One to go.

I speed through the streets I grew up driving.

Tapping the steering wheel with my index finger, I count out loud.

"One tap. Right, right. Three taps. Left. Two taps."

I take a right and another right straight away, drive down three blocks, and take one left. I drive another two blocks, take a back alley, and push the van to its limits so I don't get stuck in case they're coming from either side.

"Two taps. Right. One tap. Left. *Highway.*"

I do exactly that, following my childhood mnemotechnics from when my dad would drive me around and taught me how to drive myself.

It takes me less than two minutes to lose the other car.

"I'm going to slow down on the highway to not bring attention to us. If anyone notices anything weird, let me know."

I still go slightly above the speed limit, making sure we don't lose the advantage we caught.

I leave the highway one exit early, then speed down smaller roads, and after what feels like forever, we're at the abandoned warehouse.

We take off our masks, splitting the bags equally between Kay's car and Ethan's.

"I should go with you," I tell Kay.

"No, no, no." Elliot hurries toward me. "Don't. Please, don't."

"I need some time, Elliot." My eyes dart to Ethan and the way his fists tighten at his sides. Taking things quietly, as usual.

"You can have all the time you need at home. I'll give you my room. Whatever you want. Just don't leave us. Please, Jade."

"I'm going with Kay," I say sternly. "Now take your hands off me."

"My love..."

"Elliot," Ethan says. "She needs time. Give it to her."

"We'll see you at your house," Kay adds. "Now stop wasting time."

He lets me go, his eyes still on me as I settle in Kay's Mercedes. We're the first to leave, but I don't look back.

The guys overtake us on the highway, and I look to the side. Elliot put a huge sheet of paper on the window that says *We're sorry,* and he's holding it next to his puppy face.

I snort, giving him the middle finger before looking ahead again.

We notice a block of police cars going the opposite way, straight past us. I want to say we got away with it, but I think I should wait until we're home.

"Your boyfriends are assholes," Kay says, keeping her eyes on the road.

"I know," I huff. "I put up with a lot. Too much."

"Yeah." She pauses, overtakes a car. "But I think you should forgive them."

"What?" I choke. "Don't." I shake my head. "Put yourself in my shoes for two seconds. *You* wouldn't forgive them. You're the ruthless Kings' boss. You wouldn't stand for that shit."

She shrugs. "Or maybe I would."

"You're saying that because you love them like brothers. It's different for me. I can't just keep on forgiving. Ethan let me go for the Kings, Elliot tricked me into becoming his girlfriend. And now I learn that they both knew I hadn't stolen the money and yet didn't say anything because they wanted me to be scared. To *need* them. That's fucked up, Kay."

"Yeah, it is," she agrees. "That's how I know how much

they love you. Because of all the fucked-up things they did to have you."

"Oh, please. You've read too many of those weird dark romance books. I swear."

She bursts into a laugh. "What? How do you know about those?"

"I've been to your house, you know? I've been to your room. They're right there on the bedside table. You have a shelf full of them."

She blushes. I don't think I'd ever seen Kayla King blush. "Whatever. I'm a single mom. A girl has needs and mine are dark."

"No judging here." I don't say that I crawled for Ethan and Elliot with a tail in my ass and that I don't think I can judge anyone.

"All I'm saying is, those two men dedicated their lives to you. Yeah, Ethan fucked up and let you go for a place in our crew. But every fucking day through senior year, and even after, he sat in that stupid chair facing the road to check if you were coming to visit. Elliot had your back, even when he didn't know you were doing all those horrible things because Sawyer made you. Ethan knew and protected you in silence. He never asked once what it was Sawyer had against you. They made a deal with Caden to protect you after you set up Billie. And fuck knows he wanted to kill you."

"What even was that?" The idea of being killed by Kayla's brother sends a shiver down my spine.

"Said they would punish you themselves. But Ethan knew he would never, that he was going to help you leave. And Elliot would have said anything Cade wanted to hear to keep you alive."

"Jade," she insists after a while. "Elliot blackmailed his

own brother for you. He convinced him to go get you after he helped you escape. They killed people to find your address. They brought you back because they *needed* you. They are so in love, they've lost their fucking conscience compass."

I inhale, my chest shaking as I watch the back of Ethan's truck right in front of us. "None of us are really black or white, are we?" I say. "We're all made of tons of colors. It just so happens that Elliot and Ethan are made of *a lot* of grays."

"Yeah," Kay laughs. "I guess that's it."

Maybe it makes me crazy to like that Elliot and Ethan did all these things out of love. Maybe it truly is fucked up that it makes my heart feel strange things knowing they manipulated me into needing them. Maybe I feel that way because they truly manipulated my mind into accepting anything from them and still loving them in return.

That's how much they love me?

Fine. I'll take all of it.

"Well done for today," Kay says as we enter the North Shore from the back of the town rather than through the South Bank. "You really are the best driver around."

"Thanks."

"Look..." She licks her lips. "I'm sorry about the fifty grand. That I didn't believe you. Running this town makes you doubt everything, even your closest allies. You didn't do anything wrong, and I hurt you. I'm really sorry for that. If you still want to be part of the Kings...we're your crew, Jade. I won't let you down again."

I look away, chuckling. "You're un-fucking-believable," I grit out.

"What?"

"Not believing me this time was shit, but understandable. I probably would have done the same in

530

your place. But how dare you say the Kings are my crew when you didn't help when I needed you the most."

"What are you talking about? You keep jabbing at me with this accusation and...I'm fucking confused."

"When Joel Pearson assaulted me," I rage. "I came for help, and you didn't believe me. Don't lie to my face now and say you don't remember that. It's pretty fucking big, don't you think?"

She slows down, her eyes rounding. "Joel...Joel did what?"

"Don't, Kay. You're not a good actress."

"I have no idea what you're talking about." She doesn't sound like she's defending herself anymore, more like she's trying to swallow the news. "I'm so sorry this happened. I didn't know."

"You're a cunt."

"I would have never sent you away and not done anything about it. I take that shit seriously. I promise you. I didn't know, Jade. Was this when my dad was in charge?"

"Yes," I huff. "In senior year, at Elliot's birthday." I roll my eyes. As if she doesn't already fucking know. "I told your best friend Vickie the next day. I asked her to talk to you. She said she would, and three days later, her and Lea came back saying it was all lies. That you didn't believe a word I said and..." My voice trails when I see Kay's face fall.

She's struggling to keep her eyes on the road.

And the truth hits me because her reaction doesn't lie.

"She never told you," I murmur, clicking my nails together on my lap. My thumbs press against the other.

Click. Click.

"I am so sorry," she rasps. "I wish she had."

"Fuck." My head hits the seat. "The fucking bitch."

"I'm so sorry she didn't believe you. And for all the times

I called you a liar. God, I wish I'd known. I'm sorry if you felt you couldn't come to me."

"I wanted to come directly to you," I explain. "But Ethan's mom had already called me a liar, and when I came to your house, you weren't there. But Vickie was so I told her. When she said you didn't believe it, I just...I don't know, I just didn't want to go through telling the story again. I didn't want to risk hearing I was a liar straight from your mouth. I couldn't take it. The girl was a bitch; I should have known she made it up. But I wasn't being myself. This whole thing...it fucked with my head. I didn't who I could trust anymore."

There's a silence before she says, "You're so brave."

"I'm not. Please, everyone, stop saying that. I'm not brave. I just didn't have a choice."

If I wanted to keep going, I had to play with the cards I was dealt. And mine happened to be the *no one will believe you* card.

The *you're on your own* card.

The *pick yourself up and kill your assailant* card. Because no one will do it for you.

"I wish I could make it right."

I put a hand on her thigh, the same way she did earlier. "There's nothing for you to do. Especially now that I know you weren't aware of it."

She nods.

"It's done," I whisper, relaxing against the seat. "It's all done."

Something inside me feels so much better knowing that Kay didn't think I was a liar. That she didn't get a chance to believe me or not. That she really was there for me all the times she helped.

Until that day, I saw her as a big sister. She gave me

lunch money when my dad couldn't. Taught me how to fight. Paid for my mom's treatment. And when she died, and I was away...she sorted her funeral even though she hated me.

We're driving down the brothers' street when I talk again. "So, about that place for me in the Kings?"

She smiles at me. "Elliot is a good right-hand, but sometimes his girlfriend makes him lose his mind."

I can't help a laugh. "Are you firing him because of me?"

"I'm offering you to do it with him. Someone needs to keep him in check."

"Okay." It's hard to keep my mouth straight, and before I know, I'm grinning. "Okay, that sounds good."

The giddiness of everything that just happened starts to take over. We're home, and all we have to do is bring the bags inside. Then it's a new start for all of us.

She parks, turns to me, and offers me her hand. "Welcome back to the Kings, Jade. Anything you need, I got you."

I shake it, a shiver of happiness running down my back.

She opens her door, then turns to me again. "Oh, and Jade?"

"Yeah?"

"Anyone who did you wrong in this crew, I want their names. They don't deserve to be one of us. They don't deserve to be alive."

I nod, tears coming to my eyes and swallowing back down. I'm about to be Kay's right-hand. I can't fucking cry in front of her.

For so long, I thought I'd lost my family. That none of them had my back. It feels good to belong again.

"I can't wait to tell Elliot and Ethan I love them."

She chuckles, messing my hair. "Let's go then."

We take two bags each and enter the house. I'm the first one to get inside, throwing the bags to the side, and going straight for the kitchen.

Behind me, I hear Elliot, Ethan, and Kay walking into the living room, and talking to each other.

"We're taking the first bags to the basement," Kay shouts my way.

"Okay, just getting a drink, and I'll head back to the car for the rest," I throw back from the kitchen.

I pour myself a glass of water. My throat is dry from today's anxiety.

Shit.

We robbed a bank.

And we got away with it.

A huge smile spreads on my lips.

This is it. I'm going to tell those two men what they mean to me, how much I love them. That they might be completely insane, but I want them. I *need* them. And I don't even care if it's because they steered me in that direction.

I don't care that Elliot is a controlling manipulator.

I don't care that Ethan is a crazy murderer.

What I care about is how I feel.

And I choose to love them. Because that's the strongest, realest feeling I've had in a long time. That's all I want to hold on to.

I finish my glass and hold it to my chest, biting my lower lip. It's time.

Time for our life together to begin.

I take a step back, smiling to myself, but stop when I feel something crunch under my boot. Looking down, I frown when I see glass on the floor.

I look around the kitchen in a panic.

Glass on the floor. I know what that fucking means.

I go to the window hidden by the fridge and freeze. It's broken.

"Guys," I call, my eyes on the window. "Guys! I think someone broke—"

I jolt when a hand slams over my mouth. "Shh, shh, shh. No screaming."

I recognize this voice.

I claw at the hand, but there's nothing to do. I can breathe just fine, I just can't talk or go anywhere.

"Your boyfriends and Kay are in the living room with three guns pointed at them. You're going to follow me there and sit down with them like a good girl. All quietly."

She releases me, and I snap around.

Narrowing my gaze at Kay's lifelong enemy, the head of NSC, my jaw hurts when I grit her name. "Emma."

She jerks her head toward the kitchen door. "Off you go."

I walk to the living room slowly, her gun pressing against the back of my head. I don't want to come face to face with the fact that we were so close to happiness, and she's pulling it out from under our feet.

And yet it hits when I find Kay sitting on the sofa between Elliot and Ethan, three people standing in front of them, three guns pointed at their heads.

Kay is fuming, a rage like I've never seen boiling her blood.

"So you're that desperate now, Emma, huh? So *fucking* desperate you have come to steal from our homes."

"It's called working smarter not harder, Kayla. You should have a look at it."

Ethan and Elliot are staring at me, completely quiet, their faces blank. They would never let anyone know they're scared to die.

But I see the way Elliot taps against his thigh. Ethan's eyes are screaming murder. I bet he can practically taste blood on his tongue right now.

Logan is the one pointing his gun at Elliot, his hand trembling from the need to shoot the man he hates in the face. I have to shake my head when I realize who's holding his gun at Ethan.

"Racer?" I rasp.

He doesn't look at me, jaw tight. "I'm sorry, Jade."

"You're sorry?" I choke. "You *helped me* build that van! I should have fucking known not to trust anyone from NSC."

He shakes his head. "Please, Jade. This is just how it works in this town, and you know it. Don't make this worse."

Emma pushes me forward with her gun. "You're the one naïve enough to trust someone from the opposite crew." For lack of space on the sofa, she kicks the backs of my knees, forcing me to kneel on the floor. The closest person to me is Ethan.

I eye the woman pointing a gun at Kay. I know her from somewhere, I'm just not sure where.

"Tamar," Emma calls out. "Tie their hands behind their back. I got Kay, don't worry."

Tamar? Yeah, I've definitely heard that name in NSC, but I didn't think she ever did these kinds of jobs. She's meant to be a computer girl. Mainly runs scams online and clears any stolen devices.

I feel like this will never be over as she ties our hands behind our backs using zip ties. It takes her forever, and I'm dying inside seeing Elliot and Ethan in such vulnerable positions. I want to hold them against me, to whisper that everything will be okay, and from the looks Ethan gives me, I know he feels the same.

Elliot is gazing at Logan. If looks could kill. I know what's at the back of his mind, though. He's planning how to get us out of this situation.

You can't keep a man like Elliot tied up in his own house. You can't rob him. He always finds a way. Especially if my life is at risk.

Emma and Racer are the ones who take our bags full of money. Outside, I hear them break the windows of our cars. Probably to take the rest of the bags. I bet they're bringing them to Emma's priceless Range Rover.

It takes them a while, and we're all just forced to wait here, helpless. Her car isn't parked in front of the house, or we'd have seen it. They take one last look around the living room.

"Take whatever the fuck you want from here," Emma says. "We have all the time in the world."

My head falls forward. Ethan's is too, as if he can't take it anymore. I can't believe this is happening to us. But when my eyes dart toward Ethan, they widen. He's discretely pulling a pocketknife out of his back pocket with his tied hands.

I look away again, too scared to give him away, but not before I catch him winking at me. It's reckless, clearly to reassure me. With his black hair falling in front of his face, I don't think anyone saw that.

"If I were you, Emma," Kay says in a smug voice. "I'd kill me."

I look up at her. "Kay, stop."

Emma chuckles, pressing her gun to Kay's temple. "Why would I do that? I want you alive when your empire crumbles to the ground like the fucking house of cards it is. You're nothing without the Wolves, Kay. And without that money? You're *less than nothing*."

"There's fifty grand in my bedroom," Elliot says, his gaze not leaving Logan's. "Third door down the hall. It's under my bed."

Holy shit. I remember seeing a duffle bag when I looked for cigarettes in his room. I can't believe that was the money I was accused of stealing.

"Elliot," Ethan growls. "What the fuck are you doing?" But I recognize that tone from him. He's just playing along with his brother's plan.

Emma bites her thumb's acrylic nail, narrowing her gaze at Elliot.

"There is fifty fucking grand in that bag. Just take it," Elliot insists.

"Elliot!" Ethan barks at him. "Shut the fuck up!"

I'm confused. What are they doing?

"I just want them out. They're going to search the whole house for money. Might as well give it to them."

I don't believe this for one second, and clearly neither does Kay, who stays silent.

But Emma does. And that's most important.

She leaves the room, toward the hallway.

What are these two planning?

44

ETHAN

Supposed to Be - Presence

I decided three things today.

The first one was in the van on our way to the bank. I decided that if we were going to spend the rest of our lives with Jade, I would tell her the truth about everything. That included stealing the fifty grand and letting her take the fall for it.

The second one was in the bank vault. I decided that I would forgive Elliot if he couldn't go through with his part of the plan. I know I couldn't have touched another woman, and I would have his back if he fucked everything for us. That was about thirty seconds before he ran into the vault telling me to put my mask on.

And the third was when NSC walked out of our hallway, showing their faces once we'd brought most of the bags inside, ready to take the money we had just stolen. I decided then that they wouldn't get away with it.

Emma finally left the room for Elliot's bedroom.

One down. Three to go.

I look at Elliot, our gazes crossing. I'm almost there with the ties. He can keep going.

He relaxes against the seat, his eyes going back to Logan.

"Hey, Logan," he says coolly. "I bet you're loving this little revenge."

Logan's eyes narrow on him suspiciously, but he doesn't say anything. That doesn't stop my brother.

"Come on. I know how much you hate my brother and me for killing Zara."

"Shut up." His clipped words get Jade's attention.

She knows what we did to get her address from Xi. It wasn't our proudest fucking moment, that's for sure. But Elliot would have done anything to get her back, and as much as I want to pretend I was following along because he was threatening to tell Kay I stole the fifty grand or that I helped Jade escape, I don't think I did. I wanted to find her badly. So badly. It was just easier to hide behind my brother's craziness.

But I'm the one who stabbed Zara. I killed Xi's, Logan's, Racer's, and Tamar's best friend.

I know how I would feel if anyone killed my brother. I'd be murderous. Worse than them, for sure.

"Elliot," Jade rasps. "Stop."

I give her a look, silently telling her to let us do our thing. She gets it. I know she does because she brings her knees to her chest and drops her head on top of them.

She's hiding because she can't take the situation, and that's okay. We'll handle it for her. We'll keep her safe. All she has to do is trust us.

"Xi was right there, you know? He tried to stop us."

"He's riling you up, Logan. Don't let him," Racer jumps in.

He keeps his eyes on me, but he doesn't notice the

moment my knife cuts through the thick zip ties they used. They really should have checked us better. They took our guns and thought that's all we had.

Elliot smiles at Logan. "Do you want to know what her last words were?"

"Shut up!" He takes the step that separates him from Elliot, leaning down in the hope to press his gun against his forehead, but he's too slow.

In a split-second, Elliot headbutts him, smacking his forehead between his eyes.

Logan falls back, his nose busted and bleeding all over the place. As they all turn to him, I get up and punch Racer so hard in the jaw he blacks out right away.

"Emma!" Tamar shouts. She's already retreating, clearly not used to the violence of it all.

She's no fucking threat to me, and they should have kept her on a computer.

It all happens in mere seconds. I take Racer's gun, shooting Logan in the shoulder to make sure he doesn't die, but that he also won't be a threat anymore.

Kay is up too. "Do me. Quick." She presents me her tied wrists, and I cut her ties quickly.

She jumps over the sofa just as Emma runs back into the room, tackling her to the ground. "Bitch, I told you to kill me." The whack of her fist against Emma's face sounds disgusting.

Jade tries to get up as I cut Elliot's ties. I can't see her, but I can sense her standing.

"Sit back down," I throw behind me.

She's in more danger if she's in the middle of this than if she stays low and quiet.

"E-Ethan..."

The way she calls out my name tells me something's wrong.

Because I've heard it in every way imaginable. She's giggled it, shouted it, moaned it.

But she never said it with such fear in her voice.

Elliot and I both turn around.

Kay and Emma stop too.

Everything stands still as we watch Tamar's shaking hands holding the gun toward Jade's chest.

They're three steps apart. Maybe four.

Jade's hands are still tied behind her back, but she doesn't shake. Her fear is all in her eyes.

She eyes me and Elliot, silently pleading with us to do something.

"Tamar," I say softly. "Lower your gun." I squat and put mine to the floor, showing that I'm no threat to her.

"It's okay, my love," Elliot tells Jade. "They've got the bags. They've got everything." Then he turns to Tamar. "You're going to leave now." It's a plea more than an order, and it feels awfully strange coming from him.

Tamar nods. She's crying, clearly going through something we don't understand.

"Let's leave," she tells Emma. "Please, let's just go."

Emma is up, pushing Kay to the side. She helps Logan up, and both of them shake Racer awake.

It takes them less than a minute to be by the door. No one wants this to get any worse.

"Now put the gun away," I tell her, both my palms extended toward her. "Just leave."

She swallows thickly and shakes her head.

When she talks, her voice is barely above a whisper, choking on her tears.

"Did you like my notes, Jade?"

Jade's brows furrow. "You?"

"Yes." Tamar nods, her hands trembling some more. "Me. I saw you leave Racer's garage the day you came back to town. I was driving in as you drove away."

Jade shakes her head. "I-I don't know you. What do you want from me?"

She sniffles, eyeing me and Elliot.

And that's when it hits.

"No," I stammer. "No, no, no, Tamar, please..."

"This is for Zara," she sobs.

And she shoots.

Right at her chest.

45

JADE

Sorry - Halsey

"If we don't get her to a hospital within the next ten minutes, she's dead."

"Jade..."

Such a beautiful voice. It sounds like an echo lost in a mountain. It beats in my ears with a need for me.

"Jade...baby, please open your eyes."

A deep breath swallows the last note of his plea. The scattered kind, broken down by meaningful sobs.

"If you open your eyes...I swear...I swear I will make it right."

There's a void inside me. Something that grabbed me a few minutes ago when that gun was aimed at me.

I cough when I try to breathe. It tastes like blood in my mouth. It tastes like death in my heart.

My chest constricts when the car hits a bump.

"Small breaths..." That's a new voice. "Hold on for us, Mi Cielo. Please, hold on. Kay, take the next right."

"My love..." Elliot's voice barely makes it past the ringing in my ears this time.

Those breaths are becoming really fucking hard to take. I cough and feel the burst of blood spurting out of my mouth.

That must be all over Elliot now.

The light is too bright when I try to open my eyes. Like a flash right in front of my face.

Click. Here's your last shot as a woman alive.

I can feel a slap on my cheek, barely. Like being hit by soft cotton. My body shakes from the cold coming from within me.

"Ethan." Elliot's panic has gone up a notch. It's desperate now. "She's not..."

Isn't it insane? That I still feel conscious, perfectly knowing my breathing has stopped and so aware that there's nothing to do about it.

This is the end.

46

ETHAN

All I want - Kodaline

Elliot's arm is around my shoulders and mine around his back. I'm not sure if I'm supporting him or he's supporting me.

My throat is so tight, I can't breathe. I can't talk. I can barely keep my eyes on the coffin lowering into the ground.

I look up at the blue sky.

The sun is shining down on her, like she wanted to be with us today. She's always hated the winter, and I'm grateful the rain stopped for a few hours.

Just while we lay her down to rest.

Tears threaten to fall off my eyelids, and I keep my head back, hoping they just stay there.

I'm not ashamed to cry. Fuck, I could fall to my knees, hold her casket. I could lie down in the dirt next to her and be buried with her, and still I wouldn't fucking care what anyone thinks of me.

But I know that's not what she would have wanted. She

would have wanted me to smile through the tears. To think of all the beautiful moments we shared together.

All those times she told me that I wasn't weird, I was just me.

All the times she held my hand, kissed my cheek, and told me I was just *special.*

She made me smile and laugh.

But most importantly, she made life bearable. And that's all I could have ever asked for.

The priest finishes his prayer, handing her soul over to God, and I sign the cross. So does Elliot.

I take a shaky breath, blinking as I look down. They've started covering her casket already.

"I'm not ready," I rasp. I hold back a sob, but the tears fall. "This doesn't feel real."

"I know, brother." He holds me closer. "I know."

"Fuck." And that sob finally escapes, ripping through my chest. "I'm not ready, Elliot."

My knees buckle at the next hit of dirt against her casket. But Elliot holds me up.

Like he always has, he keeps me up. He takes care of us. He picks up the pieces and puts them back together, no matter how small or jagged they are.

Elliot might do things his own way, but even the tiniest shard will be put back in place when he's done.

And I know I can trust him with my life.

I wipe my eyes with the sleeve of my suit. "I want to be with her."

Elliot nods. "I know."

I force oxygen through my lungs, my nostrils flaring as I realize this is it.

It's over. She's gone forever and there's nothing we can do about it.

So the tears stop, and I let my brother pull me away.

No one else is here but Kay.

She had no one else but us.

She squeezes my arm and walks alongside us.

I give one last look at her grave before we get in the truck, and my mouth twists into a painful smile. "Bye, Mom."

I can finally breathe again when we enter Jade's hospital room. All I've wanted since we left this morning was to be with her again. I never thought I'd be able to make it through my mother's funeral without Jade holding my hand, but when she told us she didn't think she could do it, that it reminded her too much of the assault, I just decided to get it over with.

I know my mom didn't disappear. She would never leave me behind. We were close, we loved each other. She was my only parent, and she would have given her life for me. The relationship I had with her is nothing like the one Elliot had with his dad.

I was still holding on to the fact that she might come back one day, but after Jade told us everything...I knew.

I knew I had to say goodbye to her, even if we didn't have a body.

"Ethan," Jade beams as she sees us enter. She tries to get off her bed before the nurse drags her back.

"Jade," the nurse scolds her. "You're going to have to get used to not walking away from the oxygen container. It can rip out the nasal cannula."

Jade frowns, like she forgot about the tube in her nose that's hooked over her ears. "Sorry," she mumbles.

Nurse Waltz gives her a small smile. "We're discharging

you today. At least show me you're going to survive more than ten minutes out there."

Jade chuckles, sitting on the end of the bed. "I will. Promise."

Elliot and I walk to her, each dropping a kiss on her cheeks.

"Ugh. Some of us can't even get one, you know?" Nurse Waltz huffs.

"Yeah, but better one of very good quality than two average ones."

Elliot fakes a gasp. "How dare you?"

"How are you?" she asks me, playing with that stupid half Lego heart I wear around my neck.

Elliot wears it too. Funny how almost losing her made us appreciate her ugly gift.

"Better now that I'm with you."

She's dressed already, ready to go home. Someone knocks on the door, and Alex Delacroix enters.

"I've got two hot teas," she cheers. She looks up at both Elliot and me. "Oops. Not enough, clearly. I didn't realize you guys were back already."

"Don't worry about it." I grab the cup for Jade and give it to her. "Here you go, Mi Cielo."

We owe everything to Alex. The second she learned about Jade being shot, she was at the hospital. And when Jade was well enough to be transferred, she insisted on sending her to a clinic in Stoneview.

Jade has been recovering here since she woke up from her surgery.

And Alex paid for everything. Even the hospital in Silver Falls.

They said she was lucky. The bullet hit the lower lobe of her right lung. Far from the heart and important vessels.

Still, she was in surgery for four hours. She was asleep for thirteen hours. In intensive care for five days. Recovering for six weeks.

And all this time, Elliot and I could barely be contained. Usually, when one loses it, the other is there to limit the damage.

Yeah, that didn't happen when Jade was hurt.

The only person who stopped us from burning the town to the ground is Kay.

You killed Zara and Xi left you alone. Now you have to accept Tamar wanted her revenge and leave her alone. We have enough problems as it is.

It was the hardest thing I've ever done to accept what she said, but it was true. So we waited for our girlfriend to recover. And that was it.

Our jobs within the Kings haven't changed. The war isn't over. We will get back at NSC eventually.

"Alright, how are we doing in here? Ready to go home?"

"Fuck yes," Jade huffs.

Alex widens her eyes at her, silently scolding her for sounding unappreciative of the doctor. "Hello, Dr. Fernandez." She smiles politely, the complete opposite of my rude girlfriend.

I shake my head at Jade, but can't help the smile spreading on my face.

She's alive.

Rude, and annoyed half of the time, and always ready to retort something.

But alive.

She's smiling as the doctor tells her that she has to keep the nasal cannula on for the first two weeks and then to use it whenever she needs.

Reduced lung function is a life-long complication from

a shot wound to the lung. She must keep oxygen on her at all times. Just in case. She has to put the cannula in if she's going to do anything that could tire her and make it difficult to breathe. The doctor connects her to a portable oxygen container in a bag, tells her how to charge it and check the battery, and schedules her following appointment.

She signs the paperwork and looks up at us. "Take me home."

And that's all we needed to hear. Elliot grabs her, an arm under her legs and one at her waist.

"Not that violently, Elliot, for fuck's sake," I snap. "She's still recovering."

Alex shakes her head at us as I grab the bag containing her oxygen concentrator.

But Jade giggles against his chest and grabs my hand.

"I'm fine. Let's go home."

We all walk together outside of the room and to the car. We say bye to Alex, and Elliot settles in the back with her.

"So," I ask. "Where's home?"

She smiles at me through the rearview mirror and grabs Elliot's hand.

"Wherever you two are."

EPILOGUE
JADE

HONEY (ARE U COMING?) - Måneskin

One month later...

I jog to the front door, barging inside the house. I'm panting, the plastic in my nostrils barely giving me enough to breathe.

But I am so happy.

I run to the living room, bending over, my hands on my knees as I catch my breath.

Elliot, who was watching TV on the sofa, jerks upright.

"What is wrong with you?" he snaps. "You were running again!"

I smile as I look up at him. "I know," I pant.

"Do you want me to kill you? 'Cause I will." Ethan's voice startles me. He's right behind me. Must have come out of the kitchen.

I straighten up. "Look!" I point at my nose. "I put it on so I could run to you two."

They look at me, unimpressed.

Sometimes my eyes catch the grayish stain on the floor.

It's big. No matter how many times the guys wash it, there's no way of avoiding the exact place in the house I was shot and almost bled to death.

Hands down the scariest shit that's ever happened to me.

And fuck, how I didn't want to die.

"Let me take this off and I have good news to tell you."

I go to rip it off, but Ethan slaps my hand away. "I swear if you're not careful, you'll become a twenty-four-seven pet, baby. No more going out, no more walking on two legs. You'll just be lounging around as my little kitten. That way, I know you're not doing anything to put yourself in danger."

I roll my eyes, but Elliot is on me next. He gently lowers the ring that keeps the tube tight under my chin, unhooks the plastic from behind my ears, and slowly pulls it out of my nose.

To say they've become overprotective since I left the hospital would be an understatement, but I try to handle it one day at a time.

"Nice and slow, my love."

"Whatever." I jump on the spot, too excited to keep the news for myself any longer. "I got the job!"

The proud smiles that break free on their faces make my heart melt.

"Congratulations!" Ethan beams.

He kisses my lips, slowly and tenderly, until he's replaced by Elliot's hungry mouth. Just like he always does, he sucks at my lower lip until it swells, and I smile against him.

"Well done, baby. We knew you were the best candidate."

Because breathing has become less than an easy task to do, Kay said she didn't want to risk having me working for the Kings. She said I could if I really wanted to, but felt like Ethan and Elliot would be a fucking pain.

Absolutely they were.

So I looked for another job. I have the chance to be supported by the two men I love, and I went for it.

I applied for a job as a mechanic in a garage on the South Bank. And after today's interview, I got it.

I told Kay I still wanted to help as much as I could. We're sisters. I'm not leaving her in the mess she's currently in. The North Shore is still ours, but who knows for how long now that we lost the deal with the Wolves *and* the money from the bank.

I know she won't leave me in the dark with what happens next. That as soon as she can, she'll get me back on board. Probably behind Elliot's and Ethan's backs.

"We kind of knew you'd get the job," Ethan says. "So we got you a little something."

He goes into the kitchen and comes back with a little ball of white fluff in his arms.

It moves.

And it has ears.

"It's a bunny." My voice is barely a whisper. I can hardly believe it. "It's a bunny... You got me a bunny."

"You know your animals pretty well," Elliot chuckles.

"Oh my god," I gasp as Ethan puts it on the floor.

"Just so you know," Elliot says. "I was against this decision. That thing is going to chew everything in the house."

"She'll take care of it. Right, Mi Cielo?"

"Yes, yes, yes!"

"You'll feed it, and clean after it, and bunny-proof the house."

"I will!" I shriek excitedly.

"Alright, whatever. Have your bunny," Elliot sighs.

I run to it. Taking it in my arms, I sit down cross-legged on the floor. "Oh, you're so fluffy. You're so beautiful. I'll call you like the most beautiful person I know. The person I love the most in this world."

There's a beat of silence, and I can sense Ethan and Elliot holding their breaths, as if whichever of their two names I pick for the bunny will finally define the brother I love the most.

"You're going to be named..." I drag it out as long as I can, dying to laugh. "Henry Cavill."

I hear them releasing their breaths and turn back. "What? You didn't think I was going to *choose* between you two, did you?"

"Fucking brat," Ethan laughs.

I stand back up, turning to my boyfriends as Henry goes around the living room.

"So tell me," Elliot purrs as he wraps a hand around my waist and leads me to the hallway. Ethan grabs my bag with my oxygen in it, making sure to take it with us. "What's the men to women ratio in that garage?"

"Oh God," I laugh. "Five men, one woman."

He shakes his head as the three of us enter his bedroom. "That doesn't sound too good to me, brother."

"I agree."

"Why don't we make our girl show us how badly she belongs to us. Let her prove herself and then we'll let her know if we allow her to take the job."

"I already said yes," I tell them, deadpan.

Elliot *tsks*. "Then you'll have to prove yourself twice as hard. Maybe more after that stunt you just pulled."

Ethan stands next to his brother, his arms across his

chest as they both tower over me. "Why are you still standing, toy? You know where your place is."

A smile tugs at my lips as I fall to my knees. "Yes, Master."

"Good girl," Elliot purrs. "Now show us how you can worship two cocks at the same time."

I think I need to slap myself to understand if this is real.

I've fallen for two men. Two men who worship me, love me with all they have, and would give their lives for mine.

I look up at them, wanting nothing but to give them all of me.

Ethan, Elliot, and I...we've got blood on our hands and love on our minds. Three criminals with no intention to leave each other's sides.

They've become everything to me. My boyfriends, my family, my future.

They will probably be the end of me one day, but I'm willing to give up everything I am, or whoever I could ever be, just to have them near me. It doesn't have to come to that, but I would. They're beautiful, tempting, dangerous. Two perfect evils I will always be willing to commit my life to.

I'm an offender ready to die and burn in hell for my sins, especially when they're so delightful.

THE END

ALSO BY LOLA KING

All books happen in the same world at different times

STONEVIEW STORIES

(MF Bully):

Giving In

Giving Away

Giving Up

One Last Kiss (Novella - includes spoilers from Rose's Duet)

ROSE'S DUET

(FFMM why-choose):

Queen Of Broken Hearts (Prequel novella)

King of My Heart

Ace of All Hearts

NORTH SHORE STORIES

(interconnected standalones):

Beautiful Fiend (MF, enemies to lovers)

Heartless Beloved - (MF, good girl/bad boy)

Delightful Sins - (MFM enemies-to-lovers)

Lawless God - Coming 2024!

ACKNOWLEDGMENTS

The biggest thank you my readers for following me along this journey and sharing the craziness with me. I am infinitely grateful for your support.

Thank you my King for your support and love. Nothing else matters when I have you by my side.

Thank you to Lauren, Ratula, and Mackenzie for helping me shape this book and make it the best version it could be.

Thank you to the amazing ladies from VPR for all your help. Valentine, Ratula, Amy, Kim.

Thank you to my girlfriend, Jess for the never-ending support I get from you. Every doubt I've had in my career you reassured me. Evey time I'm scared, you push me to keep going.

Thank you to my friend Nat. My mornings start with your voice notes, and I believe that is why I end up having such good days.

A special thank you to Jay, Pryiesh, and Bhupinder for helping me with the Hindi words in the book.

As always, to my family for still loving me despite my disappearances while I work.

Lots of Love,

Lola

Made in the USA
Las Vegas, NV
01 December 2023

81933217R00333